SNOWBOUND SURPRISE FOR THE BILLIONAIRE

BY
MICHELLE DOUGLAS

MILLS & BOON

Published in Great Britain 2014
by Mills & Boon, an imprint of Harlequin (UK) Limited,
Eton House, 18-24 Paradise Road, Richmond, Surrey, TW9 1SR

© 2014 Michelle Douglas

ISBN: 978-0-263-91337-8

23-1214

Harlequin (UK) Limited's policy is to use papers that are natural, renewable and recyclable products and made from wood grown in sustainable forests. The logging and manufacturing processes conform to the legal environmental regulations of the country of origin.

Printed and bound in Spain
by CPI, Barcelona

At the age of eight **Michelle Douglas** was asked what she wanted to be when she grew up. She answered, "A writer." Years later she read an article about romance writing and thought, *Ooh, that'll be fun*. She was right. When she's not writing she can usually be found with her nose buried in a book. She is currently enrolled in an English Masters programme for the sole purpose of indulging her reading and writing habits further. She lives in a leafy suburb of Newcastle, on Australia's east coast, with her own romantic hero—husband Greg, who is the inspiration behind all her happy endings.

Michelle would love you to visit her at her website: www. michelle-douglas.com.

To my Romance Authors' Google Group—
thank you, ladies, for your wisdom,
your support and your friendship.

CHAPTER ONE

ADDIE SAUNTERED DOWN to Bruce Augustus's pen, keeping her head high and her limbs loose while her lungs cramped and her eyes stung. There was probably no one watching her, but just in case.

She rounded the corner of the pen where the galvanised iron shelter finally hid her from the homestead. Pressing the back of her hand to her mouth, she swung herself over the fence, upturned the feed bin, collapsed down onto it and finally gave way to the sobs that raked through her.

The huge Hereford stud bull—ex-stud bull, he'd been retired for a few years now—nuzzled her ear. She leant forward, wrapped her arms around him and cried into his massive shoulder. He just stood there, nuzzling her and giving off animal warmth and a measure of comfort. Eventually though he snorted and stamped a foot and Addie knew it was time to pull herself together.

She eased away to rest back against the wooden palings behind and scrubbed her hands down her face. 'Sorry, Bruce Augustus, what a big cry baby you must think me.'

He lowered his head to her lap and she scratched her hands up his nose and around his ears the way he loved. He groaned and rocked into her slightly, but she wasn't afraid. He might be twelve hundred pounds of brute animal strength, but he'd never hurt her. They'd been hanging out since she was eight years old. She'd cried with him when her mother had died two years ago. She'd cried with him when her father had died four months ago.

And she'd cried with him when her best friend, Robbie, had died.

She closed her eyes. Her head dropped. Robbie.

Finally she'd thought she'd be free to keep her promise to Robbie, had practically tasted the freedom of it on her tongue. But no. Flynn Mather in his perfect suit and with his perfectly cool—some might say cold—business manner had just presented his contract to them all. A contract with an insidious heartbreaking condition.

She stood and turned to survey the fields that rolled away in front of her, at the ranges way off to her right, and at the stands of ancient gum trees. She propped her arms on the fence and rested her chin on them. In early December in the Central West Tablelands of New South Wales, the grass was golden, the sky was an unending blue and the sun was fierce. She dashed away the perspiration that pricked her brow. 'How long do you think Robbie would've given me to fulfil my promise, Bruce Augustus?'

Of course he didn't answer.

She made herself smile—might as well practise out here where no one could see her. 'The good news is we've found a buyer for Lorna Lee's.'

A sigh juddered out of her. She and two of her neighbours had joined forces to sell their properties as a job lot. Frank and Jeannie were well past retirement age, while Eric and Lucy were spending so much time in Sydney for four-year-old Colin's treatment their place was in danger of falling into wrack and ruin. Addie and her father had helped out all they could, but when her father had died it was all Addie could do to keep on top of things here at Lorna Lee's. One person really did make that much of a difference. And when that person was gone…

She stared up at the sky and breathed deeply. No more

crying today. Besides, she'd already cried buckets for her father.

She leant a shoulder against Bruce's bulk. 'So our gamble paid off.' Putting the three properties together for sale had made it a more attractive venture for at least one buyer. Flynn Mather. 'Your new owner is a hotshot businessman. He also has a cattle station in Queensland Channel country—huge apparently.'

Bruce Augustus snorted.

'Don't be like that. He knows his stuff. Says he wants to diversify his portfolio.' She snorted then too. Who actually spoke like that? 'And he plans to expand the breeding programme here.' She practised another smile. 'That's good news, huh?'

The bull merely swished his tail, dislodging several enormous horseflies.

'We have a buyer. I should be over the moon.' She gripped the wooden paling until her knuckles turned white. 'But you know what I'd really like to do?' She glared at gorgeous golden fields. 'I'd like to take that contract and tell him to shove it where the sun don't shine.'

Bruce Augustus shook his head, dislodging the horse flies from his face. Addie grabbed the plastic swatter she'd hung on a nail by the fence and splattered both flies in one practised swat. Bruce Augustus didn't even flinch. 'That's what I'd like to do with Flynn Mather's contract.'

Two years! He'd demanded she stay here for *two whole years* to oversee the breeding programme and to train someone up. He'd made it a condition of that rotten contract.

A well of something dark and suffocating rose inside her. She swallowed. 'That means spending Christmas here.' She straightened and scowled. 'No way! I'm not some indentured servant. I'm allowed to leave. I'm *not* spending Christmas on the farm!'

The anger drained out of her. She collapsed back onto

the feed bin. 'How am I going to stand it, Bruce? How am I going to cope with two more years in this godforsaken place, treading water while everyone else gets to live their dreams? When am I going to be allowed to follow my dreams?'

Robbie hadn't lived her dreams. She'd died before her time. Leukaemia. But Addie had promised to live them for her. Dreams of travel. Dreams of adventure in exotic lands. They'd marked out routes on maps, made lists of must-see places, had kept records of not-to-be missed sights. They'd planned out in minute detail how they'd office temp in London, work the ski lifts in Switzerland and be barmaids in German beer halls. They'd teach English as a second language in Japan and save enough money to go trekking in Nepal. They'd even taken French and Japanese in high school as preparation. Robbie had become too sick to finish her studies, but on her better days Addie had done what she could to catch her up with the French—Robbie's favourite.

But now…

But now Robbie was dead and Addie was stuck on the farm for another two years.

She dropped her head to her hands. 'You know what I'm afraid of, Bruce Augustus? That I'll never leave this place, that I'll get trapped here, and that I won't even have one adventure. I'm scared that I'll get so lonely Aaron Frey will wear me down and before I know it I'll find myself married with four kids and hating my life.' And if that proved the case then Robbie should've been the one to live. Not her.

She glared at a bale of straw. 'All I want is to see the world. Other than you, Bruce Augustus, there's nothing I'll miss from this place.' Not now that her parents were dead. 'Of course I'd come back to see you, and Molly Margaret and Roger Claudius and Donald Erasmus too. Goes without saying.'

She tried to battle the weariness that descended over her, the depression that had hovered over her since her father's death.

'If it were just me I'd tell Mather to take a hike, but it isn't just me.' She stood and dusted off her hands. Jeannie and Frank deserved to retire in comfort and ease. Little Colin with Down's syndrome and all the associated health challenges that presented deserved a chance for as full a life as he could have, and his parents deserved the chance to focus on him without the worries of a farm plaguing them.

'You're right, Bruce. It's time to time stop whining and suck it up.' She couldn't turn Flynn Mather away. Given the current economic climate there were no guarantees another buyer could be found—certainly not one willing to pay the asking price. Flynn hadn't quibbled over that.

She let out a long slow breath. 'The pity party's over. I have a contract to sign.' She kissed Bruce Augustus's nose, vaulted the fence and set off towards the main house—chin up and shoulders back, whistling as if she didn't have a care in the world.

Flynn watched Adelaide Ramsey saunter back towards the house. He rested his head against the corrugated iron of the shed and swore softly. Damn it all to hell!

Looking at her now, nobody would guess all she'd confided to her bull.

He moved around to glance in the pen. The bull eyeballed him and his head lowered. 'Yeah, yeah, I'm the villain of the piece.'

One ear flicked forward. 'The problem is, Bruce Augustus—' What a name! '—I have plans for this place, big plans, and your mistress knows her stuff. She knows this place better than anyone on the planet.' Her expertise would be key to his success here.

The bull snorted and Flynn shook his head. 'I can't believe I'm talking to a bull.'

When am I going to be allowed to follow my dreams?

It had been a cry from the heart. His chest tightened as if in a vice. He couldn't afford to lose Addie and her expertise, but he didn't traffic in other people's misery either. He didn't want her to feel trapped here. He scratched a hand through his hair. Was there something he could offer her to soften her disappointment, something that would make her want to stay?

His phone rang and the bull's head reared back. Flynn knew enough about bulls to know it was time to beat a hasty retreat. He glanced at the caller ID as he moved away and lifted the phone to his ear with a grim smile, turning his steps towards the Ramsey homestead—his homestead once she signed the contract.

'Hans, hello,' he said to the lawyer.

'Good news, Herr Mather. The will is due to go through probate in two weeks' time. After that the premises you're interested in will go on the market and you can bid for them.'

His heart beat hard. His smile turned grimmer. 'Excellent news.'

'I take it you will be in Munich for Christmas?'

'Correct.'

I'm not spending Christmas on the farm!

Flynn straightened. 'We'll confer again soon.'

All I want is to see the world?

He snapped his cell phone shut and vaulted up the stairs to the veranda. Voices emerged from the front room.

'Look, lass, we know you want to leave this place too. We can wait to see if another buyer shows interest.'

'Don't be silly, Frank.' That was Adelaide. He recognised the low, rich tones of her voice. 'Who knows if another buyer could be found, let alone when?'

'Lucy, Colin and I need to leave as soon as it can be arranged. I know that sounds hard and I'm sorry, but…'

That was Eric Seymour. Flynn didn't like the other man, but then he didn't have a seriously ill child in need of surgery either. In the same circumstances he'd probably be just as ruthless.

You are that ruthless.

He pushed that thought away.

Eric spoke again. 'If you decide to turn down Mather's offer, Addie, then I'm going to insist you buy out my farm like you once offered to. I can't wait any longer.'

The bank would lend her the necessary money. Flynn didn't doubt that for a moment. But it'd put her in debt up to her eyeballs.

'Don't get your knickers in a knot, Eric. I intend to sign the contract. All of us here understand your situation and we don't want to delay you a moment longer than necessary. We want the very best for Colin too. We're behind you a hundred per cent.'

'Lucy and I know that.'

'But, love,' Jeannie started.

Time to step in. Flynn strode across the veranda, making sure his footfalls echoed. He entered the front parlour. 'I'm sorry. I had a couple of business calls to make.'

Addie opened her mouth, but he continued before she could speak. 'I get the distinct impression, Ms Ramsey, that you're not exactly thrilled with the prospect of being bound to Lorna Lee's for the next two years?'

'Addie,' she said for what must've been the sixth time that day. 'Please call me Addie.' Although she tried to hide it, her eyes lit up in a way that had his heart beating hard. 'Have you changed your mind about that condition?'

'No.'

Her face fell.

His heart burned. 'Obviously the offer of a very generous salary package hasn't quite overcome your objections.'

'Oh, I…' She trailed off. She attempted what he suspected was a smile but it looked more like a grimace.

He held himself tall and taut. 'So I've been mulling over some other bonuses that you might find more tempting and will, therefore, lead you to signing the contract without hesitation.'

She glanced at her neighbours, opened her mouth and then closed it again. 'Oh?'

'I want to make it clear that you won't be confined here. It's not necessary that you spend the entirety of the next seven hundred and thirty days chained to the farm.'

Her shoulders sagged.

'You will be entitled to four weeks of annual leave a year. Would an annual business-class airfare to anywhere in the world, return of course, sweeten the deal for you? I will offer it for every year you work for me—whether that's the two years stipulated in the contract or longer if you decide to stay on.'

Her jaw dropped. Her eyes widened, and he suddenly realised they were the most startling shade of brown he'd ever seen—warm amber with copper highlights that flared as if embers in a hearth fire. He stared, caught up in trying to define their colour even more precisely as Frank, Jeannie and Eric all started talking over the top of each other. Addie's expression snapped closed as if the noise had brought her back to herself and he suddenly discovered he couldn't read her expression at all.

She laughed and clapped her hands, and he was suddenly reminded of the way she'd whistled as she'd walked away from Bruce Augustus's pen. 'Where do I sign? Mr Mather, you have yourself a deal.'

'Flynn,' he found himself saying. 'Call me Flynn.'

'I have another offer slash request to run past you as well.'

She blinked. How on earth hadn't he noticed those eyes earlier? 'Which is?'

'I have business in Munich later this month.'

'Munich? Munich in Germany?' She rubbed a hand against her chest as if to ease an ache there.

'The same. The business that calls me there is moving more quickly than originally anticipated so I find myself in a bit of a bind. I promised my PA that she could have several weeks' leave over Christmas, you see?'

'Your PA?' Addie said.

He could tell she only asked from politeness and had no idea where he was going with this. He straightened. 'Would you consider accompanying me to Munich and acting as my assistant for three or four weeks?'

Her jaw dropped.

She wanted to say yes; he could see that.

She hauled her jaw back into place. 'Why would you offer that position to me? I've never been a secretary before or even an office assistant.'

'You keep all of the farm's financial records. You put together the marketing and PR documents. You have a filing system that's in good order. I don't doubt you have the skills I need.' To be perfectly frank what he needed was a lackey, an offsider, someone who would jump to do his bidding when it was asked of them.

'Germany, love,' Jeannie breathed. 'What an adventure.'

Addie bit her lip and peered at him through narrowed eyes. 'I expect I'd be on call twenty-four seven?'

'Then you'd expect wrong. You'll have plenty of time for sightseeing.'

Why didn't she just say yes? Or wasn't she used to good fortune dropping into her lap? If she didn't want it there were at least five other people ready to jump at the chance to take her place.

'I do have an ulterior motive,' he said. 'I want to learn all I can about Lorna Lee's breeding programme. That means I'll be spending a significant amount of time here over the course of the next two years. Once I'm up to speed I'll know what changes to implement, where an injection of capital will be most beneficial...where to expand operations.'

She frowned. 'Changes?'

He almost laughed at her proprietorial tone. 'Changes,'

he repeated, keeping his voice firm. Once she signed the contract, and after the obligatory cooling-off period, the farm would be his. 'As we'll be working closely together over the next few months, Addie—' he used the diminutive of her Christian name deliberately '—the sooner we get to know each other, the better.'

She stared at him as if seeing him for the first time. 'You actually mean to be hands-on at Lorna Lee's?'

It wasn't his usual practice, but he'd taken one look at this property and a knot inside him had unravelled. Lorna Lee's might, in fact, become his home base. 'That's right.'

She shook herself. 'Okay, well, first things first. Let's deal with the contract.'

That suited him just fine. He added in a clause outlining her new bonus before scrawling his signature at the bottom and moving across to the other side of the room.

Eric signed first. Frank and Jeannie added their signatures next. Jeannie held the pen out to Addie. She cast her eyes around the room once before taking the pen and adding her signature in turn.

Deal done.

Eric slapped his hat to his head. 'I'm off to tell Lucy the good news. We plan to be gone just after Christmas.'

Both Frank and Addie nodded.

Jeannie patted Addie's arm. 'I'm overdue for my nanna nap, love. We'll see you later. Why don't you come over for dinner?'

'Okay, thanks.'

Everyone left and as soon as the door closed behind them Addie's shoulders slumped. Flynn swallowed, hoping she wasn't going to cry again. He cleared his throat and her chin shot up and her shoulders pushed back. She swung around to face him. 'You mentioned you wanted another tour of the property today too, right?'

He nodded. He'd specifically requested that she accompany him.

'Would you like that tour now or do you have more business calls to make?'

She glanced at the cell phone he held. He stowed it away. Before he'd heard what he had at Bruce Augustus's pen, he'd thought he had her pegged—a no-nonsense, competent country girl.

When am I going to be allowed to follow my dreams?

Other than a desire to see the world, what were her dreams?

He shook off the thought. Her dreams were none of his concern. All he wanted was to reconcile her to the contract she'd just signed. Once that was done she'd be a model employee. A problem solved. Then he could move forward with his plans for the place.

'Now would be good if that suits you. I'd like to get changed first, though.'

She directed him to a spare bedroom, where he pulled on jeans, a T-shirt and riding boots.

When he returned, Addie glanced around and then her jaw dropped.

He frowned. 'What?'

'I just…' She reddened. She dragged her gaze away. It returned a few seconds later. 'I know you have a station in Channel country and all, but…heck, Flynn. Now you look like someone who could put in an honest day's work.'

He stiffened. 'You don't believe honest work can be achieved in a suit?'

'Sure it can.' She didn't sound convinced. 'Just not the kind of work we do around here.'

Before he could quiz her further she led him out of the front door. 'As you probably recall from the deeds to the properties, the Seymour farm extends from the boundary fence to the right of Lorna Lee's while Frank and Jeannie's extends in a wedge shape behind.'

He nodded. The individual farms shared an access road from the highway that led into the township of Mudgee, which was roughly twenty minutes away. There was another property to the eastern boundary of Lorna Lee's. If it ever came onto the market he'd snap it up as well. But, at the moment, all up, he'd just acquired seven hundred acres of prime beef country.

'The three individual farmhouses are of a similar size. I expect you'd like one of them as your home base if you mean to spend a lot of time here. Which one should I organise for you?'

He blinked. At the moment she was certainly no-nonsense and practical. 'I want you to remain at the homestead here. You're familiar with it and it'll only create an unnecessary distraction to move you from it. I'll base myself at the Marsh place.' Frank and Jeannie's. It was closer to Lorna Lee's than the Seymour homestead. 'Next year I'll hire a foreman and a housekeeper—a husband and wife team ideally, so keep your ear to the ground. They can have the Seymour house. There are workers' quarters if the need arises.'

He didn't want her to move out of her family home? Addie couldn't have said why, but a knot of tension eased out of her.

They talked business as they made their way over to the massive machinery shed. There'd been an itemised account of all farm equipment attached to the contract, but she went over it all again.

Because he wanted her to.

Because he was now her boss.

And because he'd held the promise of Munich out to her like a treasure of epic proportions and it shimmered in her mind like a mirage.

She glanced at his boots. 'Were you hoping to ride around the property?'

'I'd appreciate it if that could be arranged.'

'Saddle up Banjo and Blossom,' she told Logan, her

lone farmhand. Correction. Flynn's farmhand. She swung to him, hands on hips. 'You're wearing riding boots and you own a cattle station. I'm assuming you know your way around a horse.'

The man finally smiled. She'd started to think he didn't know how, that he was a machine—all cold, clinical efficiency.

'You assume right.'

For no reason at all her heart started thundering in her chest. She had to swallow before she could speak. 'I gave you a comprehensive tour of Lorna Lee's two weeks ago and I know both Frank and Eric did the same at their places. You and your people went over it all with a fine-tooth comb.' What was he actually hoping she'd show him?

'We studied points of interest—dams, fences, sheds and equipment, irrigation systems—but nothing beats getting to know the layout of the land like riding it.'

Question answered.

She rubbed the nape of her neck and tried to get her breathing back under control. It was probably the release of tension from having finally signed, but Flynn looked different in jeans and boots. He looked... She rolled her shoulders. Hot. As in *adventure* hot.

She shook her head. Crazy thought. Who cared what he looked like? She just wanted him to look after the farm, develop it to its full potential, while hoping he wasn't an absolute tyrant to work for. All of those things trumped *hot* any day.

Logan brought out the steeds and Flynn moved to take the reins from him. She selected an Akubra from a peg—an old one of her father's that had her swallowing back a lump—and handed it to him, before slapping her own hat to her head. The afternoon had lengthened but the sun would still be warm.

She glanced at the two horses. She'd been going to take Blossom, but... She glanced back at Flynn.

He gazed back steadily. 'What?'

'What are you in the mood for? An easy, relaxed ride or—' she grinned '—something more challenging?'

'Addie, something you ought to know about me from the get go is that I'll always choose challenging.'

Right. 'Then Blossom is all yours.' She indicated the grey. 'I'll take Banjo.'

'Leg up?' he offered.

If it'd been Logan, she'd have accepted. If Flynn had been in his business suit she'd have probably accepted— just to test him. But the large maleness of him as he moved in closer, all of the muscled strength clearly outlined in jeans and T-shirt, had her baulking. 'No, thank you.'

She slipped her foot into the stirrup and swung herself up into the saddle. Before she could be snarky and ask if he'd like a leg up, he'd done the same. Effortlessly. The big grey danced but Flynn handled him with ease. Perfectly.

She bit back a sigh. She suspected Flynn was one of those people who did everything perfectly.

He raised an eyebrow. 'Pass muster?'

'You'll do,' she muttered, turning her horse and hoping the movement hid the flare of colour that heated her cheeks.

She led the way out of the home paddock and then finally looked at him again. 'What in particular would you like to see?' Was there a particular herd he wanted to look over, a particular stretch of watercourse or a landscape feature?

'To be perfectly frank, Addie, there's nothing in particular I want to see. I just want to be out amongst it.'

He was tired of being cooped up. *That* she could deal with. She pointed. 'See that stand of ironbarks on the low hill over there?'

'Uh-huh.'

'Wait for me there.'

He frowned. 'Wait?'

She nodded at his steed. 'In his current mood, Blossom

will leave Banjo in the dust.' And without another word she dug her heels into Banjo's sides and set off at a canter.

As predicted, within ten seconds Blossom—and Flynn—had overtaken them and pulled ahead. Addie didn't care. She gave herself up to the smooth easy motion of the canter, the cooling afternoon and the scent of sun-warmed grasses—all the gnarls inside her working themselves free.

'Better?' she asked when she reached Flynn again.

He slanted her a grin. 'How'd you know?'

'I start to feel exactly the same way when I'm cooped up for too long. There's nothing like a good gallop to ease the kinks.'

He stared at her for a long moment. She thought he meant to say something, but he evidently decided to keep it to himself.

'Munich,' she blurted out, unable to keep her thoughts in.

'What do you want to know?'

'What would my duties be?'

'A bit of office support—some word processing, accessing databases and spreadsheets, and setting up the odd meeting. If I want printing done, you'll be my go-to person. The hotel will have business facilities. There might be the odd letter to post.'

This was her and Robbie's dream job!

'But…' she bit her lip '…I don't know any German beyond *danke* and *guten Tag.*'

He raised an eyebrow. *'Auf wiedersehen?'*

Oh, right. She nodded. 'Goodbye.'

'Those phrases will serve you well enough. You'll find you won't need to know the language. Most Europeans speak perfect English.'

Wow. Still, if she did go she meant to bone up on as much conversational German as she could.

'You'll be doing a lot of fetching and carrying—Get me that file, Addie. Where's the Parker document, Addie?

Ring down for coffee, will you, Addie? Where're the most recent sales figures and costing sheets? Things like that.'

That she could do. She could major in fetching and carrying. 'When are you planning to leave?'

'In a week's time.'

Oh, wow!

He frowned. 'Do you have a passport?'

'Yes.' She'd had one since she was seventeen. Robbie had wanted one, and even though by that stage it had been pointless, Robbie's parents hadn't been able to deny her anything. She'd wanted Addie to have one too. Addie had kept it up to date ever since.

'Good. Now be warned, when we work the pace will be fast and furious, but there'll be days—lots of them, I expect—when we'll be twiddling our thumbs. Days when you'll be free to sightsee.'

It was every dream she'd ever dreamed.

She straightened, slowly, but she felt a reverberation through her entire being. There was more than one way to get off the farm. If she played this right...

'Naturally I'll cover your expenses—airfare and accommodation—along with a wage.'

A lump lodged in her throat.

'I meant what I said earlier, Addie. I want us to build a solid working relationship and I'm not the kind of man to put off the things I want. I don't see any reason why that working relationship can't start in Munich.'

If she did a great job for him, if she proved herself a brilliant personal assistant, then maybe Flynn would keep her on as his PA? She could live the life she'd always been meant to live—striding out in a suit and jet-setting around the world.

He stared at her. Eventually he pushed the brim of his hat back as if to view her all the more intently or clearly. 'Mind if I ask you something?'

'Sure.'

'Why haven't you said yes to Munich yet? I can tell you want to.'

She moistened her lips and glanced out at the horizon. 'Have you ever wanted something so badly that when you finally think it's yours you're afraid it's too good to be true?'

He was silent for a moment and then nodded. 'I know exactly how that feels.'

She believed him.

'All you have to do is say yes, Addie.'

So she said it. 'Yes.'

CHAPTER TWO

FLYNN GLANCED ACROSS at Addie, who'd started to droop. 'Are you okay?'

She shook herself upright. 'Yes, thank you.'

He raised an eyebrow.

She gritted her teeth and wriggled back in her seat. 'When can we get off this tin can?'

They'd arrived at Munich airport and were waiting for a gate to become vacant. They'd been on the ground and waiting for fifteen minutes, but he silently agreed with her. It felt more like an hour. 'Shortly, I expect, but I thought you were looking forward to flying?'

'I've flown now. It's ticked off my list,' she ground out, and then she stilled and turned those extraordinary eyes to him. 'Not that it hasn't been interesting, but I just didn't know that twenty-two hours could take so long.'

Addie's problem was that she'd been so excited when they'd first boarded the plane in Sydney she hadn't slept a wink on the nine-and-a-half-hour leg between there and Bangkok. She'd worn herself out so much—had become so overtired—that she'd been lucky to get two hours' sleep over the next twelve hours.

He suspected she wasn't used to the inactivity either. He thought back to the way they'd cantered across the fields at Lorna Lee's and shook his head. Overtired and climbing walls. He understood completely.

A steward's voice chimed through the sound system

telling them they were taxiing to Gate Twenty-eight and to remain in their seats. Addie blew out a breath that made him laugh. Within twenty minutes, however, they'd cleared Customs and were waiting by the luggage carousel. Addie eased forward in one lithe movement and hefted a bag from the carousel as if it were a bale of hay.

He widened his stance and frowned at her. 'If you'd pointed it out I'd have got it for you.'

She blinked at him. 'Why would you do that when I'm more than capable?'

A laugh escaped him. 'Because I'm the big strong man and you're the dainty personal assistant.'

One side of her mouth hooked up and her eyes danced. 'You didn't tell me dainty was part of the job description.' And then she moved forward, picked his suitcase off the carousel and set it at his feet.

'Addie!'

'Fetch and carry—that was part of the job description and that I can do.'

He folded his arms. 'How'd you know it was my case? It's standard black and nondescript.'

She pointed. 'With a blue and green tartan ribbon tied to the handle.'

She'd noticed that? 'Adelaide Ramsey, I have a feeling you're going to be a handy person to have around.'

'That's the plan.'

Was it? Her earnestness puzzled him.

And then she jumped on the spot. 'Can we go and see Munich now?'

All of her weariness had fled. Her back had straightened, her eyes had brightened and she glanced about with interest. He swallowed and led the way out of the airport to the taxi stand. 'It'll take about forty minutes by cab to reach Munich proper.'

'It's so cold!'

He turned to find Addie struggling to pull her coat from

her hand luggage and haul it on, her breath misting on the air. 'December in Munich,' he pointed out. 'It was always going to be cold.'

Teeth chattering, she nodded. 'I'm counting on snow.'

She spent the entire trip into the city with her face pressed to the window. Flynn spent most of the trip watching her. She gobbled up everything—the trees, the houses, the shops, the people.

She flinched as they passed a truck. 'It's so wrong driving on this side of the road.'

They drove on the left in Australia. In Germany it was the opposite. It took a bit of getting used to. As he watched her an ache he couldn't explain started up in his chest.

He rubbed a hand across it and forced his gaze away to stare out of his own window, but it didn't stop him from catching the tiny sounds she made—little gasps and tiny sighs that sounded like purrs. Each and every one of them pressed that ache deeper into him.

Maybe that was why, when the taxi deposited them at the front of their hotel, he snapped at her when she didn't follow after him at a trot, but stood glued to the footpath instead. He turned, rubbing a hand across his chest again. 'What are you doing?'

She glanced around as if memorising the buildings, the street and its layout. 'This is the very first time my feet have touched European ground.'

He opened his mouth to point out that technically that wasn't true.

'I want to fix it in my mind, relish the moment. I've dreamed of it for so long and I can hardly believe…'

He snapped his mouth shut again.

She suddenly stiffened, tossed him a glance, and before he knew what she was about she'd swung her hand luggage over her shoulder, seized both of their cases and was striding straight into the foyer of the hotel with them.

For pity's sake! He took off after her to find her enquiring, in perfect German no less, for a booking in the name of Mather.

The concierge smiled and welcomed her and double-checked the details of the booking.

Flynn moved up beside her. 'I didn't think you spoke German?' It came out like an accusation.

'I don't. I learned that phrase specifically.'

'For goodness' sake, why?'

'I thought it might come in handy, and to be polite, but...' She swallowed and turned back to the concierge and glanced at his name badge. *'Entschuldigen Sie—'* I'm sorry '—Bruno, but I have no idea what you just said to me.'

The concierge beamed back at her. 'No matter at all, madam. Your accent was so perfect I thought you a native.'

'Now you're flattering me.' She laughed, delighted colour high on her cheeks. *'Danke.'* Thank you.

'Bitte.' You're welcome.

And from her smile Flynn could tell she knew what that meant. It was all he could do not to roll his eyes.

'Your hotel is sublime, beautiful.' She gestured around. 'And I can't tell you how excited I am to be here.'

The man beamed at her, completely charmed and this time Flynn did roll his eyes. 'And we're delighted to have you stay with us, madam.'

Given the prices they were charging, of course they were delighted.

Eventually Flynn managed to get their room keys and he pushed Addie in the direction of the elevator that silently whooshed them up four flights to the top floor.

Flynn stopped partway down the corridor. 'This should be your room.'

Her jaw dropped when she entered. 'It's huge!' She raced to the window. 'Oh, this is heaven.' She pointed. 'What's that?'

He moved to join her. 'That's called the Isartor. Munich

was once a gated medieval city. Tor means gate. Isar is the name of the nearby river.'

She stared at him. 'So that's the gate to the river Isar. It sounds like something from a Grimm's fairy tale.'

She turned back to fully take in her room. 'Oh, Flynn, I don't need something this big.'

'I have the main suite next door and I wanted you nearby.'

She glanced around more slowly this time and her face fell. 'What?' he barked.

'I thought there might be an adjoining door.' Colour flared suddenly in her face. 'I mean, it's not that I want one. It's just they have them in the movies and...' She broke off, grimacing.

He had to laugh and it eased the burn in his chest. 'No adjoining doors, but feel free to come across and check out the suite.'

Flynn had never thought too much about hotel rooms before beyond space and comfort. And most of the time he didn't waste much thought on the second of those. Space mattered to him though. It probably had something to do with the wide open spaces of the cattle country he was used to. He didn't like feeling hemmed in. It was strange, then, that he spent so much of his time in the cities of Sydney and Brisbane.

'Oh, my! You have a walk-in closet. *And* a second bedroom!' Addie came hurtling back into the living area. 'You have all this—' she spread her arms wide to encompass the lounge area, dining table and kitchenette '—plus all that.' She pointed back the way she'd come from the bedrooms and bathroom.

The suite was generous.

She bounced on the sofa. She sat at the table. 'And it's all lovely light wood and blue and grey accents. It's beautiful.'

He glanced around. She was right. It was.

She poked about the minibar and straightened with a frown. 'There's no price list.'

'The minibar is included in the overall price. It's the same for your room.' When he travelled he wanted the best.

'No-o-o.' Her jaw dropped. 'You mean, I can drink and eat whatever I want from it and it won't cost you a penny more?'

Heck! Had he ever been that young? *'Ja.'*

'Fantastisch!'

She sobered. 'Thank you for my beautiful room.'

He rolled his shoulders. He hadn't been thinking of her comfort or enjoyment, but his own convenience. 'It's nothing. Don't think about it.'

'Thank you for bringing me to Munich.'

'It's not a free ride, Adelaide.'

'I know, and just you wait. I'm going to be the best PA you've ever had.'

Her sincerity pricked him. 'Addie, go and unpack your bags.'

Without so much as a murmur, she turned and left. Flynn collapsed onto the sofa, shaking his head. He eased back a bit further. Addie was right. The sofa was comfortable. He'd be able to rest here and—

Out of the blue it hit him then that not once between the airport and now had he given thought to the reason he was in Munich. He straightened. He pushed to his feet. Twenty years in the planning all ousted because of Addie's excitement? Jet lag. He grabbed his suitcase and strode into the master bedroom, started flinging clothes into the closet. Either that or he was going soft in the head.

He stowed the suitcase and raked both hands back through his hair. The important thing was that he was here now and that finally—after twenty years, twenty-two, to be precise—he had the means and opportunity to bring down the man who had destroyed his family. He would crush George Mueller the way George had laid waste to his father. And he intended to relish every moment of that with the same gusto Addie had so far shown for Munich.

With a grim smile, he made for the shower.

A knock sounded on the door and Flynn glanced up from his laptop. Housekeeping?

Or Addie?

He forced himself to his feet to open it. Addie stood on the other side, but it was a version of her he'd never seen before. What on earth? He blinked.

'May I come in?'

He moved aside to let her enter, his voice trapped somewhere between chest and throat. She sauntered in with a pot of coffee in one hand and a briefcase in the other. She wore a black business suit.

Hell's bells! Addie had legs that went on forever.

She set the briefcase on the table and the coffee pot on a trivet on the bench, before turning. He dragged his gaze from her legs. 'Where did you get that?' He pointed so she knew he meant the coffee, not the legs.

'The breakfast room.'

She collected two mugs and leant down to grab the milk from the bar fridge. Her skirt was a perfectly respectable length, but... He rubbed the nape of his neck. Who'd have known that beneath her jeans she'd have legs like that?

He shook himself. 'What are you doing?' The words practically bellowed from him. 'And why are you wearing that?'

Her face fell and he could've kicked himself. 'Sorry,' he ground out. 'Jet lag. That didn't come out right.'

She swallowed. 'Flynn, I know this trip isn't a free ride. So—' she gestured down at herself '—like a good *dainty* personal assistant, I donned my work clothes, made sure to get the boss coffee and now I'm here to put in a day's work.'

'I don't expect you to do any work today.'

She handed him a coffee. Strong and black. She must've remembered that from their meetings at Lorna Lee's. 'Why not?'

He took a sip. It wasn't as hot as he'd have liked, but he kept his trap shut on that head. She'd gone to the trouble of fetching it for him. Besides, it was excellent—brewed to perfection.

'I'm here to work,' she reminded him.

'Not on the day we fly in. You're allowed some time to settle in.'

'Oh.' She bit her lip. 'I didn't realise. You didn't say.'

'Where did you get the suit?' Had she bought it especially for the trip? He hadn't meant to put her out of pocket.

'I have a wardrobe full of suits. When I finished school I started an office administration course. I had plans to—'

She broke off and he realised that whatever plans she'd made, they hadn't come to fruition.

'But my mother became sick and I came home to help out and, well, the suits haven't really seen the light of day since.'

Because she'd been stuck on the farm. *Trapped* on the farm. He recalled the way she'd pressed her face against the window of the taxi, the look on her face as she'd stared around the city street below. Why was she in his room ready to work when she should be out there exploring the streets of Munich?

'Flynn, I don't even know what it is we're doing in Munich.'

That decided him. 'Go change into your warmer clothes—jeans, a jumper and a coat—and I'll show you why we're here.'

Her eyes lit up. 'And a scarf, gloves and boots. I swear I've never known cold like this.'

'Wear two pairs of socks,' he called after her. 'I'll meet you in the foyer in ten minutes.'

Addie made it down to the foyer in eight minutes to find Flynn already there. She waved to Bruno, who waved back.

'Good to know you can move when necessary,' Flynn said, gesturing her towards the door.

Addie could hardly believe she was in Munich! She practically danced out of the door.

She halted outside. Which way did he want to go? Where did he mean to take her? Oh, goodness, it was cold! She tightened her scarf about her throat and stamped her feet up and down. 'It was thirty-three degrees Celsius when we left Sydney. The predicted top for Munich today is four!'

'In a couple of days you won't even notice.'

She turned to stare at him.

'Okay, you'll notice, but it won't hurt so much.'

'I'll accept that. So, what are you going to show me?'

'We're going to get our bearings first.'

Excellent plan. She pulled the complimentary map she'd found in her room from her coat pocket at the exact moment he pulled the same map from his.

He stared at her map, then at her and shook his head.

'What? I didn't want to get lost.' In rural Australia getting lost could get you killed.

'There's nothing dainty about you, is there, Addie?'

'Not if you're using dainty as a synonym for helpless,' she agreed warily. If it was important to him she supposed she could try and cultivate it, though.

He shoved his map back into his pocket. 'While we're on the subject, for the record I do not want you carrying my luggage.'

'Okay. Noted.' Man, who knew that negotiating the waters of PA and boss politics could be so tricky? 'Okay, while we're on the subject. When we're in business meetings and stuff, do you want me to call you Mr Mather and sir?'

His lip curled. 'Sir?'

Okay, she didn't need a business degree to work out his thoughts on that. 'So we're Herr Mather and his super-efficient—' and dainty if she could manage it '—PA, Addie.'

'Herr Mather and his assistant, Adelaide,' he corrected.

A little thrill shot up her spine. Adelaide sounded so grown up. It was a proper name for a PA. 'Right.'

Brrr…if they didn't move soon, though, she'd freeze to the footpath. She glanced at the map in her hand and then held it out to him. She could read a map as well as the next person, but she was well aware that the male of the species took particular pride in his navigational skills.

'You haven't been to Munich before?' she asked as he unfolded the map.

'No. What made you think I had?'

He studied the map and a lock of chestnut hair fell onto his forehead. The very tips were a couple of shades lighter and they, along with his tan, seemed at odds with all of this frosty cold. It made him seem suddenly exotic.

Deliciously exotic.

Delicious? She frowned. Well, she knew he was perfectly perfect—she'd known that the moment he'd stepped onto Lorna Lee's dressed in a perfectly perfect suit. He was also decidedly male. That had become evident the moment she'd clapped eyes on him in jeans and boots. She just hadn't felt all of that down in her gut until this very moment. She swallowed. Now she felt it all the way to her bones.

Flynn Mather was a perfect specimen of perfectly perfect maleness. In fact, if he'd been a stud bull she'd have moved heaven and earth to have him on the books at Lorna Lee's and—

'Addie?'

She snapped out of it. She swallowed. 'Sorry, brain fog, jet lag, the cold, I don't know.' What had they been talking about? She couldn't remember. She stared at the map and pointed. 'So where are we? What do I need to know?'

'Medieval walled city, remember?'

'Yep.' Nothing wrong with her memory.

'This circle here encloses the heart of the city. Most of our negotiations will take place within this area.'

She followed his finger as it went around, outlining where he meant. A tanned finger. A strong, tanned, masculine finger.

She had a feeling that perfectly perfect PAs didn't notice their boss's fingers.

'Our hotel is here.' His finger tapped the big blue star emblazoned with the hotel's name. 'Marienplatz—the town square—is the heart of it all and it's here…which is only a couple of blocks away.'

She jolted away from him in excitement. 'Oh, let's start there! I've read so much—'

She choked her words back. Perfectly perfect PAs waited to find out what was required of them. They didn't take the bit between their teeth and charge off.

'I mean only if it's convenient, of course, and part of your plan.'

He stared down at her and, while Munich was cold, the sky was blue but not as blue as Flynn's eyes. He grinned, and warmth—as if an oven door had been opened—encompassed her. 'You're trying really hard, aren't you?'

She couldn't deny it. 'Very.'

'I'd be happier if you'd just relax a bit.'

She bit her lip. 'I just want to do a good job and not let you down.'

'Wrong answer.'

She stared back at him. 'What was I supposed to say?'

'Noted,' he drawled and she couldn't help but laugh.

She could do relaxed…perfectly. 'To be honest, Flynn, I don't care which way we go, but can we move, please, before my feet freeze solid?'

He took her arm, his chuckle a frosty breath on the air. 'Right this way.'

He turned them towards Marienplatz. She stared at the shop fronts they passed, the people and the clothes they wore, the cars…but when she glanced up her feet slid to a halt.

'What now?' Flynn asked with exaggerated patience.

She pointed. 'Spires,' she whispered. *Oh, Robbie!* 'And green domes.'

'Pretty,' he agreed.

There was nothing like this in Australia. *Nothing.* A lump lodged in her throat. She'd never seen anything more beautiful.

'If you like those you should go to Paris. They have green domes enough to gladden every soul.'

No. She forced her legs forward again. She was *exactly* where she ought to be.

When they entered the town square, full of bustle and people on this bright chilly morning, and made their way to its centre even Flynn was quiet for a moment. 'That's really something,' he finally said.

All Addie could do was nod. Gothic architecture, sweeping spires, gargoyles and a glockenspiel were all arrayed in front of her. 'What more could one want from a town hall?' she breathed.

On cue, the glockenspiel rang out a series of notes. She and Flynn shared a glance and then folded their arms and stood shoulder to shoulder to watch. Addie had to keep closing her mouth as the jesters jested, the couples danced and the knights duelled. She watched as if in a dream, Flynn's shoulder solid against hers reminding her that this was all for real. She soaked it in, marvelled at it, her heart expanding with gratitude. The show lasted for fifteen minutes, and, despite the cold and the sore neck from craning upwards, she could've watched for another fifteen.

She spun to Flynn. 'Can you imagine how amazed the first people who ever saw that must've been? It would have been the height of technology at the time and—'

She suddenly realised she was holding his arm and, in her enthusiasm, was squeezing it. With a grimace and a belated pat of apology, she let it go. 'Sorry, got carried away.' It certainly wasn't dainty to pull your boss's arm out of its socket.

His lips twitched.

No, no—she didn't want to amuse him. She wanted to impress him.

She gestured back to the glockenspiel. 'And they call that the *New* Town Hall. I mean, it's gothic and—'

He turned her ninety degrees to face back the way they'd come. 'Oh!' A breath escaped her. 'And that would be the Old Town Hall and as it's medieval then I guess that makes sense.'

She turned a slow circle trying to take it all in.

'What do you think?'

He sounded interested in her impression. She wondered if he was merely humouring her. 'I can't believe how beautiful it all is.' She turned back to the New Town Hall and her stomach plummeted. An ache started up in her chest. 'Oh,' she murmured. 'I forgot.'

'Forgot what?'

'That it's Christmas.'

'Addie, there're decorations everywhere, not to mention a huge Christmas tree right there. How could you forget?'

She'd been too busy taking in the breathtaking architecture and the strangeness of it all. She lifted a shoulder. 'It's been such a rush this last week.' What with signing the contract to sell Lorna Lee's and preparing for the trip, Christmas had been the last thing on her mind.

Christmas. Her first ever Christmas away from Lorna Lee's. Her first Christmas without her father.

The ache stretched through her chest. If her father were still alive they'd have decorated their awful plastic tree—loaded it with tinsel and coloured balls and tiny aluminium bells and topped it with a gaudy angel. She'd be organising a ham and a turkey roll and—

A touch on her arm brought her back with a start. 'Where did you just go?'

His eyes were warm and soft and they eased the ache inside her. She remembered the way his eyes had blazed when she'd asked him if he knew what it was like to want something so terribly badly.

Yes, he'd known. She suspected he'd understand this too. 'The ghost of Christmases past,' she murmured. 'It's the first Christmas without my father.'

His face gentled. 'I'm sorry.'

'I've been doing my best not to think about it.' She stared across at the giant decorated tree that stood out at the front of the New Town Hall. 'I'm glad I'm spending Christmas here this year rather than on the farm.'

He nodded.

She turned back to him. 'Are your parents still alive?'

'My father isn't.'

Her lungs cramped at the desolation that momentarily stretched through his eyes. 'I'm sorry.'

He shoved his hands into the pockets of his coat. 'It was a long time ago.'

'Your mother?'

'My mother and I are estranged.'

She grimaced and shoved her hands into her pockets too. 'Oh, I'm sorry.' She shouldn't have pressed him.

He shrugged as if it didn't make an ounce of difference to him, but she didn't believe that for a moment. 'She's a difficult woman.'

She pushed her shoulders back. 'Then we'll just have to have our own orphans' Christmas in Munich.'

He opened his mouth. She waited but he closed it again. She cleared her throat, grimaced and scratched a hand through her hair. 'I, the thing is, I've just realised in the rush of it all that I haven't bought presents for the people back home.'

He stared down at her for three beats and then he laughed

as if she'd shaken something loose from him. 'Addie, that's not going to be a problem. Haven't you heard about the Munich Christmas markets?'

'Markets?' She wanted to jump up and down. 'Really?'

'Some are held in this very square. You'll find presents for everyone.'

'There'll be time for that?' She could send the gifts express post to make sure they arrived on time. Hang the expense.

'Plenty of time.'

She folded her arms and surveyed him. 'When are you going to tell me what your business in Munich is?'

'Come right this way.' He took her arm and set off past the New Town Hall. They passed what looked like the main shopping area. She slanted a glance up at him. 'We'll still be in Munich for the post-Christmas sales, right?'

'Never stand in the way of a woman and the sales. Don't worry; you'll have time to shop.'

Cool.

She shook herself. That was all well and good, but when were they in fact going to do any work?

Eventually he stopped, let go of her arm and pointed. She peered at the building he gestured to. It took her a moment, but… 'Ooh, a beer hall! Can we…? I mean, is it too early…?'

'It's nearly midday. C'mon.' He ushered her inside.

The interior was enormous and filled with wooden tables and benches. He led her to a table by the wall, where they had a perfect view of the rest of the room. He studied the menu and ordered them both beers in perfect German.

She stared at her glass when it was set down in front of her—her very tall glass. 'Uh, Flynn, you ordered me half a litre of beer?'

'We could've ordered it by the litre if you'd prefer.'

Her jaw dropped as a barmaid walked past with three litre tankards in one hand and two in the other.

'Bottoms up!'

He sounded younger than she'd ever heard him. She raised her glass. 'Cheers.'

She took a sip and closed her eyes in bliss. 'Nectar from the gods. Now tell me what we're drinking to?'

'This—' he gestured around '—is what we're doing here.'

It took a moment. When she realised what he meant she set her glass down and leaned towards him. 'You're buying the beer hall?' A grin threatened to split her face in two. That had to be every Australian boy's dream.

How perfectly perfect!

CHAPTER THREE

Dear Daisy
Munich is amazing. Gorgeous. And so cold! After a
couple of hours out my face burned when I came back
inside as if it were sunburned. Everything here is so
different from Mudgee. I know it's not Paris, but it's
marvellous just the same.

You know, it got me thinking about starting the
blog back up, but...I'd simply be searching for some-
thing I can't have. Again.

You should be here in Europe with me. You
should... Sorry, enough of that. Guess what? I fi-
nally found out what we're doing here. The perfectly
perfect F is buying a brewery that has its own beer
hall! How exciting is that?

We have our very first business meeting at eleven
o'clock this morning. I'm going to wear that gorgeous
garnet-coloured suit I bought in Sydney when we
went to see Cate Blanchett at the theatre that time. I
have no idea what I'm supposed to do in said meet-
ing, but in that suit I'll at least look the part!
Wish you were here.
Love, Buttercup

ADDIE EXITED HER *Till the Cows Come Home* Word document, closed the lid of her laptop and resisted the urge to
snuggle back beneath the covers. It was only seven a.m.

She could sneak in another hour of shut-eye. Flynn had said he didn't need to see her until quarter to eleven in his room, where the meeting was scheduled to take place, but...

She was in Munich!

She leapt out of bed, smothering a yawn. A brisk walk down by the River Isar would be just the thing. She wanted her body clock on Munich time asap. What she didn't want was any more of the crazy disturbed sleep like that she'd had last night.

A walk *in Munich* would wake her up, enliven her and have her bright-eyed and bushy-tailed for Flynn's business meeting.

Perfect.

Addie tried to stifle a yawn as the lawyer droned on and on and on about the conditions of probate and the details of the contract negotiations that were under way, plus additional clauses that would need to be considered, along with local government regulations and demands and...on and on and on.

Did Flynn find this stuff interesting?

She glanced at him from the corner of her eye. He watched the lawyer narrowly, those blue eyes alert. She sensed the tension coiled up inside him as if he were a stroppy King Brown waiting to strike, even as he leaned back in his seat, the picture of studied ease. She wondered if the lawyer knew.

She shivered, but she couldn't deny it only made him seem more powerful...and lethal, like a hero from a thriller. It must be beyond brilliant to feel that confident, to have all of that uncompromising derring-do. One could save small children from burning buildings and dive into seething seas to rescue battered shipwreck victims and—

'Make a note of that, will you, please, Adelaide?'

She crashed back into the room, swallowing. She pulled her notebook towards her without glancing at Flynn and jotted on it.

Am making notes about nothing so as to look efficient. Listen in future, Addie! Pay attention.

She underlined 'listen' three times.

Biting back a sigh, she tried to force her attention back to the conversation—the negotiations—but the lawyer was droning on and on in that barely varying monotone. If he'd been speaking German she'd have had a reason for tuning out, but he was speaking English with an American accent and it should've had her riveted, but...

For heaven's sake, the subject matter was so dry and dull that he could've had the most gorgeous and compelling voice in the world and she'd still tune out. She mentally scrubbed property developer off her list of potential future jobs. And lawyer.

She glanced at Flynn again. He wore a charcoal business suit and looked perfect. Didn't he feel the slightest effect from jet lag? Perhaps he really was a machine?

She bit back another sigh. Perhaps he was just a seasoned world traveller who was used to brokering million-dollar deals.

The figures these two were bandying about had almost made her eyes pop. She'd wanted to tug on Flynn's sleeve and double-check that he really wanted to invest that much money in a German brewery.

Sure, he was an Aussie guy. Aussie guys—and girls, for that matter—and beer went hand in hand. But there were limits, surely? Even for high-flying Flynn.

Still, she knew what it was like to have a childhood dream. Good luck to him for making his a reality.

She had a sudden vision of him galloping across the

fields at Lorna Lee's on Blossom. She leaned back. Did he really prefer this kind of wheeling and dealing to—?

'Record that number, please, Adelaide.'

She started and glanced at the lawyer, who barked a series of numbers at her. She scribbled them down. Was it a phone number or a fax number? For all she knew it was a serial number for… She drew a blank. She scrawled a question mark beside it.

In her pocket her phone vibrated. She silently thanked the patron saint of personal assistants for giving her the insight to switch it to silent. She slid it out and her lips lifted. A message from Frank. She clicked on it, eager for news from home.

This man of Flynn's wants to get rid of Bruce Augustus.

Her hand clenched about the phone. She shot to her feet. 'Over my dead body!'

The lawyer broke off. Both he and Flynn stared at her. She scowled at Flynn. 'This foreman of yours and I are going to have serious words.'

He cocked an eyebrow.

She recalled where they were and what they were supposed to be doing and cleared her throat, took her seat again. 'Later,' she murmured. 'We'll have our serious words later.'

But she messaged back to Frank.

If he does he dies. Text me his number.

Flynn stretched out a long leg, leaning further back in his chair, reminding her even more vividly of a King Brown. Addie pocketed her phone and kept a close eye on him.

'So what you're in effect telling me, Herr Gunther, is that there's going to be a delay in probate.'

When Flynn spoke she had no trouble whatsoever paying attention. The lawyer hummed and hawed and tried to squeeze his way out of the corner Flynn had herded him into, but there was no evading Flynn. She wondered if he'd ever camp drafted. She'd bet he'd be good at it. With those shoulders…

She blinked and shifted on her seat. She didn't care about shoulders. What she cared about was Bruce Augustus.

And getting off the farm.

She rolled her eyes. Yeah, right, as if she'd scaled the heights of PA proficiency today. She'd need to do better if she wanted this job for real.

You have a month.

'Are you familiar with the law firm Schubert, Schuller and Schmidt?'

The lawyer nodded.

'I've hired them to represent me. You'll be hearing from them.'

'I—'

Flynn rose and the lawyer's words bumbled to a halt. Addie stood too and fixed the lawyer with what she hoped was a smile as pleasantly cool as Flynn's. Thank goodness this was over.

'Thank you for your time, Herr Gunther. It was most instructive.'

Was it? Addie ushered the lawyer towards the door with an inane, 'Have a nice day, Herr Gunther,' all the while impatience building inside her.

The door had barely closed before she pulled her cell phone from her pocket and punched in Howard's number.

'What's he done?' Flynn asked as she strode back towards the table.

'Nothing you need to worry about. I'll deal with it.'

He opened his mouth and it suddenly occurred to her

what nicely shaped lips he had. It wasn't something she generally noticed about a man, but Flynn definitely—

'Hello?'

She snapped to attention. 'Howard, it's Adelaide Ramsey.'

He swore. 'Do you know what time it is in Australia?'

'I don't care what time it is.' That only made it worse. It meant Frank and Jeannie had been fretting till all hours. 'Now listen to me very carefully. If you harm one hair on Bruce Augustus's head, if you try to send him to the knackers, I will have your guts for garters. Do you hear me?'

'But—'

'No buts!'

'Look, Addie, I understand—'

'Have you ever owned a farm, Howard?' She shifted, suddenly aware of how closely Flynn watched her. She swallowed and avoided eye contact.

'No.'

'Then you don't understand.'

A pause followed. 'The boss has given me the authority to make changes, Addie, and Bruce Augustus is dead wood.'

Dead wood! She could feel herself start to shake.

'I have the boss's ear and—'

She snorted. 'You have his ear? Honey, I have more than his ear. I'm going to *be* your boss when I return home—you realise that, don't you? You do *not* want to get on the wrong side of me.'

Silence sounded and this time Howard didn't break it. 'Goodnight, Howard.' With that she snapped her phone shut and swung to face Flynn.

His lips twitched. 'Sorted, huh?'

Was he laughing at her? She narrowed her gaze and pocketed her phone. 'Absolutely.'

He lowered himself to the sofa. 'Can you tell me exactly why Bruce Augustus is necessary to Lorna Lee's future?'

'Because if he goes—' she folded her arms '—I go.'

He leaned forward and she found herself on the receiving end of a gaze colder than a Munich winter. 'We have a deal. You signed a contract.'

She widened her stance. 'You mess with my bull and the deal's off. There's a six-week cooling-off period to that contract, remember? You threaten my bull and I'll pull out of the sale.'

He leaned back. She couldn't read his expression at all. 'You mean that,' he eventually said.

She tried to stop her shoulders from sagging and nodded. She meant it.

'Why is he so important to you?'

She would never be able to explain to him what a friend the bull had been to her. It was pointless even to try. 'You said one of the reasons you wanted me to remain at Lorna Lee's was due to the affinity I have with the animals.'

'I believe the term I used was stock.'

'You can use whatever term you like—you can try and distance yourself from them—but it doesn't change what they are.'

'Which is?'

'Living creatures that provide us with our livelihoods. We have a culture at Lorna Lee's of looking after our own. I consider it a duty. *That's* where my so-called affinity comes from. When an animal provides us with good service we don't repay that by getting rid of them when they're past their use-by date. They get to live out their days in easy retirement. If that's a culture you can't live with, Flynn, then you'd better tell me now.'

He pursed his lips and continued to survey her. It took all of her strength not to fidget. 'I can live with it,' he finally said. 'Do you want it in writing?'

Very slowly she let out a breath. 'No. I believe you're a man of your word.'

He blinked. She held out her hand and he rose and shook it.

For no reason at all her heart knocked against her ribs. She pulled her hand free again, but her heart didn't stop pounding.

'Howard?' Flynn held his cell phone to his ear.

'Yes, I do. Just...don't touch the bull.'

He listened then. Obviously to the other man's justifications. She scowled. There were no justifications for—

'Howard wants to know if you're okay with him dredging the dam in the western paddock of the Seymour place...'

Oh, yes, that was long overdue.

'...extending the irrigation system on the southern boundary...'

There'd be money for that?

'...and installing solar panels on the roofs of all the homesteads?'

She swallowed and nodded. 'Those things all sound great. I don't have a problem with improvements.'

Flynn spoke to Howard for a few moments more and then rang off.

She swung back to him. 'When I return to the farm, who's going to be in charge—him or me?'

'I'll be in charge, Addie.'

Oops, that was right. Still, if rumour were anything to go by, Flynn didn't stay in any one spot for too long.

'You and Howard will have authority over different areas. You'll be in charge of the breeding programme. He'll be in charge of overseeing major improvements. I'll be overseeing the two of you.'

Unless she managed to change his mind by turning into the perfect PA. Which reminded her...

'I'm sorry I had that outburst in the meeting.'

He shrugged. 'It needed something to liven it up.'

It didn't change the fact that she should've had more presence of mind than to shout out during a business meeting. She bit her lip and glanced at him. 'So, you didn't find that meeting riveting?'

'Absolutely not.'

She sagged. 'I thought it might've just been me. Jet lag or something.' She retrieved her notebook and handed it to him. 'I'm really sorry, but my mind kept drifting off.'

He laughed when he read her notes—or lack of them.

'I promise to do better next time.'

He handed the notebook back. 'I only asked you to jot things down to keep myself awake.'

She wrinkled her nose. 'Are all business meetings that dull?'

'Not at all. Herr Gunther was just doing his best to bore and obfuscate.'

He'd succeeded with her. 'Why?'

'Because he favours one of my rivals and is hoping this other party can get a jump on me somehow.'

'There's a rival?'

'There're several, but only the one we need worry about.'

'Will this rival get a jump on you? Should we be worried?'

His eyes suddenly blazed and one of his hands clenched. 'I say bring it on. The harder and the dirtier the battle, the more satisfying it'll be.'

Really?

'Regardless of the cost, Addie, this is one battle I mean to win.'

She swallowed. Right.

'The upshot of the meeting is that there's been a delay in processing probate.'

The one thing Addie had fathomed from the meeting was that the person who'd owned the premises that housed the brewery and beer hall had recently died. Hence the reason the property would soon be on the market. The probate referred to the reading of this man's will so his estate could be finalised.

'Herr Gunther will try to draw that delay out for as long as he can, but we're not going to let him.'

That made them sound thrillingly powerful and masterful. She clapped her hands. 'So?'

He raised an eyebrow. 'So?'

'What next? Do we head over to these Schubert, Schuller and Schmidt's of yours and come up with a game plan?'

'They already have my instructions. You, Adelaide Ramsey, have the rest of the day off to do whatever you want.'

Really? That was the entirety of her work for the day?

'Go out and explore. Sightsee.' He glanced up when she didn't move. 'If I need you I have your mobile number. I'll call you if something comes up.'

Right. She gathered up her things.

'And, Addie?'

She turned in the doorway. 'Yes?'

'Have fun.'

Oh, she meant to, but she wouldn't be sightseeing in this gorgeous and compelling city. At least, not this afternoon. If she wanted to convince Flynn that she was perfect PA material, she had work to do.

Flynn barely glanced up from his laptop when the room phone rang. He seized it and pressed it to his ear. 'Hello?'

'Flynn, it's Addie. I wondered if you were busy.'

He closed the lid of his laptop, her threat to pull out of the sale still ringing in his ears. He wondered if she realised how fully invested in Lorna Lee's she was. And if he hadn't been aware of his own emotional stake in the place before, he was now. 'Not busy at all. What's up?'

'Would it be convenient to come over to show you something I've been working on?'

She'd been working? On what? 'The door's open.'

He replaced the receiver with a smothered curse and unlocked the door—stood there holding it wide open, like a lackey. Darn it! She wasn't going to pull out of their deal, was she? Lorna Lee's was small fry in the grand scheme of things, but…he'd started to think of it as a place he could hang his hat. He didn't have one of those. It was disconcerting to discover that he wanted one, but he refused to bury the need. Lorna Lee's would be perfect.

Addie came tripping in with her laptop under one arm and her notepad clutched to her chest. She'd swapped her saucy red suit for jeans and a long-sleeved T-shirt. She moved straight to the table and fired the laptop to life without a word, but a smile lit her lips and a pretty colour bloomed high on her cheeks. When she turned those amber eyes to him, their brightness made his heart sink.

If she loved her home that much he'd never be able to take it away from her.

Would she consider going into a partnership with him instead?

'I've spent the afternoon researching breweries and beer halls and—'

'You've what?' The door slipped from his fingers and closed with a muted whoosh. 'For heaven's sake, why?'

Her hands went to her hips. 'You're buying one, aren't you?'

'Specifically, I'm buying the premises.'

She waved a hand in the air. 'Semantics.'

He decided not to correct her.

'Bavaria is known for its fine beer. And, of course, Munich is famous for Oktoberfest.'

He rubbed his nape. 'Addie, why aren't you out there seeing the sights and experiencing the delights of Munich?'

She clicked away on her computer. 'I want to be useful.'

He closed his eyes and counted to three. 'What happened to "have you ever wanted something so bad", et cetera? This is a once-in-a-lifetime opportunity.'

She spun to stare at him. 'And buying a brewery and beer hall isn't?'

His mouth opened and closed, but no sound came out. He shook himself. 'C'mon.' He took her arm and propelled her out of the room, grabbing his coat and scarf on the way. 'Go put on a jumper and scarf and coat.'

'But don't you want to hear about the research I did and—?'

'Later.'

He waited outside her door while she grabbed her things.

'If you really want to be useful to me, Addie, then I want you out and about in Munich seeing and experiencing everything you can.'

She stared at him as they made their way down the stairs, struggling to get her arms into her coat. 'You want me to immerse myself in the culture?' She bit her lip. 'Are you hoping that whatever insights I gain might be helpful in your negotiations somehow?'

If she thought that was the reason then he'd play along. He held her coat so she could get her left arm in the sleeve. 'Yes.'

'Oh.' She glared at him. 'Then why didn't you say so?'

Because he hadn't been fool enough to think she'd waste the best part of a day researching breweries when it wasn't even breweries he was interested in.

Not that she knew that.

'Really, Flynn,' she harrumphed. 'You need to give your people better information.'

'Noted,' he said and had the pleasure of seeing her lips twitch. He wanted her to sightsee until she was sick of it. He wanted her to get the wanderlust out of her system so she'd settle back at Lorna Lee's without chafing at imaginary restraints.

They're not imaginary.

Whatever! She'd get four weeks' annual leave a year and plane tickets wherever she wanted. He didn't want her getting the wanderlust so completely out of her system that she refused to sell her farm to him.

She belted the sash of her coat all the more securely

about her when they stepped outside. 'It gets dark so quickly here. It's barely five o'clock.'

He missed Australia's warmth and daylight savings. Back home night wouldn't fall for another four hours. 'That's the joys of a northern hemisphere winter,' was all he said.

'Where are we going?'

He'd considered that while waiting outside her door. 'You said you needed to buy Christmas presents, and I expect you'd like to mail them home in time for Christmas.'

Her face lit up. 'The Christmas markets?'

Better yet. 'The *medieval* Christmas markets.'

Her eyes widened. 'Oh.' She clasped her gloved hands beneath her chin. 'That sounds perfectly perfect.'

He glanced down at her and something shifted in his chest. Silly woman! Why had she wasted her precious time cooped up inside? She didn't strike him as the type who'd be afraid to venture forth on her own.

I want to be useful.

He bit back a sigh. Yeah, well, he didn't want her crying on her own in Bruce Augustus's pen in the future. 'Just so you know,' he said, turning them in the direction of Wittelsbacherplatz—the site of the markets, 'this isn't some touristy money spinner.' Though no doubt it did that too. 'There's been a Christmas market on the site since medieval times apparently.'

Her jaw dropped when a short while later they passed one of the façades of the Residenz—a series of palaces and courtyards that had been the home of former Bavarian rulers. 'That's… It's amazing.'

He stared too. It was really something.

They turned down the next boulevard and her eyes widened as if to take in all the beauty. He totally sympathised. When they stepped into Odeonsplatz and she clapped eyes on St Peter's Church, she came to a dead halt. She glanced around, blinking at the Field Marshal's Hall. 'How can one city have so much beauty?' she breathed.

'What do you think?'

'Words can't do it justice. It's beautiful. I love it.'

He grinned then. 'Come right this way.'

Less than a minute later they entered Wittelsbacher-platz. It was purported to be one of the most commanding squares in Munich and at the moment it was alive with colour and bustle and the scent of Christmas. Not to mention row upon row of market stalls.

He glanced down at her and his grin widened. Breweries and Lorna Lee's were the furthest things from her mind and he pushed them firmly from his too. 'C'mon. Let's start down here.' He took her arm and led her down one of the alleys formed by the stalls.

They lost themselves in a whole new world. There were woodcarvers, glass-blowers and bakers. There were shoemakers, cuckoo clocks and gingerbread. There was noise and life and vigour, and he watched as it brought Addie alive and filled her with delight. They stopped to watch a medieval dance troop perform a folk dance, the scents from the nearby food stalls filling the air. When the dance was complete she took his arm and headed down a different alley. 'This is amazing! Have you ever seen anything so amazing? It's just…'

His mouth hooked up. 'Amazing?'

'Nutcrackers!'

He glanced from her face to the items she pointed to. An entire stall was devoted to small, and not so small, wooden soldiers.

'Colin would love these!' She selected four and paid for them all on her own, never once asking him to interpret for her. He shook his head. She definitely wasn't afraid of venturing forth on her own.

I want to be useful.

He had overcome that barrier now, hadn't he?

She oohed and aahed over chimney sweeps made from dried plums and almonds. She bought some gingerbread.

'Uh, Addie, I'm not sure you'll get that through Australian customs.'

'Who said anything about posting this home? It's for us now.' She opened the bag and broke off a piece. He thought she might melt on the spot when she tasted it. She held the bag out to him and lunch suddenly seemed like hours ago. He helped himself to a slice. She grinned at whatever expression passed across his face. 'Good, isn't it?'

He took some more. 'Really good.'

He bought them mugs of *glühwein* and they drank it, standing around one of the makeshift fires that dotted the square, Addie's holiday mood infecting him. He drank in the Christmas goodness and watched as she tried to choose a wooden figurine for Frank. 'What do you think?' She turned, holding up two carvings for his inspection. 'Father Time or the billy goat?'

He could tell by the way she surveyed the goat that it was her favourite. He didn't doubt for a moment that Frank would love either of them. 'The goat.'

He took her parcels from her so she could browse unencumbered. They stopped to watch a glass-blower shape a perfect snowflake—an ornament for a Christmas tree—but he preferred to watch her.

When was the last time he'd relished something as much as Addie was relishing this outing?

He frowned and tried to wipe the thought away. He didn't want to put any kind of dampener on Addie's mood. Not when she'd put in a full day's work on his behalf. He frowned again. He still didn't feel as if he'd got to the bottom of that yet.

'Oh, Flynn, look at that.'

He dutifully glanced at what she held out to him. It was an exquisite glass angel—ludicrously delicate and unbelievably detailed.

'Jeannie would go into ecstasies over this, but…'

'But?'

'It'd be in a thousand pieces before it ever reached her.'

He eyed it and then the packaging it came in. 'Not necessarily. It'd be well protected in its box with all of that tissue paper and sawdust around it. If we put it in another box with bubble wrap—' lots of bubble wrap '—and marked it fragile it should be fine.'

'You really think so?'

'The packaging and postage won't come cheap,' he warned.

'Hang the expense.' She bought it. It made her eyes bright. His shoulders swung suddenly free.

'Now who do you need to buy for?'

He blinked. Him? Nobody. 'I give bonuses, Addie, not Christmas gifts.'

'But surely you have friends who…' She trailed off.

Friends he hadn't spent enough time with over the last few years, he suddenly realised.

'I'm sorry. I didn't mean to make you sad.'

He shook himself. 'Not sad,' he countered. 'Wine. I've sent them wine. It's already been ordered.' One of his secretaries would've taken care of it.

She folded her arms. 'Surely there's a significant other out there you ought to buy some frippery for?'

He tried to look forbidding. 'I beg your pardon?'

She reddened. 'I'm not trying to pry.' She stiffened. 'And I don't want you thinking I'm putting myself forward for the position, mind, if there is a vacancy.'

Perhaps he'd overdone it on the forbidding thing. 'I'm not getting those vibes from you, Addie. If I were I'd make sure you were aware that I *never* get involved with employees.'

'Right.' She eased back a bit further to stare at him.

He rolled his shoulders. 'What?'

'Don't get me wrong, but you're young, successful and presentable.' She raised an eyebrow. 'Heterosexual?'

'As two failed marriages will attest.'

She shook her head. 'That doesn't prove—' Her jaw dropped. *Two failed marriages! Two?*

'Which is why I make sure *no* woman ever expects a Christmas present from me. I'm not travelling that particular road to hell ever again.'

'Two—' She gulped back whatever she'd been going to say and shook herself upright, gave one emphatic nod. 'Fair enough. The short answer is there's really nobody you need to buy for.'

'Correct.'

'The long answer is there's not going to be a new mistress at Lorna Lee's.'

Had she been worried about that? It made sense, he guessed. In her place he'd have wondered the same. 'Who else do you need to buy for?'

'Eric and Lucy.'

She'd bought a present for their little boy. Wasn't that enough?

'To own the truth, Flynn, I'm starting to feel a little shopped out.'

No, she wasn't. She'd only said that because she thought he must be bored with the shopping. He opened his mouth to disabuse her of the notion.

'What I am is starved.'

He glanced at his watch and did a double take. Seven o'clock? How had that happened? 'C'mon, we passed a cute-looking traditional place on the way here.'

The cute place turned out to be a beer hall. Of course. But Addie didn't seem to mind. 'I'll have the pork knuckle with the potato dumpling,' she said to the waitress, pointing to the dish on the menu.

Flynn held up two fingers. *'Zwei, bitte.'* He ordered two wheat beers as well.

'My research today informs me that one can't get more Bavarian than pork knuckle and dumpling.'

'Unless you settle for a plate of bratwurst,' he pointed out.

'I'll try that tomorrow.'

She stared at him. Eventually he raised his hands. 'What?'

'Aren't you even the slightest bit interested in all the stuff I've researched today?'

Not really. He didn't say that, though.

'For example, do you know how expensive beef is here?'

'Compared to Australian prices, beef is expensive throughout all of Europe.'

'You could make an absolute killing by supplying beef dishes at your beer hall. Beef sourced from your cattle station.'

He leaned towards her. She smelled of gingerbread and oranges. 'Why is doing a good job for me so important to you?'

'Oh.' She bit her lip and her gaze slid away. 'I, um…I was thinking that if I did a really good job for you, that you wouldn't mind providing me with a reference. A glowing reference I'll be able to use when I come back to Europe for real.'

'Addie, you are in Europe for real.'

She shook her head, her gaze returning to his. 'This is time out of time, not real life.'

What on earth was she talking about?

'When my two years are up on Lorna Lee's I'll be leaving to lead my real life.'

Her real life?

'And my real life is working my way through Europe at my leisure.'

Why was she so determined to leave a place that had nurtured her, a place she obviously loved, for a hobo temping trek around Europe? For heaven's sake, she'd be bored to death as a PA. Wasn't today's meeting proof positive of that?

'Unless of course you find that I'm the best PA you've ever had and decide you can't be doing without me.'

He laughed.

Addie glanced down at the table.

The waitress arrived with their beers and he lifted his glass in salute. 'To enjoying Munich.'

When she lifted her gaze he could've sworn her eyes swam, but she saluted him with her glass, blinding him with a big bright smile. 'To Munich.'

CHAPTER FOUR

FLYNN CLOSED THE door to his room and flung his coat and scarf on a chair. Pushing his hands into the small of his back, he stretched. His body ached, which didn't make a whole lot of sense. All he'd done was walk and talk, eat and laugh. It wasn't as if he'd been on muster.

He glanced at his watch and blew out a breath. Eleven p.m. He'd been walking and talking and eating and laughing for six hours. He moved to the window to stare down at the now quiet street below. He hadn't expected to enjoy Munich. He'd come here to get a job done. Enjoyment hadn't been on the agenda. Somewhere along the way, though, Addie's delight in the Christmas markets had proved contagious.

From his pocket he pulled the carved wooden bull he'd bought when Addie hadn't been looking. He'd meant to give it to her during dinner as a gesture of goodwill, a promise that Bruce Augustus would always have a home at Lorna Lee's, but, while there was no denying that Addie was good company, there'd been a shift in...tone, mood, temper? He hadn't been able to put his finger on it, but Addie had somehow subtly distanced herself and the carved bull had remained in his pocket—the right moment never presenting itself.

He frowned. It'd been a long time since he'd shared a convivial meal with a friend. Not that Addie was a friend—she was an employee—but it had him thinking about his real friends. Wasn't it time to enjoy the fruits of his labours and slow down on the cut-and-thrust? It wasn't a question he'd ever considered. Now he couldn't get it out of his mind.

He swung away from the window. What? A slip of a girl milked every ounce of enjoyment from a new experience and now he was questioning his entire way of life?

He shook himself. There was nothing wrong with being goal-oriented!

He rubbed his nape. But, when *was* the last time he'd enjoyed something as wholeheartedly as Addie?

He collapsed to the sofa. Maybe it was time to slow down. After he'd brought ruin down on Mueller's head, of course.

He recalled the peace that had filtered through his soul when he'd first clapped eyes on the rolling fields of Lorna Lee's. When he left Munich maybe he could focus on spending time there, working the land and building a home. The idea eased the ball of tightness in his chest.

First, though, he had to deal with Mueller. That fist clenched up tight again. With a growl, he headed for the shower.

It wasn't until he emerged, rubbing a towel over his hair, that Flynn noticed Addie's laptop and notepad sitting on the dining table. He paused, hesitated and then flipped open the notepad. Nothing. She'd obviously brought it along to make notes.

He eyed the laptop, rolled his shoulders and stretched his neck, first to the right and then to the left. He didn't care about the brewery. He only cared about ruining Mueller.

Still, he'd have to do something with the premises. The local council wouldn't allow them to remain idle. He'd need to provide them with assurances, make promises. Besides, it wouldn't hurt to look at the material Addie had gathered *in her free time*.

He seized the computer, planted himself on the sofa and fired it up. He'd be careful not to look at any personal documents. Clicking on the last word-processing document she'd been working one—the one titled Flynn's Brewery/ Beer Hall—he read her rough notes.

He straightened. Actually, while some of her ideas were fairly basic, some of them were interesting and surprisingly savvy.

He opened her Internet browser to follow a couple of references she'd made in her notes. He pursed his lips, his mind starting to race. Once he'd bought the premises out from beneath Mueller, it wouldn't be too hard to establish another brewery there—the equipment belonged to the premises, which meant it'd meet local council regulations.

He grinned and lifted a foot to the coffee table. Mueller's finances were in a sorry state. He'd invested too heavily in improvements to the premises without securing a guarantee—*in writing*—that he'd have first option to buy if they ever came on the market. A gentleman's agreement didn't count in this situation. A harsh laugh broke from him. That was just as well. Mueller was no gentleman. He might be able to make a halfway decent offer on the premises, but Flynn would be able to offer three times as much.

He rested his head back and stared up at the ceiling, satisfaction coursing through him. Running a brewery on Mueller's premises? Talk about poetic justice. Talk about rubbing salt into the wound.

He glanced at the computer again. The idea of owning a brewery hadn't filled him with any enthusiasm except as a means to an end. It could just as well have been a sausage factory for all he cared. But now…

Addie's enthusiasm, he discovered, wasn't just reserved for her travels—it filled her notes too and some of it caught fire in his veins. Owning a beer hall could be fun. Hadn't he just decided he needed more fun in his life? He settled back and checked her word-processing file history and then selected a document titled 'Till the Cows Come Home.' He figured it'd have something to do with the beef industry. Her idea of using beef supplied from his cattle station to launch a cheaper beef menu had a lot of merit.

A document with a header of daisies and buttercups and cartoon cows appeared. He frowned. This looked personal. He went to close it when several words leapt out at him— Munich, Brewery and F.

Dear Daisy,
I know I've said it before, but I have to say it again— you'd love Munich as much as I do! I know it's not Paris, but beggars can't be choosers—isn't that what they say? Anyway, you'd have a ball, turning all the guys' heads in one of the traditional Bavarian costumes the barmaids wear—very sexy.

We'd have to build up our arm muscles, though, before embarking on a barmaid career here. You wouldn't believe it, but I saw one girl carrying ten litres of beer—five litres in each hand—and she didn't even break a sweat. Amazing! I love the beer halls.

Hmm...wonder if F would leave me here as a tavern wench?

He grinned. Not a chance.

Speaking of which, the perfectly perfect F is perfectly cool and collected in business meetings too. Extraordinary that someone actually enjoys those things.
Still...I wish...with all my heart I wish you were here.
Love Buttercup.

Buttercup, huh?
So who was Daisy?

PS I've decided against starting the blog up again and—

Flynn jerked upright and hit 'quit' in double-quick time. He wasn't going to read Addie's private diary! Sheesh!

He stared at her computer screen, went to close down the internet browser when, on impulse, he typed 'Till the Cows Come Home' into the search engine. A page with a background of daisies, buttercups and cartoon cows loaded. He checked the archives. The very first post was dated six years ago. He read it. He read the next one and the one after that, battling the lump growing in his throat. He read into the wee small hours until he could no longer battle fatigue. In the morning when he woke he picked up where he'd left off.

Addie had posted every day for eighteen months, but the blog had been defunct for the last four years. He stared at the wall opposite. Was it an invasion to read her blog like this? If she'd truly wanted privacy she'd have kept a diary instead, right? As she did now. He scrubbed a hand down his face before shutting off the computer and pulling on a pair of sweats.

She'd published it in a public forum. After all, that was what a blog was—a way of reaching out and connecting with other people. Only…comments had been left but Addie hadn't responded to any of them.

Who was Daisy? Addie had bared her soul in that blog— her pain and heartbreak when her friend—Daisy—had died of leukaemia.

He could ask her.

Or you could keep your fat trap shut.

None of it was his business.

So why did it feel as if it were?

He jerked around at the tap on his door. A quiet tap as if the person on the other side was being careful to not disturb him if he were still asleep. Instinct told him it'd be Addie. Asleep? Ha!

He pulled in a breath, careful to keep his face smooth, before opening the door. Addie had started to turn away, but she swung back and her smile hit him in the gut. 'Hey, good morning.'

'Morning.'

She eyed him carefully. 'You okay?'

He cleared his throat. 'Yep. Fine. All's good with me.'

She blinked and her brow furrowed and then she shook it all away. 'Sorry to disturb you, but I wondered if I could grab my laptop. I left it here yesterday. I forgot to collect it when we got back last night. Speaking of which, I laid down for just a moment and bang! I was out for the count. Jet lag's a killer, huh?'

He strove for casual, for normal, when all he really wanted to do was haul her in his arms and hug her tight, tell her how sorry he was about Daisy. He cleared his throat. 'Jet lag? But you stayed awake all day yesterday, right?'

She snorted. 'One could hardly call whatever I was in that meeting with the lawyer awake.'

He laughed, when he'd thought laughing would be beyond him.

'Fingers crossed, though, that the body clock is on local time now.'

He suddenly realised they both still stood by the door. He strode back into the room, seized her laptop and notepad and then swung back and thrust them at her. He didn't invite her inside. He hoped a bit of distance would help him get his thoughts and impulses under control and ease the burning in his chest when he glanced at her.

Everything he'd read, it was none of his business. That, however, didn't mean he could just push it out of his head, disregard it or forget it. It was still too close.

She clasped the computer and notepad to her chest. 'Is today still a free day?'

He nodded. Tomorrow he'd have a meeting with his lawyers, but it was only for form's sake—to keep him abreast of what they were doing and where they were at. They'd been quietly beavering away on his behalf for the last few weeks.

'Okay, well, while I have a chance to ask, what would you like me to prepare for tomorrow?'

'Nothing.' In fact, she wouldn't even need to attend.

'You haven't given me so much as a letter to type up yet!'

But she wanted to help, to be useful. He leaned against the door. 'You want the truth?'

She stuck out a hip and nodded.

'Many of these kinds of negotiations are about appearances.'

She stared at him as if waiting for more. 'Okay.' She drew the word out.

'While we're here I want—need—to appear powerful, in control and ruthless.'

She lifted a shoulder. 'As you're all those things then I don't see the problem.'

She thought him ruthless?

He rubbed his nape. Of course she did. He was all but forcing her to spend the next two years at Lorna Lee's. 'I know I am and you know I am...'

'Ah, but you need the people you're negotiating with to know that you are too.'

'And the sooner, the better. How do you think I can best achieve that?'

'By dressing smartly in expensive suits and staying in swish hotels?'

'And having lackeys.'

Her face cleared. 'I'm your lackey!'

'Not literally, you realise.'

'But *they* don't know that.' She chewed her lip. 'So I just have to dress smartly, say "Yes, Mr Mather" and "No, Mr Mather" at the appropriate times, fetch you coffee when you demand it, email London when you tell me to, and ring New York when you deem it necessary.'

'Now you're getting the hang of it.'

She beamed at him. 'I could do that with my eyes closed.'

He frowned.

'Except I won't, of course.'

'I have perfect faith in your abilities, Adelaide.'

She stared at him for a moment before shaking herself. 'So you don't have plans for this afternoon and this evening?'

'I…'

'Because I'm going to try and get us tickets to the ice hockey.'

He stared at her.

'Sport is a universal language, Flynn.'

In her diary she'd called him perfectly perfect and it hadn't sounded like a compliment.

'So you never know. A passing comment that you saw the Red Bulls in action could swing a negotiation your way, or create a useful connection. It'll also show you're interested in the community and that won't do you any harm.'

Perfectly perfect?

'You make a strong case,' he allowed. 'But here…' He fished out his credit card. 'Charge the tickets to this.' He didn't want her out of pocket.

'But—'

'Legitimate business expenses,' he declared over the top of her protests.

'Oh!' She took a step back and then gestured to what he was wearing. 'I've interrupted your morning run.'

'Just going to hit the hotel gym for an hour.'

She rolled her eyes. 'Flynn, for heaven's sake!'

'What?'

'Look out the window.' She pointed.

He turned to stare, but he didn't know what he was supposed to be looking at.

'The sun is shining,' she said as if speaking to a six-year-old. 'Fresh air.' She slammed a hand to her hip. 'What is wrong with you? If you're going to buy a Munich business the least you can do is breathe in the Munich air.'

Did she know how cold it was out there?

'Instead of some perfectly temperature controlled recycled air that's free of the scent or taste of anything.'

There was that word again—*perfectly*.

He thrust out his jaw. 'It's convenient.'

'But is it interesting? Does it teach you anything? Is it fun?'

That last stung.

She shook her head. 'Give me five. I know the perfect jogging trail.'

He opened his mouth to refuse. *Dear Daisy…* He closed it again. 'You jog?'

'Under sufferance. I'll meet you in the foyer in five minutes.'

It took her six, not that he pointed that out as she called a *guten Morgen* to Bruno. An altogether different emotion gripped him when he surveyed her legs in their fitted track pants. Addie didn't have a classically beautiful shape—her hips were too wide and her chest too small—but it didn't stop him from wondering what it'd be like to drag those hips against his and—

Whoa! Inappropriate. Employee. Jeez.

'C'mon, we're going to jog by the river. I went for a walk down there yesterday. It's gorgeous.'

It took them three minutes to reach it. She made them go across the bridge and down to the park on the other side. 'See, what did I tell you?'

She stretched her arms out wide and he had a sudden image of her sprawled beneath him, tousled and sultry and—

Why did he have to go and read 'Till the Cows Come Home'? Why did he have to see Addie in a whole new light?

For a moment he was tempted to tell her she could jog on her own, that he was going back to the hotel.

Wish you were here,
Love Buttercup.

He bit back an oath. She didn't deserve that from him. She'd had enough grief in her life without him adding to it. All he had to do was get his hormones in check.

'You really need to get the kinks out, don't you?'

He turned to find her, hands on hips, surveying him. What was so wrong about being perfectly perfect? What the hell did perfectly perfect mean anyway?

'I know it's cold but breathe it in.' She took a deep breath and so did he. 'Can you smell it?'

He knew exactly what she meant. Could he smell the land? Yes. He could smell the brown of the river and the green of the grass and the tang of sap and bark and tree. The air was thinner than home, and colder, but invigorating too. Without another word she set off down the path at a jog.

He set off after her, breathing in the cold air and trying not to notice how her hips moved in those track pants.

She set an easy pace. He could've overtaken her if he wanted, but, for reasons he refused to delve into, he chose not to.

He wasn't sure for how long they jogged, maybe ten minutes, when she pulled up short and pointed to an upcoming bridge. 'Look, it has statues on it like something out of *Lord of the Rings*.'

As they approached he noticed the detail and workmanship. He was about to suggest they go up onto the bridge to discover whom the statues commemorated when she grabbed his arm and pulled him to a halt. She pointed to her right. 'Look at that,' she breathed. 'Isn't it the most splendid building?'

Splendid described it perfectly.

'The first thing I did when I got back from my walk yesterday was find out what it was.'

He really should've done more homework before landing here. So much culture and history just outside his door and he hadn't even been aware of it. *What is wrong with you?* What indeed?

'Do you know what it is?'

A lump blocked his throat and he couldn't have explained why. He shook his head.

'It's home to the state parliament so I guess it should be grand, *but...*'

He understood her *but—but I've never seen anything like it before; but there's nothing like this in Australia; but it's outside my experience and I'm in a foreign country and it's amazing and exciting and an adventure.*

All the total antithesis of the reason he was here.

'Are you okay, Flynn?'

Apparently he was perfectly perfect for all the good it did him. He glanced down at her. The exercise had brightened her cheeks and eyes. A well of yearning rose up inside him. How had she held onto her excitement and joy and hope in the face of all her grief?

'Flynn?'

He shook himself. 'It's just occurred to me that I've been working too hard.'

'One should never work so hard that there's no time for this.' She gestured to the parliament building, the bridge and river.

He made a vow then. As soon as he'd vanquished Mueller, he'd find his excitement again. He'd make time to feed his soul with adventure and joy the way Addie did.

After the meeting with Flynn's lawyers the next day, which Addie had insisted on attending despite Flynn's assurances that she needn't, Addie needed a shopping trip. She'd endured forty minutes of boring, boring, boring. The four men had talked figures and had used phrases like 'projected outcomes', 'financial prognoses', 'incorporated portfolios' and 'Regulation 557' until she'd thought her brain would leak out of her ears and her feigned interest would freeze into a kind of rictus on her face.

The shopping, though, sorted her out.

She let herself into her room, collapsed onto the sofa and grinned at the assortment of bags that surrounded her. Oops. She might've gone a little overboard.

Oh, what the heck? She leapt up and tipped the contents of one of the bags onto the bed. Slipping out of her jeans, she tried on her new outfit and raced to the mirror. 'You'll never believe this, Robbie, but I have a cleavage!'

Her? A cleavage? She grinned, and then grinned some more, literally chortling. She turned to the left and then to the right before giving her reflection a thumbs-up. She'd only ever be able to wear it for fancy dress, but—

The phone rang.

She lifted it to her ear. 'Hello?'

'I need you in here. Right now.'

Flynn. 'But—'

There was no point speaking. The line had gone dead.

What on earth? She glanced down with a grimace, but headed next door without delay. She'd barely knocked before the door was yanked open.

'I...' Flynn did a double take. 'What on earth are you wearing?'

'It's a traditional Bavarian costume.'

'It's gingham!'

'The skirt of the dirndl is gingham,' she corrected. Blue-and-white gingham to be precise. 'The blouse is white and the bodice of the dirndl is royal blue.' Lord, she was babbling, but she could barely form a coherent sentence when Flynn stared at her chest like that. Her hand fluttered to her cleavage in an attempt to hide it. She cleared her throat. 'What's the emergency?'

He snapped to and swore, but he grabbed her arm and pulled her into the room. 'You're not even wearing shoes,' he groaned.

'I can go change.'

'No time.'

She wanted to shake him. 'For what?'

A heavy knock sounded on the door. He moved her away from it with another smothered curse. 'There's no time to explain, but just follow my lead. I need deadpan, no surprise. Cool, smooth and efficient.'

'Roger,' she murmured back.

He planted himself at the table with a file and his computer and then gestured towards the door. 'Please let Herr Mueller in.'

'Herr Mueller,' she repeated under her breath as she moved to the door. 'Herr Mueller?' she said when she opened it.

A pair of bushy eyebrows rose as they stared down at her. 'Yes.'

'Please come in.'

He took in her attire and twinkling eyes transformed a gruff face. 'You look charming, *fräulein*.'

She smiled back. 'I'm afraid you've rather caught me on the hop.'

'And I've been rewarded for it.'

What a nice man. 'Do come in, Herr Mueller. Mr Mather is expecting you.'

Those lips firmed and the bushy eyebrows lowered over his face when he entered the room. She swallowed and recalled Flynn's demand—cool, smooth and efficient. She gestured towards the table.

'Hello, Flynn.'

'Herr Mueller.' Flynn didn't rise or offer his hand. He didn't ask the other man to sit. He simply leaned back and crossed his legs. 'You wanted to talk. Well, talk.'

Her head rocked back. This was no way to do business,

surely? She gripped her hands in front of her. At least it wasn't how he'd done business with her or Herr Gunther or Herrs Schmidt, Schuller and Schubert.

The air in the room started to bristle and burn. She surged forward. 'Coffee?' she asked, hoping to ease the way.

'That would be appreciated,' Herr Mueller said with a forced smile.

'No coffee,' Flynn said with a glare, his voice like flint.

She realised then he didn't mean no coffee for him. He meant no coffee full stop. She blinked at his rudeness and choked back her automatic rebuke. His room. His rules. Fine, no coffee.

She had no idea what to do with herself—where to sit or where to stand. She decided to remain right where she was—behind Herr Mueller. She'd promised Flynn deadpan but now she wasn't sure that she could deliver. At least back here Herr Mueller wouldn't witness her shock.

Flynn would. If he bothered to glance her way. At the moment he was too busy summing up his…adversary, if that was what Herr Mueller was, to pay any attention to her.

'I didn't want to talk,' Herr Mueller said and she suddenly realised that behind the heavy German intonation there was a thread of an Australian accent. 'I just wanted to see your face and it tells me everything I need to know.'

Malice flashed in Flynn's smile. 'Good.'

He was enjoying this? Addie wished herself anywhere else on earth. She'd even plump for Lorna Lee's. In fact, Lorna Lee's suddenly seemed like a very attractive option.

'You're determined to ruin me?'

'I am. And I'll succeed.' The words were uttered smoothly, ruthlessly, triumphantly. Addie stared down to where her toes curled against the plush pile of the carpet.

'You hold a grudge for a long time.'

'Only the ones worth keeping.'

She glanced from one to the other. What on earth were they talking about?

'You may succeed in your aim, Flynn—'

'I have every intention of succeeding, George, and I'll relish every moment of it.'

She shivered and chafed her arms.

Herr Mueller frowned and leaned towards him. 'What you don't realise yet is that in the process you'll lose more than you gain. Are you prepared for that?'

Her head lifted at the pity in the older man's voice.

'No doubt that's what you'd like me to think.'

The older man shook his head. 'Despite what you think, I was sorry to hear about your father.'

Flynn laughed, but there was no humour in it. Herr Mueller turned to leave and Addie did what she could to smooth her face out into a calm mask. He held his hand out to her and she placed hers in it automatically. 'It was nice to meet you, Fräulein...'

'Ramsey. Adelaide Ramsey.' She tried to find a smile but she suspected it was more of a grimace. 'Likewise.' She leapt forward to open the door for him. '*Auf wiedersehen.*'

When the door shut behind the older man she swung back to Flynn, hands on hips. 'What on earth was that all about? My parents would've had my hide if I'd ever been as rude as you just were.'

'You were obviously raised more nicely than me.'

She gaped at him.

'By the way, Addie, you need to work on deadpan.'

'While you need to work on your manners! That man would have to be seventy if he's a day. Would it really have killed you to offer him a seat and a cup of coffee?' She dragged both hands back through her hair, paced to the door and back again.

Those hateful lips of his twitched. 'I've shocked you to the core, haven't I?'

'I may not know much about wheeling and dealing but that's no way to do business.'

'And yet it's exactly how I mean to conduct myself while in Munich, Addie. You don't have to like it.'

Like it? She hated it.

His face grew hard and cold. 'So you have two choices. Either shut up and put up or jump on the first plane back to Australia.'

She almost took the second option, but remembered her promise to Robbie. *Of course I'll see the world. I'll visit all of the places we've talked about.* The places they'd always meant to visit together. It hit her then, though, that they'd never considered—let alone discussed—what that promise might eventually cost.

When did the price become too high?

'You didn't come here to buy a brewery, did you? This isn't about making some boyhood dream come true.'

He laughed—a harsh sound. 'A boyhood dream? Where on earth did you get that idea? The brewery is only important insomuch as it's currently Mueller's. Make no mistake, though, I mean to take it from him.'

She took a step back. 'You came here with the express purpose of ruining him.'

'I did.'

She stared at him. 'It's Christmas, Flynn.' Who planned revenge at Christmas?

'I told you I was ruthless. And if I remember correctly you agreed with me.'

True, but… 'In business dealings, not personal ones.' And Herr Mueller was obviously personal. Nor had she thought Flynn ruthless to this level. She'd just thought him one of those perfectly perfect people who got everything they wanted with nothing more than the click of their fingers.

But Flynn wasn't perfect. He was far from perfect.

He leaned forward as if he'd read that thought in her

face. 'Think whatever you want, but I'm not the Scrooge in this particular scenario.'

Oh, as if she was going to believe that! 'What do you do for an encore—steal candy from babies?' she shot back.

He straightened and he reminded her of a snake readying itself to strike. 'As you haven't left yet I take it you've chosen to put up and shut up?'

Her stomach burned acid. 'Yes,' she said shortly. 'You're right. I don't have to like it, but… Are you sure that man deserves to be ruined?'

He rocked back on his heels. 'One compliment and he completely charmed your socks off. I credited you with more sense.'

The criticism stung. 'He was polite. I was polite back.'

'You were certainly that.'

She folded her arms. 'He seems nice.'

His lips twisted. 'Appearance is everything in these games, remember?'

So he'd said, but it suddenly occurred to her that she might not be the one wearing the blinkers. 'He reminded me of—'

'Let me guess—Santa Claus?'

'The grandfather of an old school friend.' Robbie's poppy. 'A nice old man.' Who'd seen too much heartache.

She walked to the window, blinking back tears. When she was certain she had herself in hand, she turned back to Flynn. 'What did Herr Mueller do to you to deserve this?'

'That's none of your business. And,' he continued over the top of her when she went to speak again, 'for the third and final time—put up and shut up or…'

His *or* hung there like a black threat. She swallowed the rest of her questions. 'Will you need me for the remainder of the day?'

'No.'

Without another word, she left.

CHAPTER FIVE

ADDIE REEFED OFF her apron and pulled the dirndl over her head, leaving them where they fell. She tugged on thick jeans, thick socks and her thickest jumper. She wound a scarf around her throat, seized her coat and slammed out of the hotel.

If she stayed she'd only do something stupid like stride back over to Flynn's room and fight with him. And then he'd send her home.

She didn't want to go home, but...

She buried her hands deep in the pockets of her coat and hunched her shoulders against the cold. Why on earth had he let her go prattling on about marketing strategies for beer halls and import deals that could be struck, huh? She must've sounded like a right idiot! Had he been laughing at her the entire time?

She scrubbed her hands down her face before shoving them in her pockets again. Jerk! Why hadn't he told her the real reason he was in Munich from the start?

Because it was easier?

Because he knew it was wrong and felt uncomfortable about it?

She snorted. He didn't have enough sensitivity for discomfit.

She stomped down the street, but it didn't ease the tension that had her coiled up tight. It didn't answer the question of why her discovery left a hole gaping through her.

What she needed was a long gallop over rolling fields. Rolling fields. Lorna Lee's.

She slammed to a halt and lifted her face to the sky. She was going to have to spend the next two years working for this man? If she did him some perceived wrong would he then turn on her and try to destroy her? Would she for ever have to watch herself? Bite her tongue?

Ha! As if biting her tongue were a skill she possessed.

She set back off. In her pockets, her hands clenched. She had a feeling it was a necessary PA skill, though, and if she wanted to travel the world as a PA it'd be a skill she'd better master.

She wrinkled her nose. She stomped on for a while longer before thinking to take stock of her surroundings. When she did she came to a dead halt. She hadn't paid much attention to the direction her feet had taken her—other than to stay on well-lit streets. It grew dark early in Munich at this time of year.

This time of year…

Somehow she'd wended her way behind Marienplatz and now she stood on the edge of the square—facing the awe-inspiring Gothic magnificence of the New Town Hall. The enormous Christmas tree twinkled and glittered. The coloured lights and Christmas decorations strung up all around the square winked and danced, and on the balcony of the Old Town Hall a folk group sang a Christmas carol. Beneath awnings the Christmas markets were a feast of sound and scent and movement.

It was Christmas. In exactly one week.

Back home Jeannie would've put up her and Frank's tree. There'd be presents wrapped beneath it in brightly coloured paper. The ham would've been ordered and the Christmas pudding made. Addie twisted her hands together. Frank, Jeannie and her family had shared Christmas lunch and spent Christmas afternoon together for as long as she could remember. She scuffed a toe against the ground. They'd miss her father so much this Christmas Day. Maybe it'd been selfish to come to Europe.

Especially as this would be their last Christmas on the farm.

She scratched her head and rolled her shoulders. It didn't have to be. She could invite them for Christmas next year, couldn't she? Flynn wouldn't mind. Or would he?

She plonked herself onto a bench when a family vacated it and rested her elbows on her knees to frown down at the ground. She'd thought Frank and Jeannie had wanted to leave the farm—it *had* become too much for them—and to move into a retirement village with its easier pace. An email she'd received from Jeannie this morning, though, had left her feeling uneasy. Oh, Jeannie had been cheerful, full of neighbourhood news and Howard's progress with all of his 'new-fangled' ideas, but the cheer had sounded forced when she'd spoken about leaving.

Addie rested back and stared at the Christmas tree. If she was going to be stuck on the farm for another two years Frank and Jeannie could stay with her until they found exactly the right place to move into, couldn't they? She folded her arms. She'd probably have to get Flynn's approval—he with the noteworthy absence of Christmas spirit and lack of the milk of human kindness.

She ground the heels of her boots together. It wasn't precisely true, though, was it? He'd been kind to her. He'd taken her to the medieval markets. It'd seemed important to him that she enjoy herself. If he truly was ruthless then that didn't make sense.

Did he have an ulterior motive?

She snorted. Talk about fanciful, because, if he did, heaven only knew what it could be.

She bought a mug of *glühwein* and sipped it, appreciating the way it warmed her from the inside out. Back home at Lorna Lee's they'd be sipping ice-cold beer in an attempt to cool themselves. For the teensiest moment she wished herself on the homestead veranda surrounded by people she trusted and understood.

Addie didn't so much as clap eyes on Flynn for the following two days. She'd returned to her hotel room after her glass of *gluhwein* to a terse message on her voice mail informing her that he wouldn't require her services for the next two days.

It made her paranoid. Why had he brought her to Munich if he didn't want her to do anything? She rang home to speak to Jeannie and Frank, and then Eric, Lucy and Colin. She wanted to double-check that Howard had followed Flynn's directive about Bruce Augustus. She wanted to know that everyone was okay and that nothing dire was going down.

With everything at home seemingly perfect and her fears allayed, Addie went sightseeing. She visited Schloss Nymphenburg—the summer palace of the former Bavarian rulers—where she promptly went into raptures. The palace was the most exquisite building she'd ever seen. But it was the grounds that transported her.

Her jaw dropped as she viewed them from the balcony and her soul expanded until it almost hurt. Formal avenues stretched away, the central one leading down to an ornamental lake with a fountain. Flowerbeds lined the avenues. The colour must be spectacular in spring. Beyond the formal gardens, far beyond, green fields extended for as far as she could see. How perfect they'd be for cantering across, for leaving the cares of the world behind.

She'd spent a long time there—an hour in the palace itself and the rest wandering through the grounds. Did Flynn really mean to forgo all of this in the pursuit of his mean-spirited revenge? There were so many marvels and wonders to enjoy if he'd only stop for a moment and—

Stop it! Trying to understand him was fruitless. He'd have his reasons.

And as he'd pointed out, she didn't have to like them.

She glared up at a sky almost as blue as his eyes and hoped those reasons kept him awake at night.

She visited the Residenz, the palace in Munich—a series of gorgeous buildings and courtyards. The museum of grand rooms depicting differing architectural styles and works of art—paintings, sculptures, tapestries, porcelain and more—blew her away. To think people had once lived like this.

It became a bit too much so she spent the rest of the day in the English Gardens—one of the largest urban green spaces in Germany. She stared at frozen streams and dark green spruce trees and marvelled at how different they were from the creeks and gums back home. She ate bratwurst and drank hot tea and wished Flynn had chosen to join her rather than whatever nefarious plan he was no doubt putting into action instead.

Maybe if he had more fun in his life he'd let go of his grudge and focus on the future rather than…

She snorted. Yeah, as if that were going to happen.

Why are you being so hard on him?

She almost spilled her tea when that thought hit her. Was she being hard on him? She swallowed. Why—because he'd been rude to a man she'd taken a liking to? That hardly seemed fair.

She chafed her arms. No, it wasn't that. It was the hardness that had appeared in his eyes, their coldness when they'd stared at Herr Mueller. It had chilled her, frightened her. She took a sip of tea to try and chase the cold away. Still, wasn't that her problem, rather than Flynn's? He might in fact have a very good reason for his…hatred.

She set her mug down, her stomach churning. That was Flynn's primary emotion towards Herr Mueller. Hatred. She had no experience with it. And she didn't want any either, thank you very much.

Why did he feel so strongly?

She dragged a hand through her hair. The likelihood of finding that out was zilch. She wasn't sure she even wanted to know.

She returned to the hotel that evening to another terse message from her enigmatic employer informing her that a meeting was scheduled for the following morning and to meet him in the foyer at 9:45 on the dot. 'And let's see if this time you can keep your face halfway impassive.'

She poked her tongue out at the telephone, but raced over to the wardrobe to make sure her little black suit was all in order. Looking the part of the perfect PA might help her act like the perfect PA.

'Good morning, Adelaide.'

Addie leapt up from the chair she'd taken possession of in the foyer ten minutes ago. She'd made sure to arrive early. 'Good morning.'

She bit back a sigh. Flynn looked disgustingly crisp and well rested—perfectly perfect. 'Are you Mr Mather or Flynn at the meeting?' she asked, following him out to the taxi rank.

'I'm Flynn when you address me directly. I'm Mr Mather when you refer to me to a third party.'

She moistened her lips. 'And who might these third parties be?'

He flicked a wry glance in her direction. 'Herr Mueller and his lawyers.'

So they were meeting with the big guns.

'Is that going to be a problem for you?'

She didn't flinch at his sarcasm. 'I don't care what you say or threaten me with, I'm not going to be rude, Flynn.'

The words shot out of her, unrehearsed. She stiffened and waited for him to turn with those eyes and freeze her to the spot. Instead his lips twitched as he opened the cab door for her. 'Try, at least, to keep your shock in check.'

She scooted across to the far seat. 'I've had time to prepare,' she assured him.

Those blue eyes of his rolled a fraction. 'I'm hoping you won't have to say anything at all.'

Fingers crossed.

He remained silent after that. He didn't ask what she'd done for the last two days and she didn't ask him. Who knew five minutes could take so long? She spent the time practising being impassive and keeping her fingers *lightly* clasped in her lap.

They emerged from the cab and she recognised the offices of Flynn's legal team. They were on his turf, then. She smoothed a hand down her hair. How exactly did he mean to ruin Herr Mueller? How did one go about bankrupting someone? She had no idea. It wasn't something they'd taught at secretarial college—at least, not during the brief time she'd attended. Mind you, she could count all the ways disaster could strike at Lorna Lee's—drought, flood, a worldwide drop in beef prices, an outbreak of foot and mouth disease. Flynn, she supposed, planned to be Herr Mueller's natural disaster.

'Addie?'

She half tripped up a step. 'Yes?'

'Tell me your role today.'

She pulled in a breath, eyes to the front. This man had bought Lorna Lee's and was going to expand it in exciting ways. He'd offered her incentives and bonuses to stay—a generous wage and the promise of international air travel. He'd brought her to Munich, he'd taken her to Christmas markets and he'd helped her to shop. She owed him some measure of loyalty. 'My role today is lackey—super-efficient PA and lackey. When you say jump I ask how high.'

'And?'

Oh! 'And I will do my best to keep a straight face, keep my thoughts to myself and to follow your lead.'

'Excellent.'

She followed him into the building with a sigh and tried to stop her shoulders from sagging. It all sounded perfectly perfect. As long as she could pull it off.

During the first twenty minutes of the meeting, Addie learned precisely how to bankrupt a man. What one did was buy out from beneath him the building he'd leased for the last eighteen years and had spent a ludicrous amount of money improving, with the sole intention of not leasing the building back to him. Apparently a verbal agreement had existed between the deceased owner and Herr Mueller for Herr Mueller to buy the premises at a reduced price, but there was nothing in writing. Likewise, all of the equipment that Herr Mueller had spent so much money investing in was now considered part of the premises—owned by the estate and not by him.

'I had a verbal agreement with Herr Hoffman that this building would be mine!' Herr Mueller slammed a hand down to the table.

'Present the documentation to support your claim and I will gladly cede the tender to you.'

She swallowed. Dear Lord, Flynn sounded controlled and deadly.

'It was a gentleman's agreement.'

'Herr Mueller, I don't for one moment believe you a gentleman.'

Addie nearly swallowed her tongue. How on earth did Flynn expect her to keep her face unreadable when he said things like that?

'As far as I'm concerned that building is up for grabs to the highest bidder.'

No points for guessing who the highest bidder would prove to be. She bit her pen, glancing from one man to the other.

'You have no love for German culture! What do you know about brewing techniques or—?'

'I know how to turn a profit. If you want the premises all you need to do is outbid me.'

That cold hard smile! She tried not to flinch.

The only hope she had of keeping her promise was to think of something else. To tune out of the conversation while keeping her ears pricked in case Flynn called her name. She pulled her notepad towards her.

Think, think, think! What was something that bored her to tears? She'd maintain a veneer of impassivity if she were bored to tears.

Artificial insemination!

She wrote that at the top of the page. In the last couple of years there'd been developments in the techniques used for the artificial insemination of breeding stock. Not to mention the collection of bull semen. She bit back a sigh. It could be hard work inseminating a herd of twitchy heifers. Her record was four hundred and eighty-seven. In a single day. Her arm—her whole body—had been aching by the end of it. But, with an injection of funds maybe they'd be able to explore the newer methods.

They might prove quicker. She tapped the pen against her chin. Would they prove as successful, though? She jotted down some pros and cons. She'd need to do some intensive research, check a few websites and talk to some people in the industry. She scrawled down a few names, added a couple of websites to the list.

She bit the end of her pen. The improvements at Lorna Lee's didn't have to be confronting or intimidating. They could be exciting. Think what Flynn's injection of capital could do for the place. They'd be able to increase their output. A smile built through her when she thought of all of the sweet spring and autumn calves they could have. Calving was her favourite time of year.

Who knew? Maybe in a couple of years they'd really start to make a significant mark on the Australian stage. Lorna Lee's had a good reputation, but it couldn't compete with the bigger stud farms. Not yet. But if they could win a ribbon—a blue ribbon—at the Royal Easter show, Sydney's biggest agricultural show, then interest in their stock and breeding programmes would increase tenfold.

She imagined standing there, holding the halter of a magnificent bull—one of Bruce Augustus's grandbabies—as a blue ribbon was placed across his back. What a moment that would be.

Flynn glanced across at Addie when the lawyers started droning on about ordinances, injunctions and directives. His lips twitched at the dreamy expression she wore. It was a thousand times better than her indignation and disapproval, and it warmed something inside him. He'd missed her vigour and enthusiasm over the past two days. His smile widened when she started to slouch in a most un-PA way, her chin resting on her hands. What on earth was she thinking about?

He glanced at her pad, edged it around so he could read the notes she'd made. She didn't even notice, too deep in her daydream or whatever it was. He read what she'd jotted down and almost choked. He had to hide his mouth momentarily behind his hand. Artificial insemination? He coughed back a laugh. What crazy notion made her think she wanted to be a secretary or personal assistant instead of working at Lorna Lee's?

He nudged her. She immediately straightened.

He rose. She shot to her feet, gathering notebook and pens and slipping them into her briefcase.

'Gentlemen.' He glanced at the lawyers. 'You can stay to thrash this out to your hearts' content, but my resolution is fixed. Unless Herr Mueller can offer a higher bid on the property than I can, I will be buying it.'

This was supposed to be the day of his greatest triumph and all he could think about was taking Addie to lunch and listening to her sightseeing adventures.

'So you're serious in your intent, Flynn?' George Muel-ler said. There was no desperation in his eyes, only sadness.

'Deadly serious.'

Again, no triumph. The thing was…Mueller did look a lot like…well, Santa Claus. Flynn hardened his heart, delib-erately reminding himself what the other man had done to his father. Without another word he turned and left, aware of the click-click of Addie's heels as she followed him.

When they reached the street he didn't hail a cab, but turned left in the direction of their hotel. He glanced at Addie, who kept easy pace beside him. 'Artificial insemi-nation?'

She grimaced. 'I was trying to think of something that would help me keep my face straight, would help me look calm and bored.'

It hadn't succeeded, but he didn't tell her that. Inatten-tive was a hell of a lot better than 'shocked to the soles of her feet'. He still remembered her flinch when he'd told George that he didn't consider him a gentleman. It had been an almost physical rebuke.

It irked him that she thought so badly of him.

And it irked him that *that* irked him.

They needed to talk. He gestured her into a coffee shop.

'A debrief?' she asked.

'Something like that.'

He moved to a table, but Addie walked right up to the counter to peer at the cakes and sweets on display. 'Ooh, look at all of that!'

'Would you like something to eat?'

'You bet.'

And again she made him grin. Effortlessly.

'I'm on a mission to try every German delicacy I can.' She ordered a cappuccino and apple strudel with cream. After a moment's hesitation Flynn did the same.

'So?' She sat and folded her hands on the table. 'What do you need to debrief me about?'

There was no point beating about the bush. 'Howard isn't taking too kindly to you checking up on him.'

She laughed. 'The others are razzing him, huh? Good for them.'

Their order arrived and he swore her mouth watered as the strudel was placed in front of her. She lifted her spoon and took a bite. 'So good,' she moaned.

He followed her lead. Hell, yeah, it was better than good.

She took a second bite. 'But you can tell Howard not to get his knickers in a knot. I wasn't checking up on him. I was checking up on you.'

He choked on apple and pastry. When she slapped him on the back she did it so hard he almost face-planted the table. He glared at her. 'Me?'

She shrugged and ate more strudel.

'You want to explain that?'

'Not really. You won't like it.' She set her spoon down with a clatter and folded her arms. 'But I can see you're going to insist.'

Too right.

Her eyes—the expression in them—skewered him to the spot. 'I might've agreed when you said you were ruthless, but I didn't believe it. Not really.' She blew out a breath and shrugged. 'You were sort of ruthless in getting your own way about me staying on at Lorna Lee's, but you did sweeten the deal.'

Exactly.

'It wasn't until I saw how emotionless and cold and… hateful you were towards Herr Mueller that I believed it.'

She was right. He didn't like it.

'And then you said I wasn't needed for the last two days and it got me wondering if…'

'What?' He shoved apple strudel and cream into his mouth in the hope it would rid him of the bad taste that coated his tongue.

She waited until he'd finished eating before speaking

again. 'It made me wonder if there was some deeper game you were playing with me and Lorna Lee's.'

His stomach churned.

'I started thinking you might've wanted to get me away from the place for a while.'

That was what she now thought of him? He pushed his plate away.

'I thought you might have something devastating planned and didn't want me there when it happened.'

He leaned towards her. 'Addie, Lorna Lee's is mine. Once the cooling-off period is over I can do with it whatever I darn well please.'

'In another three and a half weeks.'

Was she counting down the days? He sat back. 'Why would I jeopardise our contract like that?'

'You're a man who likes to get his own way.' She sipped her coffee. 'You told me yourself that you don't like to wait when you want something.'

'We all like getting our own way, there's nothing unique about that, but why would I ask you to stay at the farm if I was going to do something to it that would get you offside?'

'Because you are ruthless.' She set her cup down. 'And I don't doubt for a moment that you think you know better than me.'

He stared at her. His ruthlessness had really shocked her, hadn't it? It had made her question his entire ethos.

He fingered the carved wooden figure in his jacket pocket. He'd carried it around with him for the last two days. He pulled it out now and set it on the table between them. 'I bought this for you as a symbol of our verbal contract about your bull, Bruce Augustus.'

She reached out and picked it up, turned it over in her fingers. 'It's beautiful.'

He recalled the warmth that had spread through him when she'd told him she believed him a man of his word. She didn't now, though. Now she thought him some kind of power-hungry, revenge-driven monster. 'I'm ruthless only where Herr Mueller is concerned.'

She glanced up. She opened her mouth, but closed it again, her eyes murky and troubled. He recalled the way he'd told her it was none of her business.

He swore under his breath. Addie didn't flinch at that. She didn't even blink. Bred to country life, she was used to swearing and expletives. What she wasn't used to was explicit rudeness. And hate.

'Herr Mueller destroyed my family.' He hadn't known he'd meant to utter the words until they left him.

Her jaw dropped. 'How?'

He dragged a hand across his nape. 'He and my father were business partners. They owned a pub in Brisbane.' Bile burned his stomach. 'Unfortunately you're not the only person to find him charming and benevolent. My father thought the same. That's the thing about conmen, Addie. They're plausible. It's a trick of the trade—that along with their charm.'

She gripped the carving in her hand and held it to her chest. 'What happened?'

He convinced my father to invest all of his money in their enterprise and then fleeced him of the lot.'

'But...but that's awful!'

'He sold up, made a killing and came to Germany, where his father's people were.'

'And your father?'

'He killed himself.'

Her hand reached out to cover his. 'Oh, Flynn.'

She didn't say anything else. Probably because there wasn't anything else to say.

'After that my mother became bitter.'

'How old were you when your father...?'

'Twelve.'

Her hand tightened about his. 'That's criminal!'

'Exactly.' He removed his hand from hers before he did

something stupid like clasp it, hold it and not let it go. 'And while I don't have the proof to put him in jail where he belongs, I can ruin him.' He clenched his hand. 'And I will.' And he'd show no mercy.

'I meant…' She swallowed. 'What Herr Mueller did is dreadful but… It was a terrible thing, your father leaving you and your mother alone like that.' She moistened her lips. 'I know money is important, but people are more important.'

A fist tightened inside Flynn's chest. 'He thought he'd failed us. The man he'd looked up to almost as a father had betrayed him. It was all too much.' His father had become a shadow, a wraith.

He dragged a hand down his face, remembering his father's attempts to explain the situation to him and his mother. He recalled her tears and the drawn, haggard lines that had appeared on her face. His father's pallor and hopelessness had burned itself onto his soul. Those things still had the power to scorch him, to shrivel what small amount of contentment he reached for. George Mueller was responsible for that.

He glanced across at her and tried to find a smile. 'Addie, my father had been so full of life. My mother was always a difficult woman, but when my father came home in the evenings he made everything better. He'd make us laugh and make everything seem carefree and merry and full of promise.' When his father had died, life had never been the same again and it was time for Herr Mueller to pay.

'Why didn't your father fight? Take him to court?'

'Mueller was too clever. He didn't leave a paper trail and he left the country before we'd even realised it. Hell, Addie, he used to come around for dinner. He'd laugh and joke and act like one of the family.' His twelve-year-old self had loved George Mueller. 'But he left without a single word of goodbye. The financial records at the bar were destroyed by fire.' Nothing had gone right for his father. 'There was nothing my father could do.'

'I'm sorry, Flynn.'

He shook his head. 'I didn't tell you this for your sympathy.' Though he knew her sympathy was real. 'I told you so you'd understand my attitude towards that man. So you'd understand why I can't let him profit from my family's misery.'

She nodded, but he could tell she didn't understand. Not really. Addie had experienced grief, but not hatred. In her world one let bygones be bygones. And he couldn't help but be glad of that.

Addie pulled her strudel back towards her. She'd lost her appetite completely, but she could tell Flynn wanted them back on an even footing—didn't want her making a fuss. She understood that. She'd appreciated her friends' and neighbours' condolences when her father had passed, but it had grown old hat real quick too. She realised she still held the carving of Bruce Augustus tightly clenched in her hand. She set him down on the table by her plate. 'Thank you for my carved Bruce Augustus.'

'I thought you'd like him.'

'I appreciate what it represents more.' She pulled in a breath. 'I do trust that you don't mean harm to Lorna Lee's. I do trust that you'll keep your word.' She did trust that he wouldn't hurt her the way—

She cut that thought dead in its tracks.

'That means a lot to me, Addie.'

She believed that too. And that seemed the strangest thing of all.

She spooned strudel into her mouth, made herself chew and swallow. 'Can I be nosy for a bit?' She wanted to get rid of the tight, hard look around his eyes and mouth.

'You can try.' But he said it with the hint of a smile that gave her the courage to persist.

'It's just that I thought you'd grown up on a cattle station, that you'd grown up with money. Now obviously that's not the case. So how did you get from there to here?' To think she'd thought everything had simply fallen into his lap in a perfectly perfect fashion. How wrong she'd been.

'After my father died my mother moved us to Bourke to be nearer her sister.'

Bourke was a small township in the far west of New South Wales. It must've been quite the culture shock to the Brisbane boy.

'In my teens I started doing a bit of jackarooing during the school holidays and on weekends and found I had a knack for it.'

She'd never believed for a moment that hard body of his came from hours spent in the gym.

'I also discovered a talent for the rodeo circuit. I started with camp drafting and breakaway roping and progressed to bareback bronc and bull riding.'

Bull riding? Whoa! Now that was tough.

'You can make a pretty packet on the rodeo circuit. I saved up and by the time I was nineteen I'd bought a small property. I made improvements to it using my own blood and sweat and then sold it for twice the price. Rinse and repeat. At the same time I did a business course by correspondence, made a couple of investments that paid off.'

She stared at him. 'So you're really the epitome of the self-made man.' The twice-married self-made man. What had *that* been about? Not that she had any intention of getting that nosy.

It was none of her business.

And she had no intention of thinking about Flynn in *that* way.

'Once all of this is over, Addie, I mean to draw a line under the whole affair and concentrate on living the life I want.'

A niggle of unease shifted through her. She wasn't convinced that hate could be dealt with so easily. What was more, something about Flynn's story didn't ring true. Not that she thought he was lying. She didn't doubt that he believed all he'd told her, but…

She couldn't put her finger on it. Just that something didn't feel right.

'And what is the life you want?'

'Maybe I'll decide to turn Lorna Lee's into one of the world's most renowned stud properties.'

That'd keep him out of trouble.

He pushed his plate away and met her gaze with a defiant glare. 'I'm going to make my home at Lorna Lee's.'

Really?

'And…'

'And?'

He shook his head and leant back. 'Somewhere along the way, Adelaide Ramsey, you fired me with your enthusiasm. I want to create a successful brewery business here in Munich. I want my beer hall to be one of the best.'

Her jaw dropped. 'No?'

'Yes.'

He grinned at her. She grinned back. 'Flynn, what are your plans for Christmas Day?'

His nose curled. 'Spare me, Addie. As far as I'm concerned, it's just another day.'

She'd bet he hadn't had a proper Christmas since he was twelve years old. She shook her head. 'Wrong answer.'

CHAPTER SIX

FLYNN LEANED BACK, his face an interesting mix of conflicting emotions—politeness and an evident desire not to hurt her feelings battled with bull-headed stubbornness and resentment.

Politeness?

Extraordinary that he took such efforts to don it for her.

No, not extraordinary. She could see now it was his rudeness to Herr Mueller that was really out of character.

'Addie, forgive me, but I don't *do* Christmas.'

Just as he didn't do marriage or romantic relationships any more?

She shook herself. 'Ignoring it won't make it go away.'

He blinked.

And she wasn't above using a little emotional blackmail. She leaned towards him. 'I was going to try and ignore Christmas this year, because…but…'

He reached out to still the hand that worried at the carved bull.

She stared at his hand resting on hers. 'But I find I can't.' She glanced up and suddenly it was real emotion and not an attempt to manipulate pity that gripped her. 'I can't ignore it in this beautiful city, Flynn. Christmas is everywhere and—'

'I'm sorry I thought—'

'No, don't be sorry. I'm happy I'm here. It's an amazing place and I'm having a fabulous time.'

'So what's the problem?'

She scratched the back of her head. She glanced down to hide the tears that threatened her composure. His grip on her hand tightened, but she couldn't speak until the ache that stretched her throat had receded.

When she was certain she had herself under control she glanced up and his eyes softened as they searched her face. He lifted his other hand and she thought he'd reach out to touch her cheek. It shocked her how much she wanted his touch, but he lowered it back to the table.

She moistened her lips, swallowed. 'It seems wrong for me to take so much pleasure in all of this, to be enjoying myself so much when my father died only four months ago.'

'He wouldn't want you falling into a pit of depression. He'd be glad to know you were enjoying yourself.'

'What makes you so sure? You didn't know him. You never met him.'

'Maybe not, but I've come to know his daughter and she has a good heart. She does right by the people in her life even when it's at the expense of her own dreams, and she's done it without losing her sense of humour. She's a lovely woman with a zest for life that has taught me a thing or two. It only follows that your father would be a good man too.'

She bit her lip to stop it from trembling, her chest doing a funny 'expand and cramp' thing. She didn't know what to say. 'Thank you.'

'Life goes on and there's no shame in you finding pleasure in that life, Addie. It doesn't mean you don't miss him or wish he was still here.'

'In my head I know the truth of that, but…'

She eased back, removing her hand from beneath his. His touch had sent a swirling, confusing heat dancing through her and she wasn't sure how much more of it she could take. 'This might seem ridiculous to you, but I know I'll miss him more on Christmas Day. Ignoring the day and pretending it doesn't matter or telling myself that I'm not celebrating it this year isn't going to change that fact.'

He pinched the bridge of his nose between thumb and forefinger.

'I suspect you know what I mean. I suspect it's why you don't do Christmas.'

He glanced at her and his eyes darkened.

She grimaced in apology. 'The thing is, I don't see that it's working for you.'

His head reared back.

'I'm not saying this to be mean,' she added quickly. 'Just trying to work out my best way forward.'

'You think it'll all magically go away—the pain and grief and disillusion—if you celebrate Christmas?'

His face twisted as he spoke and her heart throbbed for him. At twelve his life had been turned upside down. She suspected it hadn't been on an even keel since.

Did he think that it would help ease the burn in his soul if he slayed the dragon Herr Mueller represented?

She tried to find a smile from somewhere. 'I know Christmas is touted as a time for miracles, but, no, I don't believe it'll all magically go away.' She rested her elbows on the table. 'Heavens, though, wouldn't it be nice?'

He stared at her and the faintest of smiles touched his lips and it occurred to her that she didn't see them as perfectly perfect any more. Instead she saw them as intriguing and with the potential to sate some ache inside her. She blinked and forced her gaze away. He'd been married. *Twice.* The gulf of differences that lay between them almost stole her breath. He had all this experience with romantic relationships while she had none.

Well, not precisely none. But she'd had to make sacrifices where romance was concerned, her duty to her parents and the farm coming first. She didn't regret that, but she wasn't going to now go and develop a crush on Flynn. *That* would be stupid.

'So why put in the effort of celebrating at all?'

She shook herself. 'Because if you don't, you're not giving the good stuff a chance to get through.'

He stared at her but he didn't say anything.

'I think it comes from the same place as your desire to bring down Herr Mueller.'

His eyes narrowed. She suspected a more sensible mortal would stop now, but she pushed on. 'It seems to me that you think if you vanquish him all will be well again—justice served and the world put to rights.'

'You don't think that the case?'

'No.' Her stomach rolled. 'But I can't explain why not. I just can't help feeling you'll lose something of yourself in the process. For the life of me, though, I haven't worked out what that might be.'

He brought one finger down to the table between them. 'You think it's wrong to want justice?'

'You don't want justice, Flynn. You want payback.' If he wanted justice he'd have spent his time finding the proof to put Herr Mueller on trial instead of making the money and acquiring the power to destroy him. 'What you really want is to bring your father back, but you already know that's impossible.'

'Addie—' he spoke carefully '—do you really think this is the way to go about convincing me to celebrate Christmas with you?'

Oh! She could feel her cheeks heat up. 'Sorry, I…' How on earth had they got onto the subject of Herr Mueller again? 'So…' She grimaced. 'You knew that's what I was doing—trying to get you to celebrate Christmas with me?'

He kinked an eyebrow.

Of course he had. She lifted a shoulder. 'I was going to be all pathetic and use emotional blackmail.' She wrinkled her nose. 'Instead I was just pathetic.'

'There's nothing pathetic about grief.'

'Flynn, it's my first Christmas as an orphan.' Awful

word! She met his gaze squarely. 'It hurts me to know that my children will never know their grandparents.'

'You don't have any children.'

'Not yet, but I will.' One day. 'And I don't want to sit at home on Christmas Day moping and feeling sorry for myself.'

He didn't say anything.

She hauled in a breath. 'So will you celebrate the day with me?'

'I...'

'Something I've learned over the last couple of days is that sightseeing is more fun if you have someone to share it with. Someone you can nudge and say, "Check that out!" and they can say, "I know. Amazing, isn't it?" back to you. Bearing witness together. A friend. I have a feeling Christmas will be the same.'

He still didn't say anything.

She folded her arms and glared at him. 'Oh, for heaven's sake. It's only Christmas. It's not like I'm asking you to marry me.'

He scowled. 'I don't want something all hushed and reverent.'

'Me neither.' She suppressed a shudder. 'I was thinking of something cheesy. The kitschier, the better.' Loud and rowdy. A revel. A party.

His scowl eased a fraction. 'Do I have to buy you a present?'

She feigned outrage. 'Of course you do.'

He thrust out his jaw. 'I bought you that bull.'

Suddenly she wanted to laugh. 'I'm high maintenance. I want one of the dried plum and almond chimney sweeps that abound at the markets and a pair of mittens.'

His scowl vanished and his laugh lifted her heart. '*That* I might be able to manage. Just call me Saint Nick.'

She wanted to hug him.

Heavens, wouldn't that have him backtracking at a million miles an hour? 'Well, Saint Nick, if you're serious, tell me your plans for the brewery.'

Addie and Flynn spent the next morning touring one of Munich's premier breweries.

'Of course, it's five times larger than the Mueller brewery,' Flynn said as they pushed through the rotating door into their hotel.

Addie crammed in beside him. 'It was all terribly interesting, though. Who knew—?'

She suddenly realised that she was pressed up against Flynn's side as they moved the five or so steps it took to get from the street and into the hotel foyer. She became excruciatingly aware of the hard leanness of his body beside hers, the slide of his hip and thigh, their contained strength, and the firmness of the shoulder pressing against hers. Her thighs tingled, her knees trembled and she stumbled. His arm slid about her waist and he kept her upright without any apparent effort at all, which only weakened her knees further. 'Careful,' he said.

'Sorry, klutz,' she managed, her voice emerging more breathlessly than the moment warranted. 'I, uh…I should've waited and taken the section behind.'

He shrugged. 'We were talking.'

And then the door emptied them into the foyer and they moved apart. Addie busied herself straightening her jacket.

'You were saying?' Flynn said.

She had been? Oh, yes. 'I was just going to say how interesting I found the brewing process, and what fun you're going to have getting up to speed on it all.'

He shook his head. 'I'll just hire the best in the business to brew the beer and oversee production.'

As he had with her? Her shoulders went back. Did he think she was one of the best in the cattle-breeding business?

Was she? She'd never thought about it before. Surely not? She—

She bit her lip. She had a lot of experience, though, and—

'What on earth is going through your head?'

She shook herself. 'Crazy thoughts. Artificial insemination.' It had become their shorthand for her daydreaming flights of fancy.

'Well, if you can drag yourself away from such things I think you'll find our intrepid concierge is trying to catch your attention.'

She glanced over to Bruno and waved to let him know she'd be with him in a moment.

'I have an afternoon of email and phone calls—nothing you can help me with,' he added when she opened her mouth. 'A shopping-centre development in Brisbane that I'm investing in.'

Right.

'So you have a free afternoon. Will you be okay?'

Ever since she'd mentioned that sightseeing would be more fun with a companion, he'd been awfully solicitous. Too solicitous She tossed her head. 'Of course.'

'What will you do?'

'Shopping. Just good old-fashioned girly clothes and make-up shopping. I might even get a haircut.' Her fringe was starting to fall in her eyes.

'Do you have plans for this evening?'

'Not yet.'

'Then don't make any. There's something I think you might enjoy.'

She glanced up into the blue of his eyes. She wasn't sure who moved closer to the other, but suddenly they were chest to chest and the air cramped in her lungs. The air shimmered. His hand lifted as if...as if to draw her closer.

His eyes snapped away. He eased back, clasped her shoulder briefly, but even through the layers of her coat, her jacket and her blouse she could feel the strength in his fingers. 'Meet me down here at six.'

She nodded, unable to push out a sound.

He disappeared up the stairs, the breath eased out of her and she sagged.

'Fräulein Addie?'

She snapped upright and moved over to the reception desk. '*Guten Tag*, Bruno.'

'*Vielen dank.* Look!' He held up a pamphlet. 'I think I have found just the place for you and Herr Mather to spend Christmas. Look, here and here.' He opened the pamphlet and pointed.

Her jaw dropped. 'This is perfect, Bruno. I mean, simply perfect!' She took the pamphlet and flicked through it, her smile growing.

'You would like me to book it for you and Herr Mather, yes?'

'Yes, please! Oh, Bruno, you're worth your weight in gold.'

'I will book a car for you too.'

'Gold and rubies,' she declared. She'd have to buy him a Christmas present for this.

'You're most welcome. It was a pleasure. All part of the service. Also, while you were out these arrived for you today.' He handed her a business-size envelope along with a parcel.

They'd be from home! 'Ooh, thank you. *Danke.*'

He beamed at her. *'Bitte.'*

Addie raced up to her room. She recognised Jeannie's handwriting on the parcel, but the envelope had a typed label. She shrugged off her coat, dropped the envelope to the coffee table and tore the parcel open.

Fruitcake! Jeannie had sent her a slab of home-made fruitcake. A great well of longing opened up inside her. How she missed them!

She laughed over the enclosed letters—Jeannie's full of news of the farm and local doings. Frank had enclosed the local paper along with a photograph of a complacent Bruce

Augustus as, quote: 'still the farm mascot'. She kissed the photo. Colin had sent her a drawing of a Christmas tree. She propped it up on her bedside table. She folded her arms and beamed. Her dear, dear friends. 'Merry Christmas,' she whispered, realising that a part of her would be at the farm with them on the day.

She turned to the large envelope and laughed when she pulled out a sheaf of accounts. There wasn't even a note enclosed. Poor Howard. He must think her an awful bully. Or, more like, Jeannie and Frank had bullied him into sending them to her.

Later! She tossed them back to the coffee table. She wasn't wasting a perfectly good afternoon on accounts. Not when she could hit the department stores.

Addie was waiting for him when Flynn strode into the foyer. She leapt up the moment she saw him, a smile lighting her face and anticipation making her eyes sparkle. Something inside him lifted. She looked ludicrously Christmassy in a red wool swing coat, the colour complementing the colour in her cheeks.

He flicked the lapel. 'Let me guess—a bargain-basement buy on your shopping trip today?'

She stuck her nose in the air. 'I'll have you know that there was nothing bargain basement about this particular number.' And then she grinned. 'But I couldn't resist.'

'Good. It suits you.'

Her grin widened and she took his arm, leading him out of the side door rather than the revolving one. But he was no less aware of her now than he had been when they'd stepped into the revolving door earlier. It didn't stop him from hoping she'd keep hold of his arm, though.

Which could be a bad thing.

Or it could be entirely innocent and innocuous.

Yeah, right.

He ignored that.

She stopped when they reached the footpath. 'Right, which way?'

He turned them in the direction of Marienplatz. He glanced down at her. 'Aren't you going to grill me about where we're going?'

She glanced up from beneath thick, dark lashes. Her new haircut somehow emphasised her eyes. His heart slammed against his ribs. He swallowed, but he didn't look away. 'Would it do me any good? Besides—' she shrugged '—I like surprises.'

She probably didn't get too many of those living on the farm. He suddenly questioned the fairness of asking her to stay on as he had. His lips twisted. He hadn't asked. He'd forced her hand. *Ruthless.*

'Also, I like to surprise other people.'

He shot back to the present.

'And so I don't want to spoil your fun either.'

He stopped dead and stared down at her.

She touched a hand to her face. 'What?'

He kicked his legs back into action. 'Nothing. We don't have far to go,' he added to forestall any questions.

He led her across the road and down a side street. 'And here we are.'

She glanced at the building they'd stopped in front of and her mouth formed a perfect O. 'Where are we?'

'Peterskirche—the Church of St Peter.'

'I visited Frauenkirche the other day. It was amazing.'

He made a mental note to visit it as well. He'd seen the twin soaring towers multiple times, had used them on more than one occasion to orient himself, but he'd yet to go inside.

'Peterskirche is the oldest church in Munich.'

'It's beautiful.'

'My guidebook tells me it's in the Rococo style. C'mon.' He urged her forward. 'We're going inside.'

There were lots of people inside already. He found them

a seat about halfway down the nave. 'Are we going to attend a mass?' she whispered.

He pointed to the front. She craned her neck to look and then her face lit up like a little child's. 'A concert?'

'A Christmas concert brought to you today by your friendly Munich Philharmonic.'

She started to bounce. 'A proper orchestra?'

'The best in Munich,' he promised. He had no idea if they were or not, but it seemed a pretty safe bet.

As he'd guessed, the concert proved a hit with Addie. What he hadn't expected was how much her delight would make his chest swell, or how much he would enjoy the atmosphere and the Christmas music for himself. When it was over they just sat there and let the church empty around them.

'Magical,' she finally whispered, turning to him.

'Stunning,' he said, turning more fully towards her. 'I couldn't believe how high those violins soared in the last piece.'

She clasped his arm. 'Or how those cellos could make your chest feel hollow and full at the same time. It was so beautiful I nearly cried.'

He stood, dragging her with him. He didn't mean to. He didn't mean for his arm to slide about her waist either, but she didn't pull away. Her hands rested against his chest. The searing brown of her eyes felt like whiskey in his veins and when that gaze lowered to his mouth he swore he started to smoke and smoulder.

His grip tightened. Her breath hitched and her fingers curled to grasp the lapels of his coat. He wanted to kiss her. He had to kiss her. Kissing her would be like soaring with that extraordinary music.

Hunger and heat filled her eyes. Her lips parted.

He drew the scent of her into his lungs, hunger roaring through his every cell and sinew. His gaze locked onto those lips—so inviting, so promising. He lowered his head until their breaths merged, letting the tension build inside him.

What do you think you're doing?

He froze. Acid burned his stomach.

He dropped his arms from around her, straightened and tried to take a step back, but her fingers still gripped his coat anchoring him to the spot. A breath shuddered out of her and then comprehension dawned in her eyes. She snatched her hands away and tossed her head. 'That's right. I remember—two ex-wives and no canoodling with the hired help.'

She turned, eased out of the pew and headed for the arch of the doors. He set off after her, not reaching her until they were outside. She stood on the steps looking everywhere but at him. A fist tightened in his chest. 'I'm sorry, Addie, that was my fault. I got caught up in the moment.'

She glanced at him and sort of wrinkled her nose. 'Yeah, well, you weren't the only one.' And it made things sort of all right between them again and the fist loosened, though he didn't know how it could, given the intensity of what had just passed between them.

Almost passed between them, he corrected.

He gestured in the direction of the town square. 'You want to go get a bite to eat? Maybe some *glühwein*?'

'Food, yes. *Glühwein*, no. I don't need that kind of heat flowing through my veins at the moment.'

She had a point.

He fell into step beside her. She didn't take his arm. He glowered at the footpath. 'You're more than the hired help, you know?'

'It was just a turn of phrase. I know I'm one of the *most* important cogs in your wheel.'

She'd said it to make him laugh only it didn't. He scowled. She wasn't a cog.

'So tell me about the ex-wives.'

He rolled his shoulders, tightened the belt of his coat and shoved his hands into his pockets. 'Nosy, aren't you?'

'Nosy is better than hot and bothered.'

Ah.

'Besides, you said back at Lorna Lee's that you wanted us to get to know each other.'

Yeah, but he hadn't meant…

He glanced down at her and let the thought trail off as a new thought struck him. 'It seems to me that you know me better than I know you.'

She snorted as they broke onto Marienplatz. 'How do you figure that one?'

'Herr Mueller.'

'Oh.'

The sights, sounds and scents of Christmas surrounded them. He glanced about and shook his head. It was so Christmas-card perfect it was as if Munich were the very place Christmas had been invented.

'I'll make a deal with you, Flynn.'

He snapped back to her.

'You buy me a hot chocolate—' she pointed to a street vendor '—and ask me any question you want and I'll answer it.'

Deal.

'And then you'll tell me about your ex-wives.'

His hands went to his hips. 'You're getting two for the price of one.'

Her smile widened. 'Ooh, is there a juicy story to be had, then?'

Hardly.

'Tell you what.' Her eyes danced and it was almost impossible to resist her. 'You get the hot chocolates and I'll grab some doughnuts.'

'Whatever,' he muttered. 'Anything for some peace.'

They found a vacant bench and sipped their hot chocolates. 'C'mon,' she ordered. 'Fire away. Ask me a question.'

Fine. 'What I'd like to know is why you're so gung-ho to leave Lorna Lee's, when you obviously love the place, to travel the world as a PA when you obviously find the work as dull as ditch water?'

'Whoa.' She lowered her mug to her lap. 'Now that's a two-or three-pronged question.'

'I'm happy to get a two-or three-pronged answer. Don't forget,' he added, 'you'll essentially be getting two stories from me. Two wives, remember?'

She snorted. 'How could I forget? Two for the price of one.'

He wished, but they'd been far more expensive than that.

'Okay, Lorna Lee's is the only place I've ever known, the only place I've ever lived, other than a few months in Dubbo where I attended secretarial college. I want to experience something else, something wildly different.'

He understood that, but, 'It doesn't necessarily follow that different is better.'

'Maybe. Maybe not. I'd like the chance to find that out for myself.'

He got that too, but what if in the future she regretting burning her bridges at Lorna Lee's?

'As for the PA bit? Well, I might've been wrong there. When you wear jeans and work boots every day the lure of those little suits can be hard to resist.'

She could say that again. She looked great in those little suits.

'I've been thinking about it. I think bar or restaurant work might suit me better.'

It'd be a waste of her talents.

'Or maybe even retail. I like working with people and I like being on my feet all day.'

How come, then, did he get the impression she'd choose Bruce Augustus's company over people's most days?

'It's not the how of it. Just the fact that I get out there and see the world.'

'You don't have to stop working at Lorna Lee's to achieve that. Four weeks' annual leave a year, free air travel.'

She offered him the bag of doughnuts. He took one. She did too and bit into it. The sugar glazed her lips. He stared and an ache started up inside him before he could wrench his gaze away.

'When we were growing up my closest friend and I used to dream of all the places we'd visit once we were old enough to leave Mudgee. We ordered travel brochures and made up itineraries. We'd spend hours at it. We...'

She trailed off and some instinct warned him to remain silent, not to push her.

A couple of moments later she shook herself. 'When we were sixteen, though, Robbie got sick—leukaemia.'

His every muscle froze. Robbie was Daisy!

'We still made our plans. We were convinced she could beat it.'

But she hadn't and his heart bled for the woman seated beside him, the woman who still mourned her childhood friend.

'She died when we were eighteen.' She sipped hot chocolate and stared out at the square, at the crowds and the stalls and the decorations, but he knew she didn't see them.

'Addie, I'm sorry.'

'Thank you.' But she said it in that automatic way. She glanced at him. 'Before she died I promised that I'd make our dream come true. And that's what I mean to do.'

A chill chased itself down his spine. Couldn't she see how crazy it was to focus on this childhood dream to the detriment of everything else in her life? Living the life Robbie had dreamt of wouldn't bring her back. And Addie deserved better than to be living someone else's dream.

CHAPTER SEVEN

'ADDIE?'

Addie glanced up to find Flynn scratching a hand through his hair. 'Yes?' she said, instead of now demanding the ex-wife story. She'd asked for it because she'd hoped it'd cool the heat stampeding through her blood. She'd wanted him to kiss her so badly her fingers had ached with it. She still did.

'I understand how heartbreaking it must've been to have lost your friend.'

She snapped away to stare out at the square with all of its Christmas glory, but the lights and festivities had lost their charm. Did he understand? Really? She thought of his face and how it had come alive when he'd described his father and thought that maybe he did.

It didn't change the fact that she didn't want to talk about Robbie. Not to him. Not to anyone. All of them had tried—Mum and Dad, Jeannie and Frank, even Robbie's mum and dad—but some things went too deep. Besides, what was there to say? Robbie was gone. She'd died far too young. End of story. Nothing any of them could do would bring her back. So she didn't answer Flynn now.

'But,' he said.

She stiffened. But? No buts! She glared at him to indicate the conversation was over.

'But,' he repeated, evidently oblivious to her silent signals. 'How old were the pair of you when you made these plans?'

'What's that got to do with anything?'

'Sixteen?'

'We'd been making travel plans since we were twelve.' He just stared at her. She glared and shrugged. 'These particular plans?' The particular itinerary Addie meant to follow? She shrugged. 'Nearly seventeen.' That 'nearly' mattered. Every single day had mattered.

'You were only children.'

'And, again, what's that got to do with anything? We were on the cusp of adulthood.' And talking about that itinerary had fired Robbie with enthusiasm, with the desire to get well, with hope.

'You made a plan to see the world at sixteen, which you turned into a pact at eighteen. The point I want to make is that you can fit that promise into your life the way you see it now rather than how you viewed it then.'

What on earth?

'Like ninety-nine per cent of teenagers the world over, you dreamed of independence and getting away from school, home and all the usual restraints. What could be more attractive and exciting than descending upon Europe? What you're not factoring in, however, is the way your world is now, the way your life has changed.'

'I'm not sure what you're getting at.' Her stomach scrunched up tight. 'And frankly, Flynn, I'm not sure I'm interested.'

His eyes narrowed. 'Just for a moment let's imagine Robbie had lived. You're both nineteen and about to embark on a working holiday around Europe for a year.'

That wasn't hard to imagine. She'd imagined it a thousand times. It didn't stop Flynn's words from tearing something inside her.

'Before you can leave, however, your mum gets sick and you have to stay at home to help look after her and the farm. Would Robbie have held that against you?'

'Of course not!' How could he even think such a thing?

'Right, so, hypothetically speaking, your trip has been delayed for a year, but during that time Robbie has met someone and fallen in love and she wants him to come on your working holiday too. Are you okay with that?'

It wasn't the way they'd envisaged it. She busied herself scrunching closed the bag of doughnuts, not understanding her sudden urge to hit the man beside her.

'And three months into your trip she falls pregnant and suddenly she wants to go home and marry her guy and have the baby and be near her mother.'

She gaped at him.

'Are you going to hold that against her?'

She couldn't answer him. The lump in her throat had grown too big. She couldn't even shake her head. Even blinking hurt. But...

If only that were true! If only Robbie were alive in the world with a man who adored her and a couple of rug rats.

If only.

She closed her eyes and fought for air. Her lungs cramped but she refused to let them get the better of her. She focused on relaxing them rather than fixing on the pain screaming through her, the sense of loss. Eventually she was able to swallow. 'I would do anything for that to be true, but it's impossible, and talking about it like this doesn't help, Flynn. It's cruel, as if you're deliberately taunting me with what should've been.'

His eyes darkened. 'I'm not trying to hurt you. It's the last thing I want to do. I'm trying to show you that you'd have been prepared to alter the plan to accommodate changes in Robbie's circumstances. If she was half the friend to you that you were to her—'

'Don't you doubt that for a second!'

Her hands fisted. He stared at them and nodded, half smiled. 'The pair of you must've been a force to be reckoned with.'

The anger evaporated out of her on a breath. Her shoulders sagged.

'I'm just saying she'd have been prepared to alter the plan to allow for changes in your circumstances too.'

'What changes?' She whirled on him. 'I haven't fallen in love, no ankle biters, and I still have my health. Nothing has changed for me. Nothing!'

'How can you say that? Your parents died and the entire responsibility for Lorna Lee's fell to you.'

'Not for long.'

He reached out to grip her shoulders and it reminded her of that moment back in the church. The moment they'd both best forget.

'I don't know why you're so hell-bent on hiding from it, but you love Lorna Lee's. You love the breeding programme, the land, Bruce Augustus, Blossom and Banjo and all of the people there.'

'That doesn't mean it's my destiny.' Robbie had never had the chance to leave, but Addie wasn't letting her down.

'Travelling the world won't bring her back, Addie.'

She thrust out her chin. 'Perhaps not, but it makes me feel closer to her.'

His grip tightened. 'And when it's done—when you've visited all the places you spoke about—what then? What will you be left with?'

The question shocked the breath out of her. She had no answer for it. It wasn't a question she'd ever considered. 'I'm not sure that matters.'

'I think it matters most of all. I think if Robbie had lived, and as the two of you matured, it's something you'd have considered.'

Why was he so worried about her, concerned for her? And why did his hands hold so much warmth? She glanced at his lips and moistened her own. 'Are you sure you wouldn't reconsider having a brief holiday affair with an employee—just this once, Flynn?'

He let her go as if she'd burned him. 'Lord, you're incorrigible.'

All of this talk about Robbie had reminded her of the mischief they'd got into. Of course, it was far more innocent mischief than what she had planned at this current point in time. Heat stirred through her. She shifted on the bench. 'The thing is, I like you as a person and I really like your body. I'd really like to…'

His face told her he caught her drift. It told her how seriously she tempted him too. She lifted one shoulder. 'I understand you're not looking for a commitment. I'm not looking to be tied down either.'

Those words didn't ring quite true. She frowned before shrugging it off. 'I haven't…you know…in a long time. But there's no one I'd rather break the drought with than you.' She shrugged again. 'I think we could keep it uncomplicated.'

He stared down at her and temptation raced across his face, desire simmered in his eyes. He cupped her face in his hands and her blood thumped. Would he kiss her?

Instead he pulled her in for a hug. 'Uncomplicated? Not a chance. Addie, I've never been more tempted by anything in my life, but…'

But he was going to say no. Her eyes burned. She blinked hard against the warmth of his woollen coat.

'It won't make the pain of missing Robbie go away.'

No, but it'd help her forget for a little while.

She summoned her strength and pushed away from him. 'I take it that's a no, then?'

He hesitated and nodded.

She pushed upright and dropped the bag of doughnuts into his lap. 'I'm going to go back to the hotel now.' She shook her head when he stood and went to take her arm. 'I'd like to be alone for a bit.'

She didn't wait for him to say anything. She just turned and walked away.

* * *

It was still early when Addie returned to the hotel.

She peeled off her clothes and had a shower, but it didn't ease her body's prickle and burn or the ache in her soul.

She drank the complimentary beer and ate the complimentary crisps. The crisps crunched satisfyingly in her mouth, but the beer didn't make her drowsy as she'd hoped it would.

She settled on the bed, piled the pillows at her back and watched television for a while.

Would it be awkward when she saw Flynn tomorrow?

Oddly enough she didn't feel embarrassed or self-conscious about what had taken place between them, or hadn't taken place, more to the point. Men asked for what they wanted all the time. She didn't see why women couldn't do the same. She'd asked a question and he'd said no. End of story.

She had no intention of asking the question again, though. He needn't be concerned on that head.

She blinked and realised she'd lost her place in the television show. She clicked the TV off with a sigh. Her gaze travelled across the room, passed over Jeannie's parcel and then zeroed back. Fruitcake! A taste from home.

She settled on the sofa with a slice, relishing the rich scent of brandy-soaked fruit. Yum! How many times as a youngster had she helped Jeannie make the cake, and the giant pudding that'd be brought out on Christmas Day?

An ache stretched through her. Her eyes burned. She bit into the cake.

After a moment she pulled Howard's accounts towards her. If she wasn't going to sleep, she might as well do something useful.

It took less than a minute to realise these weren't accounting records from Lorna Lee's. She hadn't a clue what they were for. One of Flynn's lackeys from the city must've sent them, but why address them to her rather than him?

Was she expected to do something with them? She checked her email to see if any instructions or explanations were forthcoming. Nothing.

She shrugged. She might as well check through them. If anything were designed to put her to sleep then accounts should do the trick.

She glanced down the list of figures, toted them up and frowned. Hold on...

She totalled the amounts again. They didn't add up. The figures in the total columns were pure invention. Money had gone missing—significant amounts of money. Were these accounts for one of Flynn's current business concerns? She reached for the phone and went to punch in his room number when she caught sight of the clock. It was one o'clock in the morning. She replaced the receiver and slid the accounts back into their envelope, tapping it against her chin.

This could wait till morning. She didn't want Flynn jumping to conclusions about the reason why she might be calling at such an hour. Besides, knowing Flynn, this was probably an issue he already had well in hand. She rolled her eyes. Of course he'd have it in hand! He hired the best, remember? Some lackey somewhere would've already emailed him about this.

With that sorted, she slid into bed and turned out the lights. And stared at the darkness and the clock as the night crawled by.

Addie rang Flynn at eight o'clock on the dot.

'Addie, there're no meetings planned. The day is yours to do with what you will.'

No *Good morning, how are you today?* Just crisp, impersonal instructions. 'Good morning to you too, Flynn. How did you sleep?' some devil prompted her to say.

He didn't answer.

'Me? I slept the sleep of the righteous, which, as it turns out, isn't so good after all.'

A choked sound resonated down the line.

'Look, Flynn, I don't want you to think there's going to be a repeat of last night's proposition. It's over and done with as far as I'm concerned and I'm not the type to flog a dead horse.'

Air whistled down the line. 'I can't believe you just described me as a dead horse.'

To her relief, though, his voice had returned to normal.

'Moving on. Yesterday I received a package containing some accounts. They were addressed to me and I thought they must be from Howard, but they're not from Lorna Lee's. I'm guessing they must be for you.'

'I've been expecting those.'

Good, so he knew what they were about, then. 'Can I drop them over in half an hour?'

'By all means.'

She was careful to dress in as unthreatening a manner as possible—jeans and a loose long-sleeve T-shirt. She didn't want him thinking she had sex or seduction on her mind.

They were *very* firmly off her mind. And if that wasn't entirely true then they were very firmly off the agenda and that was almost the same thing. It resulted in the same outcome. No sex.

She bit back a sigh and went to grab a pot of coffee from the breakfast room.

Flynn opened his door two beats after her knock. He scanned her face. She stared back, refusing to let her gaze waver. 'The coffee smells great,' he eventually said.

'Let me in and we might even have a chance to drink it while it's hot.'

He half grinned and stood aside to let her enter. She immediately moved to fill two of the mugs sitting on the sideboard, but her heart pounded unaccountably hard. Darn it! Why couldn't he be dressed in one of his suits rather than jeans? She handed him a mug, trying to not look at him directly, but, man, he filled out a pair of jeans nicely.

'Addie, about yesterday evening…'

'Do we really need to do this, Flynn?'

He blinked.

'I'm fine with it. If you're not, then that's your concern, not mine. I will apologise, though,' she added, 'if I made you feel uncomfortable.'

'Blunt as usual.' He sipped his coffee. 'Okay, we'll draw a line under last night and—'

'Wait.'

He stilled.

'You still haven't told me about the ex-wives.' She moved to the sofa and sat. 'It was part of our deal, remember?' And she wasn't letting him off the hook.

'You want to talk about my ex-wives now?'

'Sure, why not?' She wanted one hundred per cent proof that he was a man she should stay away from, romantically speaking. He might be one seriously hot dude, but that didn't mean he was the kind of guy she should be fantasising about. The more weapons she had in her armoury, the better, because the longer she surveyed the long-legged, lean-hipped beauty of the man, the greater the yearning that built through her. She wanted it gone.

Flynn couldn't believe that Addie wanted to discuss his ex-wives at all, let alone right at this particular moment. Not with the spectre of last night hanging over them.

Nothing happened last night.

'I mean, you said you had no work on today.'

He'd said *she* didn't have any work on today. It wasn't exactly the same thing.

She kinked an eyebrow. 'And I know you're a man of your word.'

Oh, for heaven's sake! He threw himself down into the armchair opposite. What the hell—it'd do him good to re-live past mistakes. It'd remind him not to make those same mistakes in the future.

And last night he'd been in danger of making a very big mistake. Huge. Even with his gut telling him what a big mistake it'd be, letting Addie walk away had been one of the hardest things he'd ever done.

But he had done it.

And he'd continue to do it.

'I married Jodi when I was nineteen.'

Addie's jaw dropped and all he could think of was kissing her. The deep green of her shirt highlighted the rich darkness of her hair, which in turn contrasted with the amber of her eyes. He dragged his gaze away to stare into his coffee

'That's so young,' she said, evidently trying to get her surprise under control. 'I was way too young—' she tapped a finger to her head '—in here at nineteen to marry.'

'As it turned out so were we. We just hadn't realised it.' He could see now that he'd been searching for the family he'd missed since he was twelve. He'd tried to recreate it with Jodi—the first girl he'd ever become serious about— but it just hadn't taken.

'What happened?'

'We met while I was on the rodeo circuit. She was a city girl doing a stint in the country.' A gap year like that was popular in some circles. 'We mistook lust for love and, believe me, there was a lot of lust, but in the end it burned itself out.'

He glanced across to find Addie had her nose buried in her mug. He shifted on his chair. Perhaps lust wasn't the wisest thing to be talking about with Addie. He cleared his throat. 'It turned out she hated country life. She never took to it. I'd bought the first of my properties but I was still making a lot of money on the rodeo circuit and I wasn't prepared to give those things up yet. We started fighting. A lot. One day she left and that was that.'

'Wow.'

'It lasted all of thirteen months.'

'I'm sorry,' she offered.

He shook his head. 'With the benefit of hindsight I can see now it was inevitable. She's happily remarried with a little girl. We've made our peace with each other.'

'Well, that's something, don't you think? We live and learn. It's the way of things.'

He raised an eyebrow.

She nodded and grimaced. 'Okay, I'll stop with the platitudes.'

'I'd appreciate that.'

She kept her mouth firmly shut. He rolled his shoulders. 'Besides, I didn't learn my lesson as I did marry again.'

'How old were you this time?'

'Twenty-seven.'

She shrugged. 'Twenty-seven is old enough to know your own mind and have a proper understanding of what you're doing. I don't see how that's repeating a mistake.'

He scowled. Matrimony was a mistake, full stop.

'Who was she, then? Rank, name and serial number, please.'

He didn't smile. Nothing about this episode in his life could make him smile. 'Her name was Angela Crawford.'

He stared at Addie. She stared back and then pursed her lips. 'Is that name supposed to mean something to me?'

'Crawford and Co Holdings Pty Ltd?'

'Oh.' She sat up straighter. 'Oh! You mean Crawford Cattle?'

'One and the same. Angela is the daughter of Ronald Crawford.'

'Who's in charge of...like, everything.'

Exactly. The Crawfords owned one of Australia's largest and oldest cattle empires.

'Wow, were the family in favour of the match?'

He nodded. 'I was Ronald's head stockman for a while. I already owned a decent holding of my own, but I wanted more experience. And Crawford paid well.' It had allowed him to expand his operations too. Crawford had bankrolled a couple of Flynn's ventures—projects that had paid off handsomely for the both of them.

'Angela came home from university and I'd never met a woman like her before. She'd been born and bred to country life, but she had polish and sophistication too that...' That he'd lacked and had hungered for.

'I've seen her in the society pages. She's beautiful.'

He couldn't read the expression in Addie's eyes. Somewhere between last night and this morning they'd shut him out.

'Yes, she was beautiful, but it wasn't just that. I was twenty-seven—I'd met a lot of beautiful women. We...'

Addie leaned towards him, her expression intent. 'You?'

'We could converse on the same topics for hours. I mean, I didn't know about art and music or antiques, but we both knew about cattle and horses and business and she laughed easily. She made me laugh easily.' And that had been no mean feat back then. 'She could make a room light up just by entering.'

Addie's shoulders inched up towards her ears. 'You fell hard.'

'Like a ton of bricks. I couldn't find fault with her.' Not that he'd wanted to. 'As far as I could tell we wanted exactly the same things out of life.'

He laughed.

Addie swallowed. 'Why is that funny?'

'Because, at heart, we did want the same things. She just didn't want them with me.'

She straightened. 'Then why did she marry you?'

'Because the guy she really loved was already married.'

She sagged back against the sofa and winced.

'That's not the worst of it,' he said, driving home nails that would remind him for a long time to come that he and matrimony were not a happy mix. 'The man she was in love with owned the farm that bordered mine. The farm we moved to once we were married.'

Addie had drawn her legs under her but now her feet hit the floor. 'No!'

'She married me to be closer to him. She married me so she would have access to him. It took her two years, but she broke up his marriage and ours. And all of that time she played me so beautifully I never had a clue.'

Addie set her mug down as if she had no stomach for coffee. He didn't blame her. He set his mug on the table too.

'What a dreadful thing to do.'

Yep.

'But, Flynn, it wasn't your fault. I mean, you can't blame yourself for trusting her. For heaven's sake, you loved her!'

Which only went to prove what a fool he was. 'I should've seen the signals sooner.'

'What would that have achieved?'

He blinked.

'I mean, it wouldn't have prevented what happened, would it?'

Probably not.

'It wouldn't have stopped you from being hurt.'

No, but maybe he wouldn't have felt like such a fool.

'Mind you, if I was ever betrayed like that I'd be pretty darn bitter.'

The thought of anyone taking advantage of Addie like that made his gut burn.

'You're being wrong-headed about the marriage thing, though.' She leaned towards him and he tried to ignore the enticing shape of her lips. 'The whole "I'm not suited to it" stance is just nonsense. The first was simply a youthful mistake that could've happened to any of us if we didn't have good people around to give us wise advice. And the second…'

She shook her head and shuddered. 'You did nothing

wrong. You have nothing to blame yourself for or to be ashamed about.'

It didn't feel that way. He sat back and folded his arms. 'It didn't stop my heart from being shredded, though, did it?'

'No,' she agreed slowly. 'And I expect I'm not the girl to change your mind on the whole marriage-stance thing anyway.'

For no reason at all his heart started to pound.

'I'm really sorry she did that to you, Flynn, but you know what? Karma'a a hellcat. Angela ought to be shaking in her designer boots when it comes to call.'

He laughed. He couldn't help it.

'You know, if you married one of these beautiful Munich women that'd make the local government authorities look on your tender with a more favourable eye.'

What beautiful Munich women? The only woman he'd seen in Munich that he could recall in any detail was Addie. And marriage? He must've looked seriously appalled by the prospect as Addie burst out laughing. 'At least the desire for revenge hasn't addled your brain completely.'

He tried to scowl. When that didn't work he tried to frown. Then he simply gave up. 'Enough. Where are these accounts?'

'Oh.' She pulled a sheaf of papers from an envelope she'd thrown earlier to the sofa beside her. 'Did you have one of your lackeys send them to me?'

'Nope.'

'Because they're dodgy.' She handed them to him.

What on earth?

She pulled another sheet of paper from the envelope. 'To the best of my knowledge, these are what the figures should say.' She placed the sheet on the coffee table and turned it around so he could read it. 'Which according to my calculations leaves a shortfall of this.'

Whoa. He stared at the amount she indicated. It was just shy of two hundred and twenty thousand dollars.

She glanced into his face and bit her lip. 'I, uh, figured this was something you'd already be on top of, but maybe not.' She cleared her throat. 'If these records are for one of your companies or, what do you call them—going concerns? Then someone is lining their pockets at your expense. They're cooking the books and not all that expertly either, I might add.'

Addie was a hundred per cent on the money.

She glanced at him again. 'Do you know which of your going concerns these figures refer to?'

'No, but…' He leaned over them, his finger running down the list of figures. There was something familiar about them. A niggle teased at the edge of his consciousness, but it slipped out of reach when he tried to seize it.

'Do you have any idea why they were sent to me rather than you?'

He stiffened. 'Can I see the envelope?'

She handed it to him without a word.

He glanced at the postmark. 'This wasn't sent from Australia, Addie. It was sent locally.' He handed it back to her, a grim smile coursing through him. 'From Munich.'

She took the envelope but, rather than study the postmark, she continued to stare at him. 'You've worked it out, haven't you?'

He leant back, his hands clasped behind his head. He let his grin widen. 'I have indeed. The reason these accounts are so familiar and yet unfamiliar is that they're over twenty years old.'

She blinked.

'These accounts are from the business my father and Herr Mueller owned. The man is now toast.'

Her eyes widened.

'This—' he lifted the documents '—is the proof I need to bury George Mueller.'

* * *

Addie gazed at Flynn and it wasn't a trickle of unease that shifted through her but an entire flood. 'Who would send them to me?'

'He'll have cheated more than just my father. He'll have left a trail of victims straggling in his wake. Someone has obviously decided it's time for karma to pay Herr Mueller a call.'

Addie scratched her head and frowned up at the ceiling.

'How did you so quaintly put it—he ought to be shaking in his shoes?'

That had been in relation to his evil witch of an ex. What she'd done had been…

Desperate.

Yes, and despicable. And selfish, callous and harmful. She deserved karma.

And Herr Mueller doesn't?

Of course he did. If what Flynn said was true. It was just… *If!* Flynn was so prejudiced against the other man she had trouble believing in his objectivity. She had trouble believing Herr Mueller was the man Flynn painted him to be.

'We have work to do today after all, Adelaide.'

She snapped to attention, but her heart sank at the triumph alive in Flynn's face, the satisfaction in his eyes.

'We're going to pay Herr Mueller a visit.'

Yippee.

'Can you be ready to leave in forty minutes?'

'Do you need me to prepare anything other than myself?'

'No.'

'Then yes.'

She went to gather up the accounts, but his hand came down on hers. 'Leave those with me, Addie. I'll take care of them.'

With a shrug she removed her hand from beneath his,

hoping he hadn't noticed the way her breath had hitched at the contact. She moved towards the door.

'And, Addie?' She turned. 'Wear that little red number, if you don't mind?'

'Right.'

Man, she hated being a PA. She really, *really* hated it.

CHAPTER EIGHT

THEY CAUGHT A cab to Herr Mueller's brewery. Flynn didn't hesitate when it deposited them on the footpath, but strode straight into Reception as if he knew the place, as if he owned the place.

Of course he knew the layout of the building. She'd seen him poring over the floor plans.

But he didn't own it yet, regardless of how he acted or the expression on his face.

She kept up with him effortlessly. She figured that was a lackey's duty and she at least had the legs for that, although she suspected she didn't have the stomach for what was to come.

Is this how you really want to live your life? Because it didn't matter if she were a PA, a barmaid or a shop assistant, she'd still be a lackey.

She hadn't been a lackey at Lorna Lee's.

You will be now.

She shook the thought off. In a smooth motion she slid past Flynn. *'Guten Tag,'* she said to the woman behind the reception desk. *'Sprechen Sie Englisch?'*

'Yes, ma'am.'

She smiled. Partly in relief, but most because she was determined to keep things polite. Or, at least, as polite as she could. 'My name is Adelaide Ramsey and I'm Mr Flynn Mather's personal assistant.'

A flare of recognition lit the other woman's eyes when Addie mentioned Flynn's name.

'We don't have an appointment, but we're hoping, if it's not too much trouble, for Herr Mueller to see us, briefly,' she added as an afterthought. She'd like to keep this meeting as brief as she could.

The receptionist directed them to nearby chairs and asked them to wait.

Flynn raised an eyebrow at Addie as if to mock her, laugh at her. She simply stared—or rather, glared—back. With something almost like a smile he moved to stare out of the window. So she didn't sit either. She just stood there clasping her briefcase in front of her with both hands and staring down at the green linoleum that covered the floor.

Flynn best not try telling her what to wear at Lorna Lee's or he'd get an earful. *Wear the little red number.* Why hadn't she told him what he could do with the 'little red number' instead?

Because you like the way his eyes gleam and follow you around whenever you wear it.

Oh, she was pathetic!

'Herr Mueller would be delighted to see you now.'

Addie snapped to attention and followed the receptionist and Flynn down the corridor to a large office. *'Danke,'* she said to the other woman before she closed the door behind them.

Herr Mueller sat behind a massive desk, looking as mild and Santa-Claus-like as ever. He gestured them to seats. This time Flynn sat so Addie did too.

'To what do I owe this pleasure?'

She had no doubt whatsoever that Herr Mueller wasn't delighted to see them; that their being here gave him no pleasure at all, but he put on a good front all the same and she wanted to nudge Flynn and tell him this was how things should be done.

Flynn didn't answer him. He merely clicked his fingers at Addie.

Clicked his fingers as if she were a dog!

She gritted her teeth. What on earth had happened to, 'May I have the relevant documentation, Adelaide?' She wouldn't even demand a please or thank you.

Lackey, remember? Impressions of power, remember?

Gritting her teeth harder, she slapped the relevant documentation into his hand. He didn't thank her. He didn't so much as glance at her.

He'd notice her if she got up and tap-danced on the table.

You can't tap-dance. And you have no right to judge him like this either.

She glanced down at her hands. How would she feel if someone had financially ruined her father and made him so desperate he committed suicide? Would she act any differently from Flynn? Twelve years old. Her heart burned. He'd just been a little boy.

Flynn didn't speak. He pulled the accounting records from the file. These were photocopies. The originals were in the room safe back at the hotel. Just as slowly he spread them out on the desk, making sure they faced Herr Mueller.

'These were delivered to my assistant yesterday. As you'll see they're accounting records from the pub you and my father owned in Brisbane back in the nineties.'

Herr Mueller didn't say a word. He didn't blanch. He didn't shift on his chair. His eyes remained fixed on Flynn's face and they weren't cold and hard. She couldn't make out the emotion in them—sympathy, perhaps, or regret?

Her stomach lurched. She had an awful premonition this meeting wasn't going to go as well as Flynn hoped.

It was never going to go well!

Maybe not, but she sensed it was going to go badly in a totally unexpected way…in a way Flynn hadn't planned on. She wanted to urge him to his feet and bundle him out of here.

Ha! As if that'd work.

'These records provide incontrovertible proof that you

were robbing the business and my father blind.' Flynn sat back and smiled a grim, ugly smile. 'This is the proof I need to start criminal proceedings against you, Herr Mueller, which I fully intend to do. I'll ruin you and then I'll see you in jail.'

Herr Mueller still didn't move. Addie's heart hammered against her ribs. She wished this were one of those meetings where she had to struggle to stay awake. Where she made notes about artificial insemination or, better yet, irrigation systems. That'd be perfect.

Herr Mueller steepled his fingers and met Flynn's gaze steadily. 'Your father was an extraordinary man, Flynn. So exuberant and full of life.'

One of Flynn's hands clenched. 'Until you crushed it out of him.'

'I loved your father, Flynn, but I couldn't stop him from self-destructing. If my own father hadn't suddenly fallen ill I'd have stayed to try and help you and your mother, but as it was I had to return to Germany.'

Addie suddenly recognised the emotion in his eyes. Affection. Her mouth dried.

'You ensured you left before charges could be brought against you. Don't try and wrap it up in familial duty.'

'There's an extradition treaty between our two countries, Flynn. If your father had wanted to press charges, he could have.'

'You'd destroyed the records, made it impossible for him to prove what you'd done. For a long time I thought you hadn't done anything technically illegal, just ethically and morally. But regardless of technicalities and legalities, you robbed him of everything he had—convinced him to sign papers he never should have. But these records show proof of evident wrongdoing in black and white. The records obviously weren't destroyed after all.'

'Your father loved you very much, Flynn, and I remember how much you looked up to him. Love, however, does not always make us strong. He would've hated for you to think badly of him.'

Herr Mueller's gaze shifted to Addie. 'It was I who sent you those documents, Fräulein Ramsey.' That gaze moved back to Flynn. 'It wasn't me who was embezzling those funds, Flynn. It was your father.'

Flynn shot to his feet. 'That's a dirty, filthy lie!'

'Son, you have no idea how much I wish it were.'

'You're going to shift the blame to save your own skin? I'm not going to let that happen. We're leaving, Adelaide.'

Addie shot to her feet too, her knees trembling. Herr Mueller gathered up the papers and handed them to her. Her hands trembled as she took them. She briefly met his gaze and an ache stretched through her chest. In them she recognised the same concern and affection for Flynn that coursed through her. *'Auf weidersehen,'* she whispered.

'Good day, Fräulein Ramsey.'

'Now, Adelaide!'

She turned and left.

Flynn didn't speak a single word as they exited the building. She glanced up at him, not liking the glitter in his eyes or the thunder on his brow. Christmas carols spilled onto the street from a nearby store and while it might be the season it seemed utterly incongruous to this moment. She swallowed and shifted her weight. 'Would you like to go for a coffee?'

'No.'

It was too early to suggest a beer. She glanced around. They weren't too far from the English Gardens. Maybe Flynn would like to walk off some steam.

She opened her mouth. 'No,' he snapped before she could get the suggestion out. She closed her mouth and kept it closed this time. He hailed a cab. She climbed in beside him wordlessly. When it deposited them at their hotel she entered the elevator without a sound. She followed him into his room, biting her lip, biting back the questions that pounded through her.

She watched as Flynn's jacket landed on the sofa. His tie followed. He turned, noticed her for what she suspected was the first time since he'd hailed the cab. 'What are you doing here?' he all but snarled.

'Awaiting instructions.'

'Go. Leave.'

She turned to do exactly that and then swung back. 'This situation is not of my making so what right do you think you have to speak to me like that?' She dropped her brief-case and strode up to him. 'And while we're on the sub-ject, don't you *ever* click your fingers at me again. Got it?'

He blinked.

'I know this is stressful for you and, believe me, I'm sympathetic to that, but it doesn't give you the right to treat people like they're insignificant or have no worth. Is this how you regularly treat your employees, Flynn? Because you can't pay me enough to put up with that.'

He stared at her and something in his shoulders un-hitched. He nodded. 'Point taken, Adelaide, you're right. I'm sorry.'

So far so good.

He frowned and spread his hands when she continued to stare at him. 'What?'

'You're supposed to add that it'll never happen again.'

A glimmer of a smile touched his lips and something in her chest pitter-pattered. 'It'll never happen again. I prom-ise.'

She found herself smiling. 'Thank you.'

He shook his head and collapsed into the armchair. 'You're really not lackey material, you know that?'

She bit back a sigh. That was becoming increasingly evident.

He turned his head from where it rested on the back of

the chair. 'I know you'll have trouble believing this, but Mueller's lying.'

She pushed his jacket aside and perched on the edge of the sofa. His pallor and the tired lines fanning out from his eyes caught at her. 'Let's say that's true and that all we have are some doctored accounts.' His gaze speared to hers and she had to swallow. 'How—?'

'How can I prove it was Mueller who doctored them?' He raked both hands back through his hair. 'Yes, therein lies the rub.'

She shook her head. 'That's not what I mean.' He stilled and glanced back at her. 'I mean, how can you be sure Herr Mueller isn't telling the truth?' She held up a hand to prevent him from going into fly-off-the-handle mode. 'I'm not trying to challenge you. I like you, Flynn. You're smart and you work hard.' She admired that. 'Generally you're good-natured and you've offered me a wonderfully attractive bonus to stay on at Lorna Lee's because you want me to be content and settled there. That tells me, as a general rule, that you care about people. I feel as if we've almost become friends.'

'Addie—'

'No, Flynn, let me finish. I feel you need to hear this and there's no one else to say it. Because of all of the things I've just outlined, my loyalty lies with you regardless of what first impressions I may have gained from Herr Mueller.'

He rested his elbows on his knees, his eyes intent on her face. Her heart hammered, but she met his gaze squarely. 'If you are going to ruin this man you need to be very certain of your facts. I mean, how will you feel in five years' time if you find out you were wrong?'

His jaw slackened.

'What actual proof do you have, Flynn? What your father told you when you were twelve years old? Truly, what do any of us know about our parents' greater lives when we're young? We just love them unconditionally and depend on them completely. We're totally biased.'

He leapt out of his chair and paced the length of the room. 'My father was a good man.'

'I believe you. But sometimes good people make bad decisions.'

He didn't say anything. He didn't even turn. She moistened her lips. 'Has there been a shadow of impropriety over any of Herr Mueller's other dealings since that time?'

Flynn waved that off. 'If my father had been embezzling funds why didn't Mueller have him arrested? Answer me that.'

'He said he loved your father.'

His snort told her what he thought about that.

She pressed a hand to her brow and dragged in a breath. 'I have another question.'

'Just the one?' he growled, throwing himself back into the armchair.

'When your ex, Angela, betrayed you like she did—'

'She was never mine.'

'When she did what she did, she hurt you and her family and tore another woman's marriage apart so…'

'So?'

'Did you go after her like this and make sure she paid for what she did?'

He hadn't. She could see the answer in his eyes.

'So if you didn't try to get your revenge on her why is Herr Mueller different?'

His face twisted and he leaned towards her. 'He killed my father.'

'No, Flynn, he didn't. Your father killed himself.' Her heart quailed as she said the words. 'That responsibility rests solely with him.'

He stabbed a finger at her. 'He drove my father to it.'

'Maybe, maybe not.' She twisted her hands together.

'It's a big question, a big accusation. Do you really want to get it wrong?'

'I thought you said you were on my side?' His lips twisted. 'Or do I need to pay you more to earn that kind of loyalty?'

She ignored that. He was simply trying to get a rise out of her. 'You know what I think?'

'I can hardly wait to hear,' he bit out.

'I think your anger and your bitterness towards Herr Mueller has provided you with the spur to succeed, to reach a position of power where you can make him pay. But are you sure it's really him you're angry with?'

He leapt up, hands clenched, his entire body shaking. It took an effort of will not to shrink back against the sofa. 'I will get you the proof you need. My father *wasn't* a thief!'

'I don't need the proof, Flynn. You do.'

The air in the room shimmered, but with what she wasn't sure. 'I think what you went through when you were twelve years old was dreadful, Flynn, horrendous. I want to horse-whip the world for putting you through that.'

The storm in his face died away.

'You need to remember, though, that you're not twelve years old any more. Nobody—and I mean *nobody*—can put you through that again.'

He stared at her as if he didn't know what to say. She swallowed and rose. 'Would you like me to leave now?'

'I think that would be a very good idea.'

She collected her briefcase and left, walked into her room and promptly threw herself across her bed and burst into tears.

Flynn glanced up at the knock on the door. It'd be Addie. For the previous two mornings she'd turned up at nine o'clock on the dot to report for duty. He'd given her both days off to sightsee.

Today wouldn't be any different. 'Come in.'

'Good morning.' She breezed in wearing a chic navy suit and bearing the customary pot of coffee. He wondered if it gave her a kick to dress up in her office clothes. She set the coffee on a trivet on the table in front of him. 'Did you have a good day yesterday?' she asked.

'Yes.' It was a lie. He tensed, waiting for her to quiz him about what he'd been doing or ask him if he'd found any evidence of Mueller's guilt yet.

He hadn't.

He thrust out his chin. He mightn't have known much at twelve, but he knew his father wasn't a thief!

But Addie didn't ask him anything. He shifted on his chair. 'What about you? Get up to anything interesting?'

'Oh, yes. I walked out to the art galleries, which was quite a hike. I spent hours there.' A smile lit her up from the inside out. 'I love holidays.'

He stared at her, transfixed.

'I like art but I don't know very much about it so I'm going to learn.'

She was?

'I ordered some books online. They should be waiting for me when I get home.'

'Good for you.'

'And then—' her eyes widened '—I caught a tram back to Marienplatz.'

He grinned. This woman could find fun in the most ordinary things. 'A day of art and trams, huh?'

Her eyes danced. 'And bratwurst and black forest cake.'

He'd have had more fun venturing forth with her.

You're not here for fun.

'What would you like me to do today? Any letters you'd like me to type and post? Any emails to send or meetings to set up?'

'Nothing's happening at the moment, Addie. Everything is quietening down for the Christmas break. Go out and enjoy the day.' He scowled. While he trawled more newspapers and business reports looking for dirt on Mueller. *All you have to do is ask and she'd help.*

Addie didn't notice his scowl. In fact she seemed totally oblivious to his inner turmoil. She stared beyond him and her eyes widened and her jaw dropped. He turned to see what had captured her attention.

'Snow!' She raced to the window. 'Flynn, it's snowing!' She bounced up onto her toes. 'I've never seen snow before.'

She turned and tore out of the room. 'Addie, wait!' He moved after her. 'It'll be freezing out. Take your coat.' But she was already clattering down the stairs. 'Silly woman. It's only snow,' he muttered.

He trudged back and collected his coat. He let himself into her room and collected her coat and scarf and then stomped down the stairs after her.

She turned when he emerged onto the street and her face was so alive with delight his grumpiness evaporated. He shook his head and tried to hide a grin. 'Jeez, Addie, you wanna freeze?'

He wound her scarf about her throat. For a moment their eyes locked. A familiar ache pulled at his groin. A less familiar one stretched through his chest. Fat flakes fell all around them; one landed on her hair. He brushed it off before he realised what he was about. Addie shook herself and broke the eye contact. With a shake of his head he held her coat out for her. She slipped it on and immediately moved out of his reach.

Neither ache abated.

She turned back to grin at him. 'You're lucky it's only just started snowing. If it'd been going for a while I'd have hit you with a snowball the moment you stepped out of the door.'

He'd welcome a cold slap of reality about now.

She eyed him uncertainly when he didn't say anything. 'I suppose this is old hat for you?'

He hadn't meant to rain on her parade. 'I've seen snow before. In America. Montana.' He injected enthusiasm into his voice. 'But I can quite safely say I've never seen snow while standing by the medieval gate of a European city.'

She grinned back at him and he was glad he'd made the effort. 'It's really something, isn't it?'

Yeah, it was. He nodded and then frowned. Why did he insulate himself so much from enjoying simple pleasures like these? What harm was there in enjoying them?

'You really don't need me today?'

At the shake of his head, she raced back inside.

Flynn remained on the footpath and noticed the way the snow had started to transform everything—frosted it. Munich was a pretty city and the snow only made it prettier.

'Oh!' Addie skidded to a halt beside him. 'Are you sure you don't need me today?'

She now had her handbag slung over her shoulder. 'Your day is your own,' he assured her. She'd go out and see something amazing, enjoy experiences outside her usual world, while he holed up in his room and—

I love holidays.

Addie's earlier words taunted him. When was the last time he'd taken the time for a holiday? His life revolved around work.

Work and revenge.

But seriously, would a day off here and there really kill him? A week off here and there even?

Addie took two steps away. Stopped. Swung back. 'I'm going to sit in a little café on Marienplatz. I'm going to sip coffee and eat pastries while I watch the square turn white.' She moistened her lips. 'Would you like to join me?'

He should say no. He should… 'Yes.'

She walked back to him. 'You're acting very oddly, Flynn.'

'Maybe I've had too much sun.'

'Or maybe you've been working too hard, but may I make a suggestion?'

'By all means.'

'I think you should put on your coat. It's cold.'

He started and realised he still held his coat. He reefed it on.

'A touch of the sun,' she snorted, setting back off. He kicked himself forward to keep pace beside her. 'Brain freeze more like.'

They didn't speak again until they were seated in an upstairs café. Addie had pounced on a window table. 'We'll have the perfect view of the glockenspiel when it ramps up to do its stuff.'

He glanced at his watch. 'That's an hour and a half away.'

She turned from staring out of the window and sent him a grin. 'I don't know about you, but I haven't anything better to do for the next ninety minutes.' She nodded towards the window. 'Look how pretty the square is.'

She was right. He leaned back and his shoulders started to relax. Ninety minutes of sipping coffee and nibbling pastries and watching the world go by? It had a nice ring to it.

They made desultory chit-chat over their first coffee. Addie told him about some of the art she'd seen the previous day and how it had affected her. When she asked him about his trip to Montana he told her about the mountains and the big sky country.

It wasn't until they were on their second cup of coffee—decaffeinated this time, Addie had insisted—when she turned to him abruptly. 'I've been thinking about what you said to me the other night.'

His cup halted halfway to his mouth. Which night? He set it back to its saucer.

'You asked me what I'd have left once I'd completed my mission—my promise to Robbie. After I'd seen it all through.'

His heart ached at the trouble in her eyes. 'Addie, I had no right to ask such a question. I—'

'No, your question came from a good place. I just found it a bit confronting at the time, is all. It felt as if you were suggesting I break faith with Robbie, break my promise. I can see now that's not what you were doing. You were saying that it would be okay for me to modify the plans we made back then to fit them into my life now, if that's what would make me happier. You were saying that Robbie wouldn't mind me doing that, that she'd understand.'

That was exactly what he'd been saying. He'd wanted to ease the pressure she put on herself. He'd wanted to bring her a measure of peace.

She gave a soft half laugh, but the sadness of her smile pierced his chest. 'You were saying I could dream other dreams too and that wouldn't mean I was being unfaithful to the first dream or to Robbie.'

'It's natural to dream, Addie, and there's no reason why you can't have two, five or ten dreams.' Hell, she could have a hundred if she wanted.

'By doing that—and please be honest with me, as honest as I was with you in your room after our meeting with Herr Mueller.'

His heart thumped when she glanced up at him, but he nodded.

'If I dream my other dreams, if I envisage a different life for myself now than I did when I was sixteen, am I not letting Robbie down? Am I not being false to her memory?'

'No.'

She stared at him. 'It seems wrong to dream when she no longer can.'

He dragged a hand down his face and forced a deep breath into his lungs. 'Addie, being true to yourself won't mean you're being false to Robbie's memory. You'll only be letting her down if you see that promise through at the expense of your own happiness. That'd make a mockery of all that you and Robbie shared.'

'Oh!' Her jaw dropped. 'That has an awful ring of truth.'

He leaned towards her. 'Because it is true. If your situations had been reversed, would you want Robbie to make ludicrous sacrifices just to tick off an itinerary that didn't hold the same allure or promise for her any more? Of course you wouldn't.'

Very slowly she nodded, but behind the warm amber of her eyes her mind raced. He sat back and waited for whatever would come next, determined to do what he could to set her mind at rest. This woman didn't have a malicious bone in her body. She shouldn't be tying herself in knots over this. She should be running out into the snow with outstretched arms every day of the week—figuratively speaking. She should be living her life with joy.

'You see?' she finally said. 'Our time here has been a revelation.' She broke off a corner of an apple Danish and popped it into her mouth. 'Please, no offence, but I've discovered I don't like being a PA.'

'None taken.'

She shrugged. 'Apparently loving the clothes doesn't mean loving the job.'

He laughed.

She sighed. 'I have a feeling I wouldn't enjoy being a barmaid or a shop assistant that much either.'

'Like I said, you're not really lackey material.'

'Also, if I were working a nine-to-five job here, I'd be staying in the outer suburbs, as that'd be all I could afford, which would mean a commute into the city. That means that at this time of the year I could be leaving home while it's still dark and then not getting home again until it's dark.'

'That's true.'

'I've been lucky. I've had more free days since we've been here than work days *and* I'm in the heart of things. It occurred to me I'd rather visit all the places on my list as a vacationer rather than as a working girl.'

Mission accomplished. 'And experience its delights to the full without other distractions and responsibilities weighing you down.'

She nodded.

He straightened. 'So what's the problem?'

She ducked her head, but not before he'd glimpsed a sheen of tears. In one fluid motion he moved from sitting opposite to sitting beside her. He took her hand. 'Tell me what's really troubling you, Addie.'

She gripped his hand tightly. 'I write to Robbie. A lot. In my diary. I've written to her every day that we've been here. That probably sounds silly to you.'

'Not at all.'

'It makes me feel closer to her. And...' A sob broke from her.

He slipped an arm around her shoulders and pulled her against his chest. She cried quietly and unobtrusively, but her pain stabbed at him. He found himself swallowing and blinking hard.

Eventually she righted herself, pulled out a tissue and wiped her eyes. He swore at that moment to go out and buy handkerchiefs and to always have one on hand.

She didn't apologise for crying and he was glad.

'I don't want to lose that sense of closeness.' She glanced up at him. 'I'm afraid of forgetting her, Flynn.'

It fell into place then—her single-minded focus. 'Heck, Addie, you're not going to forget her! You'll never forget her. It'd be like trying to forget a piece of yourself. She'll always mean what she meant to you, even as new people come and go in your life.' He cupped her face. 'You don't have to lose that sense of closeness. Sure, write to her about Munich. And about Paris and London and Rome when you visit them too, but you should be telling her about your life—the things that are happening at home and the plans you're making and your dreams.'

And then he let her go before he did something stupid like kiss her.

She blinked. She straightened. 'You know, you could be onto something there.' Then she grimaced. 'Except I can't tell her what my dreams are if I don't know what they are myself.'

He wanted to touch her. He sat on his hands instead. 'So you work out what it is you really want.'

'How?'

That question stumped him. 'Why don't you ask Robbie for her advice?'

She stared at him and then a smile broke across her face. It was like morning breaking over rolling green fields. 'Perfect answer.' She reached across and kissed his cheek. *'Danke.'*

'You're welcome.' Though he had a feeling he only thought the words. He couldn't seem to get his lips to work.

CHAPTER NINE

ON CHRISTMAS MORNING Flynn met Addie in the foyer at ten o'clock as she'd instructed. The moment she saw him she beamed at him. When her eyes lit on the brightly coloured gift bag that he carried, which held three even more brightly coloured presents, she rubbed her hands together. 'Ooh.'

'Will I take that for you, sir?' the concierge asked with a grin.

He handed it over. 'Please.'

'I'd also like to take this opportunity to thank you, Herr Mather.' The concierge—Bruno, wasn't it?—nodded towards the reception desk. A bottle of schnapps and an assortment of chocolates stood amid torn Christmas paper.

They'd bought him a Christmas gift? He shook his head. *Addie* had bought him a Christmas gift. 'Merry Christmas, Bruno.'

'Merry Christmas, sir.' And then his gift bag was whisked away.

'Did we buy everyone in the hotel Christmas gifts?'

'Scrooge,' she shot back, which told him they had.

And then she wrapped her arms about him in a hug. It wasn't meant to be sexy. It wasn't that kind of hug. But it sent the blood racing through his veins and his skin prickling with heat, and it was sexy as hell.

She released him. 'Merry Christmas, Flynn.'

Lord, those eyes! They danced with so much excitement her cheeks were pink with it. Beneath the foyer lights her dark hair gleamed. In that moment he swore that regardless of how hokey a Christmas Day she'd planned, he would not rain on her parade. He would pretend to enjoy every moment of it.

Who knew? In her company there mightn't be any need for pretence.

'Merry Christmas, Addie.'

She slid her arm through his and pressed it against her side. 'C'mon, the car's already here. Let the festivities begin!'

He rolled his eyes, but grinned too. 'Where are you taking me?'

She seemed to grin with her whole body. 'You'll see.'

Their driver—Otto—was promptly handed a gift of fruitcake and spiced biscuits and wished a very merry Christmas. Within two minutes of their journey starting, Addie had wormed out of him that he was a retired chauffeur whose family was scattered. Driving on Christmas Day stopped him from getting too lonely. Oh, and he was looking forward to a family reunion next year.

Flynn shook his head. She might not be lackey material but she had a way with people. It wouldn't hurt him to take a trick or two from her book and apply it to his business life.

For the next hour, they drove in what Flynn calculated to be a roughly southerly direction. They passed through the outer suburbs of Munich until they'd left the city behind, advancing through smaller towns and villages. When they came to a town bordering a large lake, Otto stopped so Addie could admire it. She leapt out of the car and then just stood there. 'It's so beautiful,' she breathed.

Flynn stared down at her, evidently trying to memorise the view. 'Yes,' he agreed. Very beautiful.

'The landscape here is so different from home. I…' She flashed him a grin and then opened her mouth in a silent scream of delight. 'I can't believe I'm here!'

He held the door open for her as she slid back into the car, fighting the growing overwhelming urge to kiss her. Kissing her would be a bad thing to do.

Why was that again?

He scratched his head. Um…

Addie thumped his arm and pointed out of the window as the car climbed an incline. 'Look! It's a whole forest of spruce and pine and Christmas trees! It's like something from Grimm's fairy tales.'

She was right. They were surrounded by Christmas trees. He sucked in a breath. They were going to end up in the great hall of some castle, weren't they? There'd be a roast pig with an apple in its mouth and mulled wine. An oompah band would be playing and carollers would be carolling and everything would be picture-postcard perfect. *That* was where she was taking him.

His shoulders started to slump. All of it would highlight how far short his own Christmases had fallen ever since his father had died.

He passed a hand across his face, glanced across at Addie and pushed his shoulders back. He would not ruin this day for her. He'd enter into the spirit of the thing if it killed him.

'Are you ready, Ms Addie?' Otto rounded a curve in the road and as the forest retreated the view opened out. Flynn's jaw dropped. Otto pulled the car over to the verge. Addie's hand on Flynn's arm urged him out of the car. He obeyed.

'Oh, wow!' she murmured, standing shoulder to shoulder with him. 'I don't think we're in The Shire any more, Mr Frodo.'

Flynn smiled at her *Lord of the Rings* reference, but she was right. All around them soared spectacular snow-covered mountains. Dark forests dotted the landscape here and there along with sheer cliff faces. It all glittered and sparkled, fresh and crisp in the cold sunlight. He drew air so clean and fresh into his lungs it almost hurt. 'This is spectacular.'

'The Alps,' she said, somewhat unnecessarily. 'That's where I'm taking you for Christmas, Flynn.'

He thought of the cheesy medieval castle he'd conjured in his mind. It could still eventuate. He glanced down at her. 'Perfect,' he said. And then he blinked. 'What? To the very top?'

She laughed and pushed him back towards the car. 'All will be revealed soon enough.'

Fifteen minutes later they entered a town full of chalets and ski shops. 'Garmische-Partenkirchen,' Addie announced proudly. 'Try saying that five times without stopping.'

He frowned. 'The name's familiar.'

'The winter Olympics have been held here.'

'Of course!'

There wasn't a medieval castle in sight. She took him to a chalet. 'We're going to dine with twenty-four select guests on one of Germany's finest degustation menus.'

His mouth watered.

'I have a feeling there won't be a mince pie or plum pudding in sight.'

He glanced down at her. Wouldn't she miss those things?

'And there'll be a selection of wines from the Rhone Valley.'

Better and better. He took the proffered glass of schnapps from a waiter.

Addie did too and then she leaned in closer. 'We've been living on bratwurst, pork knuckle, sauerkraut and apple strudel. I thought it time we tried something different.'

Really? Did she really prefer this to a medieval castle?

They were led into a long room with an equally long picture window that looked out over those glorious soaring alpine scenes. They were both quiet as they surveyed the panorama.

'What made you choose this?' He turned to her. It was

suddenly important to know why. She hadn't done this just because she'd thought it was what he'd prefer, had she? His hand clenched about his glass of schnapps. He didn't want her to make those kinds of sacrifices for him.

Her brow creased. 'You don't like it?'

'I love it.'

Her brow cleared. 'When I looked into all the options available I initially started with traditional, but…' She stared down into her glass. 'Well, you see, Jeannie sent me some fruitcake from home and I suddenly realised that if I went traditional I'd spend most of the day missing them.'

She glanced up and the expression in her eyes skewered him to the spot.

'I knew I'd spend the day grieving for my father and I figure I'm already missing him enough as it is.'

Question answered. He pulled her in for a light hug. She rested against him for a moment and he relished it. When she pushed away from him he let her go again. He didn't want to, but he did it all the same.

'I don't mean to ignore it, though,' she said. She tipped her glass towards him. 'To absent friends. To my parents and your father and Robbie.'

He tilted his glass. 'To absent friends.'

She straightened. 'Now, I wouldn't advise you to imbibe too freely of the wine as the day doesn't end with the meal.'

He laughed, but he didn't pester her for details. He'd let the day unfold at the pace Addie had planned for it. And he'd enjoy every moment.

The meal was amazing. They sat at a table for six with a French businesswoman, her Austrian ski-instructor husband and a retired British couple from Bristol. Everyone was in greatest good humour. The wine flowed and the conversation flowed even faster. The food was amongst the best Flynn had ever sampled.

By three o'clock he swore he couldn't fit another morsel in. Not one of the petits fours or another sip of dessert wine. He turned down the brandy. So did Addie. 'I'm sure I say this every Christmas,' she groaned, 'but I have never been so full in my entire life and I swear I'm not going to eat for a week.'

They'd moved into the adjoining lounge area—a room of wood panelling, comfy sofas and a roaring fire. A picture window provided the perfect views of snow-covered mountains and ski runs. Some guests had remained talking in the dining room, some had moved in here with him and Addie, while others had adjourned to the rooms they had booked in the chalet.

Flynn collapsed onto a sofa, slumping down into its softness. He could suddenly and vividly imagine spending a week in the Alps with Addie.

He promptly shook himself upright. Crazy thought!

A bell sounded. People rose. He glanced at Addie and she grinned back. 'Are you too full to move?'

He shook his head. He'd actually been contemplating the pros and cons of braving the cold for a walk.

'Excellent. Phase Two begins.'

'Please tell me it doesn't involve food.'

'No food.'

Two small mini-buses were parked at the front of the chalet. He and Addie were directed to one of them. They drove for three minutes before pulling up again. 'We could've walked,' he said as they disembarked.

'Ah, but we may in fact appreciate the ride home later.'

He stared at the building in front of them and then swung to her. 'This is the Olympic centre. Are we getting a tour?' That'd be brilliant!

'In a manner of speaking. We get to test the facilities out.'

What was she talking about?

She laughed and urged him forward. 'We're going ice-skating, Flynn.'

They had a ball. After a mini-lesson, they were left to

their own devices. They fell, a lot, but he still figured that he and Addie picked it up pretty quickly.

'I'm going to be black and blue,' he accused her, offering his hand to help her up after another spill.

'Go on, admit it, you're having fun.'

'I am.' He held her hand a beat longer than he should have. He forced himself to let it go. He gestured around the ice-rink stadium. 'This was an inspired idea, Addie.'

'It's my one gripe with Christmas,' she said. 'There's never enough physical activity, and when I eat that much I need to move.' She glanced at him. 'You're like me in that regard—you like to jog every day, et cetera. So I figured you'd appreciate a bit of exercise too.'

She was spot on.

'Watch this.' She performed a perfect, if somewhat slow, pirouette. 'Ta-da!'

'You're obviously destined to become a star.'

She laughed and moved to the railing for a rest. 'I'm glad you've enjoyed it. I'd hoped you would. You see, the second bus went skiing.'

Skiing!

'And snowboarding.'

Snowboarding!

'And doesn't that sound like a whole trailer-load of fun?'

It did.

'But, of course, the weather conditions couldn't be guaranteed and if visibility had been poor the skiing would've been cancelled. This seemed the safer option.'

'The skating's been fun.' He wouldn't have given this up for anything. Not even to try his hand at snowboarding.

'But this might be the moment to let you know that overnight accommodation and a day on the ski slopes tomorrow is an option open to us. I had Housekeeping back at the hotel pack you an overnight case.'

He stared at her. She had? He moistened his lips. A whole day on the ski slopes.

'I didn't know what your timetable was like.' She shrugged. 'And I didn't want to pressure you, but…'

A grin built inside him. 'No, Addie, that is most definitely an option we should avail ourselves of.'

'Yes?'

'Yes.'

'Woo-hoo!' She jumped as if she meant to punch the air, but her skates shot out from beneath her. He grabbed her, yanking her back towards him and she landed against his chest, gripping his arms tightly when he wobbled too.

It brought her face in close and as their eyes met the laughter died on their lips. An ache swelled in his chest, his groin throbbed and he could barely breathe with the need to taste her.

Her gaze lowered to his lips and an answering hunger stretched through her face when she lifted her gaze back to his.

Once. Just once, he had to taste her.

His hands moved from her waist to her shoulders. Gripping them, he half lifted her as his lips slammed down to hers. Heat, sweetness and softness threatened to overwhelm him. She tasted like wine and cinnamon and her lips opened up at the sweep of his tongue as if she'd been yearning for his touch and had no interest in pretending otherwise.

Heat fireballed in his groin. Desire surged along his veins and his lungs cramped. It was too much. He couldn't breathe. He let her go and took a step back feeling branded…feeling naked.

They stared at each other, both breathing hard, both clutching the railing with one hand for balance. And then she reached forward with her free hand, grabbed the lapels of his jacket and stretched up to slam her lips to his.

It knocked the breath out of him.

She explored every inch of his lips with minute precision, thoroughly and with relish. He wanted to moan, he wanted to grab her and…and make her his!

Her tongue dared his to dance. He answered the dare and took the lead, but she matched him kiss for kiss, her fire and heat rivals for his. They kissed until they had no breath left and then she let him go and stepped back. 'I... I've been wondering what it'd be like, kissing you.'

Sensational! 'Satisfied?'

'Uh huh.' She nodded. 'Oh, yes.'

Kisses like that, though, could open a whole can of worms and—

He jolted back when she touched his face. 'Christmas kisses don't count, Flynn.'

They didn't? Her eyes told him there'd be no more Christmas kisses, though.

Good thing. He bit back a sigh.

'Race you across to the other side.'

She set off. He set off after her. Afterwards he couldn't remember who had won.

They returned to Munich on Boxing Day evening, after a day of skiing and snowboarding. Flynn had even contemplated staying for another night and day. Addie had wanted to jump up and down and shout, 'Yes!'

But then she'd wondered if either of them would have the strength to resist another night of sitting by a log fire, the winter warmth and holiday freedom and the lure of following it through to its natural conclusion.

She figured Flynn must've had the same thought. And the same fear. She knew now, in a way she hadn't on that night when she'd propositioned him, that if they made love now her heart would be in danger and Flynn had made it plain where he stood on the relationship front. She had to respect that.

Even if he was being a great, big, fat, wrong-headed fool about it.

'What are you frowning at?' Flynn demanded as the elevator whooshed them up to the fourth floor.

'Oh…uh, just tired.'

'I don't believe you.'

He was too in tune with her. She scratched her neck. 'I was thinking about Frank and Jeannie.'

'Problem?'

'Not really, but would you mind if they stayed at the farmhouse with me for a while when I get back?'

'Why?'

'They're having trouble finding the right retirement village.'

'What would they do on the farm?'

Do? She frowned at him. 'Nothing.'

'Then why…?'

He let the sentence hang. 'The why is because they're my friends.' She wanted to thump him. 'The benefits are that Jeannie's a great cook and Frank has a wealth of knowledge and experience I could call on if it's needed.'

The elevator door opened and Flynn stepped out. 'You have more experience at breeding techniques than anyone else in the district.'

'And Frank has more when it comes to pasture management, crop rotation and weed and pest control,' she said, keeping step beside him.

'I'd hazard a guess that Howard knows just as much about those subjects.'

'In Queensland Channel country maybe, but not in Mudgee.' She glared at him. 'Why is this an issue? It's not like they wouldn't be paying their own way.'

'It's an issue because I'm not running a retirement village at Lorna Lee's, Addie.'

She dropped her bag by her room door, folded her arms and widened her stance. 'We've talked about karma before, Flynn.'

'Yeah, and I'd better watch out, right?' He started to turn away.

'At Lorna Lee's we look after our own—whether they be human, animal or the land.'

He blew out a breath and turned back. 'How long would they stay?'

What was it to him? It was *her* house. 'A few months.' Maybe more. This should be up to her.

But it's not your house. Not any more. She swallowed.

'Okay, fine, yes. They can stay.' He glared at her. 'Happy?'

It occurred to her then that the answer to that might in fact be, No. She swallowed. 'Thank you.'

He slammed his hands to his hips. 'I was going to suggest that Room Service send up a plate of sandwiches and some hot chocolate, if you wanted to join me.'

An ache stretched through her chest. Did she dare?

'I still have your Christmas present in my case.'

That decided it. 'Give me half an hour to change and freshen up?'

With a nod he turned away.

Addie tripped into her room, a smile spreading through her. Had Flynn bought her something more than a dried plum and almond chimney sweep and a pair of mittens? Over the course of the last two days there hadn't been a suitable time to exchange their gifts. They'd done their best not to spend too much time on their own—especially after that kiss. They might not have actively sought out the company of others, but they'd tried to keep all of their exchanges public.

That kiss had happened in public.

Thanks heavens! Imagine where it would've led if they'd been somewhere private…intimate.

Like Flynn's room.

She shook that thought off. His bedroom in the suite next door was private—the door always firmly shut—but the rest of the suite was like the living room of a house. They'd be fine. As long as she remembered that she wanted to keep her heart intact and Flynn remembered he didn't sleep with his employees.

You don't have to be an employee. You wouldn't be an employee if...

She cut that thought dead and headed for the shower.

The phone rang as she pulled on a clean pair of jeans and a soft cashmere sweater in olive green that she'd bought on her shopping spree. Flynn had complimented her on it the first time she'd worn it. Which probably meant she should take it off.

She left it on and answered the phone.

'Fräulein Ramsey, it's Reception. There's a Herr Mueller to see you.'

What? She swallowed. 'I'll...' Um. 'I'll be right down.'

She led Herr Mueller into a small sitting room off to one side of Reception. She turned, gripping her hands together. 'I don't feel comfortable meeting you like this behind Flynn's back.'

'That does you credit, my dear, and I promise not to take up too much of your time.'

She sat and gestured for him to do the same. 'How can I help you?'

'I am very sorry—heartsick—at what Flynn experienced as a boy.'

That made the both of them.

'I did not know that Reuben, Flynn's father, would become so desperate as to take his own life. I hold myself partly responsible for that.'

Her stomach churned.

'I felt so let down and angry with him, and I let it blind me. I shouldn't have turned away from him so completely. It's not how friendship works.'

Her heart went out to the older man with his sad eyes and drooping shoulders. 'Herr Mueller, I don't believe you should take on that level of responsibility. I don't think anyone should.'

'Perhaps. Perhaps not. I do, however, understand Flynn's bitterness.'

She had no intention of talking about Flynn when he wasn't present.

'I understand it, but I will not let him take away everything for which my family has worked so hard.'

Flynn had made up his mind. She didn't see how Herr Mueller could stop him.

'Flynn is right. Reuben wasn't a thief—it wasn't he who stole the money.'

Her head shot up.

'It was his mistress—a barmaid at the pub called Rosie. Flynn and his mother never knew about her and I was grateful for that.' He sighed heavily. 'I'm afraid she had a cocaine habit that had spiralled out of control. Reuben covered up her misappropriation of funds as much as he could, but…' He shook his head. 'It couldn't go on and I'm afraid that when the money dried up she dumped him for someone younger and richer.'

She pressed a hand to her stomach. 'Why are you telling me this?'

He pulled a packet from his pocket. 'These are letters I found in Rosie's room after she left. They're the letters she and Reuben wrote to each other. There are also photographs. Some of them are quite…'

She winced and nodded.

'I didn't want either Flynn or his mother finding them.' No.

'But it's obvious Flynn needs to see them now, needs to know the truth.'

She leapt to her feet. 'Oh, but—'

'The only question that remains—' he rose too '—is if this would come better from me or from you?'

Couldn't he see he was putting her in an impossible situation?

But when he held the packet out to her she took it, and then she turned and walked away without another word.

When she reached her room she sat on her bed. What to do? The moment she gave these letters and photographs to Flynn there'd be fireworks.

Big time.

Why couldn't Herr Mueller have just left them alone to have a nice Christmas?

She glanced at the presents she'd selected for Flynn, sitting on the coffee table waiting for her to take them across next door. She straightened. It was Boxing Day—a holiday and practically still Christmas. She wasn't going to let the past ruin today. Flynn hadn't had a proper Christmas in over twenty years.

She flung the packet into her bedside drawer. There'd be enough time for that tomorrow. Today was for presents and fun and relaxation. She collected up the presents and headed next door.

When Flynn opened his door at her knock, she had to reach right down into the depths of herself to find a smile. His lips twitched. 'You look beat.'

She seized hold of the excuse. 'The last time I was this bushed was when I went on muster when I was eighteen.'

'You went on a muster? But Lorna Lee's doesn't…'

'Oh, no.' She set his presents down, curled up into a corner of his sofa and helped herself to one of the tiny sandwiches on a platter sitting on the coffee table. 'It was on a station an hour north-west of us. A paying gig.' She shrugged. 'I wanted the experience.'

He folded himself into the armchair. 'Did you enjoy it?'

'Loved it.'

He stared at her. She shifted slightly. 'Would you be interested in mustering at my station every now and again just for the hell of it?'

Hell, yeah! Except… 'I…'

'Think about it.'

Right.

He rose. 'I ordered a pot of hot chocolate, but I'm going to have a beer.'

'Yes, please.'

After he was seated again a ripple of excitement fizzed through her. 'Present time!'

He laughed. 'You're like a big kid.'

'My father and I had a tradition of three presents. The first was something yummy, the second was something funny and the third was the real present.'

He glanced at the table where she'd lined up his presents, then at her, and his grin widened. He reached down beside his chair. 'One.' He lifted a brightly wrapped gift. 'Two.' A second one appeared. 'And three.'

She clapped her hands and beamed at him. 'My father would've liked you.'

They opened their first gifts—identical dried plum and almond chimney sweeps, of course.

Her second gift was a pair of woollen mittens—red and green with a print of fat white snowflakes sprinkled across them. Flynn grinned. 'They reminded me of the look on your face when you first saw it snowing.'

She clasped them to her chest. 'They're the best!' She'd treasure them.

'I'm almost frightened to open this,' he said when she handed him his second gift.

'I promise it doesn't bite.'

He tore open the wrapping to reveal a pair of lederhosen. He groaned and she laughed. 'I couldn't resist. Now it's your turn to go first.' She handed him his final present.

He tore off the wrapping paper and then just stared. She squirmed on her seat. She'd bought him a silver fountain pen. By chance when she'd been out walking one day she'd ambled into a quirky little shop that had specialised in all sorts of pens, including fountain pens. 'Do you like it?'

He pulled it free from his case. 'Addie, it's perfect. I'm not sure I've ever owned an object quite so beautiful.'

'I figure that given all the big contracts you sign that you ought to have a pen worthy of them.' She waved a finger at him. 'Now you have to promise to use it. You're not to put it away in some drawer to keep for good.'

He grinned. 'I promise. Now, here.' He handed her the final present.

She tried to open the paper delicately but in the end impatience overcame her and she simply tore it. Her jaw dropped. 'Oh!'

He leaned towards her. 'Do you like it?'

'No.' She shook her head. 'I *love* it!' He'd bought her a cuckoo clock—a marvellous and wonderful cuckoo clock. The local souvenir shops stocked them and they constantly fascinated her. Now she had one of her very own. 'Thank you!' She looked up. 'It's the best present ever.'

He grinned and he suddenly looked younger than she'd ever seen him. 'I wanted to give you a piece of Munich you'd be able to take home with you.'

Home...

She ran a finger across the little wooden frame of the cuckoo bird's house. 'You invited me along with you to Munich so I'd learn to really appreciate the things I have at home, didn't you?'

He shrugged and settled back in his chair. 'I hoped it would do that at the same time as ease your wanderlust.'

'It worked.'

'I'm glad.'

What he didn't know was that it had worked a little too well. She opened her mouth. She shook herself and shut it again. Tomorrow. There'd be time enough for all of that tomorrow.

She leaned forward and clinked her beer to his. 'Merry Christmas, Flynn. This has been a marvellous Christmas. Much better than expected. I'll never forget it.'

'I'll agree with each and every one of those statements. Merry Christmas, Addie.'

Addie drank in his smile and her heart twisted in her chest. It might, in fact, be the very last smile he ever gave her.

CHAPTER TEN

THE PULSE IN Addie's throat pounded when Flynn answered her knock on his door the next morning. She had to fight the urge to throw her arms around him and beg him not to hate her.

His gaze travelled down the length of her and his smile widened. 'I like your suits, Addie. I like them a lot, but I want you to know it's not necessary for you to don them every morning before you head on over here. I'll let you know in advance if we have a meeting.'

The pulse in her throat pounded harder. *Oh! Don't look at me like that.* As if he liked what he saw, as if she were a nice person. He wouldn't think her nice in a moment.

She gulped and moved into the suite on unsteady knees, setting the coffee pot onto the dining table as usual. She decided then that she hated her suits. She might burn them when she got home.

He frowned as if picking up on her mood. 'Is everything okay?'

She wiped her hands down her skirt and turned to face him. 'Not really.'

In two strides he was in front of her. 'Is everyone at Lorna Lee's okay? Jeannie and Frank? Bruce Augustus?'

His questions and the sincerity of his concern made her heart burn all the harder, made her love him all the more.

She straightened and blinked. Love? She swallowed. She didn't love him. She *liked* him a lot, but love?

He touched her arm. 'Addie?'

She moved out of his reach. 'It's nothing like that. As far as I know, everyone at home is fighting fit.'

She glanced at him. Had she fallen in love with Flynn? If so, did that change the things she needed to tell him?

She thought hard for a moment before shaking her head. She had to remember he didn't want her love—had warned her on that head more than once. Telling him she loved him would be his worst nightmare. She had no intention of making this interview harder for him than it'd already be.

She pushed her shoulders back. 'There are two things I need to tell you and you're not going to like either one of them. In fact, you're going to hate them.'

He stared at her. His brow lowered over his eyes and he folded his arms. 'Are you scared of me? Is that what this is about? You're scared I'm going to rant and rave and—'

'No.' She wheeled away to collect mugs, slammed them to the table. 'I mean, you'll probably rant and rave, but that doesn't scare me. It's just…'

He raised an eyebrow.

She bit back a sigh. 'It's just that you don't deserve it and I hate being the messenger.'

She pulled out a chair and fell into it. Flynn sat too, much more slowly and far more deliberately. 'You've been in contact with George Mueller.'

'He's been in contact with me,' she corrected, stung by the suspicion that laced his words.

'When?'

'Yesterday evening. I received a call from Reception that he was down there and wanted to see me.'

His face darkened. He leaned away from her, but his gaze didn't leave her face. 'Was that before or after our little supper?'

She swallowed. 'Before.' Her voice came out small.

The lines around his mouth turned white. 'And what right

did you think you had to withhold that piece of information from me?'

His voice emerged low and cold. She sensed the betrayal beneath his words and she wanted to drop her head to the table. 'I never had any intention of withholding the information from you. I just decided to delay it.'

'You had no right.'

'You don't even know what Herr Mueller spoke to me about yet.' She moistened her lips. 'Last night I hadn't worked out what I was going to do, so I made a judgment call. You obviously think it a bad one, but it's done now. In future it's probably a good idea to choose your PAs with more care, because I feel as if I'm in way over my head here, Flynn.'

He leapt out of his chair and wheeled away. 'You know how important closing this deal is to me. I can't believe you'd deliberately hold back something important and jeopardise negotiations.'

She stood, shaking. 'You don't even know yet what it was that Herr Mueller and I discussed, but you immediately leap to the worst possible conclusions. Can't you see how your obsession with this has clouded your judgment?'

He spun back. 'Clouded?' he spat.

'Yes!' she hollered at him. 'You've made it clear on more than one occasion how important this vendetta is to you.' So important he'd rather chase after it than live his life, enjoy his life.

He took his seat again. 'Sit,' he ordered, his voice containing not an ounce of compromise.

She sat.

'And now you will tell me everything.'

Her stomach churned. Her mouth went dry. She had to clear her throat before she could speak. 'Herr Mueller told me you were right—that your father didn't steal the money.'

A grim smile lit his lips. One hand clenched. 'I'm going to crush him like a bug.'

She closed her eyes. 'There is no easy way for me to tell you what he said next.' She opened them again. 'He said the thief was a barmaid called Rosie. He said that Rosie was your father's mistress.'

Flynn shot out of his chair so quickly it crashed to the floor. It barely made a sound against the thick carpet. He stabbed a finger at Addie. 'That is a dirty, filthy lie.'

Addie folded her arms. For the first time he noted her pallor and the dark circles beneath her eyes. 'Was your father really such a paragon of perfection?' she whispered.

'He wasn't a thief and he wasn't a cheat!'

'Even if he had been both of those things, it doesn't mean he wasn't a good father.'

What on earth was she talking about?

She stared at him, her amber eyes alternately flashing and clouding. 'You love him so much that I think he must've been a wonderful father, but you did say what a difficult woman your mother always was. Would it really be such a stretch to believe that he found comfort elsewhere?'

It went against everything Flynn believed in.

'This is the version of events Herr Mueller relayed to me. I don't know if they're lies or not. I'm just telling you what he said.'

He righted his chair and sat, nodded once in a way that he hoped hid the ache that stretched through his chest. She glanced at the coffee pot and he leaned forward and poured her a mug.

She curled her hands around it. 'Thank you.'

This situation wasn't of her making. He knew how much she hated it. She'd never pretended otherwise. But she'd no right to hold this back from him. 'Go on.' His voice came out harder and curter than he'd meant it to. When, really, all he wanted to do was reach out and take her hand and tell her how sorry he was that he'd dragged her into his sordid game. She must be wishing herself a million miles away. He dragged a hand down his face.

'He said Rosie had a cocaine problem. She stole money from the pub—lots of it—and when he realised your father tried to cover it up. Of course, the money dried up at that point and Rosie apparently dumped him for someone younger and richer.' She pulled in a breath. 'Herr Mueller said he felt betrayed by your father and turned his back on him. He says he regrets that now and wishes he'd done things differently.'

This was all a fantasy, a fiction. 'And you believed him?'

Addie met his gaze. 'I don't think it matters what I believe. It's what you believe that's important.'

Had she and George been in this together from the start? Had George promised her that she could see the world if she came and worked for him?

She reached down into her briefcase and pulled out a package. 'He gave these to me. He says they're letters your father and Rosie wrote to each other. And photographs. I haven't looked at them. They're none of my business.' She set them on the table. 'I can't help feeling they're none of yours either.'

His head snapped up. She grimaced and shrugged. 'Mind you, you're talking to the woman who wouldn't read the letters her parents left behind when they…' She trailed off with another shrug.

Flynn seized the package and waved it at her. 'Letters can be forged. Photographs can be doctored.'

She swallowed. 'True.' But he could see that in this instance she didn't believe they had been.

'What else did he say?'

She nodded at the package. 'He said he took those so you and your mother wouldn't find them, wouldn't find out about Rosie. And…' she pulled in a breath '…he wanted to know if I thought this news would come better from him or from me.'

'So you made another judgment call?'

She glanced down at her hands. 'I'm sorry if I made the wrong one.'

Was she?

She straightened. Her pallor tugged at him. 'Flynn, you have your father on a pedestal—an impossibly high one. I'm not even sure if you're aware of that. Why? Is it because the last time you truly felt safe was when your father was alive? I understand about honouring the dead, but—'

'Oh, yes, you know all about that, don't you?' He wheeled on her, wanting—needing—her to stop. 'Honouring the dead, putting them on pedestals! Look at what you've done to Robbie.'

She stood too. 'Yes, I did put her on a pedestal. I didn't know how else to deal with my grief, but you showed me how doing so had narrowed my view. You helped me realise I was in danger of making a big mistake. I'm working on it, trying to put it into some kind of perspective and make it better. And you have to learn to do the same.' She lifted her arms. 'Is this really what your father would want from you?'

His scalp crawled. 'Don't you presume to tell me what my father would want from me. You didn't know him and you don't know George Mueller!'

Her eyes flashed and she strode forward to poke him in the chest. 'What happens to us when we're young can leave scars—big, ugly, jagged ones. But I'm here to tell you that you're a grown man now—a grown man with the backing of a powerful financial empire you've built yourself. Nobody and nothing can take your achievements away from you. It's time to recognise that fact. It's time you stopped chasing demons and trying to slay imaginary dragons. It's time you started acting like a man!'

All he could do was stare at her.

'If your father was the paragon of perfection that you claim, then so be it. But paragons don't kill themselves,

Flynn. In which case he wasn't perfect. In which case deal with it and move on.'

He wanted to smash something. He wanted to run away. He wanted—

He strode away from her towards the window, dragging both hands back through his hair. The street below had become alive with cars and people.

If Herr Mueller wasn't guilty…

He shook that thought off. Of course he was guilty! This was just his latest attempt to save his neck. He opened the window to let in a blast of icy air, but it did nothing to clear the confusion rolling through him.

He might be a grown man, but the terror and confusion when he'd learned of his father's death still felt as raw and real to him now as it had when he'd been twelve years old. He gripped the window frame so hard the wood bit into his hand. He'd tried to bury that scared little boy when he'd made his first million. It hadn't worked. He didn't doubt for a moment, though, that taking George Mueller down would quieten the demons that plagued him.

'The ball is now in your court,' Addie said. 'What happens now is up to you.'

He knew that if it were up to her she'd have him walk away. Well, it wasn't up to her. He slammed the window shut and spun around, cloaking the war raging inside him behind an icy wall. 'You said you had two things to tell me. What's the second thing?'

Her gaze slid away. 'You know what?' She seized her briefcase. 'I think you should consider what Herr Mueller had to say and we can discuss the other issue tomorrow. I—'

'Don't presume to tell me what I should do.'

She dropped her briefcase back to the floor, pushed her shoulders back and met his gaze squarely. 'You're no more a lackey than I am, so maybe you'll understand what I'm about to say…and do.'

Something inside him froze. He didn't know why but he wanted to beg her to stop. He wanted it to start snowing and for her face to light up as she dashed out into it. 'What do you mean to do?' he said instead. He'd have winced at the sheer hard brilliance of his voice, but he couldn't. It was as if an invisible barrier stood between him and the rest of the world.

She twisted her hands together. 'I'm not going to sell you Lorna Lee's, Flynn. I'm going to take advantage of the cooling-off period stated in our contract and renege on our deal.'

Her words knocked the breath out of him. It took all of his strength not to stagger. The dream of a home of his own, a place where he could belong and be himself, slipped out of reach, evaporated into a poof of nothingness.

They'd just spent two amazing days in the Alps and all that time she'd been planning to pull out of their deal?

'You were right. I'm not lackey material.' Her hands continued to twist. 'The more I consider having to take orders from anyone in relation to Lorna Lee's, the more everything inside me rebels. It's my home.' She slapped a hand to her chest. 'I want to be the one who shapes it, to determine which direction it should take…and to decide who can and can't live there.'

Apparently she didn't want *him* living there.

He folded his arms, something inside him hardening. 'You're doing this because you don't approve of my business dealings with Mueller. If you think this will turn me back from that course of action, you're sadly mistaken.'

'To hell with Herr Mueller,' she shot back rudely. 'And to hell with you too, Flynn. I'm doing this for me!' Her hands clenched. 'Did you really not see this coming? As far as I can tell you've been one step ahead of me when it comes to my true feelings.' She moved in closer to peer up into his face. 'I want to be the one to call the shots. I don't want to be told to get rid of a beloved bull or that I can't have Frank and Jeannie live with me. I don't want to be your lackey, Flynn, and I don't want to be Robbie's either. I just…I just want to be my own person.'

'Pretty speech,' he taunted, 'but what about your neighbours? They need this sale.'

'The bank will lend me the money to buy them out.'

He could feel his face twist. 'You've checked already?'

'Oh, for heaven's sake, are you really that intent on seeing conspiracies all around you? I checked with the bank before you ever made on offer on the place in case it became the only option.'

'I could fight you on this.'

'What?' It was her turn to taunt. 'Are you going to turn me into your next vendetta? Are you going to do everything in your power to destroy me?'

Of course not, but…

'The funny thing is it's you who's responsible for my change of heart. You dared me to discover what it was I really wanted. And Lorna Lee's is what I really want.' She threw her arms up and wheeled away. 'Yes, I also want to travel and see the world, but I want a home base. I want to live in the world where I grew up, where Robbie grew up and where all of my friends are. I want to work at something I'm good at and I want to canter over green fields at the end of a day's honest work and to know I'm where I should be.' She bit her lip and glanced up at him. 'Maybe that's the way you feel about your property in Channel country.'

He didn't feel that way about anywhere. He'd thought he might find it at Lorna Lee's but… He cut off that thought. He had no intention of sharing it with her.

'There'll be no cash injection for expansion.'

Something in her eyes told him he'd disappointed her. 'I'm well aware of that. Expansion is something I can work towards.'

So that was that, then, was it?

She swiped her hands down the front of her skirt. 'I

want to thank you, Flynn. I suspect it's no comfort, but you've helped me—'

'Spare me!'

She flinched.

'I should've known you were trouble the moment I heard you bawling to that darn bull.'

Her intake of breath told him he'd hit the mark. Finally. She brushed a hand across her eyes. 'You heard that?'

He kinked an eyebrow because a ball of stone had lodged in his chest, making it impossible to speak.

Her eyes shimmered. She swallowed hard. 'You offered me Munich because you felt sorry for me?' She stared at him as if she'd never seen him before. 'I don't get you at all.'

He forced a harsh laugh. 'But you did, didn't you? You've taken me for a complete ride. You weaselled a free trip to Munich out of me, sabotaged my business dealings while we were here and then reneged on a contract I'd signed in good faith. You must be laughing up your sleeve.'

She paled. 'That's not true.'

He shrugged and turned away as if he didn't care, as if none of it mattered to him. 'I think it'd be best all round if you just caught the first available flight back to Australia, don't you?'

'I know you're angry with me at the moment and disappointed about Lorna Lee's, but we're friends! I'm sorry, truly sorry, that things have turned out this way. If there's anything I can do to make amends...I mean, I'm still your PA for as long as you need me to and—'

'Don't bother. I'll hire someone competent.'

That was hardly fair, but he didn't care. He wanted Addie and all of her false promises gone. He didn't need reminding how bad his judgment was when it came to women. 'Like I said, it's time you were out of my hair.'

Silence and then, 'If that's what you want.'

He kept his back to her even though something in her

voice chafed at him. 'That's exactly what I want.' His heart bellowed a protest, but he ignored it.

The click of the door told him that she was gone.

For good.

He limped over to the armchair and sank into it, closing his eyes and trying to shut his mind to the pain that flooded him.

Addie stumbled back into her room. She glanced from side to side, turned on the spot and then kicked herself forward to perch on the sofa. She clutched a cushion to her stomach.

Oh, that hadn't gone well.

It was never going to go well.

Perhaps not, but she hadn't realised it would leave her feeling so depleted. So guilty. So hurt.

She dropped to her knees on the floor and pressed her face into the soft leather of the sofa. There had to be something she could do to make things right between them. It was such poor form to back out of the Lorna Lee sale. He'd made his offer fair and square, he'd gone to the expense of bringing a foreman in, he'd brought her to Munich, but...

Lorna Lee's was her home. It was where she belonged. Surely Flynn could understand that. Surely—

Everything inside her froze. She uncurled herself from the floor to stand. He didn't, though, did he? She moved to the window, but the view outside didn't register. Flynn bought things—he owned them, developed them and once he'd done that he sold them off at a profit—but he had no roots. There wasn't a single place he called home. Lorna Lee's wouldn't have been any different—just another in a long line of enterprises. Flynn shunned those kind of roots while she, she'd discovered, craved them.

'So, why so heartbroken?' she whispered into the silence.

Because none of it stops you from loving him.

For a moment she was too tired even for tears. She just stood there and stared out at a grey sky.

Flynn sat in his room. He sat and did nothing. He tried to feel nothing. Addie's news had shattered something inside him.

Not her revelation of Herr Mueller's spurious allegations. He hadn't expected any less from the other man. That had angered him, true, but it occurred to him now that much of his anger was directed at himself—for creating a situation where Addie had been forced to play go-between, that he'd involved her in dealings that turned her stomach.

Revenge might be satisfying, but it wasn't noble. He should've kept her well away from it. He glanced at the packet of letters and photographs. *Not your business.* He seized them, stalked into the bedroom and threw them into the bottom of his suitcase, threw the suitcase to the top of the wardrobe and stalked back into the living area. He threw himself back into his chair.

It wasn't Mueller's machinations that maddened him— he'd been expecting those. It was Addie's news that she wasn't going to sell him Lorna Lee's.

He leapt up and paced from one side of the room to the other. He flung out an arm. Contract-wise she was well within her rights to pull out. Besides, it wasn't as if he wouldn't be able to purchase another cattle property just like Lorna Lee's. So why did he feel so betrayed?

Because he'd thought them friends?

He dragged a hand down his face. This was business. It wasn't personal. It had nothing to do with friendship. She hadn't pulled out with the intention of hurting him.

He bent to rest his hands on his knees and dragged in a breath. He could buy another farm, but he wouldn't have Addie working for him. It wouldn't be a place that eased his soul when he entered its gates. It wouldn't feel like home.

He stumbled back to his chair.

Addie pulling out of their deal had shattered a dream he'd hardly realised had been growing within him. He would now never get the chance to work with her—to experience and observe her expertise, to witness her excitement when he gave her the opportunity to expand her programme. He would never get the chance to laugh with her, discuss moral issues, travel with her and…and experience the world through her eyes. A more attractive world than the one in which he lived.

That's your choice.

He shot upright. What the hell? He'd started to do what he'd sworn he'd never do again—become involved with a woman. His hands clenched. In walking away, Addie had done them both a favour. His realisation at the near miss had him resting his hands on the back of a chair and breathing deeply. He wasn't giving another woman the opportunity to stomp all over his heart. Not even Addie.

He didn't doubt she'd do her best to treat his heart with care and kindness, but eventually he'd make some mistake, do something wrong, and she'd turn away.

He swallowed, fighting the vice-like pain gripping his chest. When he could move again he pulled on a tracksuit and running shoes and headed outside. He ran by the Isar, drawing the scent of the river and winter into his lungs. His world might never become as congenial and gratifying as Addie's, but he wouldn't forget to appreciate the little things again.

Your world will never be like hers for as long as you continue with your vendetta.

He shook that thought off. Herr Mueller deserved everything that was coming to him.

He ran and ran until he was sick of sliding on the ice-slicked paths, and then he walked. He walked for miles and miles. He walked until he was exhausted and then he turned and headed back to the hotel—miles away.

Flynn had just passed beneath the Isartor in all of its

medieval grandness when Addie emerged from the hotel doors with Bruno at her side carrying her bags. The concierge had obviously chosen to wait on Addie himself rather than leave it to a porter. They moved towards a waiting taxi. Flynn's heart started to pound. He stepped back beneath the tor, into the shadows where Addie wouldn't see him.

You could stop this.

All he'd have to do was call out…ask her to stay. Would she?

He recalled the way she'd looked at him earlier, the way her voice had trembled, and knew she would. He closed his eyes and rested his head back against aged stone. Addie might be willing to risk her heart, but he wasn't.

He remained in the shadows until the taxi had driven away. He leant against the wall and pretended to study the structure like the other sightseers until he had the strength to push forward. He didn't want to go back to the hotel, but…

There was nowhere else to go.

Bruno greeted him as he entered. 'Good afternoon, Herr Mather.' He didn't smile.

Was it afternoon already?

'Miss Addie got away safely for her flight home.'

He swallowed. 'Excellent.'

'She asked me to give you this.'

He handed Flynn the carved bull—Bruce Augustus—and a letter.

Dammit! He'd given her that bull as a gift.

At the last moment he remembered his manners—it was almost as if Addie had dug him in the ribs. 'Thank you, Bruno.'

He moved towards the elevator. He should wait until he was in his room, but… He tore the letter open.

Dear Flynn,
You gave me this as a promise, but as I broke mine to you I don't feel I have the right to keep it.

He clenched his hand so hard the carving dug into it.

I'm sorry I disappointed you and let you down. My life is better for knowing you, but I understand that you can't say the same.

A lump weighed in his chest. His eyes burned.

I don't want you to think I took advantage of you on purpose. Please send me the bill for my share of the trip to Munich. Don't worry. I do have the funds to cover it.

Not a chance!

From the bottom of my heart—thank you. For everything. If you ever find yourself in the neighbourhood drop in for a cuppa. You can always be assured of a warm welcome at Lorna Lee's.

He wanted to accept that invitation. Everything inside him clamoured for him to.

Love, Addie.

He folded the letter. He wanted it too badly. It was why he had to resist.

'Flynn, I'm glad I caught you.'

He stiffened. George Mueller.

A fist tightened about his chest and did all it could to squeeze the air from his body. 'Herr Mueller, I'm afraid I'm not in the mood at the moment.' He turned. 'And don't bother pestering Adelaide again. She's no longer here.' He pushed the button for the elevator.

George scanned his face and something inside him seemed to sag. 'You sent her away.'

He didn't reply to that.

The older man shook his head. 'You still refuse to see the truth.'

'The one truth I do know is that whatever happened between my father and you, you turned away from him. You turned away from my mother and you turned away from me. You call that friendship? I don't think so. If nothing else, that defines you, indicates the kind of man you are.'

The elevator door slid open. Flynn stepped inside and pushed the button for the fourth floor.

Mueller reached out a hand to stop it closing. 'It is the greatest regret of my life, Flynn. I'm sorry. I should've tried harder, but when I contacted your mother she wanted nothing to do with me. I thought…'

Mueller had contacted his mother?

'I understand it's easier to hate me. Maybe I do deserve all of this, but I can't believe you sent that lovely girl away when anyone could see how much she cared for you.'

If Addie did care for him, she'd get over it. It was better this way.

Mueller straightened and met Flynn's gaze squarely. 'You can take away my business and my livelihood, you can ruin me financially, but you can never take from me my family. You will never be able to turn my loved ones against me because they love me as strongly as I love them. And for all your money and your power, Flynn, I can't help thinking that still makes me the richer man.'

Nausea churned in the pit of his stomach.

'Where is that love and connection in your life, I ask myself? You're so intent on the past that you have no future. Regardless of what you do, I would not trade places with you.'

Mueller shook his head, real disgust reflected in his eyes. 'You sent her away. You're a fool. Careful, Flynn, or you'll find yourself in danger of becoming the cruel, heartless man you think I am.'

And then he moved and the elevator door slid closed.

* * *

On the flight home, Addie fired up her laptop and opened her 'Till the Cows Come Home' diary.

> *Dear Daisy*
> *What I wouldn't give to see you right now. I need a smile and a shoulder.*

In her mind's eye she conjured that exact smile and the precise dimensions of Robbie's shoulders. How had she thought she'd ever forget?

> *I've fallen in love. I've fallen in love with a man who thinks I don't possess a faithful bone in my body—a man who thinks I used him.*

And then it all came tumbling out—the whole rush of falling in love with Flynn, of trying to resist him, of how his reasons for being in Munich had filled her with misgiving. She told Daisy how kind and thoughtful he was, how his zeal could capture hold of him and fire him to life and how that had always stolen her breath. She relayed how he dreamed impossible dreams and made them come true.

> *Daisy, I've fallen in love with a man I'm never going to see again and I don't know what to do.*

What would she like to have happen?

> *I'd like for him to turn up next week at Lorna Lee's and tell me he loves me too; that he's prepared to risk his heart one more time because he trusts me. That's what I want, but I know it's impossible.*

She moistened her lips. She'd never had a chance to tell Flynn how she felt about him. There'd be no point in trying to contact him now. He'd refuse to take her calls, would delete her emails. He would never seek out her company or speak to her again. She didn't hold any hope that he'd ever return her feelings. He'd warned her. He'd told her he didn't do relationships.

She closed the lid of her laptop. She should've listened.

CHAPTER ELEVEN

Two days later Flynn snapped his laptop closed. It was pointless. There wasn't a scrap of dirt or scandal to be found on George Mueller. How could that be?

He glanced at the contract. Finally...*finally* it was his. All it required was his signature and George Mueller would be a ruined man.

He strode to the window. Correction—Mueller would be financially ruined. He wouldn't fall into the same pit of despair Flynn's father had. He wouldn't kill himself.

He snapped away, heart pounding. He didn't want the other man to kill himself! He dragged a hand down his face. He just wanted justice.

Addie's face rose up in his mind and raised an eyebrow.

He swung back to the window. Today the sky in Munich was blue and he could see the frosty air on the breath of the passers-by below.

Are you sure he's guilty?

He glanced at his watch, drummed his fingers on the window ledge before straightening and stalking over to the telephone. He punched in a number.

'Hello, Mum, it's Flynn,' he said when she answered.

'What do you want?'

Hello, son, lovely to hear from you. He bit back his sarcasm, but dispensed with pleasantries. 'I want to know if George Mueller ever contacted you after Dad died.'

A pause followed.

'And I want the truth.'

'Things are really tight around here at the moment...'

He glared at the ceiling. 'How much do you want?'

She named a sum.

'I'll have it wired into your account by the close of business today.'

She didn't even thank him.

'George Mueller?' he prompted.

'He paid for your father's funeral.'

Flynn sat, swallowed. 'Why?'

'It was the least he could do! We'd been happy before him and your father became partners in that cursed pub. Why do you want to know about him after all this time?'

Her strident tone scratched through him. 'Because our paths have crossed again. I'm in Munich and...' He trailed off.

There was another pause and then a harsh laugh. 'You're there to take over his company, aren't you?'

Yes.

'Do it!' she ordered. 'Let him see what it feels like to lose what he's worked so hard for. Let him see what it's like when the shoe is on the other foot.'

Bile burned the back of his throat. 'I have to go.'

'The money...you won't forget?'

'No,' he ground out. 'I won't forget.'

He slammed down the phone. Her bitterness and her antipathy made his stomach churn and his temples pound. He had an insane urge to shower, to wash the dirt off, but he'd only showered a few short hours ago. *Let him see what it feels like to lose what he's worked so hard for.* His hands clenched. She'd never worked hard a day in her life! Unless you counted her incessant nagging of his father.

He rested his head in his hands before lifting it with a harsh laugh. 'The apple doesn't fall far from the tree, does it?' Was this the man he'd truly become? He'd been so busy putting his father on a pedestal that he hadn't realised that all of this time he'd been turning into his mother.

He suddenly wished Addie were here to tell him he was wrong and that he was nothing like his mother.

He swallowed the bile that rose in his throat. Addie was where she belonged. And he... He finally had Mueller exactly where he wanted him. So why was he hesitating?

Flynn took a leaf from Addie's book and went sightseeing. He strode up to the Residenz and lost himself in art and architecture. He absorbed himself in accounts of history utterly foreign to him. Four hours later he found himself in the coffee shop above Marienplatz where he and Addie had once shared coffee.

He ordered coffee and apple strudel. He stared at the town halls—old and new—and wondered what on earth he was doing there. Sitting here without Addie cracked something open in his chest, something he wasn't sure he'd ever be able to shut again. He threw money onto the table and strode back out having barely touched his refreshments.

He stalked the streets, round and round, coming to an abrupt halt when he almost collided with a statue of three stone oxen. They lorded it over a fountain that tripped down levels like a gentle waterfall.

Oxen...cattle...Bruce Augustus...Addie.

He collapsed on a nearby bench to stare at the statue, recalling the way Addie had cried against the giant bull's shoulder. He'd bet it was the first thing she'd done when she'd returned to Lorna Lee's—headed straight down to the bull's pen.

He rested his head in his hands. And she'd have cried. His abrupt dismissal would've made her cry. For a moment he wished he had a Bruce Augustus too.

For heaven's sake. He lifted his head. He didn't want coffee and cake. He didn't want Bruce Augustus. He wanted Addie. What was the point in hiding from it?

Yeah, well, you can't have her.

His mouth filled with acid and his future with darkness. Who said? Maybe he—

You said.

He pulled in a breath and nodded. He'd said. And it was for the best. It'd be for the best all round if he just stopped thinking about her.

Ha! As if that were possible.

Do what you came here to do and then go home and put it all behind you.

He slumped back against the bench, staring at the oxen. Why was he hesitating?

Because once it was done it would put him out of Addie's reach forever.

He shot to his feet. She was out of reach already!

Flynn strode back to the hotel. He made sure to enquire after Bruno's mother's health—the older woman was ailing—and sped straight up to his room. He strode over to the contract, pulled the pen Addie had given him from its case and scrawled his signature along the bottom.

Done.

His stomach churned. The blood in his veins turned alternately hot and cold. If he'd been expecting peace he'd have been seriously disappointed.

If he went through with this, there would never be a chance for him and Addie. He dragged a hand down his face. If he didn't go through with it there were no guarantees that there'd ever be a chance for him and Addie either.

If he went through with this it'd prove he was exactly like his mother.

His mouth dried. His heart pounded. What would his father choose in the same situation?

Love. The answer came to him from some secret place filled with truth. His father would've chosen love. His father would've chosen Addie.

He fell into a seat, frozen. He'd sent Addie away. She hadn't wanted to go. A lump stretched his throat in a painful ache. He blinked against the burning in his eyes.

If only he dared, could she be his?

Did he dare?

The blood pounded so hard in his ears it deafened him. He stood, but he didn't know what to do so he sat again. *Think!* Make no mistake, Addie would want it all—marriage, kids, commitment. Did he dare risk it? Could he make a marriage with Addie work?

If it went wrong he wasn't sure he'd have the strength to dust himself off again.

He stared across the room and the longer he stared, the darker it seemed to get. A choice lay before him that would affect the rest of his life. It would define the very man he'd become.

He could choose his mother's way—bitterness and revenge.

Or he could choose Addie and love; but with no guarantees.

He strode over to the contract, seized it in his hands. He'd spent a lifetime working towards this. Addie would never have to know if…

But you'd know.

'Relax, Bruce Augustus.' Addie petted the giant bull's shoulder as she settled on the fence. 'I haven't come down here to cry all over you.'

She'd been home for ten whole days and she'd spent more of that time bawling all over her poor old pal than she had in deciding Lorna Lee's future. The secret crying had helped her keep up a semi-cheerful façade for everyone else, but it hadn't made the ache in her heart go away.

She forced herself to smile. Wasn't that supposed to make you feel better? She grimaced. If so, it was a lie.

No, no. She forced another smile. 'Today we have good

news, Bruce Augustus. Today the bank agreed to lend me the money to buy out Frank and Jeannie and the Seymours.'

Jeannie and Frank were going to pay her a nominal rent on their house. She'd told them they could stay for as long as they wanted. Without the worry of having to work the land they'd developed a new lease of life. Addie was glad. She'd rent out the Seymour house too and it'd give her enough money to hire an additional hand. She'd had interest from several local farmers who wanted to agist their stock here if she were amenable. It'd all help pay the mortgage.

She turned to gaze out at the land that rolled away in front of her. Dams twinkled silver in the sunlight, grass rustled and bent in the breeze and the enormous and ancient gums stood as brooding and eternal as ever. She pressed a hand to her chest when she realised how closely she'd come to giving it all away.

'My home,' she whispered. She belonged here. It was where she wanted to be. But that didn't make the ache in her heart go away either.

She turned back to Bruce Augustus. 'I know you're sick of me talking about Flynn, but I worked something out. It's like emotionally I've been through a flood or a drought or a bushfire. Anyway—' she shook her head '—it doesn't matter what it is specifically, just that it's some kind of natural disaster. And it takes time to rebuild after something like that.'

Bruce Augustus remained silent.

'I know, I know.' She sighed. 'I have no idea how long it'll take either.'

She kicked the ground, picked a splinter of wood from the railing. She heard a car purr up the driveway. 'Sounds like we have company.' She peeked around the side of the pen when the car pulled to a halt outside the homestead. 'A black Mercedes Benz,' she told her bull, moving back into the privacy provided by the pen. 'There were lots of those in Munich. Funny thing I've noticed recently, but in the movies and on cop shows the villains always seem to drive a black Mercedes.'

She glanced back to see who would emerge from the car and then slammed back, flattening herself against the railing. Her heart hammered. Flynn! 'What's he doing here?' Had he come with his big guns to enforce the contract they'd signed?

She forced air into cramped lungs. 'Don't you worry, Bruce Augustus. I got legal advice about that.' He'd have a fight on his hands if he tried anything.

She pushed her shoulders back and moved towards the house, and slammed right into Flynn as he rounded the corner. 'Oh!'

He reached out to steady her. 'I thought I'd find you down here.'

She wanted to hurl herself into his arms. She forced herself to step back. His arms dropped back to his sides. She made herself smile brightly. 'So, you were in the area and decided to pop in for a cuppa?'

Gently he shook his head. 'No.' And her heart sank.

'I see.'

He frowned. 'You do?'

She pushed her chin up. 'Flynn, you ought to know that I did get legal advice. I was well within my rights to pull out of the sale when I did.'

His frown deepened.

'You can drag me through the courts if you want to and it may take years to settle, but no court in the country will rule against me and in the end you'll be forced to pay all of the court costs and I won't be any the worse off. I know you're angry with me, but do you really think that's the best use of your time and money?'

He turned grey. 'Of course that's what you'd think of me.'

Her heart burned. She ached to pull his head down to her shoulder.

'I haven't come here to try and take your home from you, Addie.'

The breeze ruffled his hair. She stared at it, wanting—

'Addie?'

She started. 'You haven't?'

He shook his head.

Okay, that was good to know, but... 'How was Herr Mueller when you left Munich?'

'I don't know.' He wore a business suit and she wanted to tear it off him and force him into jeans and a T-shirt. 'I didn't see him, but I expect he's relieved. I burned the contract and left Munich.'

She gripped a post to stop from falling over. 'You did what?' It didn't make sense. 'You...you read the letters, saw the photos and...'

'No, I burned those too. Bruno and I had quite the blaze. He sends his best, by the way.'

She rubbed her forehead. 'What does Bruno have to do with it?'

'There weren't fireplaces in our rooms, see, but he let me light one in the guest lounge.'

She pressed a hand to her forehead and breathed in deeply. 'Let me get this straight. You burned the contract?'

'Yes.'

She straightened. 'You found out some other way that Herr Mueller wasn't a cheat and a thief?'

He shook his head, but his eyes burned into hers. 'I'm never going to know the truth of what happened back then. I very much doubt, though, that George Mueller is the monster I made him out to be. The thing is, you were right about those letters. They weren't any of my business. They were written by two people who'd have been mortified to discover I'd ever read them. And once I understood that I realised the whole affair between Mueller and my father was none of my business either.'

She stared at him. 'Wow.'

'You were right on another head. Slaying that dragon wouldn't bring my father back. It wouldn't right wrongs and it wouldn't turn back time. It'd just start a whole new cycle of hate. I chose to turn my back and walk away.'

She couldn't get out a second wow. Her lungs had cramped too much.

As if he found it hard to meet her gaze, he turned to the bull. 'Hey, Bruce Augustus, how're you doing?'

The bull eyeballed him. Addie took his arm and edged him away. 'Old Bruce Augustus here can take a while to warm to strangers.'

She led them to a large boulder beneath an enormous spreading gum, and then gestured to his suit. 'You might get dirty. Would you like to go up to the house for a cold drink or…?'

His answer was to settle on the rock. After a moment's hesitation she settled down beside him.

'I wanted to come by and tell you that I harbour no hard feelings about you pulling out of the sale.'

She stared from her feet and up into the cool blue of his eyes. 'You mean that?'

'This is your home, Addie. You belong here. I'm glad you realised that. The cooling-off clause in a contract is there for a reason.'

A weight lifted from her. 'Thank you.'

'I also wanted to return this.' He pulled the carved bull from his pocket. 'I gave this to you last time to seal a verbal contract. I'm giving it to you this time as a token of gratitude.'

She took the miniature Bruce Augustus with a smile. 'I missed this. But, Flynn, I don't see what I could have possibly done to inspire gratitude.' That belonged solely to her, surely?

His eyes dimmed. 'You pulled me back from the brink. You stopped me from making a mistake and doing a very bad thing.'

He glanced at her with such a look in his eyes her heart started to hammer.

'You once warned me about karma. I don't want it to come calling on me to kick my butt.'

That made her grin. She forced her gaze away. In the sky, miles away, a wedge-tail eagle circled on lazy drifts of warm air. She kept her gaze trained on it rather than the man beside her. She'd spent the last ten days crying over him and she was glad he'd taken the time to tell her all he had, but she needed him to go now. It was too hard seeing him and not being able to…

'Could we go for a gallop?'

She closed her eyes. 'Why?'

'Because I want to see that look of absolute contentment and relish on your face again. I missed it when you left Munich.'

'When you sent me away,' she corrected, turning to finally meet the gaze that burned through her.

'Guilty as charged.'

What did he want? 'I appreciate you taking time out of your busy schedule, Flynn, but you could've sent the carving through the mail. You could've explained everything else in an email. Why are you here?'

'I wanted to see you.'

'Why?'

She swallowed when she recognised the flare of hunger that crossed his face. Wow! She folded her arms to keep from reaching for him. 'I'm no longer an employee. That means…'

He folded his arms too and raised an eyebrow. 'What does it mean?'

Her heart sank. 'That I now tick your box as temporary girlfriend material.'

'There's nothing temporary about you, Addie.'

She let out a breath. 'I'm glad you realise that.' She knew

in her bones that if she had an affair with Flynn her heart would never fully recover.

'Which is why I was going to ask you to marry me.'

She leapt off the rock as if scalded. 'I beg your pardon?'

His expression didn't change. 'You heard. You might have trouble taking orders, but there's nothing wrong with your hearing.'

'I...' *Say yes, you fool!* She thrust out her jaw. 'Why would I take a risk on someone with such a poor matrimonial record?'

One side of his mouth hooked up. 'Because you love me, perhaps?'

Her heart thumped. How did he know that? Was she so transparent?

'And because I love you.'

She stared at him. Her knees trembled. 'Why would you go and change your mind so completely about matrimony?'

He didn't answer. She glared. 'You must really want Lorna Lee's.'

He turned so grey and haggard she almost threw her arms around him. 'When you left Munich, Addie...when I so stupidly sent you away, your absence left such a hole inside me that I couldn't fill it up.'

She swallowed. She had to plant her feet to stop from swaying towards him.

'All I wanted was you, but I didn't believe I could have you. And then I spoke to my mother.'

What did his mother have to do with it? 'Your mother?' she prompted when he didn't continue.

He shook himself. 'She's so bitter. When she found out I was in Munich she ordered me to destroy Mueller.'

She tried to swallow the bad taste that rose in her mouth.

'That's when I realised I'd become just like her.'

Oh, no, he wasn't, he—

'And I don't want to be like her, Addie. I want to be like

my father.' He swallowed, vulnerability stretching through his eyes. 'I want to be like you.'

He did?

'To be worthy of you, I knew I'd have to give up my vendetta and initially that was a struggle.' The lines framing his eyes and bracketing his mouth deepened for a moment. 'In the end, though, I wanted to choose the future instead of the past. I wanted to be a man who built a life he could be proud of. And, Addie...' his gaze speared hers '...I want that life with you. I love you.'

Golden light pierced her from the inside out. She tossed her head, her smile growing. 'Why haven't you kissed me yet?'

He closed the gap between them in an instant and pulled her into his arms. 'Because I'm afraid that once I start I won't be able to stop,' he growled.

'I wouldn't mind,' she whispered against his lips the moment before they claimed hers.

Her head rocked back from the force of the kiss, but his hand moved to her nape to steady her. 'Sorry.' He lifted his head. 'I—'

She dragged his head back down to hers and kissed him back with the same ferocity. Her arms wrapped around him. His arms wrapped around her and they kissed and kissed. His kisses told her of his struggles and how much he'd missed her, of his frustration, fear and shame, of his loneliness. She poured all the love she had in her soul into her kisses to fill him instead with happiness and pride, joy and satisfaction.

Finally he lifted his head, dragging a breath into his lungs. She did too, leaning against him with her whole weight, relishing the strength in his powerful frame. 'I love you, Addie.' The words came out raw and ragged. 'Everything I have is yours. Please put me out of my misery. Your kisses say you'll marry me, but...' His eyes blazed down into hers. 'I need to hear it.'

'You've come home, Flynn,' she promised. 'I love you. You're mine and I'm yours. Yes, I'll marry you.'

She watched as the shadows faded from his eyes. 'Home?' he said.

Arm in arm they turned to survey the rolling fields. 'Home,' she repeated, 'because everything I have is yours too, Flynn, and I mean you to have the very best of it.'

'The very best of it is here in my arms.'

'Right answer.' She stretched up on tiptoe to kiss him. His arms snaked about her waist. 'Would you like to go for that gallop now or would you prefer to come up to the house for that, uh…cuppa?'

He grinned. 'The cuppa.'

Taking his hand, she led him back towards the homestead. She led him into the future he'd chosen. She took him home.

* * * * *

"Why should you go out of your way like this for someone you don't even know?"

Whitney had to understand his motives. First saving her from drowning and rescuing her car, and now helping her find a place to stay.

"I did have a hand in saving your life, so that gives us a kind of bond," he told her. "I also want you to be happy living the life I saved."

The man was practically a saint. Excited, relieved and feeling almost euphoric, Whitney threw her arms around his neck and declared, "You're a lifesaver." She said it a second before she kissed him.

She only meant for it to be a quick pass of her lips against his, the kind of kiss one good friend gives another. But at the last second, Liam turned his head just a fraction closer in her direction. What began as a fleeting kiss turned into a great deal more.

Something of substance and depth.

The exuberance she had initially felt stole her breath. Her body suddenly ignited, and had his arms not gone around her when they did, she would *no*t be standing up right now. A wave of weakness snaked through her, robbing her of the ability to stand. Forcing her to cling to him in order to remain upright.

She *shouldn't* be doing this.

CHRISTMAS COWBOY DUET

BY
MARIE FERRARELLA

MILLS & BOON

Published in Great Britain 2014
by Mills & Boon, an imprint of Harlequin (UK) Limited,
Eton House, 18-24 Paradise Road, Richmond, Surrey, TW9 1SR

© 2014 Marie Rydzynski-Ferrarella

ISBN: 978-0-263-91337-8

23-1214

Harlequin (UK) Limited's policy is to use papers that are natural, renewable and recyclable products and made from wood grown in sustainable forests. The logging and manufacturing processes conform to the legal environmental regulations of the country of origin.

Printed and bound in Spain
by CPI, Barcelona

To
Dr Seric Cusick, the ER physician
who sewed my face back together.
Thank you!

Prologue

She'd never learned how to swim.

Somehow, there never seemed to be the right time to sneak in lessons.

Since she was born and bred in Los Angeles, close to an ocean and many pools, everyone just assumed she knew how to swim. It was a given. There were all those beaches, all that tempting water seductively lapping against the shore during those glorious endless summers.

But Whitney Marlowe had never had the time nor the inclination to get swimming lessons. Something more pressing always snagged her attention.

For as long as Whitney could remember, she'd always had this little voice inside of her head urging her on, whispering about goals that had yet to be met.

Swimming was recreational. Swimming was associated with fun. Even growing up, Whitney never seemed to have time for fun, except maybe for a few minutes at a time. A child of divorce, she was far too involved in making a name for herself to dwell on recreation. Everyone in her family was driven and it seemed as if from the very first moment of her life, she had been embroiled in one competition or another.

Oh, she dearly loved her siblings, all five of them, but she loved them just a tiny bit more whenever she could best them at something. It didn't matter what, as long as she could come out the winner.

Her father had promoted this spirit of competition, telling his children that it would better equip them when they went out into the world. He'd been a hard taskmaster.

But right now, all those goals, all those triumphant moments, none of them mattered. None of them meant anything because the sum total of all that wasn't going to save her.

This was it, Whitney thought in frantic despair.

This was the place where she was going to die. Outside of a town that hadn't even been much more than an imperceptible dot on her map. A stupid little town prophetically named *Forever*. Because her car—and most likely her body—were going to become one with this godforsaken place. She would become eternally part of Forever's terrain and nobody was even going to realize it because she would live at the bottom of some body of water.

Forever.

Oh, why had she taken this so-called "shortcut"? she upbraided herself. Why hadn't she just gone the long way to Laredo the way she'd initially intended? It wasn't as if she was trying to outdo her brother in trying to land this new account for the family recording label. She was the only one who'd been dispatched to audition the new band The Lonely Wolves. Desperate for their big break, the band would have waited for her to come until hell froze over.

Unfortunately, it wasn't hell freezing over that was

about to be the cause of her demise; it was the torrential rains, all but unheard of in this part of the country at this time of year.

And yet, here it was, a downpour the likes of which she had never witnessed before. The kind that would have had Noah quickly boarding up the door of his ark and nervously setting sail.

The rains had fallen so fast and so heavily, the dry, parched ground—clay for the most part—couldn't begin to absorb it. One minute, she was driving through a basin, her windshield wipers going so fast, she thought they were in danger of just flying off into the wind. The next, the rain was falling so hard that the poor windshield wipers had met their match and did absolutely no good at all.

Stunned, Whitney had done her best, struggling to keep her vehicle straight, all the while getting that sinking feeling that she was fighting a losing battle. Before she knew it, her tires were no longer touching solid ground.

The rains were filling up the basin, turning the cracked, dusty depression into what amounted to a giant container for all this displaced, swiftly accumulating water.

She gave up trying to steer because nothing short of a rudder would have any effect on regaining control of her vehicle. She'd been driving the sports car with the top down and when the rains hit, they came so fast and so heavy, she couldn't get the top to go back up. Now her car swayed and bobbed as well as filled up with water. It didn't take a genius to know what would happen next.

She would be thrown from her car into the swirling waters—which meant that her life was over. She would die flailing frantically in the waters of a miniscule, backwater town.

She wasn't ready to die.

She wasn't!

Whitney opened her mouth to yell for help as loudly as she could. But the second she did, her mouth was immediately filled with water.

Holding on to the sides of the vehicle to steady herself, she tried to yell again. But the car, now at the mercy of the floodwaters, was utterly unsteady. Water was sloshing everywhere. As it crashed against her car, tipping it, Whitney lost her grip.

And then, just like that, she was separated from the vehicle. The forward motion had her all but flying from the car. The next second, she found herself immersed in the dark, swirling waters—waters that hadn't been there a few short heartbeats ago.

Whitney tried desperately to get a second grip on any part of her car, hoping to somehow stay afloat, but the car was sinking.

There was no help coming from anywhere. No one knew she'd taken this shortcut. No one back home really bothered to trace her route—that was partially because she had insisted years ago not to be treated like a child. She could make her own decisions, her own waves, as well. Certainly, at thirty, she was no longer an unsteady child.

So other than competing with her, her siblings— except for Wilson, the oldest—all stayed clear of her, making a point not to get in her way. After all, she *was* the second oldest in the family.

Tears filled Whitney's eyes before the rains could

lash at them. This wasn't how she wanted to die. And certainly not the age she wanted to die, either.

As if she had a choice, the little voice in her head mocked.

Nevertheless, just before she went under, Whitney screamed the word *Help!* again, screamed it as loudly as she could.

She swallowed more water.

And then the waters swallowed her.

Chapter One

The deluge seemed to come out of nowhere.

On his way back to town after a better-than-average rehearsal session with the band he'd helped put together, Liam and the Forever Band, Liam Murphy immediately made his way to high ground at the first sign of a serious rainfall.

Traveling alone out here, the youngest of the Murphy brothers was taking no chances—just in case. Flash floods didn't occur often around here, but they *did* occur and "better safe than sorry" had been a phrase that had been drummed into his head by his older brother Brett from the time he and his other brother Finn had been knee-high to a grasshopper.

As it turned out, Liam had made it to high ground just in time. Rain fell with a vengeance, as if the very sky had been slashed open. As he watched in awed fascination, in less than ten minutes, the onslaught of rain turned the basin below from a virtual dust bowl to a veritable swimming pool—one filled with swirling waters.

More like a whirlpool, Liam silently amended, because the waters were sweeping so angrily over the terrain, mimicking the turbulent waters in a Jacuzzi.

Liam glanced at the clock on his dashboard. Depending on when this was going to let up, he was either going to be late, or *very* late. This, after he'd promised Brett he'd be in to work early. He was due at Murphy's, Forever's only saloon. Fortunately, it belonged to his brothers and him, but Brett was still not going to be happy about this turn of events.

Liam took out his phone, automatically glancing at the upper left-hand corner to see if there were any bars available.

There were.

"Not bad," he murmured to himself when he saw the three small bars. "Service must be improving," he noted with some relief.

There'd been a time, not all that long ago, when no bars were the norm. A few short years ago, the region around Forever, for all intents and purposes, was a dead zone. But progress could only be held off for so long. Civilization had gotten a foothold in the town, though it had to be all but dragged in, kicking and screaming. Even now, on occasion, the strength of the signal was touch and go.

Liam pressed the appropriate buttons. It took a very long minute before the call connected and he could hear the line on the other end ringing. He silently began to count off the number of times the other phone rang.

He was up to four—one more and it went to voice mail—when he heard the cell phone being picked up.

There was an almost deafening crackle and then he heard, "Murphy's."

The deep, baritone voice could only belong to Brett, the oldest Murphy brother, the one who had been responsible for keeping him and Finn from becoming wards of the state when their uncle died a mere eighteen months after both their parents had passed on. Brett had done it at great personal cost, but that was something he and Finn had only found out about years after the fact.

"Brett? It's Liam. Looks like I'm going to be late for my shift," he told his brother. The rain was beating against the rolled-up windows of his truck with a vengeance as if determined to gain access. All that was missing was a big, bad wolf ranting about huffing and puffing.

"Don't tell me, you got caught in this storm."

Liam could hear the concern in his brother's voice—not that Brett would say as much. But it was understood. "Okay, I won't tell you."

He heard Brett sigh. "I always knew you didn't have enough sense to come in out of the rain. Were you at least smart enough to get to high ground?"

"Yes, big brother, the truck and I are on high ground." Even as he said the words, his windows stopped rattling and the rain stopped coming down in buckets. He looked up through the front windshield. It seemed to have stopped coming down at all. "Matter of fact," he said, pausing for a moment as he rolled down the driver's-side window and stuck his hand out, palm up, "I think it just stopped raining."

It never ceased to amaze him just how fast rain seemed to turn itself on and then off again in this part of the country.

"I'd still give it a little time," Brett warned. "In case it starts up again. I'd rather have you late than dead."

Liam laughed shortly. "And on that heartwarming note, I think I'm going to end this call. See you later," he said to his brother. The next moment, Liam hit the glowing red light on his screen, terminating the connection.

Tucking the phone into his back pocket, he continued driving very slowly. As he began guiding his truck back down the incline, he could have sworn he heard a woman's scream.

Liam froze for a second, listening intently.

Nothing.

Had to be one of the ravens, he decided. Most likely a disgruntled bird that hadn't managed to find shelter before the rains hit, although he hadn't seen one just now.

Still, even though he was now driving down the incline to the trail he'd abandoned earlier, Liam kept listening, just to make sure that it was only his imagination—or some wayward animal—that was responsible for the scream he'd thought he'd heard.

If it was his imagination, it was given to re-creating an extremely high-pitched scream, Liam decided, because he'd heard the cry for help again, fainter this time but still urgent, still high—and resoundingly full of absolute terror.

Someone *was* in trouble, Liam thought, searching for the source of the scream.

Throwing caution to the wind, he pushed down on the accelerator. The truck all but danced down the remainder of the incline in what amounted to a jerky motion. He had a death grip on the steering wheel as he proceeded to scan as much of the area around him as humanly possible.

Liam saw that the basin had completely filled up with rainwater. Something like that was enough to compromise any one of a number of people, even those who were familiar with this sort of occurrence and had lived in and around Forever most of their lives.

The water could rush at an unsuspecting driver with the speed of an oncoming train. Sadly, drownings in a flash flood were not unheard of.

With his eyes intently focused, Liam scanned the area again.

And again, he saw nothing except brackish-looking water.

"Maybe it *was* just the wind," Liam murmured under his breath.

He knew that there were times when the wind could sound exactly like a mournful woman pining after a missing lover.

If Brett were here with him, his older brother would have told him to get his tail on home.

Stop letting your imagination run away with you, Brett would have chided.

Liam was just about to get back on the road home when something—a gut feeling, or maybe just some stray, nagging instinct—made him look down into the rushing waters flooding the basin one last time.

That was when he saw her.

Saw the woman.

One minute she wasn't there at all, the next, a half-drowned-looking woman, her shoulder-length brown hair plastered to her face, came shooting up, breaking the water's surface like a man-made geyser, her arms flailing about madly as they came into contact with nothing but the air. It was obvious that she was desperately searching for something solid to grab on to.

The woman was drowning.

He'd only witnessed such abject panic once before in his life. Then it had been on the face of a friend who had accidentally discharged a pistol and missed his head by an inch, or less. The horror of what could have happened had been visible in his friend's shaken expression.

This time the horror of what could be was on the face of an angel. A very desperate, panicky, wet angel.

Before he had time to assess if this waterlogged angel was real or a mere figment of his overactive, overwrought imagination, Liam leaped out of his truck and came flying down the rest of the incline. There was no time to think, to evaluate and make calculated decisions. There was only time to act and act quickly.

Which he did.

Without pausing, he flung off his jacket because it would keep his arms too confined and from the little he had time to assess, he was going to need all the upper-arm power he could manage to summon. Leaving on his boots and hat, Liam dived into the water.

SHE WAS GOING DOWN for the last time.

Four, she'd counted four. Four times she'd gone down and managed to somehow get back up again, desperately gasping for air.

Her thoughts were colliding wildly with one another. And she was hallucinating, Whitney was sure of it, because she'd just seen someone plunging into the water to rescue her.

Except that he wasn't real. This area was deserted. There was no one around, no one to rescue her.

She was going to die.

Suddenly, Whitney thought she felt something. Or

was that someone? Whatever it was, it was grabbing her by the arm, no, wait, by the waist. Was she being pulled up, out of the homicidal waters?

No, it wasn't possible.

Wasn't possible.

It was just her mind giving her something to hang on to before life finally, irrevocably drained out of her forever.

Just a figment of her imagination. This rescuing hero she'd conjured up, he wasn't real.

And very, very soon, Whitney knew she wouldn't be real, either. But right now, she could have sworn she was being roughly dragged up out of the water.

Where was the light? Wasn't she supposed to be going toward some kind of light? Whitney wondered. But there was no light, there was only pressure and pain and the sound of yelling.

Did they yell in heaven?

Or was this the Other Place? She hadn't been an angel, but she wasn't bad enough to land in hell.

Was she?

But being sent to hell would explain why something was beating against her, pushing on her ribs over and over again.

"C'MON, DAMN IT, breathe! Breathe!" Liam ordered, frustrated and fearful all at the same time. The woman wasn't responding.

Damn it, Brett was the one who should be here, not him, Liam thought as he continued with his chest compressions. Brett would know what to do to save this woman. He just remembered bits and pieces of CPR, not from any sort of training but from programs he'd watched on TV as a kid.

Still, it was the only thing he could think to do and it was better than standing helplessly by, watching this woman die in front of him.

So he continued, almost on automatic pilot. Ten compressions against the chest, then mouth to mouth, and then back to compressions again until the dead were brought back to life.

Except that this woman—whoever she was—wasn't responding.

He was losing her.

The thought made him really angry and he worked harder.

Liam began another round, moving faster, pushing harder this time. He fully intended on continuing in this manner until he got some sort of a response from the woman he'd rescued from the water. Granted she'd looked more dead than alive when he'd pulled her out, but when he put his head against her chest, he was positive that he'd detected just the faintest sound of a heartbeat.

It gave him just a sliver of hope and he intended to build on that.

IT CAME TO HER in a blurred, painful haze: she wasn't dead.

Dead people didn't hurt.

Did they?

Whitney hadn't given much thought to reaching the afterlife. She'd always been far too preoccupied in getting ahead in the life that she had on earth. But she felt fairly certain that after transitioning to the afterlife, pain and discomfort were no longer involved, certainly not to this degree—and she was definitely experiencing both.

Big-time.

After what seemed like an absolute eternity, Whitney came to the realization that she wasn't inside of some dark abyss—or hell. The problem was that her eyes were shut. Not simply shut, it felt more as if they were glued down that way.

With what felt like almost superhuman effort, she kept on struggling until she finally managed to pry her eyes open.

Focusing took another full minute—her surroundings were a complete blur at first, wavy lines that made no sense. Part of her was convinced that she was still submerged.

But that was air she was taking in, not water, so she couldn't be underwater any longer. And what was that odd, heavy pain across her chest that she kept feeling almost rhythmically?

And then she saw him.

Saw a man with wet, medium blond hair just inches away from her face—and he had his hands crisscrossed on top of her chest.

"Why…are…you…pushing…on…my…chest?" The raspy words felt as if they had dragged themselves up a throat that was lined with jagged pieces of glass.

They weren't any louder than a faint whisper.

Liam's head jerked up and he almost lost his balance, certainly his count. Stunned, he stared at her in surprise and disbelief.

It worked! he thought, silently congratulating himself. She was alive!

He'd saved a life!

"I'm giving you CPR," he told her. "And I guess it worked," he added with pride and no small sense of satisfaction. He felt almost light-headed from his success.

"Then...I'm...not...dead?" she asked uncertainly. It took Whitney a second to process this influx of information on the heels of the panic that had enveloped her.

The last thing she clearly remembered was being thrown from the car and sinking into dirty water.

"Not unless I am, too—and I wasn't when I last checked," he told her. He'd actually saved a life. How about that? Right now, Liam felt as if he could walk on water.

It took him a minute to get back to reality.

The woman he'd rescued was looking at him with the widest green eyes he'd ever seen. She tried to sit up only to have him push her back down again. Confused, disoriented, she looked at him uncertainly.

"I don't think you should sit up just yet," he told her. She wanted to argue with him, but the energy just wasn't there. "You almost drowned. Why don't you give yourself a couple of minutes to recover?" he suggested tactfully.

"I'm...fine..." she insisted.

She certainly *was* fine, Liam couldn't help thinking. Even looking like a partially drowned little rabbit, there was no denying that this woman was strikingly beautiful. No amount of wet, slicked-back hair could change that.

Still, Liam didn't want her trying to run off just yet. She could collapse and hit her head—or worse. He hadn't just risked his own life to pull her out of the rushing waters only to have her bring about her own demise.

He continued to restrain her very gently.

"I just saved your life," Liam told her patiently. "Humor me."

The rains had obviously stopped and the waters, even now, were trying, ever so slowly, to recede. Within a couple of hours or so, it would be as if this had never happened—except that it had and an out-of-towner had almost died in it.

Talk about being in the right place at the right time, he mused. He was grateful now that band practice had run a little over. If it hadn't, he would have passed the basin when the rains hit and he would have never been there to rescue this woman.

"Okay." Whitney gave in, partially because she felt about as weak as a day-old kitten and partially because she was trying to humor the cowboy who had apparently rescued her. "But just for a few minutes," she stipulated, her speech still a little slow, definitely not as animated as it normally was.

Whitney tried to move her shoulders and got nowhere. Whoever this man was, he was strong. Definitely stronger than she was, she thought.

She'd never trusted strangers—but this one had saved her life so maybe a little trust *was* in order.

"Does this kind of thing happen often?" Whitney asked warily. Because if it did, she couldn't understand why anyone would want to live here.

Why not? her inner voice mocked. *You live in the land of earthquakes. One natural disaster is pretty much like another.*

Her expression remained stony as she waited for the cowboy to give her an answer.

"No, not often," Liam assured her, removing his hands from her shoulders. "But when it does, I guarantee that it leaves one hell of an impression."

The woman was trying to sit up again, he realized. Rather than watch her digging her elbows into the ground to try to push herself up, Liam put his hands back on her shoulders, exerting just the right amount of pressure to keep her down.

The look she gave him was a mixture of exasperation and confusion.

"Why don't you just hold on to me and I'll get you into a sitting position," Liam suggested.

Having no choice—she was *not* in any shape to outwrestle him and she suspected that out-arguing this gentle-spoken cowboy might be harder than it appeared—Whitney did as he proposed.

With her arms wrapped around his neck, Whitney was slowly raised into a sitting position. She realized that she was just a few feet away from what had been angry, dangerous waters a very short time ago, not to mention her final resting place.

The scene registered for the first time. The man beside her had risked his life to save hers. Why?

"You dived into that?" she asked in semi-disbelief.

Liam nodded. "I had to," he replied simply. "You weren't about to walk on water and come out on your own. What happened?" he asked. "Did the water overwhelm you?" Then, before she could answer, he added another basic question to the growing stack in his head. "Why weren't you swimming?"

She was about to lie, saying whatever excuse came

to mind, but then she stopped herself. This man had risked his life in order to save her. She owed him the truth.

"I don't know how," she murmured almost under her breath.

Liam stared at her, still not 100 percent convinced. "Really?"

Her very last ounce of energy had been summarily depleted as she had devoted every single ounce within her to staying alive in the swiftly moving waters. If it hadn't been, she would have been annoyed at his display of disbelief.

"Really," she answered wearily.

"Never met anyone who didn't know how to swim," he commented.

"Well, now you have," she answered, trying her best to come around enough to stand up.

Since the torrents had abated and she was now sitting on the ground, utterly soaked, Whitney looked around the immediate area.

That's when it finally hit her. She wasn't overlooking it. It wasn't anywhere in sight.

"Where's my car?" she asked the man who had rescued her.

Liam looked at her a touch uncertainly.

"What car?"

Chapter Two

"What do you mean 'What car?'" Whitney asked, bewildered as she echoed her rescuer's words back to him. "*My* car."

The events of the past few minutes were far from crystal clear in her mind, however, amid the lashing rains and the tumultuous rising waters in the basin, Whitney was fairly certain that her car hadn't sunk to the bottom of the threatening waters. She and the car had gone their separate ways, but she was sure that she'd been thrown from the vehicle as it was raised up, not pushed down.

Liam shook his head. "I didn't see any car," he told her honestly. "All I saw was you."

"But I was in a car," she insisted. "At least, I think I was." She looked at him, struggling to keep her disorientation and mounting panic contained. "How do you think I got out here?"

Liam had done very little thinking in the past few minutes, mostly reacting. He was still reacting right now. Saving a life was a heady feeling and it certainly didn't hurt matters that she was a knockout, even soaking wet.

He shrugged in response to her question and hazarded a guess, his expression giving nothing away.

"Divine intervention?" It was half a question, half an answer.

"No, I was driving a car," Whitney retorted, then took a breath. Her nerves felt as if they were systematically being shredded. "A pearl-white Mercedes," she described. There couldn't be any other cars like that around, she reasoned, not in a town that was hardly larger than a puddle. "A sports car," she elaborated. "I wound up being thrown from my car because I couldn't get the top up once that awful deluge started. Don't you people get weather warnings?" she asked, frustrated. She'd always been in control of a situation and what she'd just been through had taken that away from her.

She didn't like feeling this way.

"Sometimes," Liam answered, although he had a feeling that wouldn't have done her any good. The woman would have had to have her radio station set to local news and he had a hunch she would have been listening to some hard-rock singer.

Her story about being thrown from her vehicle was completely plausible. There was no way she would have been out here without a car or at least *some* mode of transportation.

But if that was the case, where was her car? Had it gotten completely filled with rainwater and wound up submerged? If so, it would turn up once the floodwaters receded. Unless the turbulent basin waters had succeeded in dragging it out to the gulf.

In either case, the car she was asking about wasn't anywhere to be seen.

Just for good measure, and because the woman appeared so utterly distraught, Liam looked around the surrounding area again.

Slowly.

Which was when he saw it.

Saw the car the woman had to be asking about. The topless white vehicle wasn't lying mangled on the side of the newly created bank, but it might as well have been for all the use she could get out of it in its present position.

How was she going to take this latest twist? he couldn't help wondering.

Only one way to find out, Liam decided, bracing himself. "Is that your car?" he asked, pointing toward the only vehicle—besides his own—in their vicinity.

Hope sprang up within her as Whitney looked around. But she didn't see anything that even resembled her gleaming white vehicle—

Until she did.

Whitney wasn't aware of her mouth dropping open as she rose to her feet and walked toward her car, moving like someone in a trance—or more accurately, in a very bad dream.

"Yes." Her voice was barely a whisper and she felt numb all over as she stared at the Mercedes in utter disbelief. Her beautiful white vehicle appeared to be relatively intact—but there was one major problem with it.

The white sports car was caught up in a tree.

"What's it doing up there?" she cried, her voice cracking at the end of her question.

None of this seemed real to her, not the sudden deluge coming out of nowhere, not the fact that she had almost drowned in water that hadn't been there minutes earlier and certainly not the fact that her car now had an aerial view of the area.

"By the looks of it, I'd say hanging," Liam replied quietly.

"Can't you get it down?" she asked him. She hadn't the faintest idea on how to proceed from here if he gave her a negative answer.

As she looked up at him hopefully, Liam gave her a crooked grin. "I might be strong," he told her, "but I'm not *that* strong." Having said that, Liam took out his cell phone. Within a second, his fingers were tapping out a number on his keypad.

"Are you calling AAA?" she asked.

Again, Liam smiled. He was calling the only one everyone in the area called when they had car trouble, Forever's best—and only—mechanic.

"I'm calling Mick," he told her. "He might be rated AAA, I don't know, but he's been a car mechanic for as long as I've known him and he's pretty much seen everything."

Maybe it was because her brain was somewhat addled from its underwater adventure, but the fact that this cowboy was calling some hayseed mechanic didn't exactly fill her with confidence or sound overly encouraging to her.

Whitney took a step closer to the tree and to her dismay, she realized that she'd lost one of her shoes during her brief nonswim. That left her very lopsided. The fact only registered as she found herself pitching forward.

The upshot of that was she would have been communing—face-first—with the wet ground if the man who had initially pulled her out of the water hadn't lunged and made a grab for her now, grabbing her by the waist.

"Are you okay?" Liam wanted to know, doing his own quick once-over of the woman—just in case. His arm stayed where it was, around her waist.

She wanted to say yes, she was fine. She'd been trained to say yes and then pull back, so that she could go back to managing on her own. But training or not, she still felt rather shaky inside, the way a person who had just come face-to-face with their own mortality might.

Given that state of mind, in a moment of weakness, Whitney answered him truthfully, "I don't know yet."

Turning so that he was facing her *and* the incline, he indicated his truck. "Why don't you sit down in the cab of my truck while we wait for Mick to get here? Or, better yet, I could take you to the clinic in town if you want to be checked out."

"Clinic?" she repeated with a slight bewildered frown. "You mean hospital, right?"

"No, I mean clinic," he replied. "If you want a hospital, I could take you," he said, then warned her, "but the closest one is approximately fifty miles away in Pine Ridge."

He was kidding, right? Were the hospitals around here really *that* far apart?

"Fifty miles away?" Whitney echoed, utterly stunned. "What if there's a medical emergency?" she asked.

Fortunately, they had that covered now—but it hadn't always been that way. The residents of Forever had gone some thirty years between doctors until Dan Davenport had come to fill the vast vacancy.

"It would have to be a pretty big emergency to be

something that Dr. Dan and Lady Doc couldn't handle," Liam told her.

Very gently, he tried to guide her over to his truck, but the petite woman firmly held her ground. She had to be stronger than she looked.

Dr. Dan. Lady Doc. She felt like Alice after the fictional character had slid down the rabbit hole. For a second, Whitney thought that the cowboy was putting her on, but there wasn't even a hint of a smile curving his rather sensual mouth and not so much as a glimmer of humor in his eyes.

He was serious.

What kind of a place *was* this?

"So, do you want to go?" Liam prodded.

"Go? Go where?" Whitney asked. Her light eyebrows came together in what looked like an upside-down *V*.

"To the clinic," Liam repeated patiently. If she couldn't keep abreast of the conversation, maybe he *should* just take her to the clinic even if she didn't want to go. He sincerely doubted that she could offer any real resistance if he decided to load her into his truck and drive into town. And it would be for her own good.

"No, I'm okay," Whitney insisted. "A little rattled, but I'm okay," she repeated with more conviction. "And I'll be more okay when my car is taken down out of that tree."

Looking over her shoulder to see if she had finally convinced him, she found that the cowboy had walked away from her. The next moment, he was back. He had a fleece-lined denim jacket in his hand that he then proceeded to drape over her shoulders.

"You look cold," he explained when she looked at

him warily. "And you're already chilled. Thought this might help."

Her natural inclination to argue subsided in the face of this new display of thoughtfulness. Besides, she had begun to feel a cold chill corkscrewing down along her spine. The jacket was soft and warm and given half a chance, she would have just curled up in it and gone to sleep. She was exhausted. The next moment, she was fighting that feeling.

Whitney smiled at the cowboy and said, "Thank you."

"Don't mention it," he responded, then extended his hand to her. "I'm Liam, by the way. Liam Murphy."

Whitney slipped her hand into his, absently noting how strong it felt as she shook it. "Whitney Marlowe," she responded.

Liam's grin widened. "Pleased to meet you, Whitney Marlowe," he said, then added, "Sorry the circumstances weren't better."

Whitney laughed softly to herself. "They could have been worse," she told him. When he looked at her quizzically, she explained, "You might not have heard me in time and then I would have drowned."

What she said was true, but he had learned a long time ago not to focus on the bad, only the good. "Not a pretty picture to dwell on," he said.

"Nonetheless, I owe you my life."

The grin on his face widened considerably. If she really felt that way, he could take it a step further. "You know, in some corners of the world, that would mean that your life is now mine."

"Oh?" The single word was wrapped in wariness. "But this isn't 'some corner of the world.' This is

Texas," she pointed out. "And people don't own other people here anymore and haven't for a very long time," she added just in case he was getting any funny ideas.

He could almost *feel* her tension escalating. "Relax," he soothed her in a calming voice that, judging by her expression, just irritated her more. "It's just a saying. You sure you don't want me taking you into town so you can get checked out at the clinic?"

"I'm sure," she insisted as adamantly as she could, given the circumstances. Her throat felt as if she'd swallowed a frog wearing pointy stilettos that scraped across her throat with every word she uttered.

The noise she heard coming in the distance alerted her of the car mechanic's impending arrival.

Whitney turned toward the sound and if she'd been expecting a large, souped-up-looking tow truck, she was sadly disappointed. Mick, the town mechanic who had been summoned to the scene, was driving a beat-up twenty-year-old truck that had definitely seen far better days.

Stopping his truck directly opposite Liam's, Mick lumbered out. Thin, he still had the gait and stride of a man who had once been a great deal heavier than the shadow he cast now.

Mick took out his bandanna-like handkerchief and wiped his brow, then passed it over his graying, perpetual two-day-old stubble.

"What can I do you for, Little Murphy?" he asked Liam, tucking the bandanna back in his pocket.

Putting one hand on Mick's sloping shoulder, Liam directed the man's attention to the reason he had been called. "Lady got her car stuck in that tree."

"And you want me to get it down," Mick guessed.

Taking off his cap, he scratched his bald head as he took a couple of steps closer to the tree.

"That's the general idea," Liam replied.

Mick nodded his head. "And a good one, too," he commented seriously, "except for one thing."

"What's that?" Whitney asked, cutting in. She didn't like being ignored and left out of the conversation. After all, it *was* her car up there.

"The thing of it is," Mick told her honestly, "I don't have anything I can use to get that car down." He squinted, continuing to look at the car. "I could cut the tree down," he offered. "That would get the car down, but I sure couldn't guarantee its condition once it hit the ground again." His brown eyes darted toward Liam. "You're going to need something a lot more flexible than my old truck for this."

"So what do I do?" Whitney asked. This was a nightmare. A genuine nightmare.

"Beats me," Mick said in all honesty.

Liam suddenly had an idea. "Would a cherry picker work?"

Mick bit the inside of his cheek, a clear sign that he was thinking the question over. "It might," he said. "But where are you gonna get one of those?"

"From Connie," Liam replied, brightening up. Why hadn't he thought of this before? he silently demanded. It seemed like the perfect solution to the problem.

"Who's Connie?" Whitney asked, unwilling to be left on the sidelines again. She looked from Liam to the mechanic.

"Finn's fiancée," Liam answered, clearly excited about this new solution he'd just come up with. Taking out his cell phone again, he made another call.

Connie, Finn, Mick. It sounded like a cast of characters in a strange college revue, Whitney thought. How did *any* of this get her reunited with her car? she wondered impatiently.

Because the man who rescued her from a watery grave was on the phone, she glanced at the scruffy man in coveralls whom Liam had called to the scene first. "Who's Finn?" she asked.

"That's Liam's brother. One of them, anyway," Mick amended.

"And this Finn, his fiancée has a cherry picker?" Whitney asked incredulously. This definitely sounded surreal to her. What kind of woman had a cherry picker on her property? And what would she be doing with one, anyway?

"She does," Mick confirmed.

It still sounded unbelievable to her. Whitney waited for more of an explanation. When none came, she realized she hadn't gone about this the right way. She had to ask for an explanation before she could expect one to be forthcoming. Even that struck her as strange. Didn't these people like to spin tall tales, or go endlessly on and on about things?

So why did she have to pull everything out of them? "*Why* does she have a cherry picker?" Whitney asked.

Liam had quickly placed and completed his call. Tucking his phone away, he answered her question for her before Mick could. "Because Connie's in the construction business and she's currently building Forever's first hotel."

Something was *finally* making sense, Whitney thought with relief. "And she's willing to let you borrow it?"

"Better than that," Liam told her. "She's willing to

have one of her crew drive it over here and get your car down," he corrected.

Liam took no offense at the extra measure. He was actually relieved about it. Intrigued though he was about getting a chance to handle a cherry picker, this was really not the time for him to get a new experience under his belt. Especially if he wound up dropping the very thing he was attempting to rescue.

Besides, he'd already had his new experience for the day—he had never saved a person's life before and even though he had expertly deflected compliments and thanks, knowing that he had saved a life still generated a radiant feeling within him.

Having answered Whitney's question, he turned toward Mick and asked the mechanic, "Are you going to stick around?"

Mick nodded his head.

"The car might need a little babying once it's on flat ground." He gestured toward the white car. "Those kind of vehicles really thrive on attention."

Whitney frowned. "You're talking about my car like it's a person."

Mick obviously saw no reason to contradict her. "Yes, ma'am, I am. And it is," the mechanic assured her. "And it's a she, not a he. It responds to a soft touch and kindness much better than to a rough hand," he explained, making his case.

Whitney opened her mouth to protest and argue the point. She had every intention on setting the grizzled old man straight.

But then she shut her mouth again, deciding that it really wasn't worth the effort. This wasn't the big city and people thought differently out here in the sticks.

The mechanic seemed cantankerous and if she had a guess, she would have said that the man was extremely set in his ways—as was his right, she supposed.

When she got down to it, as long as this mechanic got her car down out of the tree and running, what he called the car or how he interacted with it really didn't matter all that much.

"What are you doing here?" Liam asked her, averting what he took to be a budding clash of wills.

Whitney turned around to look at the cowboy. The question, coming out of the blue, caught her off guard. "What?"

"What are you doing here?" Liam repeated. "In Forever," he added in case she didn't understand his question.

Whitney laughed shortly. "You mean when I'm not drowning in a flash flood?"

Liam's easy grin materialized again. "Yeah, when you're not doing that. What brought you to Forever? Are you visiting someone?"

As a rule, they didn't get many people traveling to Forever—unless they were visiting a relative and Liam was fairly certain that if this woman was related to anyone in town, he would have known about it.

Still, in the past couple of years, they'd had people coming to the town and making changes to the structure of Forever's very way of life.

"Nothing," Whitney told him. "I was just on my way to Laredo."

"Laredo?" He rolled the name over in his head, mentally pinpointing the city on a map. "That's kind of out of your way, isn't it?" Liam asked.

She didn't like being wrong. Having that pointed

out to her was a pet peeve of hers and she had trouble ignoring it. "I was just following the map—"

"Guess your map's wrong, then," Liam informed her simply.

"I'm beginning to get that impression," she answered with a barely suppressed sigh.

Chapter Three

"Now, there's something you don't see every day," Mick commented.

Before either Liam or Whitney could ask what he was referring to, the mechanic pointed behind them. Turning, they saw a bright orange cherry picker being driven straight toward them.

Maybe this was going to turn out all right after all, Whitney thought.

"Somebody put out a call for a cherry picker?" the machine's operator, Henry MacKenzie, asked cheerfully as he climbed down from inside the cab. He approached Liam, obviously assuming that he was the one in charge. "Ms. Carmichael told me to tell you that this baby is at your disposal for as long as you need it. I guess, by association, I am, too. Unless you know how to operate this thing and want to do the honors yourself," the tall, burly man added.

Henry, along with several others on the construction crew, had initially been sent out from Houston by the construction company's business manager, Stewart Emerson. Highly skilled laborers, they were needed to operate the machinery that had been shipped out to do the basic foundation work for Forever's first hotel.

At this point, that part of the project had been finished more than a month ago, but the men—and their machines—had been instructed to remain on-site until the project was completed. Emerson had paid them well to remain in Forever and on call—just in case some unforeseen glitch suddenly made their services necessary.

Eager though he might have been to try his hand at operating the fancy forklift's controls, Liam had no desire to risk retrieving the car from out of the tree merely to satisfy his own curiosity. One wrong move on his part and the car was liable to become a thousand-piece puzzle.

He definitely didn't want to be the one responsible for that unfortunate turn of events.

"No, haven't got a clue," Liam confessed. "She's all yours."

Henry nodded his head, clearly expecting the reply he'd just heard.

"So why do you think you need a cherry picker way out here?" Henry asked. He looked from Liam to Mick and then to Whitney.

"Because of that," Liam answered, pointing to one of the trees along the basin.

"That tree?" Henry asked. "Why would you— Oh." The cherry picker's operator stopped abruptly as he took in the entire scene and finally saw the precariously perched vehicle. He laughed shortly as he shook his head in wonder. "You people sure don't make things easy out here, do you?"

Anxious about the condition of her sports car, Whitney cut to the chase. "Do you think you can get it down?" she asked.

"Oh, I can get it down, all right. But it's not going

to be easy and it's not going to be fast," Henry warned. "And it might not even be in one piece. But I can get it down," he reasoned.

Getting the car piecemeal wasn't going to do her any good. "How long would it take you if you took the proper precautions to get it down in one piece?" Whitney asked.

"Won't know until I start," Henry answered. "I'm also going to have to have someone working with me," he added, giving the situation further thought. "This is *not* a one-man job."

"What do you need?" Liam asked.

"I need someone in the basket," Henry said, nodding at the extreme upper part of the cherry picker. "To secure the car," he explained. "Otherwise, the damn thing'll just come crashing down to the ground the second we try to move it."

"Tell me what to do," Liam told the operator, volunteering for the job.

Henry laughed softly to himself. "The first thing you need to do is back away from the cherry picker and let me call someone on-site," the man said seriously. "No offense—and thanks for the offer—but this'll go a whole lot better and faster if someone with experience is doing it."

Liam took no offense at being turned down. "I get it. But in the interest of time, I thought I'd volunteer." And then he felt compelled to add, "Securing a car isn't rocket science."

"Might not be rocket science," Henry agreed, "but one wrong move and no car, either. Hey, it don't matter to me one way or the other, but I think this little lady might have something to say about it." Henry's small, deep-set brown eyes darted toward her.

Whitney was still having trouble wrapping her mind around this rather strange turn of events: first she nearly drowned, and then her vehicle was thrown into a tree. It all felt like some sort of a bizarre nightmare. A small part of Whitney thought that she'd actually wake up at any moment.

The more practical side of her, however, knew that was not about to happen. Her car really *was* stuck in a tree—and would remain there unless drastic measures were taken.

"Do whatever it takes," Whitney told the machine operator.

"Yes, ma'am," Henry replied. He was on his cell phone in less than five seconds, calling for one of the other crew members to come out. "Need a hand here, Rick," he said to the man who had answered his call. "You're not going to believe this," he added with a deep chuckle. "No, I'm not going to tell you. This you've got to come out and see for yourself. Boss lady okayed this job," he added in case there were any questions about priorities. Henry rattled off the same directions to Rick that he had been given earlier.

With that part of it taken care of, Liam turned his attention to Mick. "Looks like it's going to be a while before they have the car on solid ground," Liam told the mechanic. "Why don't you go back to the shop? I can call you once the car's ready to be looked over," Liam suggested.

Mick raised his rather wide shoulders and then let them drop again in a dismissive shrug. "Ain't got no other place to be right now," he confessed. "Mrs. Ab-

ernathy took her old Buick last night so there's nothing for me to work on in the shop. I might as well stay
here and watch history being made," Mick said philosophically, his eyes all but glowing with fascination as
he stared up at the treed vehicle.

"Suit yourself," Liam said. "You don't mind if I take
her to the diner to get a bite to eat, do you?" he asked,
indicating Whitney. Since he was the one who had
put in the call to Mick in the first place, he felt a little
guilty about leaving the man here more or less on call.

"Not as long as you bring me back somethin'," Mick
qualified.

"Like what?"

Mick began to slowly circle the tree, searching for
the path of least resistance. "Surprise me," Mick answered.

Having been privy to the entire exchange, Whitney
frowned—deeply. Granted there was a part of her that
longed for a strong, forceful man to take charge. However, the greater part of Whitney was wary of someone
usurping her control over her life and that was exactly
the part that was presently balking at what Liam had
just told his mechanic friend.

"What if I don't want to go for 'a bite'?" Whitney
asked.

"I'm not about to force-feed you, if that's what you're
worried about," Liam said, then asked, "You're not hungry?"

She wanted to say no, she wasn't. The problem was
that she *was* hungry. Very.

As if to bear witness to that, her stomach suddenly
rumbled—not quietly but all too loudly.

"If you're not hungry," Liam continued, "I think

you should tell your stomach because I get the definite impression that your stomach seems to think it's *very* hungry."

She lifted one shoulder in a disinterested shrug. The jacket began to slip off and she made a grab for it, returning it to its place.

"I suppose it can't hurt to go get something to eat," she allowed.

"Well, maybe in some cases," Liam told her in all honesty, "but not when it involves Miss Joan."

Following him to where he had parked his truck, Whitney stopped walking and took hold of his elbow, turning him around to face her.

"Wait, are you taking me to someone's house?" she asked, ready to put the skids on this venture before it got underway. She was in no mood to be friendly and exchange small talk with some stranger bearing the quaint name of "Miss Joan." Right now, she wasn't up to exchanging discomfort for a hot meal.

"No, we're not going to someone's house," Liam assured her. "Although she's there so much, there are times I think that the diner really could double for her home."

Her head hurt and all these details that Liam kept tossing out were just making it that much worse. "'She,' who's this 'she' you're referring to?" Whitney asked.

A control freak for most of her life—she no longer saw the point in disputing her siblings' accusations— it was hard for her to just hand over the reins to someone in matters that concerned her. But she had no idea when this person the cherry picker operator had called was going to get there. And she *was* hungry.

She supposed there was no harm in going along with

this wandering Good Samaritan, she thought, slanting a look in Liam's direction—at least until her car was back on solid ground.

"Miss Joan," Liam said, answering her question. "She's the 'she' I was referring to. It's her diner."

"Oh."

The pieces started to fall into place, making some sort of sense. She supposed she was being too edgy. Whenever she felt the slightest bit insecure, she could be demanding, needing to know every detail of the future. This man who had rescued her—and was now trying to rescue her car—didn't deserve to have her constantly challenging his every move.

"All right. As long as I get a call the minute my car is down and ready to go," Whitney ordered. She was looking directly at Henry when she said it.

"You heard the lady," Liam said, eyeing Mick. "Do me a favor and call me on my cell."

"You got it," Mick replied, then promised, "The second it's down, I'll give you a call."

Henry nodded his agreement.

At which point Liam regarded Whitney. "Good enough?" he asked her.

It would have to be, Whitney decided.

"Let's go," she told Liam just as her stomach offered up another symphony of off-key, embarrassing growling noises.

Liam brought her over to his truck, opened the passenger door and stood by it, waiting for her to get in.

"Are you planning on strapping me in, too?" Whitney asked, wondering why he was just standing there like that instead of getting in on the driver's side.

He grinned. "Just want to make sure you don't need any help getting in," he explained.

Buckling up, Whitney flashed him a look of irritation. "Why, do I look feeble to you? I've been getting into cars and sitting down rather successfully for more than a couple of decades now."

He answered her truthfully. "You don't look feeble but you do look pale."

The last thing she needed was to be criticized by a cowboy.

"Good," Whitney quipped. "I was going for a pale look," she told him flippantly.

"Then I guess you've succeeded." Liam started up his truck, then rolled down the window on his side before putting the truck into Drive. As he drove past Henry and Mick, he called out, "I'll be back soon."

Both men nodded in acknowledgment.

With that, Liam drove toward town.

THERE WAS SILENCE for the first few minutes of the drive. Not the comfortable kind of silence that two people who ended each other's sentences might have slipped into, but the awkward kind of silence that became steadily deeper and more ominous as the seconds ticked into minutes, then hung around oppressively.

Enduring it for as long as possible, Liam decided that enough was enough.

"You always have this chip on your shoulder, or is this something new for you?" he asked Whitney.

"I don't have a chip," she informed Liam indignantly, sitting up stiffly as her entire body became completely rigid.

"Yes, you do," Liam contradicted. "From where I'm

sitting, that chip is pretty damn big and very nearly impenetrable. In case you haven't noticed, these people are just trying to help you."

"I noticed," she said a bit too defensively.

Whitney paused, pressing her lips together. She was searching for a way to get her point across without sounding as if she had an ax to grind. She really didn't; it was just that because of this setback, she had gone into overdrive. Whenever that happened, she wound up having the kind of personality that put people off. All except for the people she signed to recording contracts. That group would have been willing to cut the devil some slack as long as they got what they were after: a shot at the big time. And because of what she did for a living and the label she was associated with, she was their first step in the right direction.

"But they're not trying to help me out of the goodness of their hearts, it's just business. Everyone's going to get paid for their services," she told Liam, wondering why he thought that was so altruistic.

"Mick's hanging around, waiting for your car to be brought down from its perch. A savvy businessman would have gone back to the shop—and charged you just for coming out," Liam pointed out.

"This way he gets to charge me for his downtime," she countered.

Liam shook his head. "That's not the way Mick operates," he disagreed, then said with emphasis, "That's not how any of us operate around here."

She wasn't ready to believe that. After all, this was just some tiny Texas town, not Oz. However, in the interest of not starting an argument, she merely said, "If you say so."

"I do, but that doesn't mean anything. I guess you'll just have to see for yourself. There it is," he said abruptly.

She sat up a little straighter, as if she'd just been put on notice.

"There 'what' is?" Whitney asked, her green eyes sweeping up and down the muddy road ahead of her. From where she was sitting, it just looked like open country—and more of the same.

"Miss Joan's," Liam elaborated, gesturing up ahead and to the left.

As Whitney looked, the diner came into view more clearly. It looked like a long, silver tube on wheels and it was completely unimpressive in her opinion.

It was also rather blinding.

The sun, which had decided to come out in full regalia now that all the water had been purged out of the sky, seemed to be literally bouncing off the sides of the diner. It made it rather difficult to see, if anyone wanted to drive past the establishment.

But Liam had no intentions of driving past the diner. For him, the diner was journey's end.

He pulled his truck up to the informal area that was the diner's unofficial parking lot.

When Liam turned off the engine, she looked at him. The diner made her think of a third-rate, greasy-spoon establishment that played fast and loose with sanitary conditions. It definitely didn't inspire confidence.

"Isn't there another restaurant we could go to?" she asked as he began to open the door on his side.

Liam paused, his hand on the door handle. "Not without driving fifty miles."

There it was again, she thought. That fifty-mile

separation from everything civilized. Was everything of any worth in this region automatically fifty miles away?

Whitney looked grudgingly at the diner. Maybe she would be lucky and not get ptomaine poisoning.

"Seems to me that this town would do a whole lot better if it just picked itself up and moved fifty miles away," she said cynically.

"We like Forever just where it is and the way it is," Liam informed her.

Yeah, backward and hopelessly behind the times, she thought to herself. Out loud, Whitney offered up another, less hostile description. "Old-fashioned and impossibly quaint?"

"Honest and straightforward," he contradicted.

"Well, I guess that really puts me in my place," she quipped.

He laughed, shaking his head. "I really doubt if anything could ever put you in your place—unless you wanted to be there," he qualified.

Getting out of his truck, he rounded the hood and came around to her side. Opening the door for Whitney, he put his hand out as if to help her get out.

She looked down at it for a moment as if debating whether or not she should take it. Deciding that it wouldn't hurt anything to act graciously, she wrapped her fingers around his.

"I'm sorry," she told him.

He looked surprised by this unusual turn of events. "For?"

In for a penny, in for a pound. Wasn't that what her mother used to say before she ran off? Whitney decided that she might as well say it.

"For acting like an ungrateful brat." She flushed as her own label hit home. "I guess I'm a little out of my element. I'm usually the one on the receiving end of gratitude, not on the giving side."

He wasn't exactly sure what she was trying to say, but he knew contrition when he saw it and he had never been the kind who enjoyed making people squirm. "Hey, you just went through a harrowing experience. You're allowed to act out a little."

His forgiving attitude made her feel even guiltier than she already did.

Their hands were still linked and he tugged on hers just a little. "C'mon," he coaxed. "Everything will seem a lot better after you eat something. Angel will whip up something that'll make you feel as if you've died and gone to heaven."

"Angel?" she repeated a little uncertainly.

"Miss Joan's head cook. Woman could make a mud pie taste appetizing," he told her with enthusiasm.

"I think I'll pass on the mud pie, but I could go for a cheeseburger and fries."

"Great," he responded, drawing her into the diner. "Get ready to have the best cheeseburger and fries you've ever had."

She sincerely doubted that, but she decided to play along. After all, she owed him.

Chapter Four

"So this is the little lady you saved from a watery grave, eh?"

The rather unusual greeting came from Miss Joan less than a heartbeat after Liam had walked into the diner with Whitney at his side.

As was her habit, Miss Joan, ever on top of things, seemed to appear out of nowhere and was right next to them.

Amber eyes took measure of the young stranger quickly, sweeping over her from top to toe in record time, even for Miss Joan. She noted that the young woman was struggling very hard to keep from trembling. *Small wonder,* Miss Joan assessed.

"You look pretty good for someone who'd just cheated death less than a few hours ago. Wet, but good," she amended for the sake of precision.

Stunned, Whitney held on to the ends of the sheepskin jacket, unconsciously using it as a barrier between herself and the older woman. She slanted an uneasy look at Liam.

"Did you just call and tell her about the flash flood—and everything?" she added vaguely. How else could the woman have known that she almost drowned unless Liam had told her?

"Nobody has to call and tell Miss Joan anything," Liam assured her. "She's always just seemed to *know* things, usually right after they happen."

"How?" Whitney asked. Did the woman claim to be clairvoyant?

The smile on the redheaded owner's face was enigmatic and Whitney found it irritatingly unreadable. "I've got my ways," was all Miss Joan said.

"She's kidding, right?" Whitney asked in a hushed whisper.

Because she had turned her head away from Miss Joan and whispered her question to him, Liam felt Whitney's warm breath feathering along the side of his neck. It caused various internal parts of him to go temporarily haywire before he was able to summon a greater degree of control. When he finally did, it allowed him to shut down the momentary aberration and function normally again.

But for just a second, it had been touch and go.

"You'll know when Miss Joan is kidding," he promised Whitney.

"Let me show you to a table," Miss Joan offered. The words stopped short of being an order.

Miss Joan brought them over to a table on the side that was relatively out of the way of general foot traffic.

Once they were seated, the owner of the diner looked from Liam to his companion, as if to make a further assessment, and then asked, "So, what can I get for the hero and the rescuee?"

"I'm not a hero, Miss Joan."

"No point in denying what everybody's thinking,

boy," Miss Joan said. Then, looking at the young woman at the table, she confided, "He's always been a little on the shy side, downplaying things he's done." Her thin lips stretched out in a smile. "But you'll get to see that for yourself if you stay around here long enough."

"I'm sure I would," Whitney replied, thinking she might as well be polite and play along with what this woman was saying. "*If* I were staying, but I'm not. I'm just killing a little time here before I get back on the road."

Miss Joan smiled knowingly. "You go right ahead and do that, dear. You do that." Her tone of voice made it clear that she knew more about the situation than either the young woman or Liam. Amber eyes shifted to Liam. "Want your usual?"

Liam grinned and nodded. He viewed the meal as comfort food. He was about due for some comfort, he thought. "Yes, please."

"And you, honey?" Miss Joan asked, turning her gaze to Whitney.

"I'll have a cheeseburger and fries," she told the older woman.

"Coming right up," Miss Joan promised as she withdrew from the table.

Whitney noted that the woman hadn't written down either order. Lowering her voice, Whitney leaned in closer to the man who had brought her here in the first place.

"Is she always like that?" she asked once Miss Joan had withdrawn.

"Like what?" Liam asked, curious. As far as he was

concerned, it was business as usual for the owner of the diner.

"Invasive," Whitney finally said after spending a moment hunting for the right word to describe what she'd felt.

Liam turned the word over in his head, then shrugged. "I suppose so. That's just Miss Joan being Miss Joan," he said, then assured her, "I'll tell you one thing. There's nobody better to have on your side when you've got a problem or need a friend than Miss Joan."

Whitney glanced over her shoulder toward the older woman. The latter was behind the counter, engaging one of her customers in conversation as she refilled his coffee cup.

Aside from the fact that the woman seemed nosy, Whitney saw nothing overly remarkable about Miss Joan. The woman certainly didn't strike her as someone people would turn to in an emergency.

"Her? Really?" she asked Liam.

"Her. Really," he confirmed with a hint of an amused grin.

Whitney shook her head. "I'm afraid I just can't see it."

"Well, you're still an outsider so that's understandable. You'll have to experience it for yourself."

Whitney laughed shortly, waving the idea away.

"I'll pass on that, thanks. The second my car is back on solid ground, I'm out of here." She glanced at her watch and frowned. She was really behind schedule. "I should already be on my way."

"Maybe you should call whoever you're going to

see and let them know that you're being held up," Liam suggested.

Her eyes widened as she looked at him warily. "Held up?"

"Delayed," Liam amended.

"Oh."

Whitney chewed on her lower lip, thinking. She really didn't want to call to say she'd be late, but she had to grudgingly admit that the cowboy had a point. With that, she shrugged his jacket off, letting it rest against the back of her chair, and dug into her pocket for her phone.

Pulling it out, she began to tap out the phone number of the band she was on her way to audition. When nothing happened, she tried the number again—with the same result. Frustrated, she took a closer look at her phone and realized that it was completely dormant. The light hadn't really come on.

Why was it acting as if it was drained? "I just charged the battery," she complained.

Liam leaned over and placed his hand over hers, turning her phone so that he could get a better look at it. The diagnosis was quick and succinct.

"I think it's dead."

"Dead?" Whitney echoed. "How can it be dead?" she challenged.

He had an answer for that, as well. "That's not a waterproof case, is it?" He'd phrased it in the form of a question, but he already knew the answer.

"No," Whitney snapped. And then she remembered something. "But you dived in to pull me out of the water and you had your phone in your pocket," she recalled. "I saw you take it out to call that mechanic and whoever sent over that cherry picker."

Rather than say anything, Liam took out his phone and held it up to let her see the difference between his and the one she had in her hand.

"Mine's sealed in a waterproof case," he told her. She looked as if she was about to protest, so he explained rather matter-of-factly, "Things happen out here. All you can do is try to stay as prepared as possible."

Of course, he thought, he definitely wasn't prepared to be as strongly attracted to this woman as he was. But then, he'd never saved anyone from drowning before and maybe that had a lot to do with it.

Whitney was torn between actually *liking* the fact that he was this prepared and resenting the fact that he was taking charge like this while she couldn't. What was even worse was that she was having all sorts of feelings about this man that had absolutely nothing to do with any of this—except that he had saved her.

"Like a Boy Scout," she commented.

"Something like that, I guess. Want to borrow my phone to make that call?" he offered, holding it out to her.

"I guess I'm going to have to," she muttered, less than thrilled about this turn of events. She glared at her unresponsive phone. "I guess this is just an expensive paperweight now."

"Not necessarily," Miss Joan said.

Whitney nearly jumped out of her skin. The woman had seemingly materialized out of nowhere again. Didn't *anyone* else find that annoying? she couldn't help wondering.

Taking a breath to steady nerves that were becoming increasingly jumpier, Whitney turned in her seat and focused on what the older woman had just said rather than the fact that she was beginning to view Miss Joan as some sort of a resident witch.

"Do you think you can fix this?" she asked Miss Joan, allowing a trace of hope to enter her voice for good measure.

Miss Joan looked at the phone in question. "Depends. This just happened, right?" she asked, raising her eyes to look at Liam's companion.

"Right," Whitney answered quickly.

Miss Joan put out her hand. "Let me take your phone apart and put it in a container of rice."

"You're going to cook it?" Whitney asked warily.

Miss Joan laughed. "Hardly. Rice draws the moisture out. Doesn't work all the time but it's the only shot your phone has."

With a sigh, Whitney handed her phone over to the woman, although she was far from confident about what was about to transpire.

"Okay."

Taking the phone, Miss Joan pocketed it for a moment. "By the way, these are for you," she said, offering the younger woman what had caused her to return to the table before Angel had finished preparing their orders.

Whitney then noticed that the older woman had brought over a couple of items of clothing with her—a light blue sweatshirt and a pair of faded jeans.

Instead of taking the items, Whitney stared at them. "What am I supposed to do with these?"

Miss Joan pursed her lips, a sign that she was banking down a wave of impatience. "Well, this is just a wild guess on my part, but if it were me, I'd put them on. In case you didn't know, the clothes you have on will dry a lot faster without you in them—especially if I put them in a dryer. Unless, of course, you like looking like something the cat dragged in," Miss Joan added whimsically.

"Ladies' room is right through there," she told Whitney, pointing toward the far side of the diner. And then she held the defunct phone aloft. "I'll go get your orders after I put this baby into the rice container."

Whitney felt as if she'd just been doused by the flash flood a second time, except that this time around, it had come in human form.

After a beat, she gazed at Liam. "I think I'm beginning to see what you mean about Miss Joan."

"Miss Joan likes to look out for everybody," he explained. "Like a roving den mother. Takes some getting used to for some people. Now, I'm not telling you what to do, but it might not be such a bad idea putting those on." He nodded at the clothes she was holding in her arms.

She'd felt rather uncomfortable in the wet clothes, despite the jacket Liam had given her. But she hadn't felt it was worth drawing attention to the fact. After all, it wasn't as if anyone could do anything about it. Except that obviously Miss Joan could—and had.

Whitney rose without saying a word and walked to the rear of the diner, holding the clothes Miss Joan had brought her.

She had definitely fallen down the rabbit's hole, Whitney thought as she changed quickly, discarding her wet outer garments and pulling on the sweatshirt and the jeans Miss Joan had given her.

Dressed, Whitney didn't know what surprised her more, that the strange woman with the flaming red hair had brought her a change of clothing—or that the clothes that Miss Joan had brought her actually fit.

"You look a lot drier," Liam commented with a smile when she finally returned and quietly slipped back into her chair.

Whitney's eyes met his. He couldn't quite read her expression. It seemed to be a cross between bewildered and uneasy.

"How did she know?" Whitney asked.

"That you were wet?" It was the first thing that came to his mind. "It might have to do with the fact that there was a small trail of water drops marking your path to the table."

He tactfully refrained from mentioning that both her hair and the clothes beneath his jacket were plastered against her body.

She shook her head. "No, I mean how did Miss Joan know what size I took? The jeans fit me as if they were mine." And she found that almost eerie.

Liam laughed again. These were things that he had come to accept as par for the course, but he could see how they might rattle someone who wasn't used to Miss Joan and her uncanny knack of hitting the nail right on the head time and again.

"Like I said before, that's all part of her being Miss Joan. The rest of us don't ask. We just accept it as a given."

The next minute, Miss Joan was at their table again.

This time Whitney didn't jump and her nerves didn't spike.

"You look better, honey," Miss Joan said with approval. She'd brought their orders over on a tray and now leaned the edge of it against their table. She proceeded to divvy the plates between them. And there was more.

"Figured you might like a hot cup of coffee with that." Although she had brought two coffees, she directed her comment to Liam. "It'll take the rest of the chill out of your bones," she promised with a wink that instantly took thirty years off her face.

The tray now emptied, Miss Joan deftly picked up the discarded blouse and tailored slacks from the floor next to Whitney's chair. "I'll just take care of these for you," the woman said.

"I usually have those dry-cleaned," Whitney protested as the other woman was beginning to walk away with her clothes.

Miss Joan paused, glancing down at the wet clothing she was holding. "I think we both agree that there's really nothing 'usual' about this now, is there?" she said knowingly.

With that, Miss Joan walked away.

Whitney glared at the man who was responsible for bringing her here in the first place. "Was she ever in the military?" she asked.

Liam laughed. It didn't take a genius to see where Whitney was going with this. He didn't want her wasting her time or her energy.

"I think it'll be a whole lot easier on you if you stop trying to figure Miss Joan out and just accept her as being a force of nature. That's what the rest of us have done. It's just simpler that way."

Whitney frowned to herself. If these people wanted to deceive themselves and think of the diner owner as some sort of a "chosen one," that was their prerogative. But brand-new clothes not withstanding, she wasn't about to have any of it. That was for people who couldn't think for themselves and reason things out.

Whitney suddenly turned toward him again and changed the subject entirely. "How long do you think it's going to take your friend to get my car down out of that tree?" she asked.

"Hard to tell since I've never known anyone to have gotten their car up a tree before," Liam freely admitted.

Maybe everything had finally gotten to her, or she was just getting giddy. Then again, perhaps it was the result of nearly drowning that did it, but Liam's answer, offered to her with a completely straight face, struck Whitney as being funny.

Not just mildly funny, but rip-roaringly, side-splittingly so.

She laughed at what Liam had said and once she started laughing, the jovial sound just seemed to feed on itself.

It was hard for her to stop.

Because her laughter was the infectious kind, Liam laughed right along with her. After a minute or so of this, he stopped abruptly to look at her closely. He wanted to ascertain that she wasn't tottering on the verge of hysteria. Laughter could so easily turn to tears.

But in this case, the laughter was a form of letting off tension and nothing more than that. Even so, Liam had to ask. "You all right?"

It took her a moment to answer because she had to get herself under control first. But when she did speak, she was truthful about it.

"I really don't know," she admitted. "I almost drowned in water that hadn't been there when I started out. For all I know, my car's still up a tree, my phone might very well be dead, I've got on someone else's clothes and I'm sitting in a diner run by a strange woman who acts as if she can read my mind, so I guess the answer's no, I'm *so* not all right."

Liam listened to her intently and only when she was finished did he venture to speak. He gave her some age-old advice.

"Maybe you should eat something. You might feel more up to dealing with all this on a stomach that's not empty," he suggested.

That almost drove her to another round of laughter. Whitney managed to hold herself in check at the last minute.

"You sound like my mother," she said, responding to his quaint advice. *Before she ran off,* she added silently.

"All things considered, I think I'd rather sound like your father," Liam countered, amused.

Whitney raised her eyes to his. Her father had been the one who had all but bred competition into her and her siblings. Her mother, on the other hand, had been the dreamer, the one whose temperament could withstand anything—or so she had thought until the day she wasn't there anymore.

The day her mother had left a note on the kitchen table to take her place.

"No, you wouldn't," she said. "Trust me," she added when Liam looked at her somewhat skeptically.

"I do," he told her simply. "I trust you, Whitney."

She had no idea why that affirmation warmed her the way it did, but there was no denying that she was definitely reacting to it in a positive way.

Whitney decided that Miss Joan had to have put something into her cheeseburger. That was the explanation she was going with since she had no room in her life for any more complications. And feeling any sort of an attraction for this cowboy was definitely a complication of the highest magnitude.

Chapter Five

Whitney glanced down at her watch for the umpteenth time. She tried not to be too obvious about it, but she had a feeling that she wasn't fooling the man sitting across from her.

With each minute that passed by, she was getting progressively antsy.

She had never been one to dawdle over her food—there was always too much to get accomplished for her to eat leisurely—but she had deliberately forced herself to eat slower this one time, hoping that once she was done with the meal, there would be some news about the state of her car.

But Liam's phone had not rung and she had just popped the last French fry into her mouth.

Now what?

Trying to contain her impatience, she said to Liam, "Maybe you should check your phone, just in case you shut off the ringer."

"I didn't," he told her. The diner was usually a noisy place and he hadn't wanted to take a chance on missing the mechanic's call. He knew how important it was to Whitney. "But even if I had, I'd feel the phone vibrating."

"Then maybe you accidentally shut your phone off altogether."

She knew she was reaching, but it would be night soon and she was supposed to have been at the audition she'd set up in Laredo first thing in the morning. Now all that careful planning was about to fall through, though she'd called to say she'd be late. At the same time, she didn't like falling so far behind in her schedule.

Whitney could just see her brother Wilson's smug face now, making no secret of the fact that he enjoyed watching her stumble and, even better, fall behind. Her position was technically lower than his within the company, but she still felt she was in competition with him. This sense of extreme competition was the way they had all been raised. Never once was the family unit stressed. For the Marlowes it was more of a case of every man—and woman—for themselves.

She did *not* want to wind up on the bottom of the heap—demoted to territory off the beaten path as far as finding talent was concerned.

"I definitely didn't do that," Liam assured her. To prove it, he dug out his phone and glanced at its screen before holding it up for Whitney to view. "See?"

She saw, all right. Saw that there was no message across the front of the screen announcing a missed call or a missed text communication.

"I see," she acknowledged quietly, frustration bubbling up in her voice.

"Don't worry," Liam told her. "Mick'll come through. He always has before. No reason to think he won't this time." And then he grinned his lopsided grin as the door to the diner opened and Mick walked in.

"Speak of the devil," Liam said with a laugh. "Mick, over here," he called out, raising his hand in the air to attract the mechanic's attention.

Standing just a little past the threshold, Mick was scanning the diner's occupants. When he saw Liam waving his hand, Mick's lips parted in what could be viewed as an attempted smile, the kind that made small children and smaller dogs uneasy because the expression looked more like a grimace than an actual smile.

Waving back, Mick quickly crossed to the table at the rear of the diner.

"I wasn't sure you'd still be here," the mechanic blurted out as he approached them.

Once at the table, instead of sitting down, he remained on his feet, as if he felt that he might have to dash off at any moment.

At any other time, Whitney might have attempted to indulge in a little small talk, just to be polite. But at this point, she felt as if her nerves had been stretched out to their full limit—plus 10 percent more. She desperately wanted to be on her way, so she made no comment on the mechanic's statement.

Instead, she got right down to business and asked, "How's my car?" Before he could respond, Whitney forced herself to ask another question, which she realized should have come first. "Did you get it down out of the tree?"

"Oh, yeah, we got it down," Mick told her with conviction.

She wasn't sure that she was comfortable about his tone of voice. "And the car's in one piece?" she pressed.

Her heart was speeding up a little as she braced herself—for what she wasn't altogether sure, only that whatever it would be, something told her that it wouldn't be good.

"Pretty much," Mick acknowledged. "One of the headlights is smashed, but that's no big deal."

Liam read between the lines. "What *is* a big deal?" he asked, well versed in "Mick-speak." The man was hiding something.

Mick began slowly, working up to what he assumed the woman would think was the bad part. "Well, the engine's flooded—I mean *really* flooded, so it's gonna take some time to dry out."

"What else?" Liam prodded.

Mick took a deep breath as if it physically hurt him to be the bearer of this news. "The alternator took a beating and it needs to be replaced."

"And you can do that, right?" Whitney asked somewhat apprehensively, watching his face as he answered. If he was lying, she hoped she could tell the difference.

"Oh, I can do that, sure," Mick said with enthusiasm. And then his voice fell as he added, "Once I get the parts in."

Whitney stared at the thin man. "You don't have an alternator?" she asked, having no idea what that actually was or what it did.

"I don't have *that* alternator," Mick explained. "I'm going to have to start calling around to a bunch of suppliers to see if I can find one and then get it sent here."

Whitney's stomach tied itself up in knots. "And how long is that going to take?"

Mick was nothing if not honest in his answer. "Well, I haven't started looking for it yet, so it's hard to tell."

"Then what are you doing here?" she asked, feeling the last of her nerves shredding. "Shouldn't you be calling around, trying to locate one?"

"Liam said to let him know when we got the car out of the tree, so I came here to tell him that we did," Mick informed her.

"Okay, fine, you told him. You told us," she amended. "I'll authorize you to do what you have to do to get my car running. I'll pick it up on my way back." She was aware of the fact that both men were now looking at her quizzically. Ignoring that, she pushed on. "Meanwhile, I'll rent one of your loaner cars."

"There's just one little thing wrong with that plan," Liam interjected.

Now, in addition to her stomach having tied itself up in one giant knot, it started to sink. This did not sound as if it would turn out well.

"And that is?" she asked, afraid to put what had just crossed her mind into words.

"Mick doesn't have any loaner cars," Liam said.

"You're not serious." She said the words so low, Liam wasn't sure if her voice was fading, or if this was the calm before the storm.

"I'm afraid I am," Liam replied.

Her eyes darted toward Mick, who had a sheepish expression on his face as he nodded.

"Does *anyone* in this town have a car I can rent?" Whitney asked in exasperation. When Liam shook his head, a growing sense of panic had her asking, "How about the car dealer?"

To which Liam said, "What car dealer?"

"You don't have a car dealer." It wasn't a question but a conclusion wreathed in mounting despair. "If there's no car dealership here, where do you people get your cars?"

Liam considered her question, then said, "That all depends on what direction we want to go in. There's a dealer in Pine Ridge—but he doesn't have cars to rent, either," he said, guessing where her question was ultimately going.

Whitney closed her eyes for a moment and sighed. "This is like a nightmare," she cried.

Liam had always been able to look on the bright side of things. It was a habit he'd picked up from Brett. His older brother never seemed to be defeated, no matter how bad things might get.

"It doesn't have to be," he told Whitney.

How could he even *say* that?

"Oh, no? Well, what would you call being trapped in a tiny town that isn't even on some of the maps of this region?"

His view of Forever was decidedly different than hers obviously was. "An opportunity to kick back for a few days and unwind," he suggested.

But Whitney heard only one thing. "A few *days*?" she echoed, horrified.

"Think of it as a vacation, honey," Miss Joan told her, not about to be left out. The woman scrutinized her for a moment. "Speaking of which, when was the last time you took one?"

Why did these people think they could just invade her life and ask personal questions like this? It wasn't any of their business. But her sense of survival trumped her feeling of outrage, so she answered the older woman. "I don't take vacations."

"Well, there you go," Miss Joan concluded with a

smart nod of her head. "This is the universe telling you that you need one."

"What I *need*," Whitney retorted through clenched teeth, her temper just barely contained, "is to have my car running."

"And you will," Mick assured her. "Just gotta get the parts."

"Parts?" Whitney echoed, stunned and dismayed. "A minute ago it was just one part, now it's 'parts'?" Just what was this con artist's game?

"Well, I thought I'd fix that headlight while I was waiting for the alternator," Mick replied honestly.

"Why stop there? Why not repaint the car while you're at it," Whitney said sarcastically, throwing up her hands in mounting frustration.

"You want me to?" Mick asked her in all innocent sincerity.

"I think you should just stick to getting that alternator and fixing the headlight—don't want some highway patrolman giving her a ticket now, do we?" Miss Joan said to the mechanic, keeping one eye on the young woman Liam had saved. "Go on, Mick," she urged. "Get started on her car."

"Can't really get started doing much tonight," he confessed.

"Then do what you can," Miss Joan encouraged.

"Right away, ma'am," the mechanic promised. He paused to tip his cap to Whitney, and then, the next moment, he was hurrying out the door.

It occurred to Whitney that this woman had no right to tell the mechanic to do *anything* that had to do with her car.

It also occurred to her that if she valued her sanity—

as well as other vital parts of herself—she should forego trying to argue the point with Miss Joan and just go along with what the woman said.

Besides, she had a larger concern at the moment. If she had to stick around this one-horse town, she was going to need somewhere to sleep.

She directed her question to Liam. "I don't suppose this place has a motel or, better yet, a hotel around somewhere?" She was hopeful, but at the center, she had an uneasy feeling she knew what the answer would be.

Which in turn meant that she was going to have to camp out—something that was completely unacceptable to her.

Beggars can't be choosers, Whitney.

"There's the hotel that's going up," Liam said, thinking out loud. "That's where the cherry picker came from," he reminded her.

"Going up," she echoed. "Doesn't exactly do me much good without walls."

Whitney was doing her best to remain as calm as possible despite the fact that part of her felt as if she was on the brink of a meltdown. For most of the past year, she had been going ninety miles an hour. To come to a skidding halt like this threw her completely off.

"Oh, it's got walls," Liam assured her, then amended, "At least the first floor does." He tried to remember what Finn had said about the progress being made. "I think there are a handful of completed rooms on the ground floor."

The rooms didn't do her any good if the hotel wasn't in business yet. "But it's in the middle of being built, right?"

"Right." Liam didn't see what the problem was for her. "So?"

For such a good-looking man, he was pitifully slow on the uptake, Whitney thought. She proceeded to spell it out for him.

"So that means that the hotel is not open for business yet."

"No," he agreed. "At least not to the general public." He took out his cell phone again and began to tap out a number on the keypad.

And what was that supposed to mean? She didn't see where he was going with this distinction.

"Well, I'm part of the general public," she pointed out. And that meant that it didn't matter how many finished rooms the hotel had, it was still in the process of being built. And that in turn meant that it was *not* open for business.

Holding up his hand to push back the unending flow of words that threatened to come out of this woman's mouth, Liam focused on getting the call he was making to go through. He needed to concentrate in order to word this just right once the person on the other end of the line picked up.

"You can bunk at my place for as long as you need."

The offer came out of the blue, pretty much in the same fashion that Miss Joan had a habit of turning up to take part in various conversations.

Whitney twisted around to look at the woman. "Excuse me?" she said uncertainly.

"I'm offering you a place to stay in case Liam's negotiations break down." Miss Joan nodded toward Liam, who was clearly talking to someone on the other end of the line.

Whitney frowned slightly. Had she actually heard the woman correctly?

"Wait, let me get this straight," she said to Miss Joan. "You'd actually take me in and let me spend the night in your place?"

"That's what I said," Miss Joan confirmed. "And the night after that if you need to." Miss Joan smiled tolerantly at the younger woman, the implication clear that at least for the moment, she viewed her to be slightly mentally challenged.

How could Miss Joan be so casual about inviting her to spend the night—or two—in her house?

"But you don't know me," Whitney pointed out.

Miss Joan looked entirely unfazed by what she was clearly suggesting. But the older woman played along, just for good measure.

"You got any Wanted posters out on you?" Miss Joan asked glibly.

"What? No, of course not," Whitney declared indignantly after she replayed the woman's words in her head.

Miss Joan lifted her shoulders and then let them drop indifferently. "Then that's all I need to know. For the record," she added, leaning in so that only Whitney could hear her clearly, "neither do I. So we should get along well enough. As long as you don't mind snoring. Henry makes enough noise to imitate two buzz saws, flying high."

"Henry?" Whitney echoed uncertainly.

"My husband." She had married the man over a year ago. As far as she was concerned, they were still on their honeymoon. "He's got a few quirks, but he's a good man at bottom."

"And he'd be okay with you taking in a stranger and having them stay over in your house?" Whitney asked in disbelief.

"Sure. Why wouldn't he?"

"Because I'm a *stranger*," Whitney repeated, stressing the word.

"A stranger's a friend whose name you haven't found out yet," Miss Joan informed her philosophically. "Offer's on the table, good for any time if Little Murphy can't get you a room at the 'hotel' that's going up," she said, crossing back to the counter.

Whitney could have sworn the woman was actually sauntering, moving her trim hips provocatively.

It took her a moment to realize that she was not Miss Joan's intended prime target audience. That honor belonged to several of the older men sitting at the counter itself. Cowboys, if she was going to judge them by their boots and hats.

She turned around just in time to see Liam terminate his call and put his cell phone away.

"I got you a room."

There was a layer of apprehension that was pressing down on her and it prevented Whitney from feeling relieved. "At the hotel?"

"At the hotel," he confirmed. It was obvious that he was rather pleased with himself.

"And it has walls?" she asked suspiciously. With these people, she felt that she needed to spell everything out and take nothing for granted.

He grinned. "It has walls."

She had learned a long time ago not to be trusting or to make what seemed like logical assumptions. A person could be easily misled that way. As for being trusting, well, that path just led to general disappointment. *That* was a lesson she'd learned from her mother— even though that hadn't been her mother's intention at the time.

"Four walls?" she asked.

"You can count them when we get there," Liam told her, not bothering to hide his amusement.

Getting up from the booth, he took out his wallet and extracted several bills.

She took her cue and felt around for her wallet. She'd put it into the borrowed jeans she had on when she switched clothes.

"How much is my share?"

Liam glanced at her. Making her pay her share hadn't even crossed his mind. That wasn't the way things were done around here.

"That's okay, I covered it."

"I pay my own way."

He watched her for a long moment, then said glibly, "Good to know. Let's go."

He was leaving the diner. She had no choice but to hurry after him—or be completely stranded.

"I don't want to be in your debt," she protested.

He stopped for a second to tell her, "There are two kinds of debt—the monetary kind and the emotional kind. While you try to figure out which kind bothers you more, I'll drive you over to the hotel," Liam informed her.

And with that, he placed his hand to the small of her back and proceeded to guide her out of the diner.

Watching them, Miss Joan smiled to herself. "Looks like another Murphy brother just might be about to bite the dust," she murmured to her customer as she refilled his empty coffee cup.

Joe Lone Wolf, the sheriff's chief deputy, glanced over his shoulder toward the door that was now closing. "Lot of that going around," he acknowledged quietly just before he took a sip of his coffee.

Chapter Six

Liam got out of his truck and made his way around to the passenger side. Whitney had made no move to get out of the vehicle. Instead, she was staring at the building he had parked in front of.

When he opened her door, there was suspicion in Whitney's eyes as she turned to him. "This isn't the hotel."

The building he had brought her to was a wide, squat two-story building with the name Murphy's spelled out in bright green lights.

"No," Liam agreed, "it's not the hotel."

This was a bar. Exactly what was this man up to? Her bravado went up several notches. "I thought you said you were taking me to the hotel."

"I am and I will," he assured her. "We just have to stop here first."

Whitney still wasn't budging. Granted the man had saved her life and been nothing but upstanding until this point—but maybe it was all leading up to something. She wasn't about to let her guard down.

"Why?" she asked.

"Because," he said patiently, "this is where the lady who's in charge of building the hotel is right now."

And he thought that since she was bending a few rules for him, the least he could do was show up and thank Connie in person.

"The hotel is being built by a woman?" Whitney asked in surprise. The frown on her face gave way to a hint of a smile. She had to admit what he'd just said intrigued her.

"Long story," Liam told her as he went on to give her the highlights. "Connie Carmichael was part of Carmichael Construction and she—"

"'Was'?" Whitney got out of the truck. The name sounded vaguely familiar. "What happened?"

The entrance to Murphy's was only a few feet away. "She decided to head up her own company and help renovate and restore sections of this town as well as on the reservation—"

Whitney stopped before the wide oak door. "You have a reservation?"

Liam paused. The woman was rapid firing her questions at him, not letting him catch his breath.

"You know, you might get the answers to your questions if you just give me enough time to talk," he pointed out, amused. Was this what it was like in the world she came from—everyone talking, nobody really listening?

When she continued looking at him expectantly, Liam had no choice but to continue. "Yes, we've got a reservation. Three of my best friends live there."

Liam pushed open the saloon's door. A blast of warm air, contrasting sharply with the winter breeze outside, hit them as they entered. A wall of noise accompanied it, enveloping them.

Being the only place in town to gather, other than

Miss Joan's diner, Murphy's always did a fair amount of business. The number of patrons varied. Tonight the place was packed to the point that maneuvering around presented a challenge.

Whitney looked around, trying to take in as much as she could. "Are you related to the Murphy who owns this?" she asked, raising her voice so Liam could hear her.

"I *am* the Murphy who owns this. Or at least one of them," he said. Since, for once, she hadn't interrupted him, he continued, all the while expertly guiding her to the bar. "The saloon used to belong to my dad, then my uncle Patrick when Dad died. We got it after Uncle Patrick passed away."

He had taken hold of her hand and was bringing her over to somewhere. Her curiosity made her follow without protest.

"'We'?"

He looked at her over his shoulder. "My two brothers and me."

They seemed to be doing a fair amount of business, she thought, looking around. The place looked like a gold mine waiting to explode.

"Who runs it?" she asked.

"We all do." Then, because he wasn't giving credit where it was due, Liam added, "But Brett calls the shots. He's the oldest and he's the one with the most business sense. C'mon, I'll introduce you."

She really didn't want to be introduced to anyone. All she wanted was to find a place to spend the night, then be on her way to Laredo in the morning—provided her car was running by then.

A peripheral movement caught her eye. The next

thing she knew, a tall, dark, handsome bartender was working his way over to them.

"Ah, the prodigal brother returns." Brett's easy gaze shifted to take in the woman standing beside his youngest brother. "And I take it that this is the damsel in distress that you rescued."

Liam nodded. "Whitney, this is my brother Brett, the one I was telling you about. Brett, this is Whitney Marlowe."

Brett extended his hand over the bar. "Pleased to meet you, Whitney. What'll you have? It's on the house."

She didn't want anything, but thought that might insult the man, so she said, "A ginger ale would be nice." She half expected to hear him scoff, but all he did was smile.

"Ginger ale coming up." Opening a small bottle, Brett poured the contents into a fluted glass and placed it in front of her.

"Does everything that happens to someone in this town get immediately broadcasted to the whole town?" Whitney asked.

"Pretty much," Brett answered without any hesitation or offense at her tone. "It's a small town. We look out for each other here."

"Speaking of looking," Liam interrupted. "Do you know where Finn and Connie are?"

"Probably with each other." A casual shrug accompanied the guess.

"I kind of figured that," Liam said wearily. "But where? I thought they'd be in here."

Brett paused to take Nathan McHale's glass and refill it. Nathan was their most faithful patron and even the most infrequent attendee knew exactly what the man's beverage of choice was without asking. A dark ale that was kept on tap. Nathan's mug remained filled until such time as one of them felt the man had had his quota for the night. Once in a while, that call was made too late and Nathan spent the hours between midnight and dawn as a guest of the city inside a jail cell.

"Why?" Brett asked his brother, covertly studying the woman Liam had brought in with him. "What do you need with Finn?"

"Actually, it's Connie I really want," Liam explained. "Finn got her to okay Whitney spending the night in the hotel."

"But it's not finished yet," Brett reminded Liam as he leaned forward and whispered that little detail to his brother.

"According to Finn, the ground floor's completed and that includes all the rooms on that level." Liam nodded toward the woman nursing her ginger ale. "Whitney needs a room for the night."

"What about the room over the saloon?" Brett suggested, raising his eyes upward to indicate the studio apartment all three of them had put to use one time or another. Shifting his attention to Whitney, Brett told her, "That's where Alisha stayed when she first came to Forever."

"Alisha?" Whitney looked to Liam for an answer.

"Brett's wife," Liam explained, then thought she might need a little more detail than that. "She came out here from New York to work at the clinic with our other doctor."

"Other doctor?" Whitney repeated. "Does that mean that this Alisha is a doctor, too?"

"That's what it means," Brett answered with a wide smile.

"He's had that silly grin on his face ever since he got Alisha to agree to be his wife," Liam said, shaking his head at his brother. "I guess love does that for some people."

"Just wait until it happens to you, little brother," Brett said.

"If it did, I sure wouldn't be walking around grinning like some loon," Liam kidded.

"We'll see," Brett replied.

Whitney felt as if she was being bombarded with too much irrelevant information and it was hindering her from processing the important information.

"What about that room?" she asked. Maybe it would be simpler if she just spent the night in the room above the bar. After all, she was already here.

The last time he'd seen the room, it had been in a state of disarray. The hotel rooms, according to Finn, were pristine. "Think of it as a last resort," Liam advised.

"Hey, I lived in that room for a while," Brett protested. That had been before Alisha had stayed there and before Finn had added on the bathroom for Alisha's usage.

"Which is why I'm labeling it as a last resort," Liam said. "You sure you don't know where Finn is?"

"Never said I didn't know. That was something you just assumed," Brett declared. "What I said was that he was with Connie."

"Okay, since you *didn't* say you didn't know, then can you tell me where he is?" The playful drawl had left Liam's voice, a sure sign that he was serious.

Rather than give him a verbal answer, Brett pointed over his brother's head. Turning, Liam scanned the immediate area and then spotted Finn. As predicted, the middle Murphy brother was with his fiancée.

Liam turned to glare at Brett. "Why didn't you say so to begin with?"

"And lose out on this fine, scintillating conversation we've been having?" Brett asked, feigning surprise.

Liam grunted dismissively at his brother. Instead of just walking away, he paused to take Whitney's hand, drawing her off the bar stool. He did it not because he found her to be a singularly stunning woman despite the fact that she had no makeup on, thanks to the flash flood, but because the saloon was filled to the brim with patrons. There was a distinct possibility that if he wasn't holding on to her, they might get separated and ultimately lose track of one another.

Granted the saloon wasn't big by most standards, but when it was packed the way it was tonight, getting lost in the crowd was all too easy a feat. Not only that, but he'd seen too many appreciative glances sent Whitney's way and he wanted to make sure that no one acted on impulse and cornered her.

"C'mon. Let's go," Liam said gently.

The second he had taken her hand, Whitney had felt it. Felt that strange magnetic pull, that intense crackle that instant chemistry generated.

Whitney did her best to block it without being obvious about it. She knew that if she pulled her hand out of his, she'd be drawing attention to herself for all the wrong reasons. And one look at her face in an unguarded moment would tell Liam far more than she was willing for him to know: that she was extremely attracted to him. Whether it was because he'd risked his life to save hers, she didn't know. What she did know was that what she felt was something that both of them would be far better off not having subjected to the light of day.

She had no time for complications—especially if that complication lived in such an out-of-the-way place as this one. Right now, her life was all about work. Later down the road, she'd concentrate on the personal aspects that were currently missing.

But not now.

The moment they came up to the people Liam was obviously seeking, Whitney immediately disengaged her hand from his. If he noticed the abrupt way she did it, he gave absolutely no indication.

"So you two need a room?" Finn asked innocently, looking from his brother to the woman standing next to him, a woman he didn't recall ever seeing before.

"*She* needs a room," Liam emphasized.

Finn flashed a smile at her, a smile she had already seen duplicated on both Brett's and Liam's faces. The family resemblance began with their smiles, Miss Joan was fond of saying.

"My brother has no manners," he told Whitney. Putting out his hand to her, he introduced himself. "Hi, I'm Finn. This is my fiancée—love saying that word," he confided. "Connie."

Whitney acknowledged both introductions, nodding her head as she shook hands with first one, then the other.

There was a vague resemblance between the brothers, she noticed. But Finn's hair was a light brown while

Liam's was a dirty blond that made her fingers itch to touch it.

With Connie, the second their eyes met, Whitney sensed a kindred spirit in the slender, auburn-haired woman. Maybe life here in this little dot on the map wasn't quite as laid-back as she thought.

"Pleased to meet you," Whitney murmured to both.

"What brings you to Forever?" Finn asked.

"The flash flood," Whitney replied without hesitation. If that hadn't occurred, she and her car would have been well on their way to Laredo.

"Then that story making the rounds is true?" Finn asked in surprise, looking from her to Liam for confirmation.

Liam's brother made it sound as if she was the town's breaking news story. Just how starved for news were the people in this town? she couldn't help wondering.

"Depends on the details in the story," Liam qualified cautiously. When he saw Finn begin to open his mouth to fill him in on just that, Liam cut him off. "But it's going to have to keep. I need to get Whitney to bed." When he saw his brother's face light up, he realized he hadn't exactly phrased that correctly. "To *a* bed. To her bed." Then, for good measure, he added, "She needs to get some rest."

At any other time, Liam would have gone out of his way to wipe that smug, amused look off his brother's face, but who knew where that would ultimately wind up. So for everybody's sake, he banked down his feelings.

"Here you go," Connie said, pushing a key card over to him on the table.

Liam was quick to lay his hand on the key card.

This, he assumed, was what they were using instead of a good old-fashioned key these days.

"Thanks, both of you," Liam emphasized, holding up the key card. He was looking directly at Connie as he said it.

"Don't mention it," Connie said. The smile on her lips was the kind someone had when they felt they were sharing some inner secret with the other party.

"A kindness should always be mentioned—and acknowledged," Whitney told the couple. Connie smiled at her.

"Ready to go?" Liam asked, just in case Whitney had changed her mind and wanted to stay for the music or the company, or for some other reason. He wanted to accommodate her, even though he wouldn't have been able to explain why. It was just something he felt.

Liam didn't have to ask her twice. Turning toward the front door, Whitney all but burrowed her way through the crowd in a matter of minutes.

"I guess that's a yes," he commented with a laugh, increasing his stride to keep up with her.

The lady could certainly hustle when she wanted to, he thought.

Having fallen a couple of steps behind her, Liam was afforded a rather enticing view of the way the jeans Miss Joan had given her adhered to her body, molding themselves to her hips with every step she took.

That alone was worth the price of admission—and any trouble he had to go through to accommodate the woman he had saved from a watery, albeit rather dirty, grave.

They got back into his truck and Liam drove her the short distance to the hotel.

"This is it?" Whitney asked as she got out on her side. She was staring at a building whose steel girders were up, but only the first floor bore any resemblance to an actual hotel.

"This is it," he confirmed. "Forever's very first hotel. C'mon, I'll take you inside," he coaxed.

"Give me a minute," she requested. "I'm trying to decide if I've just made a mistake."

"To spend the night here?" he guessed. "Don't worry. It gets better once you're inside."

"It would have to," she said under her breath.

Judging by what she saw, the first floor did look to be finished. But when she raised her eyes to take in the other floors—floors that were in various degrees of completion—that was when she realized just how much more work there was left before this could officially become an actual hotel.

She started to walk toward the unfinished building, emulating a moth drawn to a flame.

"Wait a second," Liam told her as he went rummaging through an area in the rear of the truck. It took him a minute, but he found what he was looking for and held it aloft.

It was a lantern.

An uneasy feeling zipped through her as she looked at what he was holding. "What's that for?" she asked.

"I doubt if the power's been turned on yet," he told her honestly. "This'll give you light for the next fourteen hours."

She had no intentions of being here that long. "That's okay, I don't need it," she told him.

"Yes, you do," Liam insisted, taking the lead and

walking ahead of her. "Unless you glow in the dark, you're going to need to see where you're going."

It was twilight and she was exhausted, but nonetheless, she stubbornly held her ground. "It's a hotel. It'll have an emergency generator."

"Only if it had electricity turned on in the first place—and it hasn't. It's an *unfinished* hotel," he stressed. "Plenty of places for you to have an accident. So take it." He all but slapped the lantern into her hand. He wanted her to get used to carrying it.

She blew out a breath, grudgingly—and silently—admitting he was right. But out loud she said, "Anyone ever tell you that you are pushy?"

"Nope. They're all too busy thanking me for keeping them from doing something stupid," he informed her as they entered the hotel through the front entrance. He took in his surroundings, recalling the recent tour he'd been given by Finn. Even so, it took him a moment to get his bearings.

"It's through here." He indicated a corridor on his left.

Because Whitney had no idea which way she was supposed to go, she let him lead the way.

Since none of the rooms were occupied, Liam chose what he assumed was the largest room—a corner suite—for her.

"How about this one?" he asked, stepping inside the suite.

She peered over his shoulder, then stepped inside, still looking around. Whitney made her way over to the sliding glass door that led to a small balcony. "It'll do," she said.

He noticed a lack of enthusiasm in her voice. "What's wrong?" he asked.

Ordinarily, she would have told him he was imagining things. But she was tired and overwrought, so the truth came out despite the fact that she found her admission to be somewhat embarrassing.

"I don't think I'm going to be able to sleep tonight."

He made a guess as to the cause. "Worried about the meeting you're missing?"

She shook her head. That was small potatoes, actually. "It's not even that. It's dark around here and it's really quiet." He was obviously waiting for more. Her smile was rueful. "I can't sleep without noise and some sort of light peeking in through my bedroom window." She ran her hands up and down her arms, trying to ward off the chill she felt. "Quiet like this just feels eerie to me."

He'd always loved the quiet, but he supposed there were obviously those, like Whitney, who didn't. "Where did you say you were from?"

"Los Angeles."

He laughed shortly. He'd never been but he knew what she was getting at. "That explains it. Well, give it your best shot," he encouraged. "See you in the morning."

Whitney nodded, resigning herself to sleeping in snatches. She could feel the disquietude settling in. "Thanks for everything."

"Don't mention it," he said as he walked out.

But rather than going back to Murphy's or turning in for the night himself—God knew he deserved some sleep himself—Liam got into his truck and began to drive slowly back and forth around the corner of the hotel, exactly where her room was located. He put his headlights on bright and turned up his radio, creating both noise and light.

Inside, Whitney had lain down, fully clothed, on the bed, hoping to hypnotize herself into falling asleep. Her concentration was interrupted by a sudden burst of light and a throbbing noise that passed for current music. The fact that there were both out here mystified her.

She got off the bed, opened the sliding glass door and stepped out onto the terrace.

That was when she saw him. Saw the lone truck driving around in what amounted to elongated circles near her hotel suite.

Liam.

Watching him for a moment before she withdrew into her room again, Whitney found herself smiling.

This was, she thought, the nicest thing anyone had done for her in a very, very long time.

Chapter Seven

"You're *what*?"

Whitney held her newly restored cell phone—thanks to Miss Joan's container of rice—away from her ear as her brother Wilson's loud rant came through loud and clear.

No signal failure here, she thought as she continued to hold the phone she'd found outside of her door this morning away from her ear.

After a second, feeling that it was safe, she brought the cell phone closer to her ear again.

"I said," she repeated patiently, "I'm going to be stuck here for a few days."

She hadn't expected sympathy from Wilson and that was just what she got—none. "You mean you're slacking off," he accused angrily.

"No, I mean exactly what I said," she told him as calmly as she could—she'd learned a long time ago that shouting at Wilson never got her anywhere. "I'm stuck here. My car needs to have several parts replaced before it's drivable again."

"So what's the problem?" he asked, his voice going up another octave.

"The parts have to be ordered."

Mick had already called her earlier this morning to say that he'd made the necessary calls to get her vehicle up and running and her back on the road—but it was going to take at least a couple of days. She'd thanked him for the update, and then immediately resigned herself to breaking the news to her brother in LA.

"A couple of days? Where the hell are you, the Amazon rain forest?" he retorted.

"No, actually quite the opposite. It's pretty dry here—except yesterday when it flooded."

Whitney had to admit that she was still mystified how a few minutes of intense rain could have suddenly immersed her in a small lake. Mystified as well as rather shaken up because she was just now coming to terms with how close she had come to losing her life. She was certain that she would have, had it not been for Liam.

"I already gave you all the details," she told Wilson.

It was obvious by his tone that he'd thought she was just exaggerating. "Yeah, yeah. All I hear is that you're slacking off."

"Slacking off?" she echoed, her voice finally rising. Wilson was pushing her to the edge of her patience. "I almost died yesterday," she reminded him angrily.

"Uh-huh. And if you don't sign up that band, and several more really good ones, our label might be in danger of going belly-up, remember?" he said. "We're only as good as the new artists we sign up."

Wilson had a tendency to exaggerate and dramatize everything. Ordinarily, it didn't faze her and she just shrugged it off. But today it irritated the hell out of her.

So much so that she heard herself saying, "Look, if

you're so worried about missing out on that band, why don't you send Amelia to sign them?"

"Amelia," he repeated as if their cousin's name was brand-new to him.

"Amelia," Whitney said with more conviction.

"You're serious."

She and Amelia had been competitors since pre-school. The fact that they were first cousins had no bearing in their rivalry. From time to time, there was a marginal effort to get along, but what they really enjoyed was outdoing the other. Getting The Lonely Wolves to sign with Purely Platinum, the family label, would have been a decent feather in either one of their caps.

Whitney sighed. She hated giving up this opportunity, but the recording label was more important than any one person, and that included her.

"You need the band, or more to the point, you need a band or an artist to put you back on the map and I can't very well hitchhike all the way to Laredo. So yes, I'm serious."

"Okay, just remember, you passed up on this," Wilson told her.

"I'll get the next one," Whitney responded, trying her best to sound upbeat.

She heard Wilson grunt dismissively. "*If* there's a next one for you. You know this business, Whit. You're only as good as your next success. Barring that, you're history."

She'd expected just a hint of support from her brother. After all, she had been there for him. Granted they were all competitive in her family, but when had it become cutthroat?

"Wilson, after all the time I've put into the company—" But she found herself talking to dead air. Her brother had hung up on her.

Frustrated, Whitney vented the only way she knew how. She let loose with a guttural cry that was a cross between anguish and anger. After having emitted the teeth-jarring sound, she hurled her cell phone across the room. It hit the door with a loud thud and then fell to the floor, miraculously still intact.

Padding across the carpeted floor in her bare feet, Whitney stooped down to pick up her phone. She was still crouching when she heard a sharp knock on the door less than half a minute after her momentary tantrum.

She thought of ignoring whoever was on the other side of the door, but since she was the only person who had a suite—or a room of any kind—in the hotel, she felt obligated to respond. It might be the contractor coming to tell her that she couldn't stay here any longer.

Holding her breath, she approached the door and asked, "Who is it?"

"Liam Murphy. You okay in there?" he asked. "I heard a scream and then something falling and I just want to make sure you're all right."

Whitney lost no time in flipping open the lock and opening the door to the suite. "Not really," she said, answering his question.

She was far from a happy camper at this point. She'd just lost out signing what might become a major new band, moreover she had lost out to Amelia, who would rub her nose in it for weeks to come—maybe even months. If she lasted that long.

"Anything I can do?" he asked her, walking into the suite.

He actually sounded genuine in his offer. She had already decided, after last night's above-and-beyond performance, that Liam Murphy was not only exceptionally handsome, he was exceptionally kind and selfless, as well. If she was in the market for someone to share her life with—which she wasn't—he would have made an excellent choice.

But this was not the time to entertain any romantic thoughts. She needed instead to assess Liam's appeal dispassionately. With his somewhat longer dirty blond hair and electric blue eyes, not to mention that easy, sensual smile, Liam would undoubtedly be the center of every female's dreams from fourteen to ninety-four. She definitely wouldn't do well against competition like that.

As it was, she laughed softly at his offer. "How are you at laying your hands on a car and healing it?"

"That, unfortunately, is entirely out of my league."

"That's what I was afraid of. Then no, there's nothing you can do for me." She walked back toward the sliding glass door and looked out. In the distance, she could make out a range of foothills. "I need to be in Laredo today and it's just not going to happen."

He came up behind her, his attention focused on her. He really wanted to help. "What's in Laredo?"

"A band. The Lonely Wolves," she told him. What was the point of even talking about it, she thought, dejected. Amelia was going to sign them up and she'd suddenly be transformed into the lead weight that was being carried by the label. Temporarily.

"You don't look like a groupie," he commented.

The term caught her by surprise and she laughed shortly. "Good, because I'm not."

Something wasn't adding up. "Then why all this angst about a four-piece band?"

He'd surprised her again. She had him pegged as a fan of country music, not hard rock. "You've heard of them?"

"Sure I've heard of them," he acknowledged.

He was keenly aware of most of the homegrown bands in the southern part of Texas. He didn't see any of them as competition but as opportunities for a learning experience. His musical education came from all over and he soaked it up like a sponge.

"They were the people I was going to be meeting with today. Actually, I wasn't 'meeting' with them so much as auditioning them, but even that was just a technicality. Unless they didn't perform as well in person as they did on the demo they had sent in, I was going to be signing them for the label I represent."

He stared at her, wondering if he was still asleep and dreaming. This was just too much of a coincidence to actually be true. What were the odds that he would wind up rescuing someone who worked for a music label?

"You're a talent scout?" he asked, doing his best to sound casual about it. Since he and his band were unknowns, he couldn't push too hard—but he did want her to hear them.

She nodded. "My grandfather founded Purely Platinum Records and my brothers, cousins and I all work for the label. My older brother, Wilson, runs the company these days after my father passed away at his desk two years ago."

"I'm sorry," Liam said with genuine feeling.

She shrugged. "It happens." She hadn't been close to her father. He tended to favor her brothers, but in her heart of hearts, she still missed him. "We usually have at least a handful of big names signed at any one time," she confided, "but times have been tough lately. Our star performers were lured away to other labels and Wilson's trying to get fresh blood to bring us back to the top."

She looked as if she had just lost her best friend and it prompted him to ask, "If you're trying to get the label back on its feet, why do you look so down?"

"Because," she said between clenched teeth, "I just had to tell Wilson to send my cousin Amelia to sign the group."

Liam still didn't see the problem. "And…?"

Whitney knew that this had to sound petty to Liam, but she wasn't about to sugarcoat it. "And she's been out to top me since before we took our first steps."

"And I take it that whoever signs this band up first goes to the head of the line?"

She shrugged again. It was pointless to talk about this. Whatever happened, happened. "Something like that," she murmured.

It took him less than a minute to make up his mind. It wasn't his day to man the bar, so he was free to make this offer. "I can drive you to Laredo."

Struggling not to give in to feeling sorry for herself, she had barely heard what Liam had said. And what she *thought* he'd said was impossible. "Excuse me?"

"I said I can drive—"

She waved away the rest of his words as they replayed themselves in her head. "I heard, I heard," she cried happily. "You'd do that?" she asked in disbelief.

"Yes."

"Why?" She had to know. "Why would you go out of your way like this for someone you don't even know?"

"Because it seems so important to you. And I did have a hand in saving your life, so that gives us a kind of bond," he said. "I want you to be happy living the life I saved."

The man was practically a saint, she thought. Excited, relieved and feeling suddenly almost euphoric, Whitney threw her arms around his neck and declared, "You're a lifesaver." She said it a second before she kissed him.

She only meant for it to be a quick pass of her lips against his, the kind of kiss one good friend gives another, because he certainly qualified for that distinction.

But at the last second, Liam had turned his head just a fraction closer in her direction and somehow what began as a fleeting kiss turned into something that was a great deal more.

Something of substance and depth.

Something to actually sing about.

Whitney felt herself responding instantly and before she could hold back—she didn't. Instead, almost moving on automatic pilot, his arms went around her, closing in an embrace that pressed her body against his.

That, too, brought a reaction with it, because every fiber of her being went on high alert.

This, the thought telegraphed through her brain, *is different.* Everything in her life before this moment was just a stick-figure drawing, executed in crayon, and this, what she was experiencing now, was a rich oil painting that instantly captured the viewers and drew them in.

It certainly did her.

The kiss went on far longer than either one of them had intended, taking on a life of its own and changing *their* lives from that moment on.

The exuberance she had initially felt, the exuberance that had generated this kiss in the first place, flowered and intensified, stealing her very breath away in the process.

Whitney's whole body suddenly ignited and had Liam's arms not gone around her when they did, she seriously felt that she would *not* be standing up right now. A wave of weakness had snaked through her, robbing her of the ability to stand. Forcing her to cling to him in order to remain upright.

And be thrilled about doing it.

For most of her thirty years, Whitney had been focused on getting ahead, on besting her siblings and cousins, because that was the way she—and they, even her cousins—had been raised by her father. And that sort of sense of intense competition did not allow anything else to interfere, did not allow anything else to flourish, even briefly.

She'd had a handful of dates so far, none of which were inspiring enough to turn her attention away from the family business and all the alert competitiveness it required.

She'd certainly never encountered anything remotely like this—or even dreamed of its existence.

But the longer the kiss continued, the less control

Whitney realized that she had over her own thoughts, her own body.

It was as if the very life force within her was being systematically sucked *out* of her.

She couldn't be doing this.

She *shouldn't* be doing this.

With her last ounce of self-preservation, Whitney put the heels of her hands against Liam's rock-hard shoulders and pushed him back.

The force she exerted didn't have the intensity required to crush a newborn ant, but it did get its point across to Liam.

Mainly because he felt he shouldn't have allowed it to go this far, at least, not this quickly.

Not yet.

Still, he couldn't do anything about the wide smile on his face. There was absolutely no way he could wipe it away or camouflage it as he stood looking at her after the fact.

The kiss made him feel like singing—as did Whitney.

"If I had known it meant so much to you and that you'd react this way, I would have offered to drive you there five minutes after I rescued you yesterday," he told Whitney.

Shaken by what she'd felt, she did her best to seem nonchalant. Despite her performance, she had a feeling that she hadn't convinced Liam that his kiss had no effect on her.

Still, he seemed nice enough to pretend to go along with her charade.

"Well, there's no time like the present. Just let me make a couple of calls to update everyone," she said, crossing back to the table, where she had left her cell phone.

God, did her voice sound as squeaky to him as it did to her?

Clearing her throat, Whitney picked up her phone and prepared to make her first call. She raised her eyes to his and waited.

Liam took the hint. "I'll just go to Miss Joan's and get us a couple of breakfasts to go," he offered.

She nodded, barely hearing him. Had she heard, she would have again been struck by his thoughtfulness. But right now, she was struggling to regain some control over herself.

The first number she dialed was her brother's.

Wilson answered on the third ring.

"Wilson, it's Whitney."

"Now what's wrong?" he demanded wearily.

Sometimes she really disliked his negative approach to everything.

"Nothing. Just tell our illustrious cousin Amelia to put her broom back in the closet. She won't be flying to Texas to sign that Laredo-based band."

She could hear her brother come to life. It was there in the very way he breathed. She could tell he was all ears now.

"What happened?" he asked.

"Nothing happened," she said, deciding to play this out a little. "I just found a way to get to Laredo and since I'm already in Texas, there's no point in her coming out, too. It's as simple as that."

"She already said yes," Wilson told her, as if no changes to the plan were acceptable.

What had it been? Five minutes since she'd spoken to him? Talk about acting quickly...

"Well, now *you* can say no. I'll call you once the band has signed the contracts—*if* they're as good as that demo they sent," she said, and then it was her turn to terminate the call without forewarning.

It was also before her brother could offer any more protests.

Her second call was to the band itself, to tell them that the canceled audition was back on again, only she needed to schedule it for a slightly later hour than had initially been agreed to.

"So you can audition for me at around three," she informed them cheerfully.

"No, I'm afraid that we can't," the lead singer replied.

It was time to go into saleswoman mode, she thought. It wouldn't be the first time. She'd started out as a somewhat precocious child and what she had going for her then was her innocent face. Now she had her looks and her innocent manner, both of which she used with expert precision.

"Look, if you're thinking of signing with someone else, I just want you to know that we have the better reputation because we've been in the business for over fifty years—not to mention that we have far better perks for our top draws."

"Yeah, yeah, I know all that," the man on the other end of the line said, cutting her short. "But right now, we can't audition for you because we don't have a drummer."

Caught off guard, Whitney's mouth dropped open.

Chapter Eight

Maybe she'd heard him wrong, Whitney thought. "What do you mean, you don't have a drummer?" she asked the man on the other end of the call.

"I don't have a drummer," Kirk, the lead singer of The Lonely Wolves, repeated. "The guy's in the hospital."

This couldn't be good. "What happened?" she asked.

Part of Whitney was instantly sympathetic, but part of her couldn't help wondering if this was some sort of ploy, either in a bid to make their signing price higher, or to keep her label at bay while they auditioned for another talent scout, trying to see who would come through with the better offer.

"We were rehearsing, getting ready for the audition, and suddenly Scottie—the drummer—grabbed his stomach and doubled up. We all thought he was just clowning around and told him to get serious, but then he fell on the floor, still holding on to his stomach, except that now he was saying things like he feels his gut's on fire and he's dying, stuff like that. So we got him into my van and I drove like crazy over to the closest ER."

Kirk paused dramatically, catching his breath, then

continued, talking even faster than he had been a second ago. "They wound up operating on him right there in the ER. Turned out Scottie's appendix blew up or something like that."

"Is he all right?" Whitney asked, concerned.

"Yeah. Takes more than a crummy appendix to take Scottie out. But he feels awful now," Kirk added in a hushed voice.

Whitney laughed shortly. By her calculation, the drummer had just been operated on less than twenty-four hours ago. "I don't wonder. He went through a lot."

There was silence on the other end, as if Kirk was assimilating what she'd just said before responding. "What? No, I mean because he can't play, which means he blew the audition for the band."

The band's temporary derailment gave her some needed breathing space, Whitney thought. Funny how things can sometimes turn out for the best in the long run.

"Tell your drummer not to worry. We'll just reschedule the audition when he's up to playing," she told the lead singer.

More silence, as if she'd just managed to stun Kirk. "You mean it?"

Whitney smiled to herself. "Absolutely. Just tell Scottie to get better and I'll check in on you in a month."

"Are you just being nice?" Kirk asked, obviously leery of hoping for a second chance.

Whitney knew exactly where the performer was coming from. The world of entertainment was a fickle, completely unpredictable place. People who were at the top one month were thrown off and trampled by the up-and-comers the following month. Staying power was an art form as well as unusually rare.

"Yes, I mean it—but I'm also nice," Whitney said as she smiled to herself.

She proceeded to take down an alternate number where the lead singer could be reached and subsequently gave him her cell number, as well. Only then did the singer decide that she was on the level.

The moment she terminated her call to the drummerless band, Whitney placed another call, this one to her brother.

Again.

It was his private line, but even so, Wilson took his time picking up. Whitney was getting ready to leave a message on his voice mail when her brother finally got on the line.

In place of a greeting, Wilson said, "Maybe we should just string up two tin cans and use those every five minutes." Impatience fairly throbbed in his voice as he said, "What now, Whitney?"

"'Now' is when I tell you that not only don't you have to send Amelia to audition The Lonely Wolves—and, yes, I know you, Wilson, you were going to let her fly down and show up even though I told you I was going—but now I'm not going, either."

She heard her older brother sigh deeply. "What is this, Whitney, reverse psychology so I decide *not* to send Amelia in your place?"

"No, this is I'm not going because the band is down one drummer. And let's face it, he's the best one in the group *and* he's the one who writes the songs. You can go right ahead and send Amelia if you want, but she won't have anyone to audition once she gets there."

"What the hell happened to the drummer?" Wilson demanded angrily. "Is he hungover?" he guessed. "Or is it worse?"

Whitney pretended to think it over for a minute, just to keep her brother dangling.

"That all depends on whether or not you consider appendicitis to be worse than a hangover," she replied in a serious voice.

"He has appendicitis?" Wilson sounded rather unconvinced.

"Had," Whitney corrected. "Right in the middle of band rehearsal the way I hear it. Kirk—"

"And who the hell is Kirk?" Wilson asked.

"The lead singer," she said, sounding as calm as he was agitated. "Will, you *have* to make an effort to learn their names if you're signing them."

"Yeah, yeah," he said dismissively. "Get on with the story."

"Kirk rushed him to the hospital and the upshot, barring some bizarre disaster, is that the drummer is going to be fine. Just not up to playing right now. The band is rather bummed out about not auditioning for Platinum so I don't think we have to worry about them holding out to sign with another label," she told her brother.

"Is your car still in need of parts?" Wilson asked.

"Yes. What's one thing got to do with the other?" she asked.

And then it hit her. The answer to her question was right there in front of her. She just had some trouble getting herself to believe it since she had always been so honest and up-front about everything.

"You thought I made it up, didn't you?" she accused Wilson.

"Yeah, well, I thought you were just trying to get a little downtime for a change. By my reckoning, you've been going nonstop for practically years now—"

"No 'practically' about it, Will," she said, interrupting. "It *has* been years. I'm just as invested in our recording label as you are. If I'd wanted time off, I would have said so."

There was only one way to deal with Wilson and that was head-on. She'd learned that during her first negotiation for him. Older sibling or not, the man took absolutely no prisoners.

"Okay. Sorry." Wilson uttered the word rather grudgingly.

She knew he really wasn't sorry, but paying lip service was better than nothing, she supposed. So he said the word and she pretended to accept it.

"I'll give you a call as soon as I can get out of this one-horse town," she promised.

"Right."

And then, as usual, Whitney found herself listening to the sound of silence. Wilson had hung up.

"Someday, Wilson, someone is going to have to teach you some phone etiquette. And while they're at it, some regular etiquette wouldn't be out of order, either." She addressed the words to her dormant cell phone, which was now lying on the bed.

"Is that a new feature on your cell phone?" Liam asked, peering into the suite. "You talk to it and somehow messages magically get delivered?"

Beckoning for him to come in, she smiled a little

ruefully. "I'm just clearing the air by yelling at my brother."

Liam laughed shortly. "I kind of got that part." He'd heard her voice before he opened the door. "Anything wrong?" he asked seriously.

"Nothing a long stint in rehab wouldn't fix," she quipped.

Liam looked surprised. She'd made it sound as if her brother was in a position of considerable responsibility. "He's got a substance abuse problem?"

"No, my brother's got a people abuse problem," she corrected with a resigned sigh.

Liam had a simple question for her. "Why do you take it?"

There were lots of reasons, she thought. "Because I like my job. Because it's the family company. And because I've never known anything else. I think I was born traveling and auditioning performers, looking for just the right ones for our label."

He could see how hard it would be to give up something she cared about. But if her working conditions were unacceptable, then she needed to think over other paths she could take.

"You can always reeducate yourself, go off in a different direction," he suggested.

"Not hardly," she muttered. If she was going to spend that much energy, she would put it toward straightening things out on the home front. "Funny advice coming from a guy who works at the family business."

He supposed they had that in common, but the similarities ended there. Brett treated him with respect. That wasn't to say that his older brother didn't enjoy putting the screws to him once in a while. But the bottom line was Brett and Finn had his back and he had theirs.

"Just part-time," Liam told her.

He didn't want to talk about his actual passion—at least not until the timing was right. He was worried that she would get the wrong idea, that he'd been playing her all along, trying to cash in on the fact that he had saved her life and then trade that for a recording contract with her label.

He didn't want anything he didn't honestly earn.

"I've got breakfast," he said, holding up a bag. "You ready to hit the road?"

How quickly things can change, she couldn't help thinking. "Actually, turns out that there's no need for any road-hitting—not that I don't appreciate your volunteering and coming to my rescue this way. *Again*," she emphasized.

"Nobody's keeping count," he said dismissively, then asked a more serious question. "Did your brother fire you?"

The question took her by surprise, as did his tone of voice. She could have sworn there was an underlying, albeit suppressed, indignation in his voice, strictly on her behalf.

"No—and he really *can't* fire me from the family company." Although, she thought, if he wanted to, Wilson could have made life a living hell for her. And *that* would convince her to leave.

"Anyway, it seems that the band's drummer had appendicitis and was brought to the hospital just in the nick of time. Everything went well, but he won't be holding a pair of drumsticks for a few weeks, so the audition's been postponed."

He wondered if that meant she'd stick around, or if that was a signal for her to leave. He knew the car would have to be left behind, but there were ways to ship out a vehicle to its final destination. He was hoping she'd go along with the first choice.

"So what now?"

Whitney shrugged. She hadn't thought that far yet. "I have breakfast, twiddle my thumbs. Wait for Rick to get my car running—"

"Mick," Liam corrected.

She flushed. "Right. Mick. Sorry," she murmured. "I really appreciated your volunteering to drive me down to Laredo, but since the trip is now off, you don't have to feel like you need to hang around." Although, she added silently, she really hoped that he would. "I've taken up too much of your time already."

"Well, seeing as I've got nothing planned since I'm not driving to Laredo, why don't we have breakfast together and then see where the day goes?" he suggested. After the way she had all but knocked his socks off earlier, he wasn't eager to part company just yet. "You want to eat here, or would you rather we go back to the diner and have our breakfast there?"

"You mean eat takeout in?" she asked, not entirely clear on what he was proposing they do. "Won't Miss Joan think that's kind of strange?"

Liam laughed. "Miss Joan's been subjected to a lot stranger things than that."

Well, if he didn't mind, why should she? And after what had transpired between them earlier, she thought it might be safer for both of them if they had people around instead of staying by themselves. She still didn't know what to make of the effect he'd had on her.

"All right, then, let's eat there," she agreed.

"You're on," he said, grinning.

"Something wrong with the order?" Miss Joan asked when she saw the two of them walk into the diner fifteen minutes after Liam had picked up two breakfasts to go. "You two should have been on your way to Laredo by now," she estimated.

Whitney saw no point in asking the other woman how she knew about Laredo. Whitney was beginning to accept the fact that if there was anything to know about anyone, Miss Joan had homed in on it and already knew. She supposed that feeling this way gave her something in common with the rest of the citizens of Forever.

Instead of answering the older woman's question, Liam looked to Whitney as if silently asking if she minded his telling Miss Joan why they were there.

Rather than nod, Whitney did the honors herself. "The trip's been postponed, Miss Joan. Liam thought it would be more comfortable eating in here than in the hotel suite. I agreed, so here we are," she explained simply.

Miss Joan nodded her approval. "Makes sense. Find a table, I'll bring coffee."

"We've already got coffee," Liam told her, indicating the two containers he took out of the large bag. He placed the containers on the table.

Miss Joan waved her hand at the containers. "That coffee's at least forty minutes old. I'll pour you both fresh cups," she said in a voice that was not about to take no for an answer.

"She certainly does take charge, doesn't she?" Whitney whispered to him as she leaned across the small table Liam had picked.

"She likes to mother people," Liam explained.

Whitney wasn't entirely convinced. "That's one way to describe it."

"Hey, since you're gonna be with us for a bit," Miss Joan said to Whitney, filling the cup in front of her to an inch below the rim, leaving room for the cream, "how would you feel about coming out with us and helping pick out a Christmas tree?"

"Us?" Whitney repeated, a little confused as to what the diner owner was proposing.

"The town," Miss Joan clarified. "Each year, a bunch of Forever's citizens go out, scout the area, look for the best specimen to cut down and bring back," Miss Joan went on to explain.

"The tree's for the town square," Liam told her, filling in some of the gaps that Miss Joan had left. "After we bring it back and get it up, everybody gets a chance to decorate the tree."

It sounded like a really lovely tradition, Whitney thought. But it wasn't her tradition and she felt as if she would be intruding if she joined in.

"But isn't that a community thing?" Whitney pointed out as tactfully as she could.

"Yes…" Liam stretched out the word, waiting to see where Whitney was going with this.

"But I'm not part of the community." She doubted that everyone would be all right with her intrusion— and she couldn't fault them for it.

"Well, if you don't want to—" Miss Joan began, one rather bony shoulder rising and falling in a careless shrug.

"I didn't say that," Whitney protested.

The words had tumbled out of her mouth rather quickly before she had time to think them through. But even as she said them, Whitney figured that joining in might be fun. It had been years and years since she had gotten involved in something just for the sheer enjoyment of it. Everything had always had to have a purpose, an endgame attached to it.

But she was definitely willing to try a little fun.

"Good," Miss Joan said with finality. "Now eat up," she ordered. "The scouting trucks leave in half an hour."

Whitney could feel Liam staring at her in what could only be termed amazement as Miss Joan withdrew to make certain that this year's team was almost ready to set out on their quest.

Whitney could only shake her head in wonder. Miss Joan would have made one hell of a dictator, she thought. "You heard the lady, Liam," she said, turning toward him. "Eat up."

The sound of Liam's laugh as he dug in to his breakfast made her toes curl unexpectedly.

It didn't leave the rest of her unaffected, either.

ASIDE FROM WHEN Liam had pulled her out of the floodwaters, Whitney couldn't remember the last time she had felt this incredibly bone tired.

However, unlike that experience, this one left her feeling immensely happy, as well. She and Liam had joined the others on this Christmas tree hunt—she learned that Miss Joan chose different people for the task each year so no one monopolized the selection group by throwing their weight around. That sort of thing was strictly Miss Joan's domain alone.

It had taken a total of four hours before the group found a tree that they could all agree on, then another two to cut it down, tie it up and load it onto an oversize flatbed.

The latter was courtesy of Connie and her construction company.

It was far bigger than the one the town usually used, Liam told her. What that ultimately meant was that this year's tree was also somewhat larger than past trees. Loading it had been far from an easy matter. It was a combined effort and it had taken more than one try before they were finally successful in getting the tree onto the flatbed.

The drive back, perforce, was an exceedingly slow one.

It was, Whitney decided, like being part of a parade that was traveling its route in slow motion. They finally got back to the town square. Another hour plus was spent getting the tree off the truck and into an upright position.

"It's going a lot faster this year with all of Connie's equipment," Liam told her as she marveled at the process.

Whitney couldn't help wondering how difficult it all had to have been to accomplish *without* the aid of the construction equipment.

Yet she knew, thanks to the photographs Miss Joan had shown her earlier, that there had been a huge Christmas tree in the town square each and every year.

Because of that, and a number of other things, she found herself looking at the residents of Forever with renewed respect.

And perhaps just a touch of affection, as well.

Chapter Nine

"You *are* going to stick around to help decorate the tree, aren't you?" Miss Joan asked, materializing out of nowhere just as Whitney had begun to turn away. Liam was already walking from the town square. When she received no immediate reply, Miss Joan went on to elaborate. "I mean, after you went through all that trouble to get this beauty out here, you can't just leave it standing naked like that."

Whitney looked over her shoulder and saw that there was already a wave of people, adults and children alike, who had begun to open up boxes upon boxes of giant decorations that had been set up on more than a dozen folding tables.

Each year, according to what she had heard, more decorations were added. Last year's tree hadn't had even a single small length of branch left unadorned by at least *something*.

"From the looks of it, I'd say that you have that angle well taken care of," Whitney commented, indicating the people clustering around the laden folding tables.

"Maybe for the moment," Miss Joan allowed dismissively. "But everyone in town puts on at least a couple of decorations on the Christmas tree, if not more. It's tra—"

"—dition," Whitney completed.

As if she hadn't heard that over and over again today. To be honest, she envied the people here their traditions and their sense of community. But she was an outsider and she wasn't going to stay here long enough to be anything else.

"Yes, I know that," Whitney told the other woman.

Before she could say another word, Miss Joan took her in hand and led her over to the long row of folding tables.

"Put on a couple for me," Liam called out to her as he continued walking away. "I've got to be getting ready for work."

Whitney glanced at him in surprise. She'd just assumed that Liam would get one of his brothers to cover for him at the bar and remain here with her to decorate the tree the way Miss Joan insisted.

Obviously, he didn't feel not showing up at the bar was an option. Or maybe, after spending the better part of a day with her, Liam had had his fill.

She found that option number two bothered her. A lot. The fact that it did concerned her.

"She's in good hands," Miss Joan promised, speaking up so that her voice followed him as Liam walked away from the town square. "Don't worry, honey." Miss Joan turned her attention back to her. "I know where to find him and once you've had your fill of small-town camaraderie, I'll point you in the right direction and send you off to be with Liam."

"I wasn't worried," Whitney replied a little stiffly, feeling uncomfortable with Miss Joan's assumptions.

Had she really come across that way? Had she looked uneasy watching Liam leave? She was going to have to really work on her poker face.

Why would the older woman even *think* that? she wondered. She functioned just fine on her own. After all, she spent more than half her time being by herself, flying alone from place to place to watch young singers and bands in action, looking for that elusive, magical "something" that separated one performer or band of performers from the rest.

"Good!" Miss Joan was saying. Her voice rang with approval as the woman patted her hand. "So, let's get on with it, girl. Put a little elbow grease into it," she ordered, back to her take-charge self.

"Don't let her intimidate you," a rather tall, willowy woman with light blond hair advised.

When Whitney turned around to face this newest stranger, the woman smiled and put out her hand.

"Hi, I'm Olivia Santiago—the sheriff's wife," she added by way of introduction as Whitney shook her hand.

"Whitney Marlowe—just passing through," Whitney added in case the other woman thought otherwise.

"Between you and me, I thought Miss Joan came on like gangbusters when I first came here. The woman thought *nothing* of elbowing her way into my life. But that's just because she cares," Olivia explained. "If you ever need a friend or someone in your corner, you couldn't ask for a better person than Miss Joan," Olivia went on to assure her.

So she'd been hearing, Whitney thought. "Well, luckily, I don't need either. I don't plan on being here that long." She had no idea why that statement would make the attractive blonde smile that way. She didn't think she'd said anything funny.

Small-town residents were really rather strange people.

"Yes, that's what a lot of us said when we first found ourselves here," Olivia replied, nodding her head. And then she winked. "This is the fun part," the woman told her, leading the way over to the decorations. "C'mon, grab a few. Decorating is almost addictive."

The woman really needed to get out more. But, since she had nothing else to do at the moment—and it would appease Miss Joan—Whitney decided to take Olivia up on her invitation and joined in the initial wave of tree decorators.

WHITNEY WOUND UP staying a great deal longer than she'd intended. Not because she was forced to or found herself commandeered by Miss Joan for some other trivial task, but because she discovered, much to her amazement—and pleasure—that she was having fun.

The simple fact hadn't even dawned on her until Whitney caught herself laughing at something one of the people on her side of the tree had said in an off-handed quip.

Whitney had gotten drawn into the conversations happening around her. Before she knew it, she'd lost track of time. Not long after that, Miss Joan made the rounds, announcing that it was getting dark and decorating the remainder of the tree would resume bright and early in the morning.

"How long does decorating go on?" Whitney asked, turning to Olivia.

"Until all the decorations are on the tree and the boxes are empty," Forever's first lawyer replied.

Whitney took a couple of steps back away from the tree and looked to the uppermost part of the spruce. "How do you get the top of the tree decorated?" she asked, taking in the barren branches far above her.

"Miss Joan usually rents a cherry picker and we use that to help," Olivia told her. "This year, though, thanks to the construction project—Forever's getting its first hotel," she confided with a deep sense of town pride, "we have a cherry picker already on the premises."

That was when she realized that the woman who had befriended her didn't realize that she was currently staying in the hotel she'd just mentioned.

Whitney couldn't help smiling to herself. It was nice to know that not everyone here was like Miss Joan— ten steps ahead of her at all times.

"Did I say something funny?" Olivia asked, slightly puzzled.

"No," Whitney denied, then added quickly, "I'm just happy."

"Decorating a Christmas tree will do that to you," Olivia agreed wholeheartedly. "I think that's why Miss Joan makes such a production out of it every year. It's her personal way of spreading cheer." Olivia stopped to glance at her watch. It was obvious by her expression that what she saw was a surprise. "Look at the time. I've got to run. It was nice talking to you," she said, then asked just before she headed for home, "Are you planning on staying here awhile?"

"Couple of days at most," Whitney answered.

"A couple of days is better than nothing. Maybe I'll see you around, then," Olivia said.

"Maybe," Whitney murmured. "Oh, by the way, which way's is Murphy's?" she asked. "I got a little turned around earlier when we came back with that behemoth tree."

Olivia pointed directly behind her. "Just keep going south. You can't miss it."

Ordinarily, that was a direction that Whitney very well *could* miss. She had never had much of a sense of direction and relied completely on the GPS firmly fixed to her dashboard. Right now, it did her no good since she was separated from the device, but then this wasn't a typical crowded urban area. Forever was a small town with very little going on and if she'd been left on her own, Whitney was fairly certain she could get to the point where she had the streets—and directions for getting around in general—memorized.

As it was, even though the directions struck a familiar cord with her, it still took Whitney about ten minutes to walk from the center of town to Murphy's.

Pushing the door aside, Whitney noted that the inside of the hospitable saloon was nearly as crowded as the town square had been at the height of today's activity.

Anticipating that the crowd would only get bigger, she wove her way to the bar, expecting to find Liam behind it. After all, he had told her that he needed to work and she had just assumed that he had meant here. But instead of Liam, she saw his older brother Brett.

Had Liam lied to her? she wondered. After spending the better part of the day with her, searching for just the right Christmas tree to bring back, had he decided he had put in enough time and just wanted some space between them?

Still, she couldn't imagine Liam lying. He just didn't seem like the type to be anything but honest. Charming, yes, but still almost painfully honest.

So what, now you're making a saint out of him just because he saved you from drowning? Face it, Whit, all men are more or less alike. Their needs come first. Maybe he's already found himself someone else to occupy his time.

Maybe she had even scared him off with that kiss this morning.

Hell, she'd almost scared herself off, as well. Looking back, she had *never* felt a pull like that before—or any sort of an actual sexual pull, when she got right down to it. She hadn't had time for any sort of steady relationship, and the handful of dates she'd gone on had pretty much left her cold and convinced that the only magic to be had between a man and a woman was strictly only to be found in the movies or in some fanciful romance books.

Real life just wasn't like that.

Until it was.

With a sigh, she neatly pushed all that aside in her head and she began to turn away from the bar when she heard her name being called.

Turning around again, Whitney scanned the immediate area, curious as to who had called to her since she wasn't exactly a regular here. She sincerely doubted that any more than a handful of people even *knew* her name.

"Whitney, over here!"

That was when she saw Brett waving to her.

Once she looked in his direction, the handsome bar-

tender beckoned her over to the section he was standing behind.

Because it would have been rude to ignore the man,
Whitney forced herself to make her way through the
crowd. It took a little bobbing and weaving, but she finally managed to reach him.

Once she did, Brett grinned at her. "I see you survived Miss Joan's annual Christmas tree foraging."

She survived, all right, but there were times when
she felt as if she had just barely succeeded. "She certainly is something else," Whitney replied evasively.

In total agreement, Brett was nodding his head.
"The woman does take a little getting used to," he
replied. "It helps to know that her heart's in the right
place."

"So people keep telling me," Whitney commented.
But that just wasn't enough of a recommendation to her.
And then, because she felt she didn't have anything to
lose—after all, she would be leaving town the minute
her car was repaired, which meant that she'd never see
any of these people again—that was her incentive to
ask Brett, "Is Liam around? I thought he'd be tending
the bar, but obviously, he's not."

"Liam doesn't tend bar very much anymore. His interests have taken him in a new, different direction,"
Brett said.

As he continued speaking to her, Brett took a rather
impressive-looking bottle from the rear counter. It was
filled with a thick amber liquid. He poured a very small
amount into a shot glass. Placing the bottle back on the
display behind him, he moved the shot glass closer to
Whitney.

"First one's on the house," he told her with a warm smile.

Rather than reach for it, Whitney eyed the drink for a moment.

"What is it?" she asked.

"Nothing lethal," Brett promised. "Just a little something to take the chill out of your bones—it is December 1, after all, even if we don't have snow around here."

There was no real chill as far as she was concerned, but she took a tentative sip from her glass. As the liquid made its way through her system she raised her eyes to his.

"Bénédictine?" she asked.

Brett appeared impressed. "Ah, the lady has a discerning palate," he declared with a note of admiration.

"A lot of the deals I make are closed over drinks," she explained. "Some of the people tend to favor Bénédictine, which is how I know what it tastes like."

Pausing for a moment, she contemplated the remaining contents of her glass. "These interests that Liam has developed," she began, getting back to what Brett had said to her a minute ago, "just which way are they taking him?"

"Well, if he's good enough, probably the sky's the limit," Brett guessed, and then as he looked at her, he went on to add, "But then, you'd be the better judge of that than I would."

A third sip had her finishing the drink he had placed in front of her. Whitney put the shot glass back on the bar and her eyes met his. What he'd just said clearly intrigued her.

"How's that?" She was completely in the dark about what he was talking about.

Brett tried to explain it another way. "It's an area that you're far more familiar with than I am."

He wasn't making any sense to her. She looked down at the shot glass. "That was only one shot and I can pretty much hold my liquor, so it's not the alcohol making my brain fuzzy. But I don't understand what you're talking about," she freely admitted.

Brett, like his brother Liam, had that going for him. Charming, he had a way of dismantling barriers, dismantling them in such a way that one minute they were there, the next, they were gone and life had taken on a far more meaningful, far more satisfactory air.

"Why would I be the better judge than you?"

Rather than answer her question outright, Brett smiled and refilled her glass, pouring from the same bottle.

"That's okay," she said. "I don't need another." Though two drinks still didn't make her unsteady, she didn't see the need to stand there essentially drinking by herself. That was for people trying to erase something from their memory.

"I'm thinking that maybe, this one time, you just might need a second one."

They really did talk in riddles in this town, she thought, frustrated. They should all come with an instruction manual.

Maybe this penchant for riddles had something to do with the fact that there seemed to be preciously little entertainment to be had in Forever. Outside of the saloon, she hadn't seen anything that promised to cut into the day-to-day, wall-to-wall boredom.

There were no malls, small or otherwise—there wasn't even so much as one mini-mall. There were no chain movie theaters. From what she could ascertain, there wasn't even *one* movie theater in the entire town. There certainly wasn't a restaurant to challenge Miss Joan's diner for business.

There was, in effect, nothing that served as some sort of a temporary diversion for the people of this small town.

So, poking their noses into other people's business and saying enigmatic statements that made little to no sense to an outsider seemed to be the residents' only means to entertain themselves.

She looked at the refilled shot glass with its shimmering contents. "Well, I'm just going to leave it where it is, but since you poured it, it can't go back into the bottle. So let me pay you for it. That way, it doesn't count as a loss to you.

"Tell Liam the excursion earlier was really an experience." She paused a second, then added, "Tell him I really had fun."

There was no harm in telling the man the truth, especially if she didn't see him again.

Then Brett said something that blew that out of the water for her.

"Why don't you tell him yourself?"

"I would if I could," she told Brett, "but since he's not around—"

Brett interrupted her again. "Turn around," he said. When she went on staring at him, confusion creasing her brow, Brett pointed behind her.

It was so noisy in here, with people shouting over one another to be heard, she had a hard time hearing

Brett, and the bartender was standing just a couple of feet away from her.

Still deliberately leaving her drink on the bar, Whitney turned around just as she heard someone—was that Liam?—loudly counting off, "Three, two, one!"

The next second, the countdown was instantly followed by a rather enthusiastic burst of music she could literally feel into her very bones.

That was certainly an attention getter.

It had certainly gotten hers.

By the time Whitney had managed to turn all the way around, she noticed a four-piece band set up some distance from the middle of the saloon.

There was a man playing an upright keyboard, accompanying three guitarists. The one in the middle was the only one who was singing.

The one in the middle was also Liam.

Like someone in a trance, Whitney, her eyes riveted on the band, slowly reached behind her for the drink that she had just rejected. She spread her fingers out, trying to make contact with the shot glass.

Taking pity on her, Brett pushed the shot glass into her questing fingers. Triumphantly securing it, Whitney brought the shot glass to her, then raised it in a single toast to the band.

The drink disappeared in one gulp.

Chapter Ten

"Would you like another?" Brett asked, his amusement plainly audible.

He addressed the words to the back of Whitney's head. She was on the bar stool, sitting absolutely ramrod straight. Every fiber in her body was focused on the band. More specifically, on Liam.

"I'll let you know," she finally told Brett after a beat, the words all but dribbling from her lips in slow motion.

"All right," Brett answered.

Even those words were too many, interfering with her concentration. Whitney waved him into silence, wishing she could do that with the rest of the people who were in the saloon. She was doing her best to try to hear the song the band was playing, really hear it. She wanted to be sure she wasn't mistaken, or talking herself into something.

But even the surrounding chatter couldn't diminish or detract from what she knew she was hearing: one rather professional-sounding band playing background for one extremely excellent-singing guitarist.

She became even *more* impressed when Liam in-

dulged in some entertaining, albeit exceedingly difficult, guitar fingering.

Sliding off the bar stool she'd only been partially
perched on, Whitney abandoned her place by the bar
and came closer to the music, drawn there more or less
like one of the hypnotized children mesmerized by the
Pied Piper's flute.

She stopped herself just a little short of the perimeter
that surrounded the band.

As she absorbed the quality of the music, she began
to notice other equally as important things, as well.
Such as the fact that the inner circle that surrounded the
band was comprised predominately of young women.
Young women who appeared to be absolutely spell-
bound, hanging on every syllable Liam sang, on every
note he played.

There were men in the outer circle that went around
the band, but the band appealed in no small way predominately to the female of the species. Whitney
wasn't sure how she felt about this, but for the moment, she was excited by what she saw.

WHENEVER HE PLAYED, whether to an audience or just
in rehearsal, where only the other band members were
present, Liam always gave 150 percent of himself to
the performance.

But tonight, he'd kept just a fraction of himself back
in order to aim a covert glance or two in Whitney's direction. He wanted to impress her. To literally wow her.

He told himself it was because of who she was and
ultimately who she represented. After all, she was a
talent scout for a major recording label.

But while that was all very true, it wasn't the only

reason he wanted to blow Whitney away with his dexterity and with his musical prowess.

At bottom lay the reason that all men flexed whatever muscles they had available—be it physical or mental—to impress the ladies in their lives.

When he finally got himself to glance up, he saw her. Saw Whitney. Saw her swaying to the beat of the song they were playing.

That she was standing closer rather than lingering by the bar gave him a very positive feeling, not to mention what it did for his confidence.

Liam deliberately made eye contact with her now and while that sort of thing was supposed to make a huge impression on the recipient of his gaze, he found to his surprise that making eye contact with Whitney also sent a shaft of heat through him.

At the very same time, he felt a shiver work its way down his back. He was behaving like some damn fool teenager. It was a good thing that Whitney wasn't into mind reading or his goose would have *really* been cooked.

Because she did look so captivated, Liam went straight into the next number without pausing when he and the band concluded the one they had been playing.

They wound up doing five numbers that way. At the end of the fifth number, Liam took command of the microphone set up in the center.

"The guys and I are going to give our fingers a little rest by taking a short break," he announced. "But don't go away too far 'cause the show's going to resume in a few minutes. Until then, drink up!" he ordered with an infectious grin. With that, he returned the mike back to its stand and stepped away from the makeshift stage Finn had put together for them.

Several of the band's—and his—would-be groupies immediately converged, blocking his path as he tried to make his way over toward Whitney. Gently but firmly, he got the young women to get out of his way.

"So?" Liam asked with enthusiasm the second he reached her. "What do you think?"

He was all but radiating pure sex appeal, Whitney thought, struggling to see him objectively rather than as the young performer whose unorchestrated kiss had completely rocked the very foundations of her world.

"I think," she replied, "you should have told me that you can sing."

He laughed shortly. "You mean I left that off my résumé when I handed it to you?" he asked, acting surprised at the omission.

Whitney's eyes narrowed. Had she overlooked something? "What résumé?"

Liam's expression bordered on triumphant. He'd made his point, or so he thought. "Exactly."

"Wait, back up," Whitney ordered. This was *not* making any sense to her. If she had been in his place when this situation had arose, she would have lost absolutely *no* time making her musical bent known to him. "When I told you that I was a talent scout for Purely Platinum, that didn't ring any bells for you?"

Again, he laughed. If she only knew the kind of restraint he'd employed to keep from telling her about his aspirations for himself and his band.

"It rang an entire wind-chimes factory full of them for me," he told her.

She stared at him, getting more and more confused.

"Then *why* didn't you tell me you were in a band and that you were a damn good singer?"

"And musician," Brett added, having rounded the bar for a moment to come over and join Whitney and his brother. When she looked at him over her shoulder, Brett went on to explain. "Liam also wrote most of the songs the band's playing tonight."

"Really?" She turned and directed her question at Liam.

If she'd had anywhere near the talent she had just witnessed, she would have been out performing her heart out in every venue she could find until someone discovered her—the way she had just discovered Liam and his band right now. Excitement surged through her veins.

Whitney watched now as a boyish flush washed over Liam's ultra-handsome chiseled features. He nodded his head almost as an afterthought, blond hair slipping over his eyes. He combed it back with his fingers and looked at her.

"Yeah, I wrote them. No big deal," he murmured with a vague, dismissive shrug.

"Yes, big deal," she contradicted. "You should have said *something*."

"Couldn't take the chance that it would have sounded like bragging to you. So I figured it would come across better if you heard us play," he said, explaining his reasoning as best he could. "I mean, you probably get a lot of people telling you they've always wanted to play or sing professionally and that all their friends tell them how good they are—even if they sound like fingernails scraping across a chalkboard. I didn't want you to think I was in that group."

"Then what are you saying? That you don't want to play professionally?"

He looked at her as if she'd lost her mind. "Oh, yeah, sure we want to play professionally. That's what our goal is—the band's and mine," he elaborated, nodding toward the other three members of his band, who weren't quite as fast or as good as he was when it came to avoiding overly energetic fans. "But you probably get a lot of people saying that and you probably have a way to block them all out. I didn't want you ruling the band out just because you're tired of every second person thinking they could be the next big sensation on the entertainment scene."

He was right, she realized. She would have probably dismissed him out of hand if he'd come across the standard way. It had become second nature for her, a way of preserving herself. Whenever people learned what she did for a living, they suddenly began singing under their breath rather loudly, or tapping out tunes to direct her attention to them.

Consequently, Liam had gone about it just the right way, she couldn't help thinking. Not only had he gotten her to listen, but he'd also turned out to be damn good. Ordinarily, the label she represented didn't have—nor had it ever had—a country-and-western performer in their stable. Purely Platinum focused predominantly on contemporary pop stars—but good was good, she thought. And Liam and his band were *damn* good.

About to say something else to her, Liam seemed to catch a movement out of the corner of his eye. When he turned to look, he must have seen one of the remaining guitarists beckoning for him to come back. Their first break was over and it was time to begin a second set.

"Music calls," he told Whitney just before he started making his way back to the band.

An equal number of girls—if not more—impeded his route back, getting in his way, asking for autographs or just simply fawning over him.

Whitney certainly didn't blame them. Liam was nothing if not incredibly appealing. He didn't even need to sing to knock them dead.

"Seeing those girls acting like that, you'd never know that they all went to school with Liam," Brett commented to her, watching his youngest brother.

"It's the performer phenomenon," Whitney told him knowingly.

"The what?" he asked her.

"The performer phenomenon," she repeated, then explained what she meant. "Doesn't matter if they grew up living next door to one another and playing together in a sandbox every day for fifteen years," Whitney exaggerated. "You stick an instrument in one of their hands, shine a spotlight on them—or a big flashlight—and make them sing, provided that they *can* sing even a little," she stipulated, "and suddenly, his lifelong neighbor is seeing him with new eyes and getting giddy, thanks to fantasies that are materializing in her head. It's like he's changed into some kind of a minigod right before her eyes. Trust me, I've seen it happen again and again."

She paused, listening to the newest number Liam and his band were playing. "Excuse me for a second," she said to Brett, searching for her phone.

"No problem," he said. He shouldn't have taken this long of a break himself. "I've got to get back to the bar.

Finn can only stand filling orders for so long before he gets antsy," Brett told her with a laugh.

She barely nodded to acknowledge that she'd heard him. Her mind was on capturing Liam's performance while she could.

Her smartphone in hand, Whitney pulled up her video app. Pressing it, she then aimed her phone at Liam and began recording him as he sang and played.

Still watching Liam, she smiled to herself. "Have I got a surprise for you, big brother," she murmured under her breath, suddenly exceedingly pleased with herself. "Looks like almost drowning turned out to be a good thing."

What was it her mother used to say, she tried to recall. Something about nothing bad ever happening that some good couldn't come of it.

This was definitely a good thing.

Her almost drowning and subsequently getting stranded out here in nowhere land turned out to be definitely a good thing because if that hadn't happened to her, if she hadn't gotten swept up in that awful flash flood, she wouldn't be here now, listening to what could very well be Purely Platinum's latest superstars.

She went on taping.

ONCE AGAIN, LIAM came over to her during his next break. He was flushed, having worked up a real sweat this time out, but he was also obviously very pleased with himself.

He and the band had outdone themselves, Liam felt—and he was usually his own worst critic. But tonight, tonight they had played as if a fleet of angels had pulled up a cloud to listen to them and they in turn had given it their all.

It didn't hurt that he had told the band who Whitney was and the label she was with.

"Why the hell didn't you tell us?" Sam had demanded, stunned.

"I didn't want to make you nervous," Liam had answered.

The other three performers had been far from happy with the answer, but they *were* grateful for the opportunity now.

They had played their hearts out.

"How is it that you're still here, playing in a saloon in Forever?" Whitney asked Liam the moment he joined her.

That was a simple enough question to answer. He'd stayed up until now because he'd honed his skills here. "Because Brett lets me try out new songs here and besides, this is where the guys and I got started. It's home to us."

She understood the appeal of home. Home, for her, had been her mother. But then everything had changed when she had abandoned the family in favor of a man a lot younger than her. Now, to her, home was someplace to leave.

"Home's a nice place to come back to when you need to rest up," she said for Liam's sake, "but, well, haven't you ever wanted to go out on the road, play to different audiences, make money—no, make a *living* at this?" she pressed.

As she asked the question, a thought hit her. "Does Brett even pay you for playing here?" she asked, fairly certain she knew the answer to that before Liam said it.

Loyalty had Liam carefully gauging his answer.

"Not at first," he admitted, "but that was because we were just starting out, developing our skills, our pacing, things like that. But he pays us now," he said, then, because Brett was such a stickler for the truth and had all but drummed it into his head as well as Finn's, he added, "Or at least he pays the guys."

"But not you?" she asked incredulously. "You're the singer." *And the real reason there are so many females packing the place tonight,* Whitney added silently.

"And related to the owners—not to mention that I'm also one of the owners," he reminded her. "Seems kind of silly to be paying myself."

"It seems even 'sillier' to do it for free," Whitney deliberately countered. "It's like throwing away a precious commodity."

"Precious, huh?" Liam repeated with a very wide grin. A grin that was swiftly getting under her skin. She could see why the other women reacted the way they did to Liam. The man was *very* hard to resist. "Is that what you really think?"

"Absolutely," she told him, doing her best to sound professional and distant.

She was only partially successful.

Clearing her throat, she continued, "I've been in the business for practically ten years now and you are one of the best—if not *the* best—performer that I have ever heard."

Liam was one to always hammer things down and put them into perspective. He'd grown confident over the past year, confident, but not cocky. The latter was the road to self-destruction in his opinion and he intended to be around, playing or doing whatever it was he liked, for a very long time.

"You're just saying that because I saved your life," he said with a grin.

"No," she contradicted quite seriously, "I'm saying that because it's true."

Liam couldn't keep the wide smile from his face. He was fairly beaming inside. It was one thing to have one of the locals rave about the band and tell him how good they—and he—were. Hearing that was good for the soul. But having someone of Whitney's caliber, someone who did this sort of thing for a living, tell him he was good was an entirely different matter.

Her words had him walking on air.

Impulsively, Liam turned around and waved for his band to join them.

"Hey, guys," he called out. "Come over here. Remember what I told you? Well, I think it's time for you all to meet." He paused to look at Whitney for a second. "You don't mind, do you?" he asked her, realizing that he'd taken her assent for granted.

"No, I don't mind," she replied. "I'd really like to meet them."

"Great!" he said with genuine feeling.

Turning, Liam beckoned to them again, this time with enthusiastic hand movements. The other members of the band made their way over to Liam and the woman he was talking to.

"Whitney, I'd like you to meet Sam Howard, Christian Grey Eagle and Tom Grant. Guys, this is Whitney Marlowe. She's the talent scout for Purely Platinum recording studio I told you about. She's auditioning singers and musicians."

Sam Howard had deep blue-black hair that was straighter than a pin. He was tall, with cheekbones that seemed to have been carved out of ivory and at the moment, his dark, chocolate-colored eyes were scrutinizing her.

"Did you like what you heard?" he asked Whitney point-blank.

"Very much so," she told the man. "I think your band has a great deal of energy that is extremely infectious. You make the audience part of your music."

Whitney didn't add that it had been a very long time since she had been this impressed with a band. But they were new and fresh and listening to them was an exciting experience.

She had a feeling that Wilson would agree with her—after, of course, he finished being dismissive and complaining that they were too raw and that they sang country, of all things. Then he'd tell her that the publicity department didn't have a clue as to how to promote county-and-western music or performers who specialized in that genre.

But in the end, she was certain that he would come around and grudgingly mutter that yes, they did have a lot of potential.

Because, Whitney thought as she watched Liam go back to the makeshift stage and pick up his guitar again, the band certainly did have potential—a great deal of potential.

They began to play again and Whitney felt herself completely transported. Within seconds, she began taping again.

Chapter Eleven

"You really think we're good?" Liam asked her later on that night as he drove Whitney back to the hotel. Nature had slipped into a respectful stillness while the full moon illuminated the road before them, guiding them on their way. "I'm not asking for myself," he interjected quickly before she had a chance to answer him. He didn't want Whitney to think he was so shallow he would get her to stroke his ego. He had a logical reason for asking about her opinion. "I just don't want to raise the guys' hopes if you're just being nice. We've been at this a long time and the band's really important to us."

"Yes," she answered him with a smile, "I think you're not just good but *very* good. I think with the right person to manage you, you'll go far."

Liam parked his truck in front of the hotel and got out.

"The right person," Liam repeated slowly as if rolling the matter over in his head to come to a conclusion. "You?"

Whitney blinked, surprised as she got out of the passenger side of the vehicle. "What? No, not me." She hadn't meant to imply that. She was just speaking in general terms. "I just find talent. You need an agent, a manager, someone to look out for you, book you in the right places. Someone with business savvy, the patience of Job and a good ear," she told him as he walked her to the hotel's entrance.

Liam stopped walking just inside the hotel lobby and shifted the lantern he was holding to his other hand. He was confused.

"Well, isn't that you?" he asked. "I think you just described what you do."

"Maybe in a general sort of way," she granted. "But you need more than just what I do as you get started building a career."

"What the band and I need," he pointed out, "is someone we can trust. Someone we feel has our best interests at heart." He was looking straight at her as he put forth his band's requirement for the future.

She had to admit that the idea of representing Liam and his band was tempting. She'd only been at the very beginning of a couple of performers' careers, but even then it had been strictly in a distant, advisory capacity. The way she viewed it, she wasn't cutthroat enough to be a successful agent.

"Look, Liam," she began, "I'm flattered, but you need someone with a lot more expertise than I have." She thought for a second, then went on. "I've got a list of agents somewhere. Why don't I—"

"Maybe I don't want someone with more expertise than you," Liam said, not letting her finish what she was saying. "Maybe I want someone who's as hungry as I am to get somewhere in that particular field, hungry to get started in this business and build a career."

Oh, dear God, Whitney thought as she looked up at

him, she was tempted. Really, *really* tempted. What Liam was suggesting—managing his band—would be taking a chance. It meant challenging herself, taking a real risk by leaving everything she knew behind and starting fresh in a brand-new, virgin world. It would mean giving up her comfort zone and the perks she had right now and diving headfirst into the deep end of the pool.

What perks? A little voice in her head jeered. *You spend half the year traveling around, sleeping in strange, uncomfortable hotel beds, periodically calling Wilson and arguing with him until he comes around. That's not a life. That's an existence. When you think about it, maybe it's even a rut.*

Still, rut or not, it was *her* rut and she could depend on it.

"Tell you what, Liam, why don't we just take this whole idea one step at a time? Is that okay with you?" she asked.

Liam nodded, the moonlight outlining his chiseled features and managing somehow to make them even sexier than they already were. If the man looked any sexier, Whitney caught herself thinking, there would probably be a law on the books requiring him to wear a paper bag over his head in public. As it was, she could hardly keep from running her fingers through his light blond hair. It looked silky—was it? she wondered.

"Okay," Liam agreed to her suggestion.

Arriving at her door, he put the lantern down on the floor.

The next moment, rather than opening the door for her, Liam managed to surprise her by slipping his fingers into her hair and framing her face.

Whitney could feel her heart starting to accelerate, beating hard with an anticipation she really shouldn't be having, she silently lectured herself.

But she made no move to put distance between herself and Liam. Instead, she asked him in a voice that was hardly above a whisper, "What are you doing?"

"I'm just following your suggestion," he told her, his face so serious Whitney had no idea just what she was to expect.

Everything inside of her was on edge, anticipation all but overwhelming her. "My suggestion?"

Liam nodded his head. Light blond hair fell into his eyes but he ignored it. His gaze never left hers. "Taking it one step at a time."

And then, with the moonlight pushing its way in through the various windows, wrapping itself around them, Liam drew her a fraction of an inch closer, lowered his mouth to hers and kissed her.

Unlike the first time they'd kissed, this kiss began slowly, softly, but with a purpose. Even though it flowered at an even pace, it drew all the energy from her in a single instant. She came close to melting away in the ensuing wave of heat.

One moment, the kiss was so gentle, so delicate, it felt as light as a butterfly's wing fluttering by. The next moment, heated passion all but exploded between them and for the life of her, she couldn't tell if he was the one who had struck the match—or if she was. All she knew was that something far more powerful than she had taken over, all but consuming her with its head-spinning majesty.

This was wrong, wrong, wrong. Her brain kept telegraphing the protest to the rest of her, desperately trying to get the message registered and acted on.

Allowing what was taking place to go any further was wrong for so many reasons, it was difficult to know where to begin. She was mixing business with pleasure, interweaving her professional life with her private one and worse than that, she was behaving like a cougar in training, or maybe just a plain, old-fashioned cradle robber.

And her resolve was growing weaker by the moment.

But as much as she could so very easily succumb to what was happening to her, Whitney summoned every last ounce of strength she still had and separated her mouth from his.

She saw the bewilderment, the question in Liam's eyes, and knew she couldn't just turn her back on him and walk off. She had to explain, to make him see *why* she couldn't allow this to happen between them.

She began with the most basic of reasons why they shouldn't sleep together—because she knew that was where this was clearly headed. "How old are you?"

Liam stared at her, a look of bewilderment on his face that made her rethink her question.

"What's my age have to do with anything?"

"A lot," she insisted, her eyes narrowing to tiny laser points focused on him. "Now, how old are you?" she repeated.

"Old enough," Liam maintained.

That's what people said when they *weren't* old enough. "Well, I'm older."

He nodded his head as if to evaluate her. "And I

see that you're getting around just fine without your walker," he cracked.

That managed to get her more annoyed. "I'm not making jokes," she snapped.

"You're also not making sense," Liam countered calmly.

"Don't you understand? I'm *older* than you," Whitney informed him pointedly, certain of the fact now.

Liam shrugged, completely unmoved by this so-called revelation. "A lot of people are. So what?"

"So it bothers *me*," she insisted hotly. There were so many ugly names for the situation she found herself almost entangled in. She wanted to nip this right in the bud. It couldn't be allowed to flower.

Again Liam lifted his broad shoulders in a careless shrug. "It doesn't bother me," he said.

How could it not? she wondered. "It should," she told him in no uncertain terms, implying that if it didn't bother him, then there was something wrong with the way he was thinking.

"Why?" Liam pressed. "You're a beautiful woman who has sophistication and maturity on her side. If anything, you're like a fine wine, although I doubt you've had much time to ferment," he teased, softly kissing her temples one at a time.

Liam was definitely making it exceedingly difficult to resist him, but she knew she had to. Had to keep a clear head and not succumb to the havoc Liam was creating inside of her. If for no other reason, she had to keep him at arm's length to prevent Wilson from accusing her of pushing a personal agenda by getting him to watch Liam perform. Wilson was very quick to label things. Nepotism was Wilson's favorite thing to rail against, despite the fact that he was guilty of it himself time and again.

"I'm twenty-seven," Liam said. "How old are you?"

Twenty-seven. She was almost four years older than that. Four whole years. Practically half a decade. However, she wasn't ready to admit any of it. "More than twenty-seven."

Very slowly, his eyes swept over the length of her, lingering a little during the passage. "I'm willing to bet it's not much more. One year? Two? Six?"

"Six?" she cried, her eyes widening in apparent shock and dismay. And then she realized by Liam's grin that he had somehow set her up—to what end?

"Okay," he said and nodded, taking in every nuance that had just transpired between Whitney and himself. "More than two and, judging by that cry, less than six. So that means that you've got a few years left before you forget how to feed yourself and have to be shipped off to a nursing home. I suggest you enjoy them."

"I am," she informed him with a toss of her head. It was a studied move, but she felt it did the trick. "I'm doing what I like. I'm discovering new talent."

"Commendable," Liam wholeheartedly agreed. "But how about discovering yourself?"

What was that supposed to mean? "I don't have to discover myself. I know just who I am," she told him. "I always have."

She found his smile to be positively wicked and incredibly disarming even if she struggled to give no indication of that.

"Yeah," Liam agreed to her assessment. "The lady who can make me forget just about everything else," he told her and just to show her what he meant by that, he kissed her again.

This time the gentleness was placed on hold, allowing the passion to come out in full force. So much so that she was swept away. She had to throw her arms around his neck just to anchor herself to something.

The kiss continued to grow in what amounted to a matter of seconds.

At that point Whitney realized that she was ready to throw caution, principles and everything in between into the wind in exchange for something intangible, but incredibly wonderful—even though it was fleeting and unpredictable.

Most likely, she would have done just that, had Liam not stopped what was happening when he did.

Just as Whitney was ready to lose herself in him, Liam stepped back, smiled into her eyes and said, "Pleasant dreams."

She didn't know whether to throw something at him, drag him to her room or just run for cover as fast as she could.

She walked sedately for cover instead just as Liam walked back to his truck.

He had absolutely no idea just how frustrated she was.

WHITNEY WAS FAR too keyed up to go to bed—not that she had expected to get too much sleep that night.

Once she returned to her hotel room, her initial plan was to begin editing the videos she had taken of Liam and his band with her cell phone. Not altogether certain how long the process would take, she had meant only to get started.

But whenever she got caught up in something, it became a matter of putting going to bed off for an extra ten minutes, just until she completed work on the next frame and then the next one. Telling herself that all she wanted to do was make a little tweak here, a slightly larger tweak there, and so on.

Then, before she knew it, daylight slipped into her room, dueling with the light from the lantern left on in the suite.

She didn't take immediate note of even *that*. She realized it was the dawn of a new day somewhat after the fact.

Whitney glanced at her watch and blinked. That couldn't be true. Yet as she looked at the old-fashioned face, she saw that it was close to eight o'clock.

She had been up all night.

But she had also done some pretty impressive editing, she realized and congratulated herself. The editing had included finding a way to filter out the noisy, albeit appreciative, patrons who had surrounded the band. The only time she allowed the noisy crowd was to highlight the band's strengths as well as its strong appeal.

The rest of the time, she made sure that the band's sound was the dominant one on the video file.

"Okay, Wilson," she said, addressing the air, "prepare to have your socks knocked off, starting from all the way up to your knees."

She played the video for herself one more time to make sure everything was as perfect as she could get it—then she pressed Send and forwarded the video she had spent all night editing to her brother.

Drained and exhilarated at the same time, Whitney

decided that a shower was in order. So she allowed herself only three extra minutes to absorb the hot water beating down on her rigid shoulders and body.

The shower, seductive in its heat, went on a little longer before she finally turned the faucet off and stepped out of the stall. Toweling herself off, she got dressed quickly, then, after a few seconds of psyching herself up, placed a call to Wilson.

Her brother's phone rang four times on his end before she heard it finally going to voice mail. Her hand tightened on her own phone.

"Pick up, Wilson, you'll thank me when you do." She gave it to the count of twenty, then placed another call to him.

And another.

By her count, she placed twelve calls in all before her brother finally picked up his phone and answered it none-too-politely.

"What?" Wilson fairly roared into the phone. "Are you completely insane, Whit? Should I start calling you Half-Whit?"

"Whitney is just fine," she informed her brother crisply. "And, for the record, I'm not insane, just persistent," she replied, her voice softening slightly. "Remember, that's part of my charm."

"You don't have any charm," Wilson snapped at her. "Especially not at six in the morning."

"It's not six," Whitney informed her older brother.

"It is here," he said coldly.

"It *was*," she corrected. She'd forgotten about the time difference, she realized. But she wasn't *that* far off and besides, she wanted to talk to him about Liam and his band. "It's later now—and anyway, when I'm finished telling you why I called, you're going to thank me and want to know why I didn't call you earlier."

"Ha!" He laughed as if *that* would be the day. "Did you by any chance come down with something in that hick town you're staying in? The cattle don't have anthrax, do they?" he jeered.

"I haven't seen any cattle and I haven't come down with anything," she said. "I've just been doing my job."

He took that to mean only one thing. "You auditioned The Lonely Wolves?" he asked, apparently coming to life on the other end of the line. "I thought you said they were short a drummer."

"No, I didn't audition *that* group. But I found a group that's even better than they are," she told him, not bothering to bridle her enthusiasm.

"How would you know that? You just said that you haven't auditioned The Lonely Wolves yet, right?" Wilson asked smugly, obviously tickled to have caught her in a lie.

"Right, but we do have that demo they sent, so I think it's safe to say the group I heard last night is twice—if not three times—as good as the one you sent me to audition."

"I'm getting confused here," her brother grumbled. "Are you saying—"

She had no patience to engage in lengthy explanations for the sake of clearing up her brother's apparently foggy brain. Instead, she cut him off and made another suggestion.

"Put me on hold and watch the video I sent you," she said. "I'll wait."

Wilson snorted in disgust. "I'll call you back later."

She knew that meant he was going back to bed and

she wanted him to watch the video first. "No, I'll wait," she insisted.

He was obviously out of patience, something he never had a large supply of to begin with. "If I fired you, would you go away?"

"Nope. And you can't fire me," she reminded him. "I'm part owner, remember?"

"All too well," he complained. "Okay, I'll watch your stupid video—but if I don't like it, that's the end of it, okay?"

"If you don't like it," she told him, "then I'd seriously think about having you committed because it'll mean you've lost your taste as well as your business savvy."

"What I'd really like to lose is you," Wilson snapped back.

"Maybe someday, but not now. Now go watch the video," she ordered. "I'll be right here when you're done." Provided, of course, that her brother didn't hit the wrong key, as he was wont to do, and disconnect them.

The next minute, she had dead air registering against her ear, which could, but didn't necessarily have to, mean that she had been disconnected.

With a sigh, she told herself it was an accident on Wilson's part. There was a fifty-fifty chance that it was just that. But, knowing her older brother's pigheaded approach to certain things, like being woken up at an early hour, she was inclined to believe that he'd just ended the call and hoped she'd go away.

"Think again, Will," she declared, punching in his number again on her keypad.

Chapter Twelve

It took her three more tries before she got Wilson to pick up his phone and talk to her again. The first two attempts wound up ringing five times, then going to voice mail. Once she heard the prerecorded message beginning, she'd terminate her call and then hit Redial to start the process all over again.

Whitney was prepared to continue redialing until she wore him down, or he threw out his phone, whichever came first.

When he finally got back on the phone, Wilson was *not* a happy camper. "I swear I'm going to take out a restraining order against you," he declared in a voice that was barely below shouting range.

"A restraining order against your own sister and business partner? I really don't think you'll be able to get one. The judge'll see this as a family matter and tell you to sit down and talk to me—which is what I want in the first place," she informed her brother cheerfully. "Now, stop being so stubborn and take a look at that video I just sent you. Trust me, you'll be glad you did." She knew he hated it when she took the lead, but this time it was justified. She honestly thought that Liam and his band had that something extra that set them apart from the crowd.

She heard Wilson blowing out a beleaguered breath and knew that he was slowly coming around. "Just where did you find this band you're so hot about?"

"I heard them last night right here at the local saloon," Whitney replied.

"Where's 'here'?" Wilson asked. She could almost see him frowning as he spoke. It took a great deal to make Wilson smile.

She answered his question. "The town's name is Forever."

Wilson snorted dismissively. "Never heard of it." It was impossible to miss the superior tone in his voice.

"The town's name isn't important, Will," she insisted, beginning to lose patience with her brother. "Just watch the video."

She was surprised that Wilson's sigh didn't blow her away, it was that deep, that put-upon.

"Okay, okay, just as long as I'm not listening to a country-western band," he said. When she made no comment—or offered any reassurances—she heard her brother groan audibly. "Oh, God, please tell me that you didn't send me a video of a country-western group."

"Would you please just watch the video—and keep an open mind," she ordered.

He didn't seem to have heard her, but was marching to his own inner tune. "It is, isn't it?" Wilson demanded. "It's some two-bit country-western band made up of three dimwits who have trouble remembering which end of the guitar to play and some guy who yodels, right? Whit, you know damn well that we don't have any crying-in-your-beer groups under contract. We never have and we never will."

"Never say never," Whitney countered. "You just might have to eat your own words. Besides," she continued in defense of the group she'd been instantly impressed with, "they're not crying into their beer or into anything else. Now watch the damn video. I've got a feeling that if we don't sign these people, we're really going to regret it—and that's not how this business works."

Wilson's voice took on an edge—she knew he didn't like her lecturing him, but she was out of options. "I'm already filled with regret," Wilson grumbled.

"Wilson..." she began, a warning note in her voice, although, quite honestly, she wasn't sure what more she could threaten her brother with if he decided to stand firm.

There was a long pause on the other end of the line. And then, in a far less adversarial tone, Wilson asked, "You're really serious about this band, aren't you, Whitney?"

Finally, he was getting the message, she thought, relieved. "Yes."

"And you want to sign this band even if we've never put country singers under contract, not even so much as once."

"Yes, I do," she replied unwaveringly.

"Well, if you're that gung ho about it, the least I can do is give this video of yours a look-see," he agreed, relenting. "Stand by," he instructed. "I'll get back to you when it's over." He proceeded to put her on hold, this time successfully.

The video she had sent him included three songs,

bringing the playing time in at just a shade over ten minutes. She marked that down on her watch and proceeded to wait.

They were, she judged, quite possibly the *longest* ten minutes of her life.

Her shoulder and arm slowly began to ache from holding the cell phone by her head. Even so, she didn't dare put the phone down. She could very well miss her brother's feedback when he returned to the call. She knew the way Wilson operated. If she didn't answer immediately, he would just hang up and move on to something else. This was already hard enough. Convincing her brother to give her—and Liam's band—a second chance was in the same category as walking on water: it was done just once in history and was not about to happen again.

She was beginning to think that Wilson had decided to leave her on hold when she finally heard sounds on the other end of the line. The next second, she heard her brother's voice.

"You filmed this?"

"With my own little hands," she cracked, then became serious. "The band's good, isn't it?" she asked with a certain amount of pride.

Rather than agree with her, her brother allowed, "The singer's got some potential."

"Some?" Whitney echoed incredulously. Was Wilson kidding? Or was it just hard for her brother to give her any credit for finding a really good band? "Pretend it's not me you're talking to. Pretend the video came from one of your other talent scouts."

Again she heard Wilson sigh. She held her breath,

waiting. "Okay, more than some. How soon can you get this guy out here? I want to hear him for myself."

She had her doubts about Liam and his band dropping everything and flying out to Los Angeles at a moment's notice. From what she'd observed, that wasn't the way things seemed to operate around here.

"Well, if you want the full Forever Band experience, I think you're going to have to come out here and listen to them play in surroundings they're comfortable with."

Wilson snorted, clearly insulted. "In what scenario does the mountain come to Mohammed?"

"In the scenario where the mountain wants to make money," she replied calmly.

There was silence again on the other end and she knew Wilson was weighing his options—his pride versus his business acumen. When he spoke again, she had a feeling that the acumen had gotten the upper hand. "I'll look at my schedule and get back to you later today," Wilson told her. "How about you? You leaving this hole-in-the-wall anytime soon?" he asked. "Or do they have you chained in someone's basement?"

"No chains," she said simply. "My car's not ready yet. The mechanic's having trouble getting the parts that are needed."

"Take it to another mechanic," he advised.

"There is no other mechanic in this town," she told him.

"Huh." The sound was exceedingly dismissive and pregnant with covert meaning. "You ask me, you're being played."

Ah, but I didn't ask you, did I?

Whitney knew better than to say that out loud. It

would only get Wilson's back up and send him off on yet another round of lectures.

"Thanks for the input, Will. Call me back later about your schedule. The band sounds even better in person than they do on that video," she promised.

"We'll see," he responded evasively.

This time when the dead air against her ears registered, she took it as a natural progression of things. Wilson never said hello or goodbye. He was of the opinion that actions always spoke louder than any words he could possibly use.

Pushing back her chair, Whitney rose from the small desk. She was mildly surprised that exhaustion hadn't caught up with her yet. After all, she hadn't slept except to rest her eyes a couple of times during the night when she'd put her head down on the desk. However she'd hardly closed her eyes for more than a few minutes at a time and no self-respecting feline would even allow what she'd done to be called a catnap.

She paused for a moment, wondering if she should try to get at least an hour or so of sleep before heading out to the diner for some breakfast. After all, it wasn't as if she was exactly facing a full agenda.

For the first time in years, she was actually at loose ends. She could, of course, ask the owner of Murphy's— the *head* owner, she amended—if any other bands played at his saloon or if that was strictly Liam's spot. But after she received her answer—and she had a strong suspicion that Liam and his band were the sole occupants of that position—there was nothing left for her to actually *do*…unless, of course, her car was ready. However, she had a strong suspicion that it wouldn't be.

Now what? You always keep talking about what

*you'd do if you had some downtime. Well, congratu-
lations, Whit. This is officially downtime. Now what?*
the voice in her head repeated.

She had no answer. Some people, she concluded,
weren't built for inactivity—and she most definitely
was one of them.

She didn't do "nothing" well.

Walking up to the door of her suite, she pulled it
open just as Liam was about to knock on the other side.
Her forward momentum caused her to lose her balance
and all but fall into him.

To keep her from stumbling, Liam instinctively
made a grab for her. He wound up pulling her against
his hard torso.

Rather than act surprised, he merely smiled at her
and said, "Hi. I came to take you to breakfast."

She congratulated herself for not yelping like an
idiot. Instead, she had pulled herself together and
calmly said, "Sounds like a plan." Then, when Liam
continued standing where he was, his arms still very
much around her, Whitney asked, "Doesn't your plan
involve walking out of here?"

He smiled into her eyes, bringing her body temperature up by five degrees.

"It does," he answered.

Her breath was just about solidifying in her lungs.
She managed to push out a single word. "Today?"

His smile only grew wider as Liam assured her,
"Absolutely."

*Keep talking, Whit. Keep talking. He can't kiss a
moving target—no matter how much you really want
him to,* she upbraided herself.

"Then what seems to be the problem?" she asked him after a beat.

"No problem," he said easily, then went on to tell her honestly, "I just like the way it feels to have my arms around you so I thought—if you don't have any objections—that I'd just absorb that feeling a little bit longer."

Okay, there went her heart, she thought, going into double time. She had to get this under control, get out in front of it before she just gave in to the desires that were beginning to blossom—big-time—inside of her.

"How much is 'a little bit longer'?" she asked.

The end of her question was punctuated not just with an implied question mark, but her stomach made a gurgling sound, the kind of sound that went along with someone missing a meal—or two.

"I believe time has been called," Liam said, instantly raising his hands in an upward position, dramatically releasing her.

Just in time, she thought with relief. She'd been inches away from giving in to the overwhelming desire she had to kiss him.

Clearing her throat, she asked, "Where are we going for breakfast?"

"Same place we'd go for lunch and dinner," Liam replied. "Miss Joan's diner."

"There really is no other place to eat in town?" Because of where she came from, she was having a great deal of trouble wrapping her mind around the concept.

"Not unless someone invites you over to their home for a meal," he said.

"So Miss Joan has a monopoly," Whitney concluded. "That doesn't exactly encourage the woman to put her best foot forward and make sure the meals are fresh, satisfying and inexpensive."

"If you think that," Liam told her, "then you *really* don't know Miss Joan. That lady is always making sure her cooks use the freshest cuts, the best selections, and looking for bargains is second nature to her.

"It might just look like another greasy spoon," he continued, growing a shade more defensive of the woman who was dear to them all, "but nothing could be further from the truth. Angel Rodriguez is in charge of the kitchen and she's always trying out new recipes as well as keeping some of the older favorites on the menu.

"It's probably the closest think to home cooking my brothers and I have had in years," he said.

Whitney laughed and shook her head. "You make Miss Joan's diner sound like it's a slice of heaven."

"If heaven came in slices," he said, using her analogy, "then Miss Joan's would certainly be a top contender." They were outside now and despite the slight chill in the air, the sun was out and it promised to be a perfect day. Liam debated walking to the diner rather than taking his truck. Walking won out. "You got any plans for this morning and early afternoon?" he asked her.

Plans were something she could make once she was mobile again. Lengthening her stride, Whitney kept up with him. "That all depends on if my car's ready or not."

Liam was way ahead of her when it came to a status report on her car. He had made it a point to swing by the mechanic's corner shop on his way over to the hotel.

"I just checked with Mick," he told her as gently as

he could, sensing the news might upset her. "I think you might have to go with 'or not' for the time being."

"Then I guess I have no plans," Whitney said as they walked into the diner. "Why?"

"Good, because you have plans now," Miss Joan informed her in the same cadence a drill sergeant might use if he were trying to soften his approach to shouting out orders on a regular basis.

"Excuse me?" Whitney asked. She cocked her head as if that would make her hear better—or at least absorb what was being said better. She was certain that she couldn't have heard Miss Joan correctly. The woman wasn't ordering her around—was she?

"You'll be helping the rest of us finish decorating the tree," Miss Joan told her in no uncertain terms. "Can't have it standing there like that, half-done, now can we?"

The question was pointedly directed at her.

"Not if I can help it." Whitney meant it as a joke, saying the sentence tongue in cheek. However, judging by the look on Miss Joan's thin face, the woman seemed to accept her statement at face value.

"Glad to have you join us," Miss Joan continued, her face softening just a tad as her eyes swept over Liam and then back to the stranger in their midst.

Something akin to approval had the old woman's mouth curving in just the smallest of smiles.

Now what was all that about? Whitney couldn't help wondering. She strongly doubted that her mere presence was enough to get the owner of the diner to appear so pleased. It had to be something else.

But, looking around, she saw nothing out of the

ordinary—except that all the stools at the counter were filled and it looked as if no one had ordered anything yet.

That could only mean one thing. This had to be Miss Joan's work crew, Whitney thought. These were Miss Joan's dedicated Christmas Elves.

The label had Whitney smiling to herself.

Liam leaned over and asked in a hushed voice, "What's so funny?"

"I wouldn't know where to begin," Whitney whispered back.

"At the beginning would be my first suggestion, but anywhere you feel comfortable would be my next one. In the meantime," he continued when she didn't say anything, "why don't we order you some breakfast?"

Not waiting for her to agree, Liam raised his hand to catch the attention of any of the waitresses currently working in the diner.

Less than thirty seconds later, a dark-haired young woman with deep brown eyes was heading their way. She looked to be no older than about nineteen. "Can I get you anything?" she asked.

Liam turned toward Whitney and asked, "What would you like?"

A repeat of last night's kiss were the first words that streaked across Whitney's brain. Startled, she quickly banked them down. "How about just coffee and toast?"

Liam nodded, but when he placed the order with the waitress, it had somehow managed to expand. "The lady will have coffee, toast and an order of scrambled eggs, sausage and hash browns. And so will I," he added, flashing a smile at Whitney.

"Is someone else joining us?" Whitney asked him the moment the waitress withdrew. "Because that wasn't my order."

"No," he agreed. "But I thought you might need your strength. You can always leave whatever you don't want to eat on your plate," Liam told her, then added, "You look a little tired. Rough night?"

"No night," she answered. "That is, I didn't get any sleep. I was too busy editing the video."

"Video?" he repeated, confused. She hadn't mentioned anything like that last night when he'd dropped her off at the hotel. "What video?"

She looked at him. Hadn't he seen her taping him and his band last night? "One I took of you and the band performing at the saloon. Didn't you see me recording?" she asked in surprise.

"All I saw was you."

Now, why did a simple phrase like that suddenly send waves of heat all through her body, taking her from a nice, stable 98.6 to practically 100 plus in less time than it took to scramble those eggs that he had ordered for her breakfast?

Don't dwell on it, she commanded herself. There were no answers that way, only more questions. Questions and a whole nest of desires that could *not* be addressed at this time—if ever.

Clearing her throat, she went back to the subject under discussion. "Well, I had my smartphone in my hand and I was filming you and your band. I got a handful of your songs and then I stayed up editing and tweaking the footage until it popped."

The term seemed out of place where she used it. "It broke?" he asked her.

"No, it popped," she repeated, then realized that he *had* heard her. He just didn't understand what she meant. "That means it was perfect," she explained.

"Oh." He grinned at the compliment. "Then why didn't you say so?"

"I thought I did," Whitney countered. She had to remember that they were rather out of the loop here—or maybe she was just from a place where pretentiousness abounded, she amended. In that case, she needed to watch that and rein herself in.

A beat later, Liam lifted his shoulders in a dismissive shrug. "Guess I need to brush up my language skills. Anyway, Miss Joan said that everyone's to come and finish working on the tree today. Personally, I think it's going to take an extra day—if not two, before we're finished." He wrapped his hands around the coffee mug, absorbing its heat. "This is some monster we brought off the mountain," he quipped. "It's enough to give a guy a complex. Couldn't even finish decorating a simple little Christmas tree."

Her basic instincts had always been protective and now were no different. "It's neither little nor simple," she told him.

"When you two are finished," Miss Joan said, delivering their breakfasts to them personally, "get yourselves on down to the town square and get started." The woman began to leave, then remembered something. Turning around, she said, "Oh, by the way, your breakfasts are on me."

Liam protested and began taking out his wallet. Miss Joan's eyes narrowed.

"Keep your money, boy. I intend to take the amounts out in trade. That tree needs to be decorated," she repeated. "The sooner that's done, the sooner our holiday season kicks into gear—even if the weather doesn't want to cooperate."

With that, she disappeared into the kitchen.

Chapter Thirteen

Whitney found herself hurrying through the meal she initially hadn't even wanted. All it had taken was one bite, coupled with the tempting aroma of warm, crisp bacon, to resuscitate her appetite. She realized that she actually *was* hungry.

Even so, the reason behind her powering through the meal wasn't spurred on because of hunger but because she was far more focused on what would happen once breakfast was out of the way.

Her speedy consumption did not go unnoticed. "Any particular reason you're eating as if you just went the last forty-eight hours without any food?" Liam asked, amused as he watched her clean her plate at lightning speed.

Whitney spared him a quick glance, then went back to eating. "So Miss Joan doesn't come out and lecture me about wasting food."

"And?" he asked, waiting for her to tell him the real reason.

Whitney raised her eyes again. Okay, he'd caught her. She supposed there was no shame in admitting this.

"And I want to get back to decorating the tree,"

she confessed. When her mouth curved, he could have sworn the smile that graced her lips was on the shy side. "I forgot how much fun it could be."

He hoped that he would never get so busy that he put his personal life and family traditions on hold. Curious about the woman he'd rescued, Liam asked, "When was the last time you decorated a Christmas tree?"

Whitney paused for so long, he thought she'd decided not to answer him. And then, to his surprise, she told him. "The year before my mother…left."

She looked uncomfortable about her admission. He wondered why.

"Left," Liam repeated. "Is that a euphemism or…?"

"It's a description," she replied, doing her best to sound distant and having very little luck about it. "My mother left." Even now, so many years later, the words she was uttering felt as if they were comprised of cotton and sticking to her tongue and throat. "She took off with this guy who was a couple of years older than Wilson, my oldest brother."

Her expression was rueful as she continued. "Christmas was canceled that year. And the year after that. There didn't seem to be much point in celebrating it. My father had never been much for that kind of thing anyway—it was my mother who handled the holiday celebrations, the buying and wrapping of presents, things like that. My father was always too busy earning a living."

She sighed, struggling not to sound bitter. "I think that's why she took up with Roy in the first place. My mother was a beautiful woman—she always looked as if she'd just stepped out of a fashion magazine—

and Roy paid attention to her. He talked with her—not at her—and just like that, my mother was in heaven.

"And then my father found out about Roy and he gave her an ultimatum. It was him or Roy." Whitney paused for a moment as she struggled to gain some sort of control over herself, keeping the words she was saying from hurting her. "She picked Roy—and just like that, she was gone."

Leaning in, Liam asked her gently, "How old were you?"

"Eleven." Her meal finished, Whitney pushed the plate away and squared her shoulders. "So to answer your question, the last time I decorated a Christmas tree, I was eleven."

Finished as well, Liam rose to his feet and smiled at her. "Then let's get started. You've got a lot of time to make up for," he said. One hand lightly pressed against the lower portion of her spine, he gently guided her out of the diner.

Even with several blocks between the diner and the town square, she could hear the happy squeals of children enjoying themselves.

It warmed her heart.

The moment she approached the semi-decorated giant Scotch pine in the square, Whitney began to *feel* like a kid again.

There was something almost magical about the experience and the fact that she was sharing it with someone—with the man she quite literally owed her life to—just made it that much more meaningful, that much more special for her.

Because, once she was up close, the tree was so tall and so wide, several very tall ladders had been recruited and arranged in what amounted to a circle around the Scotch pine. The working theory was that with these ladders positioned for use, all the high places could be reached and decorated, as well.

That particular task would be handed over to the tallest residents of Forever, since their reach was higher than the average person's.

But that would come later. For now, there was an interweaving of bodies as young and old pitched in to make the tree presentable and uniquely theirs.

A lot of the town's citizens came and joined in for short periods of time, but most of them had work or classrooms they had to get to, some with passes stamped with a definite return time.

Whitney had no timetable to follow, no time when she had to return because she needed to be somewhere else. Consequently, decorating the tree, helping with myriad details that went along with the festive occasion, turned into almost an all-day affair.

Because her car was still with Mick, she had nowhere she needed to be. Wilson hadn't gotten back to her regarding his schedule, so for the time being, she was freer than she'd been in a very long time.

Free to enjoy herself in any way she saw fit.

And free to spend time with Liam, a man she found herself increasingly attracted to, despite her own firm promises to herself that she was not about to fall into the very same trap that had been her mother's downfall.

Her mother's actions had ruined the family, splintered it because she'd run off with a younger man, leaving her husband and children behind.

Liam wasn't that much younger than she was, but

she would still be ignoring her responsibility to her family—just as her mother had done.

Whitney refused to even *remotely* repeat history.

So she immersed herself in the enormous task of Christmas tree decorating, in volunteering to be everywhere, do everything, all under the sharp eye of one Miss Joan.

"Girl, you're beginning to wear *me* out," Miss Joan protested later that day. "And I'm just standing down here, watching you. Pace yourself," she ordered, shading her amber eyes as she looked up at Whitney.

The latter was currently balancing her weight on the step second from the top of the ladder, bracing her thighs against it as she tried to extend her reach.

"And for God's sakes, don't lean like that!" Miss Joan shouted. "C'mon down and Liam here will move the ladder for you so you can hang that ornament up properly."

Ordinarily, that would have been enough to get her instructions carried out. But Whitney made no attempt to come down.

"Whitney!" Miss Joan shouted when Whitney gave no indication that she had even heard her, much less would do as she was told.

The words were no sooner out of Miss Joan's mouth than the entire ladder moved because Whitney had shifted her weight. Listing, it began to fall to the side. The next fraction of a second saw Whitney suddenly free-falling.

Impact with the ground below was imminent.

"I gotcha!" Liam yelled as he rushed over to the

exact point where she was about to do a bone-jarring, possibly bone-breaking touchdown.

Miraculously, Liam managed to catch her. But as he did so, because of the angle, his knees buckled. They made abrupt contact with the ground, hitting it so hard that he felt his teeth all but rattling in his head.

It took everything he had not to drop her, but he managed to hold on to Whitney even more tightly.

Whitney heard him sucking in air, as if that would somehow shield him from the pain she knew he had to be experiencing.

The second she'd stopped falling and Liam came to a resting position, Whitney scrambled out of his arms. Her knees felt wobbly, but she wasn't the one she was worried about.

She looked at Liam with concern. Impact could have shattered his knees or a thigh bone. "Are you all right?" she cried.

He tried to smile and found that it took more effort than he normally expended.

"I think I'm probably two inches shorter now, but yeah, I'm all right." After struggling up to his feet, deliberately ignoring the hand she'd extended to him, Liam looked her over quickly. "Are you?"

Whitney shrugged away his question. "Other than feeling terminally stupid, I'm fine." And then her expression softened. "That's twice you saved me in less than a week," she pointed out. "If you hadn't caught me just then, I could have broken my back, or injured my spleen, or—"

She found she had to stop talking because he'd laid his index finger against her lips.

"The point is, you didn't. And the next time I catch you going up a ladder, I won't."

"You won't what?"

"I won't catch you," he told her. "You'll be on your own then. Why are you grinning?" he asked.

Her smile was warm and inviting. She was onto him.

"Because you talk big, but once a hero, always a hero," she told him, then quickly added, "That doesn't mean I plan to be reckless again. Hell, I didn't plan on being reckless to begin with. Things just devolved into that state. I'm sorry if I worried you," she apologized quietly, knowing he didn't want to attract attention to what he'd just done. "And thank you—again—for saving me."

He laughed shortly. Gratitude always left him wondering how to respond. "Yeah, well, don't mention it—and if you're really grateful—"

"Yes?" she asked, finding she had to coax the words out of his mouth.

"You'll decorate the lower branches," Liam said, pointing to that area on the tree.

Whitney turned to look at it. That particular level had been long since taken care of by Forever's children, mostly the ones under the age of eight.

"I think if the lower branches get one more decoration hung on them, the tree'll sink deep into the ground. That's a lot of concentrated weight all in a small radius."

"Then shift it," Miss Joan suggested. When Whitney continued to look at her, Miss Joan gave her a demonstration. She plucked a small decoration depicting a classic cartoon character getting all caught up in wrapping tape and paper, suffering the unfortunate state with a display of anger that was typical for this particular character.

Reaching up higher, where no child could manage to reach, Miss Joan hung up the ornament.

"See? Easy." Dusting off her hands, she signaled that her association with the decorations was now purely in an advisory capacity. "Now you do it," she told Whitney. Glancing at Liam, she added, "You, too, sunshine."

Liam gave her a mock-salute and began to shift every third decoration to a higher level.

IT FELT AS IF every bone in her body had gotten caught up in this tree-decorating venture. And now, with the tree finally dressed in all its decorative finery, those muscles and tendons were all issuing formal complaints.

With enthusiasm.

She was so tired that when Miss Joan's remaining helpers had retreated back to the diner for dinner, Whitney had trouble picking up her cup of freshly brewed coffee and bringing it to her lips.

Sitting there and trying to regroup, she was definitely too tired to chew. The idea of dinner had no appeal to her.

"I don't think I have *ever* felt this bone weary," she told Liam.

"Maybe it has something to do with the fact that you just spent the last eight hours climbing, stretching, lifting and practically being two places at once. That tree wouldn't have been finished today if not for you. Have you always been an overachiever?" Liam asked.

Whitney laughed at his question. "In my world, that's just being a plain old achiever."

"Wow. It's a wonder that you all don't burn out by the time you hit thirty," Liam marveled.

"Well, since I've already hit that so-called milestone, I guess I should consider that a compliment," she replied.

"Lady," he said, "everything about you suggests a compliment. You are, quite honestly, the most beautiful woman I've ever seen."

"I take it you don't get out much," she commented.

"I get out plenty," he assured her.

Whitney took out her phone and glanced at the screen.

"I didn't hear it ring," he said, assuming that was why she'd taken out the cell phone.

"That's because it didn't," she replied. "I was just checking to see if I missed a call." Closing the cover, she slipped the phone back into her pocket. "I didn't," she said with a sigh.

"You're not eating," Miss Joan accused, coming over to their table.

"Too tired to eat," Whitney told the woman.

"Well, you did a bang-up job and I owe you a steak dinner anytime you want to take me up on it," Miss Joan said. "I always pay my debts," she added with a wink.

"Ready to go?" Liam asked her.

She nodded. "More than ready."

Getting up, Whitney found that she wasn't quite as mobile as she thought. "Give me a second to get my legs in gear."

"I could carry you to the truck," Liam offered with a grin.

It sounded rather tempting, but the last thing she wanted was to be the center of attention.

"I'll take a rain check on that," she said, moving slowly toward the exit.

THE TRIP BACK to the hotel was short. Just as Liam pulled up to the entrance, Whitney's curiosity got the better of her.

"This morning, just before we left the diner, Miss Joan called you 'Sunshine.' Isn't that kind of an odd name to call a guy?" To her, it was a nickname best suited for a girl with long, flowing blond hair.

Turning the engine off, Liam shrugged. "It's a nickname she gave me years ago."

"Still doesn't explain why she calls you that," Whitney persisted.

There was no point in not answering her question. He'd stopped being embarrassed by it long ago. "It's because of my smile."

Whitney narrowed her eyes. "Your smile?"

Okay, maybe he was just a tad embarrassed about it, he decided. But he pushed on, thinking he probably had no choice in the matter. He had a feeling that Whitney would only keep after him until he gave her a satisfactory answer.

"Miss Joan claims it looks like sunshine when I'm really smiling." He shrugged. "I'd rather just drop the subject, okay?" he asked.

"Okay," Whitney agreed. It hadn't been her intention to make him uncomfortable. She'd just been curious. "But since we're talking about dropping it—"

"Yes?"

She forced herself to make eye contact even though

she felt like fidgeting inside and just staring at the truck's floor. "What I told you about my mother this morning, I'd rather just keep it between the two of us if you don't mind."

"I don't mind at all," he was quick to assure her. And then, because the moment seemed to call for it— or maybe because his guard was completely down, he said, "It seems kind of nice, keeping your secret." He paused for a moment. "It makes me feel close to you," he admitted.

"I would have thought that saving my life and my butt all in under a week's time would have done that," Whitney quipped.

"Well, it certainly didn't hurt," he agreed. Uncoupling his seat belt, Liam turned toward her and said, "Anytime you need saving, I'm your man."

Whitney immediately focused on the last part of his sentence.

I'm your man.

Ah, if only, she couldn't help thinking.

"Actually," he continued, slowly threading his fingers through her hair, "I'm your man no matter what it is that you need." Liam's voice was just barely above a whisper.

He'd been struggling with his reaction to her for the better part of the evening, especially during this short—and intimate—drive to the hotel.

Now, breathing in her perfume, sitting mere inches away from her, Liam couldn't think of anything else *but* her.

"I'll keep that in mind," she told him, her heart going into overdrive as she suddenly felt the space in the truck's cab shrink.

"You do that," Liam replied, his eyes caressing her face.

The next moment, he couldn't hold himself in restraint any longer. Leaning forward, he brought his mouth down on hers.

Unlike the other two times he had kissed her, this time the merest hint of contact shook his world. She'd unleashed a huge need in him, a void that for some unknown reason he felt only *she* could fill. She, with her unique way of dealing with life, with her almost childlike joy when it came to something so simple as decorating a Christmas tree, albeit a hugely oversize one.

Liam had always been lucky when it came to women. He'd had his share of women to make love with. But as much as he always got along with them and retained their friendship long after the fact, none of them had ever fired up his imagination and his soul the way that this one did.

Sitting beside her like this and not having her was sheer torture. He hadn't realized just how much torture until this very moment.

THIS WAS WRONG.

It went against everything she had said that she didn't want. Everything she'd promised herself she wouldn't do because that would mean following in her mother's footsteps.

Granted there were no husband and children gathered together in the wings, waiting to be abandoned, but the similarity between the two scenarios was impossible to miss. Her mother had run off with a younger man. Liam was younger than she was. She'd looked him up—public records were incredibly easy to access

if a person knew what they were doing, and she did.
She'd been right. He was close to being almost four
years younger than she was. While the span wasn't
nearly as much as the one that had existed between
her mother and Roy, it was still there, ready to haunt
her if she took any more of a misstep.

And yet—

And yet, she just couldn't find it in her heart to resist, to turn him away. Couldn't force herself to get
out of the truck and just walk into the hotel, leaving
him behind her.

She knew him well enough now to be confident
that he wouldn't follow her if she didn't want him to.

The trouble was she did.

Chapter Fourteen

"You're thinking too hard," Liam told her just before he leaned in and kissed first one side of her mouth, then the other. "I can practically see the steam coming out of your ears," he teased softly, brushing his lips across hers lightly.

Even before he began to kiss her, Whitney was melting. It wasn't just her body, but all her pep talks to herself that were dissolving right along with her.

"That steam has nothing to do with thinking," she whispered back.

"Oh?"

There was way too much innocence infused into that single word. She knew that *he* knew exactly what he was doing to her.

Even so, Whitney could feel herself responding that much more.

Wanting him that much more.

"Yes, 'oh,'" she said, doing her best to sound distant, or at least neutral. But she was failing miserably and she knew it.

The only thing that could save her—from her own desires, let alone his—was actual distance. She needed to put real distance between them.

"I'd better go in," Whitney announced in a shaky voice.

Liam nodded, understanding. He wasn't about to push what was clearly going on between them if she was the least bit uncomfortable about it. He'd just go home and take a shower. *An extra long, really cold shower,* he told himself. Maybe one that lasted an hour…or two.

Getting out of his truck, Liam came around to her side and opened the door for her. Whitney swung her legs out, went to stand, and her knees seemed to have liquefied.

The second she began to sink, she made a grab for Liam to keep herself from hitting the ground.

He was even quicker than she was. Steadying her, he closed his arms around her tightly.

"Are you all right?" he asked, his eyes sweeping over her, taking their own inventory.

Saying yes seemed ludicrous, given what had just happened, so she said, "Just a little wobbly." Whitney looked at him, embarrassed. "Just give me a minute to get my land legs back," she said, doing her best to make a joke out of the situation.

"I've got a better idea," Liam said. The next moment, he scooped her up into his arms and began to walk to the hotel's entrance.

Caught off guard, Whitney cried, "What are you doing?"

He merely smiled at her as he shouldered open the entrance door. Moonlight streaming in through the surrounding glass illuminated the lobby as he carried her to her first-floor suite.

"I'm implementing my better idea," Liam answered easily.

"I *can* walk," Whitney protested. When he gave her a very dubious look, she amended her initial statement. "Eventually. It'll just take me a minute—or two," she murmured, thinking of her last experience.

One shoulder raised and lowered in a careless, dismissive shrug. "This saves time," he said.

She knew that Liam was just trying to be helpful, but unfortunately he was *way* too close to her. It was hard enough resisting the man when he was clear across the length of a room. Right now, she was close enough to him to breathe in the breath he exhaled.

In addition, being so close to Liam wreaked havoc on her resolve, on all her resolutions to just view him the way she did any other performer she'd signed for the family recording label.

Being close to Liam made her acutely aware of how drawn to the man she was.

Anticipation began to surface, taking her prisoner. Desire and passion suddenly became united, making demands, causing her willpower to sizzle away in the heat that was swiftly taking firm control of every inch of her body.

Whitney wasn't altogether sure just when she had laced her arms around the back of his neck. All she was truly aware of was that when he reached her suite and brought her inside, she didn't want to be here alone. Didn't want him to go.

Still holding her in his arms, he asked, "Are you okay to stand?"

"Yes," she answered much too quickly. When he began to set her down and one of her knees buckled, she had to change the "yes" to a "no" as she grabbed on to his shoulders.

"Maybe I should just put you on the bed," he suggested, indicating with his eyes the single queen-size bed behind her.

She barely turned her head to look. Pulses in her throat and wrists throbbed. Hard.

"Okay," she murmured.

But when he gently put her down, Liam found that she had wrapped her hands around the front of his jacket. When Whitney went down, so did he.

Caught by surprise, Liam wound up on top of the woman he was trying to help.

"Looks like you're not the only one who's lost their balance," he said.

She knew what he was doing. He was trying to give her a way out as a last resort.

Whitney didn't take it.

Didn't want to take it.

What she wanted this very moment, more than anything, was to feel his mouth on hers again. Feel his passion unleashing.

Still holding the front of his jacket, she yanked hard and managed to throw him off balance again just enough to get him to cover her body with his once more.

Coming in contact with the hardening contours of his torso sent a hot thrill all through her body.

At the same time, she raised her head and captured his lips with her own.

The kiss had *surrender* written all over it. Whether that was intended for him or a message to herself wasn't really clear, but since neither of them wanted a way out any longer tonight, it really didn't matter.

All that mattered was that they were right here, right now, and there was no one to argue them out of their feelings for one another.

She knew better than to be here…with him. But the chasm between knowing and doing could be leagues long and, right now, all she wanted was for Liam to make her feel wanted.

Feeling loved would have been even better, but she wasn't a child. She knew that this wasn't happy-ever-after. That happened in fairy tales. She only wanted a little happiness that existed for a few hours.

Liam would appreciate that. After all, what man Liam's age was looking for forever, anyway? A golden evening, or stellar weekend, was the longest period of time she felt she could possibly hope for.

It was enough.

Or so she told herself. The world she came from didn't have lasting relationships. All she had to look to were her parents to know that.

THE MOMENT SHE pulled him down onto her, the second she locked her lips with his, Liam realized that he was essentially a goner. He was utterly, hopelessly intrigued by this woman. Noble instincts could only last for so long and Whitney had melted his away in the heat of her mouth as it went questing over his.

His head spinning, his lips completely occupied, Liam began to caress her body. With each pass of his hands, he became more and more possessive of her, making her his own.

Rather than shrink back, Whitney pushed herself

against his hands. The small noises that escaped her lips, the tiny catches in her breath, all urged him on to greater plateaus.

He peeled her out of her clothing, one garment at a time, one side at a time.

For every item that he pulled away from her twisting, damp body, one was dragged away from his. She became as bold as he was and it only heightened his desire for her.

Their bodies became more and more entangled with one another.

Her breath grew shorter and shorter. She just couldn't seem to get enough of him. But still, a distant image of her mother wrapped up in Roy's arms haunted her. Haunted her to the point that even now, in the middle of their communal explorations, she lifted her head and asked, each word an effort, "Are you sure that you're just twenty-seven?"

The question took him aback, but only for a moment. With his heart hammering wildly, he told her, "I'll be anything you want me to be, any age. Whatever makes you happy." Framing her face with his hands, he looked into her eyes and whispered, "It's just a number, nothing else."

Then, to make his case and to get her mind off something that should have had absolutely no bearing on what they were feeling at this moment, Liam began to stroke her body, *really* stroke it, his lips softly trailing in the wake of his fingers, kissing every part of her that he had just touched.

He could tell by the way her breathing became more labored, more shallow, that he had succeeded in stirring her up even further.

Liam caressed and made love to each and every part of her for as long as he could hold himself in check. He brought her to her first climax by deftly using both his mouth and his fingers to stimulate her and bring her up and over to the ecstasy they both craved.

Her pleasure only intensified his own.

IT WAS AT THAT moment that Whitney realized that while she'd had sex before, she had never experienced lovemaking until just now. What her body was going through—what *she* was going through—felt so very different from those other times.

It felt so different that had anyone asked her to describe what was happening to her, she would have been hard-pressed to find the words to properly—or even improperly—describe it.

The closest she could come was to say that fireworks were going off inside, the kind that created rainbows and light shows in the sky.

The kind that had her holding on to him for dear life, wanting more, afraid of having it all end.

Did anyone die of ecstasy?

It was, she discovered, exquisite agony—and she was gripping it as hard as she could, by just her fingertips.

Liam finally drew the length of his body up along hers. She wiggled beneath him in heightened anticipation. With his eyes locked on hers, Liam balanced his weight between his elbows, and then he entered her.

The second he did, her breathing became more audible, her body tensed for a split second, then instantly became more fluid. Her mouth curved beneath his. A surge of excitement coursed through her veins.

Liam began to move his hips.

Whitney mimicked every move, grasping his shoulders so hard it was almost as if letting go would suddenly cause her to slip away from the earth's gravitational pull and she would go drifting through space.

The urgency within her made the rhythm more frantic as they both scrambled toward the peak that they knew waited to be claimed.

When they finally reached it a fraction of a moment later, a shower of euphoria rained on them, drenching them both.

"Incredible," Liam said, smiling and holding on to the feeling, holding on to *her*, for as long as he possibly could.

"Incredible," she echoed.

Something within him hoped the moment would last forever.

But it didn't.

And as it slowly faded away beyond their grasp, reality was there, waiting for them, waiting as they came spiraling down to earth.

He knew the second it happened for her. Her heart abruptly ceased pounding hard in double time.

Even so, it slowly settled down to a normal beat, although that took some time.

The euphoria created in the wake of their lovemaking might have been gone, but the feelings he'd had when this had all begun were still very much with him. Feelings of protectiveness, of tenderness, still flourished within his heart.

But along with those, there was another feeling, one that was entirely new to him.

It was a feeling that he'd thought he'd experienced once or twice in his life. But even so, when he tried to examine that feeling, it would suddenly just fade away, disappearing entirely as if it had never existed at all.

But this time, as he tried to explore it, the feeling remained just where it was, as strong as it had been at its inception. Liam had a very strong feeling that this time, what he was experiencing wouldn't disappear no matter how much time he gave it.

So many sensations were slamming into him, making him want things, tugging him in all different directions at the same time. He took a breath, trying to pull himself together so he could sort things out.

Gathering her to him, he kissed the top of her head. He could feel himself wanting her all over again. "See? I told you," he said softly.

She twisted so that she could see at least part of his face, her cheek rubbing against his hard, bare chest. "Told me what?"

"That age didn't matter." And then he grinned, mischief gleaming in his eyes. "You kept up just fine, granny."

Doubling up her fist, Whitney punched his arm.

"Ouch!" he cried, pretending that her punch had actually hurt.

"Is this the part where you say love hurts?" he asked, tongue in cheek.

The word pulled her up short. "Love?" she repeated in stunned disbelief.

Was he implying that he thought she loved him—or was he saying that he was entertaining stronger emotions than those made of wet tissues? Either way, she knew she couldn't ask him. That would put both of them on the spot no matter which answer he gave.

Most likely, he'd lie to hide the truth—or tell her the truth and hide it amid a joke.

One way or the other, she wasn't going to get to the truth of the situation tonight. Quite possibly never.

The only path opened to her was to just brazen it out.

"Who said anything about love?" she asked as flippantly and nonchalantly as she could.

"Well, since the voice was rather deep, I'm guessing it was me," he said, doing his best to keep a straight face. "Gonna hold it against me?" he asked.

"No, of course not," she said quickly. The last thing she wanted was for him to say anything he didn't want to say.

How had this gotten so complicated so quickly?

"You just said it in the heat of the moment," she reasoned.

"It wasn't the moment that was hot," he replied, his eyes slowly assessing the length of her. All that accomplished was to make himself crazy all over again, Liam thought. "It was me—and it was you. And if I get a vote in this, I was kind of hoping you would hold it against me—right along with that delicious body of yours," he said.

Whitney was certain that she wasn't understanding him correctly. Her brain felt muddled and all she could really think of was making love with him again—she had to be losing her mind.

Where the hell was her sense of self-preservation? she silently demanded.

She shook her head as if to try to clear it, even though she knew that wouldn't accomplish anything. "What?"

"Guess I'm not making myself clear. Looks like I'm just going to have to show you," he said out loud. "I'm better at showing than telling, anyway," he told her just before he went on to demonstrate just what he meant by sealing his mouth to hers.

Whitney slipped willingly back into the land of ecstasy—right alongside of the man who took her there.

Chapter Fifteen

The rhythmic buzzing noise wouldn't stop.

It wormed its insistent way into Whitney's consciousness like a malcontented intruder, ultimately dissolving her sleep.

Reluctantly, after several tries, Whitney finally managed to pry her eyes open. Only when she finally succeeded did she realize that she'd fallen asleep. The next moment, she became aware of the fact that she hadn't fallen asleep alone.

Bolting upright, her heart racing, she found herself looking down into Liam's peaceful face. He was still asleep—or at least it looked that way to her.

However, the next moment, with his eyes still closed, she heard Liam ask, "Aren't you going to get that? I think it's your cell phone. I turned mine off last night."

Disoriented, Whitney scanned the room, trying to home in on where the sound was coming from so she could find her phone.

"It's okay, you can get up," he murmured, barely opening his eyes so that they formed slits. "I won't peek if that's what you're afraid of."

"It's a little late for that," she murmured under her

breath. He was right, though. She couldn't spot her phone if she stayed in bed. Whitney got up.

"Glad you feel that way," he responded, opening his eyes all the way. He made no attempt to pretend that he wasn't looking at her. Seeing her like that stirred him all over again. "You're just as beautiful in the morning light as you looked last night," he told Whitney.

The compliment both pleased her and upset her at the same time. She loved making love with Liam but even so, she was annoyed with herself for not having enough inner strength to resist him.

Playing a hunch, Liam leaned over the side of the bed and looked under it. The phone was there, having somehow been kicked under her bed during the initial frenzy last night. Retrieving it now, Liam held the phone out to her.

It was still buzzing.

"Better answer it before they hang up," he advised. His eyes washed over her possessively. "Sounds important."

Whitney flushed, embarrassed, as she took the phone from him. "Hello?"

"You sure took your sweet time answering." The deep, critical voice was unmistakable. Wilson. "Where were you?"

Talk about bad timing, she thought. Leave it up to her older brother to interrupt things. The only way it would have been any worse was if he had called her while she and Liam were in the middle of making love. She supposed she should be grateful for smaller favors.

"Sorry, I was in the shower," she apologized, saying the first thing that popped into her head. Out of the corner of her eye, she saw Liam's amused expression. She turned her head away.

"Well, dry yourself off and get ready to pick me up at the airport," Wilson informed her. He rattled off the airline and flight number. "It's supposed to be landing in an hour, but you know how reliable *that* is. I'm just hoping to get there before evening—it'll mess up my return time," he told her before she could ask.

She braced herself for her brother's disapproval. "I can't pick you up, Will. My car's being repaired, remember?"

She could almost *see* the frown burning itself into his face. She certainly heard it in his voice when he asked, "And there're no other cars in this town?"

"None that are mine," she answered. "I could see if I might be able to rent someone's truck for a couple of hours," she offered.

"A truck?" Wilson echoed in clear disdain. He sounded as if she'd just suggested he gather several pigs together and wallop in the mud with them. "Never mind, I'll rent a car at the airport."

"Do you want directions on how to get here?" she asked, struggling to come across as helpful.

In actuality, she was finding it increasingly more difficult to think straight because Liam was tracing patterns with his fingertips along her bare spine, then following his tracings with a light trail of kisses, none of which was conducive to coherent thought.

"Thanks, but if my GPS can't locate your hick town, I'm turning around and booking a flight home immediately," Wilson told her.

And then he was gone.

With a sigh, Whitney put her phone on the night-stand.

"He upset you," Liam noted, turning her so that she partially faced him.

She pulled the sheet up around herself. "He's my brother. He thinks that's his job." And then she forced herself to brighten. "But the good news is that the video I sent him of you and the band impressed him enough for Will to come out here to see you perform in person."

She just wished her brother had given her a heads-up about *when* he was coming here instead of just turning up, so she could have been more prepared.

"If you and the band play even half as well as you did the other night, I think you can consider yourselves on your way to fame and fortune." She grinned at Liam. "You'll get the life you've always wanted."

"Well, if that *does* happen, then you're the lady who *made* it happen," he said.

Then, just like that, he pulled her into his arms and kissed her soundly, putting his heart into it.

Whitney knew she should be getting both herself—and Liam—ready, but all she could think of was making love with him again. When she was with him, she completely forgot to be logical.

"Liam," she breathed, her head spinning. "You have to stop that. I can't think when you do that."

"Funny, me, neither," he admitted just before he kissed her again.

After that, everything else was put on temporary hold.

WILSON MARLOWE'S DARK BROWN eyes missed nothing. He looked slowly around Murphy's. His reaction was not particularly difficult to gauge in view of the disdainful expression on his rather thin face.

Murphy's was not up to his standards. It had been a long time since he had haunted places like this, looking for unnoticed talent.

"I flew all the way from LA for this?" he asked his sister.

"No, you flew all the way from Los Angeles to see the band perform in person," she reminded him. "'This' is just where they play. Besides, I think this place is quaint. It grows on you."

"Maybe on you, but I have standards," Wilson informed her dismissively. A sound that was close to a laugh escaped his lips. "I guess this means I won't be involved in a bidding war to get them to sign a contract with Purely Platinum. I'm still undecided about signing them at all," Wilson was quick to add when he saw the hopeful expression cross Whitney's face.

Wilson's flight had been delayed a number of hours and when he finally arrived in Forever, he was in less than good spirits.

"Well, I hope this trip convinces you of their talent," she said. The moment he crossed the threshold to the saloon, Whitney could feel her whole body instantly grow tense. She wanted this break for Liam and his band in the worst way. She was going on instincts, something she had honed over the past ten years, and she believed in Liam and the Forever Band. The band—especially Liam—was talented and had a great deal of potential.

But Wilson was the type who allowed more than just appreciation of good performers guide the decisions he ultimately made. There were times when she had

seen him pass on a performer because he had taken a
basic dislike to them for no apparent reason. In general, Wilson was good, but he was not above pettiness.

"Do all these other people have to be here?" he
asked Whitney, waving his hand around the room to
generally include all the other patrons.

"Will, they're paying customers here. I can't ask
Brett to clear the place so that the acoustics are better,"
she protested. "Besides, don't you want to see how the
performers interact with their audience?"

"Audience," he repeated, as if exploring the term.
"Don't you mean the people who they've known all
their lives?" His contempt was obvious. "Not particularly. They like them," he observed, listening to the wel-
coming applause just before the band played their first
number. "Big surprise," he snorted.

He was going to be difficult about this, Whitney
thought. And yet, he'd come all this way, so he had to
believe it was worth the effort. Her brother never did
anything just to be accommodating.

"Wilson, why don't you try just listening and putting
your cynicism on hold for a change?" she suggested.

Wilson merely shrugged in response. But at least he
remained where he was rather than stalking out. With
Wilson, anything was possible. Having him here was
a small victory in itself.

Whitney mentally crossed her fingers and smiled
her encouragement to Liam and the rest of the band as
they began to play.

DURING THE NEXT forty-five minutes, Whitney slanted
a glance toward her brother several times, trying to
gauge whether or not Wilson liked what he was hear-

ing. On the one hand, she couldn't see how he couldn't, but on the other, he was Wilson and Wilson had always behaved unpredictably.

She honestly believed that her brother took a certain amount of satisfaction in being that way.

Finally, the last number was over and the band took a short break. During that entire set, Wilson hadn't said a single word and she just couldn't stand not knowing any longer.

"Well?" she asked eagerly. "What do you think of them?"

Wilson inclined his perfectly styled head slightly, as if considering her question for the very first time. "Good," he finally pronounced. "Needs work," he emphasized, then continued in a loftier tone, "but good." Looking at her, he asked, "When can he fly to LA?" he asked.

She felt elated and released the breath she'd been holding. Her brother liked the band!

"Well, you'd have to ask— Wait," she said, suddenly focusing on the exact words her brother had just used. "You just said 'he.'"

"Yes," he said coolly. "I know. Your point?"

He couldn't be saying what she thought he was saying. "Don't you mean when can the band fly out?"

His tone bordered on exasperated annoyance. "If I had meant the 'band,' I would have *said* the 'band.' Or, in a pinch, 'they.'" His eyes narrowed as he looked at her. "But I didn't, did I?"

No, he hadn't, she thought, getting a sinking feeling in the pit of her stomach. This wasn't going to go over well with Liam. The band meant a great deal to him.

He'd told her that the other men who made up the band had been his friends since first grade, or thereabouts.

"You only want Liam?" Whitney asked in a stilted voice.

"If that's his name, yes, I just want him," Wilson confirmed.

"Why don't you want the whole band?" Whitney challenged.

She knew in her heart that Liam would not go for this latest twist. Yes, he wanted to succeed, but he wanted the *band* to succeed, not just him.

That was one of the reasons she'd felt so drawn to him, because he was so very loyal. That was a rare emotion in her world, where artists sold out their own mothers for a decent review.

"Because there's nothing exceptional about them," Wilson replied, sounding as if the topic bored him. "This Liam guy, however, I think he can be marketed well. He has that whole chiseled, movie-star look going on for him, plus he's got a damn good voice."

"Yes, he does," she agreed with Wilson. "But he's not going to go for it—for breaking up the band," she warned her brother.

"Then it'll be his loss," Wilson predicted, sounding unmoved. "I'm not about to deal with some self-absorbed prima donna to start with."

"That's not being a prima donna," she said fiercely. "That's being loyal. You remember loyalty, don't you, Will? It's one of those admirable traits we shed like a second skin if it gets in our way. And by 'our,' I mean 'your,'" she emphasized.

Wilson remained unmoved and unaffected. "Potato, po*ta*to, it's all one and the same to me," he told her.

Just then, Liam reached their table. He was fairly radiating sheer energy, the way he always did after delivering what he considered to be a good performance.

"Well?" he asked, allowing his eagerness to break through, glancing from Whitney to her brother. "What did you think?" he asked the latter. After all, that was why he had come, Whitney had told him.

"I think you've got a big future ahead of you, kid," Wilson said, slipping into his public persona, which for the most part, was far less dour than the Wilson he allowed his siblings to see. "Big future," he repeated with emphasis.

"Oh, wow." Liam felt as if clouds had just been substituted for solid ground beneath his feet. To want something for so long and then to be within touching distance of it, Liam found it difficult to contain himself. "Wait'll the guys hear this. Sam kept saying that we'd never make it—"

Wilson made no apologies for cutting in. "He was right."

Liam looked at Whitney's brother in confusion. He hadn't liked the man all that much when he'd first met him today, but nowhere was it written that you had to like the man who "discovered" you. He made up for it by really liking Whitney. A lot.

Still, he wanted to get this straightened out if he could. "But you just said—"

"Will said that you're the one with potential, not the band," she clarified, her voice somber.

Liam gazed at her for a long moment, sheer confusion becoming very apparent on his face. "But we're a band," he protested.

"They're just so much background," Wilson corrected him. "You're the one with star potential. I thought we'd sign you, find the right kind of songs for you, find your brand so to speak. I know a couple of background musicians I can have come in to the studio to play with you, explore your sound."

"Wait. Wait, wait," Liam said, holding up his hand. This was going much too fast and he wanted to clear it all up before he found himself agreeing to something he had no intentions of agreeing with. "Are you really telling me that you don't want the band?"

Wilson shrugged. "They're okay, kid, but you're the one with star power—given the right material and guidance," Wilson qualified pointedly. "What do you say?"

Liam glanced at Whitney before giving her brother his answer. "I say that the band and I are a set—"

"Kid, take it from me, they'll just hold you back," Wilson interrupted. And then he counseled, "Think about it for a couple of days, then give me a call."

Going into his vest pocket, Wilson retrieved a business card. He pressed it into Liam's hand. "But I'm telling you now, this is a once in a lifetime deal and if I were you I'd jump to take it."

Liam looked at the business card, then at Whitney. "What do you say?"

She could feel Wilson watching her, willing her to go along with his decision. She knew there was no way around it.

"I say that I like you *and* the band, but it's not my call. Wilson has the final word on that." *For better or for worse,* she couldn't help thinking.

Then, Wilson did what he seldom did, he coaxed. "Don't be a fool, kid. Don't turn down the opportunity of a lifetime just because you think you owe those other guys something. Take my word for it, if the tables were turned, I guarantee that they'd jump at this opportunity and leave you behind in the dust. Loyalty isn't what it's cracked up to be," Wilson concluded. He looked at his watch. "I've got to be getting to the airport. My flight back is in a couple of hours."

Whitney looked at him in surprise. "You're not even staying the night?" It seemed as if he had put in an awful lot of miles for possibly nothing.

"What for?" Wilson was asking. "I came, I heard, I pitched a contract. That was what you wanted, right? Congratulations, you were right," he allowed. "The guy's good."

"I said the *band* was good," she corrected him.

"Then maybe there shouldn't be that much more congratulating," he said. "Either way, I'll sign pretty boy over there to a contract as long as I can get him into a studio in Los Angeles. There're big things ahead of him," he promised—and Wilson, she was the first to admit, was seldom wrong. "See you back in Los Angeles," he said.

He got up and walked out before she could speak further.

"That didn't exactly go the way I'd planned," she told Liam by way of an apology as she crossed over to him. "But he did like you," she was quick to point out.

"Doesn't matter," Liam said, shrugging off her comment. "There's no way that I'm going to break up the band, to walk out on guys I've known—and practiced with—ever since I was in elementary school with them."

She wanted him to carefully consider all his options

and not just dismiss the offer because he was angry that Wilson wasn't keen on the other members of the band.

"Liam, my brother really does have the kind of connections that will open doors and could easily make your career for you."

"I can't believe I'm saying this," he said quite honestly, "but there're some things that are more important than a career. If I jumped at this, leaving Sam and Christian and Tom behind, I wouldn't be able to look at myself in the mirror every morning."

"Liam, *think* of what you're turning down," Whitney pleaded.

"I am," he told her solemnly, his eyes on hers. He assumed that she was including herself in that package deal. If he said no to her brother, if he remained here, then it was over. That stellar experience he'd just had with her last night, that was over with, as well.

"Hey, there you are," Mick called out, striding toward Whitney. "Don't mean to interrupt you two, but I knew how anxious you were to get your car back, little lady, and I just wanted to let you know that it's all done. You can come by the shop anytime and we'll settle up. She's all yours and eager to go," Mick said with a laugh.

"I guess there's nothing keeping you here, then," Liam concluded, giving her a look that all but pulled her heart out of her chest. And then he nodded toward the band. "I've got to be getting back to the guys. It's time for the next set."

With that, he turned away from her and walked back to the band.

And managed to walk over her heart in the process.

Chapter Sixteen

She was gone.

Liam moved slowly through the hotel suite. There was absolutely no trace of her. No indication that she had ever been there.

Nothing.

He wasn't sure why he'd thought that he'd still find Whitney here, in the suite where his life had suddenly changed forever. Maybe it was because neither one of them had said the word *goodbye*.

Or maybe it was because the whole last scenario between them had seemed so surreal. In what world did the woman who turned out to be the answer to his prayers also have the ability to make his professional dreams come true?

It was more of a fantasy than reality.

In any case, part of him felt that a short time-out had been in order. But that had come and gone now. A full twenty-four hours had evaporated since everything had gone sour between Whitney and him.

He wanted a mulligan or whatever the current term was for what amounted to a do-over.

He *needed* a do-over.

Liam continued to move around the suite, searching

for some small item Whitney might have forgotten to pack, but there wasn't any. Nothing he could touch or hold in his hand.

Maybe he was going crazy, but he could detect just the faintest trace of the perfume she'd worn.

He stood very still for a moment, inhaling as deeply as he could. But all he succeeded in doing was somehow neutralizing that scent.

It was gone.

As was she.

He had to face it. Whitney was gone and so was his opportunity to apologize, to tell her that whether or not his career took off didn't matter to him—the only thing that mattered was her.

Feeling incredibly empty, he slowly closed the door to the hotel suite and went back to Murphy's. Work was waiting for him.

"Great job."

Wilson's words echoed in her head as Whitney recalled the satisfied expression on her brother's face when she'd brought him the Laredo band's signed contract. She had lived up to her promise, done what she had initially set out to do. She had auditioned the pop group—the drummer had bounced back faster than anyone had hoped and had attended, propped up in his chair. They'd turned out to be as good as their demo so she had signed them to a contract. Each side felt as if they had come out ahead. It was a mutually beneficial contract.

After delivering the contract to her brother, she'd thrown herself back into traveling and making the rounds at the various clubs where, on occasion, decent new talent could be found.

"Why don't you take some time off?" Wilson had suggested the next time she'd touched base with him. "You certainly have earned it—and by my reckoning, you haven't taken any time off in years."

"I want to work," she'd answered, summarily rejecting her brother's suggestion.

What was implied, but not said, was that she *needed* to work, needed to keep moving so that she could stay ahead of her thoughts, which were still far too melancholy for her to handle.

"Well, then, by all means, work," Wilson had told her, leaning back in his swivel chair. "I'm sure as hell not going to stand in your way because—and if you tell anyone, I'll deny it—you've become even better at spotting talent than I am."

She'd looked at him then, surprised. This was definitely out of character for her brother. If she didn't know any better, she would have checked his garage for a pod to see if he'd been cloned.

"You don't have to treat me with kid gloves, Will," she'd said.

"No kid gloves," he'd immediately denied, holding up his hands as if she had the right to inspect them. "Just respect. It's about time I gave you your due." Leaning over his desk, he'd handed her the newest list of possible up-and-comers she could go check out in person before she made any arrangements for future auditions. "That should keep you busy."

Whitney had tucked the list away in her pocket without even looking at it, only saying, "Good," before she'd left her brother's office.

Though she worked frantically, she still couldn't shake the feeling that she was sleepwalking through her life.

And she ached inside.

"HAVE YOU TRIED getting in touch with her?" Brett asked out of the blue two days before Finn's wedding.

He'd been watching Liam sitting on a bar stool, just staring off into space for the past twenty minutes. He'd voiced his concern for his youngest brother, concern over the fact that in the past two weeks, Liam had moved around like a man in a trance.

Liam went through the motions of being alive, tended bar, played with his band, but it was as if his very soul had gone missing. There was nothing about Liam that even remotely hinted at the man he'd been just a short while ago.

"Liam?" Brett said, raising his voice when he received no answer. "Earth to Liam."

The third time was the charm. Hearing his brother for the first time, Liam turned toward him and said, "Yeah?"

"Have you tried getting in touch with her?" Brett repeated.

Liam glanced away. "Who?" he asked innocently.

"The Tooth Fairy," Brett retorted. "Who do you think, lunkhead? That woman you saved from drowning. The one who's got your insides all tied up in knots."

"Nobody's got me tied up in knots," Liam denied angrily.

Brett frowned, shaking his head. "You could have fooled me."

"Apparently that's not hard to do," Liam answered listlessly.

Brett tossed aside the cloth he'd been using to polish the counter. "You want me to track her down?"

For the first time in two weeks, Liam came to life. His head whipped around as he faced his older brother and all but shouted, "Hell no!"

"All right," Brett agreed. His eyes narrowed as he pinned his younger brother in place. "Then you do it."

Liam raised and lowered his shoulders in a hapless shrug.

"Nothing to do," Liam told his brother.

"Look, you've been moping around for the last two weeks and frankly, we're all worried about you."

Liam deftly turned the tables around. "And I'm worried about you because if you have nothing better to do than sit around watching me, you're in a really bad way, Brett. What's the matter? Honeymoon over for you and Lady Doc?"

"Liam—" he began.

"Drop it, Brett," Liam warned his brother. "I mean it."

"Okay, then I've got a question for you. Are you going to be able to play at Finn's wedding or should I see if I can find someone else at this late date?"

Just because he was trying to function without a heart didn't mean he couldn't do right by Finn.

"Don't worry about it. The band and I have got this," he said, his tone of voice warning his brother to back off if the latter knew what was good for not just him but for everyone.

"I hope so," Brett said evenly. "Finn wants to give Connie the wedding of her dreams and that doesn't include a hangdog front man for the band." He looked pointedly at Liam.

"As I remember, the wedding of Connie's dreams involved getting married on Christmas Day and having newly fallen snow on the ground for their wedding pictures. That sure isn't going to happen, not down here."

"That's what I mean," Brett interjected. "He's already working with a slight handicap." Brett came across as relatively easygoing, but his hackles went up when it came to anything having to do with his brothers. "I don't want you to be another one."

"No problem," Liam assured him.

"You're going to be able to play even though it's in the town square?"

"Yeah, sure." Liam shrugged dismissively.

But Brett obviously didn't consider the matter settled yet. "Even though, ever since Whitney left, you've gone out of your way *not* to walk through the town square, specifically, not to walk by the Christmas tree?" Brett looked at him knowingly.

"What are you, following me now?" Liam demanded, stunned.

"Kid, this is Forever. *Nobody's* got secrets here no matter how hard they try." He didn't need to follow Liam to get his answers. If nothing else, Miss Joan was his conduit. He could always rely on the woman to clue him into things. "Now, one last time," Brett pressed the matter for Finn's sake. "Playing in the town square, with that tree *she* helped decorate in the background, that's not going to be a problem for you?"

"The only thing that's a problem for me right now is a nosy brother who doesn't know when to back off and stop asking so many insulting questions."

Brett slowly nodded. He'd developed a very tough skin years ago when he'd had to take over running Murphy's as well as raising his two younger, orphaned brothers. A thin-skinned person would have never been able to survive, coping with everything the way that he had.

Raising his hands up halfway, Brett declared, "This is me, officially backing off."

Liam merely grunted in acknowledgment as he left the saloon. He was late for rehearsal.

IT WAS THE NOISE that woke him. The sound of large trucks drawing closer.

Liam hadn't really been able to sleep very much the past few nights. Someone would have thought it was *his* wedding today instead of Finn's by the way that he acted and felt.

Right now, it felt as if *he* was mounted on pins and needles.

Maybe it was because, in preparing for Finn's wedding and rehearsing the songs that he and the band would play, it just brought home the fact that he was never going to get married.

Up until almost a month ago, that wouldn't have even earned a blink from him. But now, it just made him realize that he would face the rest of his life alone. That there would never be someone for him the way there was for Brett and Finn.

Lightning didn't strike twice in the same place. And he had already had lightning in his life.

The noise grew louder.

It almost sounded as if it was coming from more

than one direction. What the hell was going on? he wondered, the fog around his brain lifting.

Liam headed toward the window and looked out to see what there was to see. The window faced the square and he had been avoiding looking out at or even coming near it, but now his curiosity prompted him to push back the drapes and, Christmas tree or no Christmas tree, to look out.

He supposed even the intent to do that was a good sign in his case. Maybe it meant that he was taking back his life—or maybe it meant that he was just more curious than he'd thought.

Pushing the drapes back as far as he could, Liam found himself looking at what seemed like a fleet of huge trucks. Dump trucks from their appearance. And they were dumping their contents right in the middle of the town square.

There were several white mounds in the middle of the square and they grew with each truck's deposit.

Liam blinked. Was that—

"Damn, it looks like snow!" Finn cried out, crowded in behind him.

Determined to go the traditional route, Finn had opted to spend his last night as a single male in the house where he had grown up instead of with Connie.

"You see it, too, huh?" Liam asked, staring at the white mounds.

"Damn straight I do," Finn answered excitedly. "Connie is going to *love* this." He suddenly looked at his brother. "Did you do this?"

"Me?" Not that he wouldn't have loved to take credit for this, but there was no way he could begin to pull off something like this. He hadn't a clue where this—

and the trucks that brought it—had all come from. "Where would I get snow?" Liam asked. "I can create songs. Snow's another matter entirely. Maybe Brett had it shipped," he guessed.

"From where?" Finn asked.

Damned if he knew, Liam thought. "Good point. Maybe Connie did it," was Liam's next guess.

It was a guess that Finn quickly shot down. "Connie wouldn't waste money like that. Now that she's heading her own construction company and donating all her free time to renovating the homes on the reservation, she wouldn't do something like this just to satisfy an old fantasy she had."

Finn was probably right, Liam thought. But that still didn't solve the mystery. "Well the snow didn't just drive itself here," Liam said, trying to get to the bottom of the mystery and going over to his brother's side.

Finn had been staring out the window the entire time that the dump trucks had been unloading their cargo in the square.

Looking for anything that might answer his mounting questions, Liam suddenly homed in on the person who appeared to be signing something for each driver.

A bill?

Who in their right minds would have brought in this much snow, or ice, or whatever the substance actually turned out to be? The person signing for the "cargo" turned around and Liam could make out the person's face clearly.

Son of a gun.

Finn looked rather smug. "I believe you know the lady, right?"

Liam's jaw slackened. He stood there a moment longer, as if not trusting his own eyes. He'd already made up his mind that right after Finn's wedding, he was going to move heaven and earth to find Whitney. Was this his mind just playing tricks on him?

The next moment, still only wearing his jeans and forgetting to pick up a shirt, Liam ran barefoot out of the house. He had to see if it was really Whitney.

"I guess 'right,'" Finn murmured, then announced happily to the air at large, "I've got a wedding to get ready for." He hurried off to get started.

THE GROUND WAS hard and rough on his bare feet, but Liam hardly noticed. Every fiber of his being was focused on only one thing. The woman in the center of the truck caravan.

She was back.

Unless he was having serious hallucinations, Whitney was back.

He had no intentions of losing this second chance he'd just been granted by the whimsical forces that were out there.

"Whitney!" he called out way before he was anywhere close to her.

The trucks were all rumbling and creaking, creating a veritable wall of noise all around her. Even so, she could have sworn she heard Liam calling out her name.

Most likely, it was just wishful thinking on her part. Wishful thinking, too, that just because she had called in a number of favors from several ski resort managers so that she could help give Liam's future sister-in-law the wedding of her dreams, everything would be perfect between her and Liam from here on in.

She knew better than that, Whitney silently lectured herself.

At least her brain knew better. Her heart, rebel that it was, well, that was an entirely different matter. Her heart was hoping for a miracle. It was hoping for the opportunity to reconnect with Liam and, this time, to do it right.

Or at least, not to mess up too badly.

"Whitney!"

Damn it, that *was* Liam's voice. She was *certain* of it.

Whitney started to look around, doing her best to scan the immediate area. The fleet of trucks were beginning to draw a crowd on their own. People's natural curiosity had been aroused.

She could see Miss Joan approaching from the diner, saw a number of other people she recognized converging on the square as well, but Liam wasn't part of them.

Whitney could feel her heart beginning to sink a little.

Not over yet, she promised herself. *It's not over yet.*

She was prepared to do or say whatever it took to make amends with him, and—

"Damn it, woman, I'm yelling myself hoarse."

Suddenly, she felt herself being swept up as a strong pair of arms closed around her. "You came back!" she heard Liam cry one split second before he covered her mouth with his own.

After that, she was a little fuzzy about the details. All she knew was that everything became right with the world.

And this time, she intended to keep it that way.

Epilogue

It was a wedding that the people of Forever wouldn't soon forget, Miss Joan would say in the months that lay ahead. Not just because of the last-minute, unexpected appearance of snowdrifts throughout the town square to dazzle the wedding guests—snowdrifts in a town that had *never* seen any snow before. But also because, as the bride was walking down the aisle on the arm of Stewart Emerson, a man she had come to regard as her surrogate father, her own father, Calvin Carmichael, seemed to materialize out of nowhere. He quietly asked her for permission to walk her the rest of the way.

"I thought you said you couldn't get away," Connie said, totally stunned by her father's unexpected appearance.

It was one of the few times she had ever seen her father smile. "What? A man can't change his mind about seeing his only daughter get married?"

Overwhelmed, torn, she looked at Emerson, but the stately man had already gently removed her hand from his arm. Smiling encouragingly at her, Emerson nodded and fell back, allowing her father to replace him.

Connie silently blessed Emerson.

She struggled with tears the last ten feet to where the minister, and Finn, stood waiting.

By the time the ceremony was over, there was hardly a dry eye left in the crowd.

IT WASN'T UNTIL several hours later, after the professional wedding photographs had been taken and the reception had officially gotten underway, that Liam had an opportunity to actually talk with the woman who had set his life on its ear.

"Where did you get the snow?" he asked, still marveling at the winter-wonderland effect it was having on everyone, despite the fact that it had, perforce, begun to slowly melt.

Whitney was still very pleased with both herself and the way the bride had squealed in excited disbelief when she first saw the snow around the Christmas tree.

"I pulled a few strings with the managers of a couple of skiing resorts that I knew," she replied.

"That was a hell of a thing you did," Brett said, coming up to join them.

Whitney shrugged off the compliment. "A girl deserves to have the wedding of her dreams. Just so happened that I could make it come true. No big deal."

"Oh, yes," Liam contradicted, "it's a *very* big deal."

"I second the motion," Alisha, Brett's wife, said, raising her hand as if this was an actual vote being taken. Brett's arm slipped around her shoulders. Alisha flashed her husband a smile before going on to tell Whitney, "That was a really nice thing you did."

Wanting to deflect the subject away from her, Whitney asked Liam, "Do you think your band can play one song without you so we can dance?"

He was already taking her hand and leading her to the dance floor. Since he and the band were taking a break, the dance floor was presently devoid of couples.

"Consider it done," Liam said.

Looking over his shoulder toward his band members, he nodded and pointed his index and middle fingers at them. Half a beat later, the air was filled with music.

"I came back for a reason," Whitney told him as they danced.

"I know." His fingers laced through hers. They were swaying to the music. It was as if order was restored to the universe, he mused. "To bring Connie her dream wedding."

"That wasn't the only reason I came back," Whitney admitted. "Liam, I have something to tell you."

He looked at her for a long moment. "Funny, because I have something to tell you."

"Me first," she insisted. She'd been bursting with this news since she had arrived in Forever early this morning.

Liam inclined his head, humoring her. "Okay, ladies first."

It took effort not to have the words just come tumbling out over one another like so many scattered marbles. "I convinced Wilson that you needed the band—*this* band. After all, every performer has people who play backup for them, why not the people who know you like the back of their own hands? *And*—"

"There's more?" he asked in surprise.

"There's more." She beamed, excited for him. "Wilson's agreed that you should do your first music video right here in Forever. In essence, it'll put Forever on the map—so that Connie's hotel can see some decent business," she concluded. "Your turn. What did you want to tell me?"

"What I've got to say isn't going to hold a candle to what you just said," he warned her.

Whitney didn't want him to feel that way. For the first time in her life, she wasn't trying to compete, to come out on top. What she had done, she had done strictly for him. She wanted him to be happy.

"Let me be the judge of that," she coaxed, waiting to hear what he had to say.

"I was going to come out to LA next month," he said quietly.

He had succeeded in surprising her. "You decided to accept Wilson's terms for the contract?"

She would have bet money that he wouldn't change his stance on the matter. Had she been that wrong about him? Had the promise of fame seduced him, making him turn his back on loyalty?

"No," he answered emphatically. "I was going to come out to look for you." A rueful smile curved his lips. "Turns out that nobody likes me without you. They all think I've gotten surly and moody."

"You?" Whitney asked incredulously, then shook her head. "Never happen."

"Yeah, actually it did," he contradicted. "They were right. I'm not any good without you." He took a deep breath. "In case I'm not making myself clear, I love you. And even I don't like myself without you. No pressure, I just want to be around you."

"And that's all?" she asked, looking at him. "Just be 'around me'?"

He laughed shortly to himself. "Well, ideally, I'd want to marry you, but—"

"Yes!"

Liam blinked. He was too young to be losing his hearing. "Wait, what?"

"Yes," Whitney repeated, glowing.

Liam abruptly stopped dancing even though the band hadn't finished the number. "Yes?" he asked, wanting to be perfectly clear on this.

She nodded for good measure. "Yes."

He still wasn't sure they were talking about the same thing. He watched her closely as he asked, "You'll marry me?"

Her smile widened to the point that under different conditions, it might have been referred to as blinding. "Yes!"

"Hey, Liam, you're up, man!" Sam called to him, beckoning him over to the band.

"Hold on a second," he called back, his attention entirely focused on the woman who had just made him the happiest man on earth. Holding her hand, he wove his way over to the others.

"What are you doing?" Whitney asked, laughing as she trailed after him.

"You're going to sing the next number with me," he told her, tossing the words over his shoulder.

"I can't sing," she protested, tugging slightly to get her hand back. He held it fast.

"Yes, you can. I've heard you," Liam said. The next moment, he turned toward the wedding guests and addressed them. "She's going to need a little coaxing, folks. Whitney's shy, so give it up for the future Mrs. Liam Murphy."

A wave of resounding applause met the announcement. When it died down, the band began to play. Two bars into it, Whitney recognized the song. The song was all about giving your heart to the one you love.

She had no choice but to sing with Liam. Their voices blended beautifully. Just as their lives would, she couldn't help thinking.

And when the number was over, Liam surprised her again by kissing her in front of everyone.

She had no choice but to kiss him back.

It was the first time in her life that she enjoyed not having a choice.

* * * * *

MILLS & BOON®

Why not subscribe?

Never miss a title and save money too!

Here's what's available to you if you join the exclusive **Mills & Boon Book Club** today:

✦ *Titles up to a month ahead of the shops*
✦ *Amazing discounts*
✦ *Free P&P*
✦ *Earn Bonus Book points that can be redeemed against other titles and gifts*
✦ *Choose from monthly or pre-paid plans*

Still want more?

Well, if you join today we'll even give you *50% OFF your first parcel!*

So visit **www.millsandboon.co.uk/subs**
or call Customer Relations on 020 8288 2888
to be a part of this exclusive Book Club!

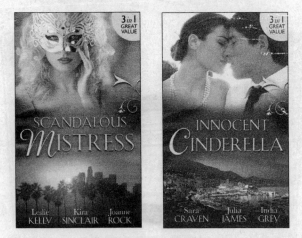

MILLS & BOON®

Exciting new titles
coming next month

With over 100 new titles available every month,
find out what exciting romances
lie ahead next month.

Visit
www.millsandboon.co.uk/comingsoon
to find out more!